# THE
# LOST
# TRIDENT
## OF
# POSEIDON

# THE
# LOST
# TRIDENT
## OF
# POSEIDON

GRANT DAWSON

Desert Wind Press

Cover art by Max Mitenkov

Interior design by Robert Brent Gardner

Independently published by Desert Wind Press LLC
www.desertwindpress.com

ISBN 978-1-956271-34-8 (paperback)

ISBN 978-1-956271-35-5 (hardcover)

ISBN 978-1-956271-36-2 (eBook)

*For Tatjana – Love of My Life*

*My bounty is as boundless as the sea,*

*My love as deep; the more I give to thee,*

*The more I have, for both are infinite.*

— William Shakespeare

*Romeo and Juliet*, Act 2, Scene 2

Table of Contents

Prologue ........................................................................1

Chapter 1 Grandfather.................................................11

Chapter 2 Mount Tapochau ........................................21

Chapter 3 School............................................................29

Chapter 4 Prophesy .....................................................47

Chapter 5 Departure .....................................................61

Chapter 6 Mission Briefing.........................................87

Chapter 7 Arrival ........................................................103

Chapter 8 Discovery....................................................113

Chapter 9 Revelation...................................................127

Chapter 10 Voice of Church........................................143

Chapter 11 Taming Proteus .......................................159

Chapter 12 Escape .......................................................187

Chapter 13 Descent......................................................199

Chapter 14 Connection................................................239

Chapter 15 Disarming the Devices .............................259

Chapter 16 Return .......................................................277

Epilogue ......................................................................291

*Dramatis Personae* .......................................................299

Timeline.......................................................................300

Acknowledgements .....................................................303

About the Author.........................................................305

# PROLOGUE

The darkness was so profound that it transcended the absence of light and had a physical quality to it. There was no up or down; no right or left. She existed in the abyss, suspended in a seemingly infinite universe of water.

With a quick tilt of her head, Agana Taitano Hofstadter activated the oxygen gage within her helmet's inner display screen. Two minutes left. *I can hold my breath for four minutes . . . I think. Well, let's find out for sure.* She had six minutes left—three-hundred and sixty seconds. A nice round number for calculations. She calculated how long it would take her to reach the seabed: she could depth dive vertically downward at about one-point-five meters per second; and, according to the abacus (her wrist-mounted computer and scanning device), the ocean floor was ninety-one meters below her. It would therefore take about one minute to reach the seabed again, and another minute to disarm the munition. She was already about one-hundred meters below the surface; it would therefore take her at least four minutes to ascend back up to the surface, with the blood-nitrogen exchanger within her diving suit working at maximum capacity.

As she ran these mental calculations, her earliest childhood memory—both unbidden and unwelcome—intruded upon her otherwise logical and concentrated mind. The reminiscence was not a soft-focus montage of black and white images with no sound, blurred at the edges of recalled perception—but rather a razor-keen playback of the unlocked chemical engrams buried deep within her hippocampus. She was five years old again. She stood at the far edge of a long wooden pier that jutted into a freezing Scottish tarn, Loch Etchachan, ensconced high within the Cairngorm Mountains.

Her parents were engaged in some kind of exotic research expedition and had sent her to live for a few months with one of their cousins, who, for the five-year-old girl, was a first cousin once removed. Taitano had been at the end of the pier the day before, contemplating the perfectly clear and halcyon water all the way down to the bottom of the tarn. It was so placid and undarkened that Taitano almost imagined that the invisible barrier of the many trillions of $H_2O$ molecules in liquid formation was not even there. At the bottom, she could even plainly discern individual stones, beckoning her to come closer. She felt an urge to jump off the pier, plunge into the pellucid water, and swim to the submerged floor of the tarn to retrieve one of those darkly lambent stones. The light of Sol frisked off the grey and brown surfaces of the stone and alighted upon the rods and cones of her retina, enticing her to descend into the siberian depths.

She then experienced a presentiment—*can one have a glimmer of what is to come during a memory?*—of triumphantly showing one of the stones to her cousin, who would tell her parents about her daring achievement, and they would all be so proud of her. But an admonition from her amygdala began to mix with the resurrected memory, both competing now for dominance across her cerebral cortex, and her innate sense of self-preservation held her back. Again, it was not as if she were reliving an event in the past, but rather struggling with a dilemma in the here and now. With a great effort, she turned away from the brink, and walked the long way back to the shore along the pier, her shoes reverberating along the planks in a rhythm that mocked her.

That night, at dinner, she told her cousin about her desire to retrieve a rock from the bottom of the tarn and announced that tomorrow she would do it. Her cousin replied something about Taitano being able to do anything to which she put her mind, but otherwise did not take such statements coming from a five-year-old too seriously.

The next day, Taitano, directly after breakfast, strode with purpose to the end of the pier, calmly removed her shoes—it would not do to have soaking wet shoes in the icy bite of the Cairngorms—and deftly pitched herself into the water feet first. The shock of the cold was like being punched in the chest. At once, the blast of frigid water suffused her nerve receptors, disorienting her; the water filled her nose and stung her sinuses. After a few seconds, she perceived that she was sinking, her body already several meters under the surface of the tarn. With clarity of purpose, she looked down towards the stones, but the cold had constricted the curvature of her corneas to such an extent that her vision was blurred. Her limbs were numb and sluggish. Her lungs began to ache. She tried to breathe, sucking in only water, which immediately paralyzed her further. She was drowning. She felt an intense feeling of regret, as she thought about how distraught her parents would be to hear of the tragic death of their baby daughter, especially when they learned that she had not been able to acquire one of the stones as the fruit of her daring audacity. (Such is the mind of a child.)

As she began to lose consciousness, she felt a tug upon her arm. Her next recollection was lying on the pier, drenched, gagging up water from her lungs—so chilled she could not even remember what it felt like to be warm. She was now a being of ice. The layers of her body's tissues were so frigid that she felt as though she were just another frozen plank in the wooden pier. She was then lifted, brought inside, and set by an unknown source of heat, wrapped in blankets. Heat, her mind recalled, was energy locked in molecules that was then transferred to other molecules according to the immutable laws of thermodynamics. She was now the beneficiary of those physical laws of science. When her body temperature had been brought up several degrees, she was given a hot liquid to drink. More heat transfer.

She remembered her cousin asking with vexatious fury, "Tai, whatever were you thinking? You could have died. If I had not happened, by chance, to hear you jumping into the water, you would be dead now. Why did you do such a thing?"

Taitano knew full well why she had done it. It really had not even been a conscious choice. She had felt an obsessive compulsion and had simply followed her nature. But she now felt the fear of getting into trouble. Not just any old fear. A paralytic, soul destroying fear. A fear that cruelly seared the synapses of her nubile neocortices. So she lied. She said that she could not remember why she had done it—could not even remember that she *had* done it. She simply could not remember anything.

Her cousin looked even more stricken than before and called her parents via the orbital network, on the other side of the world. Both her parents were now on the audio-visual call via their cousin's abacus. Her father said, "Taibo, do you really not remember? We're afraid you suffered brain damage due to lack of oxygen. We're going to have Maiana take you to the hospital for a brain scan."

Taitano's heart sickened further: *Do I keep lying and try to avoid responsibility for my actions or tell them the truth so they don't worry further?*

Her mother spoke to her softly over the abacus. "Agana, please tell us the truth. We don't care if you jumped off the pier. We just want to know if you're OK. Do you really not remember anything? We want to make sure you're OK."

Taitano was more scared than she had ever been in her brief five years of existence. Torn between disappointing her parents for her imprudent act and distressing them over her feigned amnesia and brain damage, she chose to take responsibility, realizing that she had only made things worse by lying, for now she had done not one, but *two* things wrong. "I jumped. I remember it. I was afraid to tell you because I thought you'd be mad at me. I'm sorry." She could see the relief wash over her parents over the screen of the abacus. Her parents, emotionally spent, told her they loved her, asked Maiana to take Taitano to the hospital in Inverness for a check (just to be on the safe side), and then signed off.

All of this passed through Taitano's mind, prompted by the stress of the decision she now needed to make—not in the northern defile of Scotland many years ago, but in the present, pressed between two layers of the Ocean in the strait between the islands of Saipan and Tinian. *Do I give into the compulsion and go for the munition, and maybe get into trouble—or do I play it safe, return to the surface, and deal with being disappointed in myself for not going for it, for not pushing it to the limit?*

Her obsessive compulsive nature prevailed over her trepidation and healthy sense of self-preservation. In an attempt to mitigate the anxiety rising in her, she tapped, five times in quick succession with her index and middle fingers, the outside of her helmet in the place that corresponded to the skin just below her right ear. Inhaling deeply, she used the internal sensors to locate the target ninety-one meters below her, confirmed its location on the seabed, and plunged down. She visualized her body as an ancient torpedo streaking towards her mark. She spotted the sediment encrusted bomb casing.

Fifty seconds. *Ahead of schedule.*

Activating her wrist-mounted abacus, the darkness was rent asunder by the lights of her environmental suit. She was now no longer enveloped in liquid shadow, but rather encased in a globe of silvery light. With precision and passion, she accessed the bomb's actuator and began to program an analysis of the exact frequency needed to defuse the lonely munition. As her abacus cycled through the possibilities, she monitored the parameters and adjusted them for greater efficiency—and alacrity. This was no mid-term examination. It was real.

Her mind wandered to thoughts of whence the munition had originally come. *Was it part of a payload of a scuttled ship's hold? Was it cast into the sea along with others as a misguided means of disposal? Had it rolled down the continental sea-shelf, pushed and pulled by the endless currents for over a century?* She chided herself. *There will be time to analyze the data later.* The abacus blinked and chirped. It had located the right nano-frequency for disarming the complex fuse. She pressed a sequence of buttons to activate a microburst of gamma rays from her abacus' emitter nodes, which instantaneously disintegrated the bomb's fuse. She tagged the bomb for recovery later. *One more down. But now time to go.*

One-hundred seconds. *Longer than expected. Behind schedule. That's what you get for daydreaming. Now it's time to focus.*

These old munitions, some of which had been on the ocean floor for well over two-hundred years, did not always behave as in the laboratory simulators or according to the pre-mission diagnostics. On the other hand, the fact that some of them had not imploded, or their casings degrade, after so much time was a testament to the brilliance and acumen of the scientists and engineers who had constructed them long ago. At the same time, she thought of the wasted time, energy, money, and intellect put toward making weapons to maim and kill. A mixed legacy.

Time to ascend—two-hundred and ten seconds left of oxygen. Two-hundred and forty seconds to the surface. Only thirty seconds short. She could do it. She dropped her sink weights and thrust herself upwards, kicking and paddling the long flippers attached to her feet in a smooth and steady rhythm.

Half-way to the surface, she could feel her buoyancy increase—and her lungs begin to burn. She felt a current pushing her sideways through the infinite mass of water. She had not accounted for a lateral current at these depths. *It will add ten seconds to my ascent.* She calmed the instinctive panic rising low in her abdomen. *Humans evolved on land and have no business in the sea. No. Focus on what you can control and accept that which you cannot.* She was rapidly ascending, the faint glow of Sol's radiation beginning to show itself through the oppressive layers of salt water between her and the surface.

One minute left.

Her lungs ached and throbbed. Panic began to assert control again over her rational attempts to calm herself. She initiated one of her incantations. *Pain is a thing of the mind.*

Forty-five seconds.

She objectified the pain, separated her mind from her physical body, and imagined herself in a boat above looking down at herself.

Thirty seconds.

*The pain is not me; it does not define me. I control the pain. It does not control me.*

Fifteen seconds.

*Pain is pleasure. Pleasure is pain. Pain reminds us we are alive.*

Five seconds left to the top. She desperately ripped off her helmet in anticipation of reaching the surface—so she could breathe *the moment* she was freed of the water's grasp.

In a violent upward thrust, Taitano's head broke the surface of the azure, crystal water—her ebony hair flinging back and slapping the water behind her. Her pale blue eyes involuntarily squinted from the blaze of Sol. She desperately exhaled the accumulated carbon dioxide from her overtaxed lungs and then drew a luxurious, extended breath. She gasped her next breaths, tried to calm her breathing, and then began to sob, releasing the pent-up anxiety from her mind as she had expelled the waste gases from the strained alveoli of her lungs. She floated on the surface of the Ocean, regaining her composure and resting her enervated body.

Several minutes later, Taitano heard the tittering of her professor, as he approached. She could sense his strained movement through the water. A virile bottlenose dolphin popped his head above the water, excitedly chattering at her. She looked around for her helmet. The dolphin left and returned a minute later, expertly pushing her helmet towards her with his rostrum. It reminded her of the tricks that dolphins used to do with balls and other objects in human water parks in the twentieth century, an observation she did *not* share with her professor.

She put the helmet back on and activated its system. The translator came on-line, and an explosion of words hit her eardrums. "Are all humans this insane? Or is this specific personality flaw just your own? Do you have a death wish, Agana? Or are you just demented? What are you trying to prove anyway?" Taitano took it all in, vacillating between feeling criticized and complemented. Professor Sun continued, "Was that really necessary? We could have picked up that last one tomorrow! There was no need to risk your life over it!"

Taitano had regained control of her breathing now, enough to rasp out a response, "Sun, it was fine. I had it under control. There was nothing to worry about."

Sun replied, "Fire and brimstone, Tai! It's like an itch you just have to scratch, isn't it? I knew accepting you for a postdoc and this team, despite your psych profile, was a liability. I mean, really! Guess whose tail would be clipped if something had gone wrong. Next time, you leave it down there, and we pick it up later. Understood?"

Taitano placed her right hand to her brow, saluted the professor, and responded, "Aye-aye, Sir. Understood. Permission to speak freely, Professor."

The dolphin chittered with what seemed to be reluctance. The translator paused, momentarily unable to render the impressively complex and melodic stream of whines, whistles, and low-frequency clicks into the human equivalent, and then interpreted the sounds simply as: "Go ahead." Taitano swore she heard the translator actually issue a brief sigh (although that was not possible).

"You've got some funky looking seaweed stuck on your dorsal fin. It's looks kinda funny."

If dolphins could scowl, Professor Sun would have done so. But Taitano could see his suppressed amusement, mixed with exasperation and pride in her. Sun finally managed to repress his emotions and said, in a serious tone, "Tai, one of these days you're going to push it too far, and either your luck is going to run out or I won't be there to save you."

"Oh, come on, Sun. You'll always be there to save me."

If Professor Sun were a human, he would have had a doubtful look on his face.

# CHAPTER 1

# GRANDFATHER

Taitano toweled herself off on the rocky shore, as she watched Professor Sun glide away through the surf back to Carl Sagan University on the neighboring island of Tinian. She experienced, not for the first time, an awkward twang of irony that the university—located on the island whence the first, and only, nuclear assault had been staged—had been named after one of the most eloquent advocates against the nuclear arms race.

She felt a momentary well of anxiety for Professor Sun, as she recalled the number of sharks that now hunted in the narrow strait between Saipan and Tinian since the Great Restoration. She knew that sharks, as apex predators, were essential for the health of the Ocean, but it did not calm her fretting. She immediately took a long deep breath of blessed air, which carried the scent of brine and decaying organic matter to her olfactory nerve. *I accept my fears. Anxiety is a thing of the mind. It is not real. Sun has swum that strait a million times. He's fine. Anyway, a shark is more in danger from a dolphin than the other way around. The last thing a shark would try to eat is a dolphin, especially when there are so many other easier things to kill. I accept my anxiety as an old friend who teaches me valuable lessons—and then I let her go.*

She then was able to turn her mind to the myriad other thoughts that raced through it. The surge of the soughing waves against the rocks below soothingly assaulted her ears. She peeled off her diving suit, carefully stowed her abacus in its protective box, and slipped into her dry, loose-fitting clothes. She could feel the warm, soft fibers of the cotton swishing against her skin. Her mind started to analyze and recall the manufacturing techniques that were employed to produce the tunic and pants .... *No! There's no need for that now. I accept that this cotton shirt is here, I am wearing it, and I don't have to analyze it right now! ... Maybe later.* After this self-inflicted tongue-lashing, she chuckled to herself and then focused on the present. Her solar sail was parked on the top of a ridge of jagged rock, where she had left it. She skirted up the wall of acuminous rock, careful not to cut herself or slip. A generation or two ago, her human ancestors would have flattened and paved a place for a fossil-fueled car to park. Now, there were no "parking lots," as they once were called, but rather just the natural landscape. The solar sail gently rested on some rocks, slightly askew, waiting for her to board.

Taitano crawled inside, and the vehicle powered up in a gentle surge of stored solar energy, which it had collected while she was in the water.

"Where to, Doctor?" asked the gentle voice that was not quite male or female, but rather a melodious combination of several speakers modulated at a frequency that was designed to boost the serotonin levels in a human brain.

"Back home. I'll fly myself. I'm in the mood, and it takes my mind off things."

"As you wish, Dr. Taitano."

"I told you to call me 'Tai.'"

"As you wish ... Tai."

She took hold of the analogue controls, the cyclic pitch stick, the collective thrust lever, and the antitorque pedals. She gave a slow twist to the throttle control, and the solar sail gently lifted into the air in a gentle arc. Her mind drifted to thoughts of how the controls of the sail were basically the same as those designed for old-style helicopters in the early twentieth century. She marveled at their simplicity and the engineering brilliance of those ancient humans who were able to design such an elegant and functional mechanism for guiding a craft through three-dimensional atmospheric space. In fact, the same principles were used for space flight as well, with some important modifications for the almost complete lack of air resistance and resulting friction.

As her mind perambulated amongst these thoughts, she navigated the solar sail over the brief expanse of volcanic island to the southern tip where her home lay nestled in a tumble of igneous rock formations. The dwelling was a vaulted structure integrated into the landscape; from high up in the sky or at a distance, the arched habitat appeared to be nothing more than another random fell of magma that had hardened millennia ago, following a volcanic eruption from deep within Earth-Ocean. But as Taitano drew nearer to her home, she could discern the several dozen meter-long bladeless wind turbines affixed to the top and sides of the dome. These glaive-like protuberances were designed to oscillate when struck by the wind and then generate electricity from their own vibration. To Taitano, they were the pinnacle of simplicity and sophistication—and also a constant reminder of all the wrong turns that humanity had taken in its rather unimaginative efforts to generate electricity over the last couple of centuries. But she was not so sure that the rows of quivering stalks of polymerized resin squared very well with the maxim *form follows function*, as they made her home look like a shivering sea urchin with a crewcut.

She deftly put the sail down on a relatively flat shelf of rock, engaged the magnetic restrictors, and disembarked the craft for her home.

As she entered, she heard a booming voice call out, "Tai, you're late!" A pungent smell of burnt broccoli hit her nostrils, and she saw black smoke coming from around the corner of the eating nook. An oven door slammed. "Damn! I'm such an idiot!"

"That's negative self-talk, Grandpa. You know better." A smile curved the corners of her mouth as her grandfather appeared around the corner holding a baking pan of black, smoking vegetables.

"What the hell is wrong with me? I put this in the oven and then went to read the news feed on the abacus for just a second, and then … Bam! … I do that every time!"

"Runs in the family. Why are trying to cook again anyway? You know you're rubbish at it."

"A man's gotta eat."

"Is that supposed to make me feel guilty?" she asked.

"No," her grandfather responded. He looked dejected, and then a mischievous hope filled his eyes. "Let's just heat up a pizza."

"Pepperoni?"

"Yes, plant-based pepperoni. Whatever that is. And then I will tell you of the days of high adventure. When pepperoni was pepperoni instead of this plant-based nonsense, and humans did whatever they wanted, instead of following the orders of damn alien monsters."

"OK, Grandpa. Put them in the oven. I'll be there in fifteen."

"Beer?"

"Sure, I'll take a zero-point-zero."

"Oh, Lordy. Heavens and Saints preserve us from ourselves. Non-pepperoni pepperoni. Non-alcoholic alcohol. What the hell is happening to the world? Back in my day …."

As her grandfather muttered to himself, Taitano dropped her equipment in the storage area in the back of the dwelling, walked to the bathroom, removed her clothing, and stepped into the shower. Her hamstrings ached a bit from the strain of the recovery operation and ascending so rapidly from the seabed, but it was a wholesome type of ache. Like she had earned the right to feel sore. Muscle fatigue from too much use, rather than from indolence. She checked to ensure there was a towel on the rack before entering the shower. Her grandfather had the annoying habit of washing her towel and then not replacing it with another one. She had lost count of how many times she had shouted, dripping wet, from the bathroom for her grandfather to bring her a towel. He would then open the door a crack and thrust his arm through the door holding a fresh towel. She could swear she could see his amused smile through the door.

"Water, thirty degrees, five minutes."

The rush of warm water encased her body, and she relaxed into it. Water—the same molecular compound that had endangered her life not so long ago—now enveloped her like a soothing embrace. She closed her eyes and angled her face toward the shower head, thinking of the millennia of humans who had never experienced the blessed sensation of a hot shower. A frigid dousing under a waterfall, maybe. But the invention of the hot shower had to be one of the singularly most significant accomplishments of human civilization. She could not picture in her mind what it would be like to never have had one— or never to have one again. She mused that it could be seen as humanity's harnessing of the awesome power of nature, brought down to human dimensions and tamed for their own carnal pleasure. The water ceased, and she sighed in both pleasure and regret. The timer was a necessary feature. Without it, she would likely never leave the shower or would exceed her allotted limits under the Water Reclamation Regulations. (She could have effortlessly hacked the water meter, but was too tired this evening to bother.) In any case, the timer also helped her gage her sense of elapsed time, which helped her while diving. *Every little bit counts.*

When Taitano emerged from the living quarters, dinner was on the table, and her grandfather was sitting at the table, as always, reading the daily newsfeeds, inaudibly grumbling about something. She gave him a kiss on the cheek, "Thanks for making dinner, Grandpa. You're a sweet old guy. I think I'll keep you around a little longer."

"Hum!" In a terrible facsimile of a British accent, her grandfather continued, "Thank you, my beloved granddaughter. Art thou ready to dine? It is indeed most kind of you to grace me with thy august presence."

"OK, OK. I'm late, and you can't cook. So, we're even, OK? Let's eat."

He raised his beer to her, she picked up her zero-point-zero, they clinked glasses. "Prost," they uttered together.

Half a pizza later, her grandfather asked, "So how was it today? Did you get the last one?"

"Yeah, I got it. Barely. Ran out of air again and just made it to the surface. Sun was *not* happy."

"Tai, why do you always do that? You had your spare air cartridge with you, right?"

"Yeah," she said a bit slyly, looking at the table instead of his eyes.

"Then why do that to yourself?"

"The cartridge was in the solar sail."

Disapprobation played across his face. He laid his head into his hands, closed his eyes, and shook his head back and forth, moaning in despair. "Perdition's flames, Tai! What in the name of Ennea was the spare cartridge doing in the sail instead of on your belt? Wait, don't tell me. You wanted to push your limits to see how far you could go. I never should have filled your head with all that nonsense. Seriously, Tai. There's pushing limits, and then there's sheer stupidity."

"I don't know. I just can't help it."

"And what about the electrolyzer?" her grandfather asked. Taitano's suit was powered by a green hydrogen power cell, called an electrolyzer, which cleaved $H_2O$ molecules to produce energy for the suit. The chemical reaction also produced oxygen molecules as a by-product that could be captured by the suit and channeled into a breathing apparatus.

"The electrolyzer?" Taitano responded. "Oh, yeah." She paused with a sheepish look on her face, trying not to smile out of embarrassment, "I turned it off."

He stared at her blankly. "Taibo …. you are seriously going to give me a heart attack. And then they're going to have to grow me yet another heart and replace the old one that you've beaten to a bloody pulp."

"OK, OK!"

Undaunted, he continued, "And don't think all that tap-tap-tapping on the back of that thick skull of yours is going to save you from all these daredevil stunts."

"OK, Grandpa! You've made your point already. *Geez.*"

He stared at her, the fear, concern, and anger playing across his lined and weathered face.

Taitano continued, "OK, really. I'll take the spare with me next time and turn on the electrolyzer. Don't know if there will be a next time anyway. I think we got the last one now."

"The last one in the Marianas maybe. But there's always another one. We left you all quite a mess to clean up."

"You didn't know any better."

"Oh, but we did. The scientists and environmental activists told us for generations that we were mucking up the planet. But we were too set in our ways, too comfortable. We were riding high on the wave of what we thought were limitless resources. Only it wasn't limitless, was it?"

"Come on. Let's not have this useless conversation again. We woke up soon enough. We're fixing it."

"You and your generation woke up. Not us," he said.

"Well, the Enneans sure helped with that, didn't they," Taitano responded.

"Yeah, there's that, of course. Hey, there's something I wanted to talk to you about."

Taitano's abacus chirped. "Professor Sun is asking me to come to the university early tomorrow morning. Do you think you can get yourself to your check-up without me?"

"Yeah, sure. I am a grown man, you know. And it's just a routine examination."

"There's nothing routine about the heart of a one-hundred and fifty-six-year-old, especially when it's your third one."

"I'll be fine, Ms. Worrywart. But I thought you were going to Sunil's party tonight. Will you be in any shape for an early meeting tomorrow if you are out partying all night?"

"What, are you my grandfather or my dad? I'm a big girl now. I think I can take care of myself. Anyway, I'm not going to the party."

"And why might that be?"

"It was pretty intense today. I just want to get into my pajamas, watch a classic episode of *Cosmos*, and then get to bed early. Wanna join?"

"I'd love to, but I'm worried you're becoming a bit of a recluse. A choice between a raging party with a bunch of twenty-somethings swigging their zero-point-zeros or vegging on the couch with some old geezers like me and Carl. And you choose the latter? What would Doctor Xiu say?"

"First of all. Carl will never be an old geezer. You know the old song: 'Only the Good Die Young.' You, on the other hand, would definitely qualify for the position of 'old geezer.' So, option two would actually be chilling on the couch with the most dashing and brilliant scientist of the twentieth century—and, yes, you, an old geezer. As for Doctor Xiu, she would say I'm employing the psychological defense mechanism of avoidance in order to prevent myself from the psychological fear of trying to interact with my peers who have higher serotonin production levels than I do. And she would be *wrong*." Taitano paused in self-reflection. "Or maybe she's right. I don't know. I just want to chill tonight. We can watch the episode where Sagan describes the fourth dimension. I love that one."

"OK," her grandfather said. "But I want popcorn."

"No problem."

He paused for dramatic effect, looking deathly serious. "With *real* butter."

"Grandpa, there hasn't been real butter for a hundred years. Get over it."

"Never!" he shouted in mock horror. He then assumed a conspiratorial tone, "You do realize, don't you, that there are places where I can get real butter. Provided I'm discreet and willing to pay the right price."

"You're hopeless."

"I can also buy fried chicken there," he said with a wink.

"Grandpa!" she shouted in true alarm. "That's against the law, not to mention immoral. You're a terrible person!"

"No, I'm a determined and steadfast person. That's something you got from your Hofstadter side."

"Not the blue eyes?"

"Well, that too. It goes well with that jet black hair of yours." He winked at her again—this time to show he was kidding. "I still want to talk to you about something, though."

"What's it about?"

"Your future."

"Oh, *not tonight*, Grandpa, OK?"

"OK, when then?"

"Just not tonight."

"OK," he conceded. "I'll get Carl ready, and you make the disgusting fake popcorn," he said, trying to suppress a smile—and failing.

"Deal."

# Chapter 2

# Mount Tapochau

Taitano struggled between slumber and alertness and forced herself into consciousness. She gazed at the natural rock patterns of the ceiling above her bed. Her muscles ached. Her neck was stiff. She pulled on a robe and stumbled into the kitchen. All was quiet. Grandpa still asleep. An odor of burned broccoli and pizza permeated the air.

She had dreamt of ghosts and shadows, as she often did. Traditional Chamorro healers—"*suruhåna*" (*suruhånu* in the singular)—had been herding wraith-like creatures through the densely overgrown hills of the island. Not herding them like a dog corrals recalcitrant, terrified sheep, but rather guiding them in a loving, compassionate way. The chimeras seemed potent, but oddly helpless and in need of the protection of the *suruhåna*. The dream started to fade, and she could no longer prevent it from evaporating back into her subconscious mind for long-term biochemical storage.

She measured out three small teaspoons of loose Earl Grey tea into a tea pot, boiled the water, and managed to pour the water over the leaves and into the pot without spilling it, despite her slumberous swaying. Not just fatigue from the previous day, but also caffeine withdrawal symptoms, as her last dose was twenty-four hours ago. As she set her wrist abacus for a five-minute countdown, she could actually feel the synapses between her neurons. She visualized them. Great gulfs of space bordered by knobbly dendrites, the polar surfaces at the end of an impossibly long, and at the same time microscopic, nerve fiber that carried electrical impulses to and from her brain—that, in fact, constituted her brain. These nerve fibers were who and what she was, a whole greater than the sum of its parts (as Aristotle would say). Medical science had come a long way, but the understanding of the mind and consciousness was still largely a mystery. There had been some research in the early twenty-first century, positing that human consciousness was a function of quantum fluctuations in the atoms forming the tissue of nerve fibers, all working together to create an unimaginably complex symphony of thought. Sometimes in unison, sometimes in cacophony. But they had not yet really understood the true physical nature of consciousness.

All these thoughts ran through her mind as the tea leaves seeped and yielded their own complex symphony of polyphenols, amino acids, and—of course—caffeine. The timer went off. Five minutes. Without the timer, she mused, she would have been lost in her reverie for much longer. Hence the need for the impartiality of the time piece. The timer kept her honest. It was an objective interval of time, at least in the seemingly non-relativistic world on the surface of Earth-Ocean. She cognitively knew that she was on the surface of a planet, that the planet was rotating at 1,670 kilometers per hour (at least at the equator), and that the same planet was revolving around Sol at 110,000 kilometers per hour. She also was intellectually aware that the entire Solar System (with Sol as its gravitational center) was revolving around the galactic core of the Milky Way Galaxy at 720,000 kilometers per hour. Moreover, the galaxy itself was racing away from the scene of the Big Bang 13.8 billion years ago and, at the same time, was being subjected to the gravitational fields of other galaxies. But to her limited human senses, all was still. She blessed the heavens for the phenomenon of relative speed and was grateful that she was born as a human who could *not* perceive all these unimaginable forces at work on her minuscule body, for if she could perceive the Universe as it truly was, she feared she would go mad.

*Damn. Seven minutes now. Bitter tea. Oh, well. A few million extra leucoanthocyanines never killed anyone ... probably. Or least not right away.* She removed the sieve filled with bloated tea leaves, poured herself a generous draught of the tea, dumped in a heaping dollop of protein power, finished it off with some oat milk, and vigorously shook it up in a shaker bottle. With the completion of her morning caffeine concoction, which would have made the most expert alchemist of the eighteenth century proud, she allowed the first wave of tea protein shake to slide down her esophagus. The chalky taste of the plant protein, along with the warmth of the tea and the sweetness of the oats, coated her mouth and made her stomach explode in ecstasy. One minute later, the caffeine had been absorbed through the lining of her stomach and into her blood stream and carried to the blood vessels of her brain. There, the caffeine caused the blood vessels to dilate, which increased the blood flow to the neurons of her cerebral cortex. The dendrites of her neurons yielded up their beloved neurotransmitters, which swirled into her synaptic clefts, and she was off to the races on a Cartesian high for the rest of the day.

She reflected upon the fact that the renaissances in Arab and European civilizations directly coincided with the introduction of caffeine into those societies. The chemicals had enhanced human consciousness in a way that no other substance ever had and enabled people to invent and apply mathematics, engineering, and philosophy. She wondered where humans of the twenty-second century would be without the drug. Thoughts for another time.

Taitano vigorously pulled her athletic, light brown limbs into her running gear, secured the support clasps of her sneakers, activated her abacus to track her progress, and headed out the door for a run up Mount Tapochau, the highest point on the island of Saipan. She stepped into the front aperture of her living habitat, tapping with her index and middle fingers, five times in quick succession, the skin behind her right ear lobe, in order to queue her adrenal glands to release a small burst of dopamine. (This tapping was one of several techniques, along with meditation and mindful breathing, that she had been taught as a young girl in order to manage the anxiety caused by her obsessive-compulsive impulses.) *Once you're out there, it'll be great. Just get out of the front door.* As she keyed the locking sequence on the entrance, she concentrated all her focus on the numbered and lettered keypad, deliberately pushing the symbols one at a time. *I am entering the locking code: 463csd36. I am doing this deliberately and carefully. I will do this one time. I do not have to come back and do it again.* She stepped away from the entrance, turned her back on the house, and began to walk away. She was immediately overwhelmed by a compulsion to turn around, check the lock, and re-enter the sequence. *No, I do not have to go back and re-enter the locking sequence. I just did it in a deliberate and careful way. The door is locked. There is no possibility— outside of statistically improbable quantum events—that the door is not locked. I do not need to go back and do it again. I am not going back. I am going forward. I am OK with this. I accept the uncertainty and will go for a run now. And when I return, I will see that the door is locked.*

She tore herself away, through force of will, turned her mind to the run ahead, and set out languidly, letting the muscles and joints of her body warm up in the cool morning air. A light rain tickled her face as she headed up a dirt path in the predawn haze. The path disappeared into a thick mass of jungle with palms twice her height. As she entered, she quickly thanked the crepuscular spirits of her ancestors— *taotaomo'na* who guarded the entrance of the jungle—for letting her pass its border. The morning chorus danced against her eardrums, as countless birds chirped, cawed, sang, and squealed across the landscape different avian versions of "Hey, this is my territory, stay away" or "I want to mate with someone; come on over." The serenades probably sounded much more winsome and highbrow to a human than to a bird.

The grade of the trail grew steeper, and Taitano regulated her breathing. Steadily in through the nose, and then out through the mouth. She integrated a mantra into the inflation and deflation of her lungs: "I—can—run—well … I—can—fly—fast." Each mantra devoted to a respective inhalation and exhalation, and each syllable devoted to a stride. She fell into a meditative trance. The track abruptly turned left for several strides, and then right, alternating back and forth. She had reached the switch-back portion of the steepest part of the ascent, near the summit. She could distinctly feel the rush of blood from the left ventricle of her heart, the expansion of her aorta to accommodate the influx of oxygenated blood, and then the flow of liquid down to the lower half of her body through her iliac arteries. Her legs began to burn, and a twinge of pain nagged her left ankle. Her breathing began to lose its rhythm. She concentrated on slowing her pace and restoring the rhythm of her breathing. After several more minutes, she crested the summit of the peak, just as the Earth-Ocean's rotation brought Sol into view. The photons of the star struck her eyes as a physical pressure against her retinas, and she could perceive slight pain at the rapid contraction of her irises to reduce the apertures of her pupils to protect her sensitive optic nerve.

Taitano slowly whirled in a three-hundred-and-sixty-degree circle, taking in the view of the entire island, the Pacific Ocean, and the island of Tinian in the distance, mostly obscured by the morning mist. Her mind was, as usual, racing. The moment she stopped moving, her body began to shiver in the cool humectation of the atmosphere. But she permitted herself a minute to reflect on where she was, in both space and time. She knew that to truly locate oneself in the Cosmos, one had to give not three coordinates—height, width, depth—but also a fourth: time. She thought of the people who had stood in the exact same place as she was at that moment, *but at a different time.* The Ancient Chamorros who had bravely sailed here around 2000 BCE from Southeast Asia and who made this narrow chain of volcanic islands along the Marianas Trench their new home for thousands of years. And the comparatively recent colonization by the Spanish, Germans, Japanese, and Americans. She herself was a product of this rich, and often bloody, multi-ethnic legacy.

Putting aside her reflections, she headed back down the mountain. Her knees felt the increase in G-forces, as she jogged down the steep descent, cutting through the switchbacks via lightly worn foot trails that bisected the angles of the path. Every minute or so, she paused to do sets of push-ups, with her head in the direction of the declivity of the slope for increased resistance. She was careful to keep her arms at her sides and her back straight in order to engage the core muscle groups of her abdomen. She repeated the intervals until she reached two-hundred push-ups. She then ran the rest of the way home.

When she arrived and approached the door, she found that it was unlocked. Her mind raced. *Is it possible that I failed to lock it? No, not possible. I was so careful and deliberate. This is like a nightmare. This can't be happening. Am I losing my mind, at such an early age? The techniques I learned. How could they not work? How could this happen?* She raced into the house and found her grandfather in the kitchen, pouring himself a large mug of coffee.

"Morning, Tai!" he rumbled in a rough, not yet fully awake, rasp of a voice—the timber of his greeting as coarse as his bewhiskered countenance.

"Grandpa, did you just get up?" she murmured in a tightly controlled vociferation. In desperate hope, she asked, "Have you been outside?"

Through the duskiness of his pre-caffeine brain, he could see she was distressed, "Yeah, I stepped out front to see the sunrise. You OK, Taibo?"

Taitano's chest relaxed, and she tried to steady her erratic breathing. *Grandfather opened the door. You were right. You did it right. You locked the door. You're not crazy. Well, maybe you are, but you still locked the door and did not go back. One little victory. And baby steps can carry us long distances.*

"Yes, Grandpa, I'm fine." *I am going to be fine.* "I have to get to the lab. Dinner tonight?"

"Sure, Taibo. Wouldn't miss it."

# Chapter 3

# School

Saiyam Patel was a real jerk. As usual, he was holding court in the back of the classroom, loudly regaling a devoted and fawning group of students with his exploits from last night. "Yeah, that was the *best*! After twenty points, Lucy just gave up and admitted I was the best rakshaw player she'd ever seen. She even paid up right there and then and bought the whole room another round."

"Where did you learn to play rackshaw like that?" asked a sycophantic young woman who had positioned herself in a supplicating position slightly below Patel, who was leaning back into his seat with his feet up on the chair in front of him.

"Well, my parents hired a teacher for me, but when I beat him during our first lesson, I just kind of taught myself. Guess I'm just a natural, or a genius, or both. Who knows?"

"No way! That's *unbelievable*."

Taitano took her seat in the second row of the classroom, in front of the dense, transparent polymer barrier that separated the "dry side" from the "wet side" of the room. As she glided into her seat, she tapped with her index and middle fingers, five times in quick succession, the skin behind her right ear lobe. Into both sides of the classroom, the terrestrial and aquatic areas, humans and dolphins shuffled or swam in and took their places, the dolphin side being much more relaxed when it came to remaining in one place during the class. The dozen or so dolphins maintained a loose formation, gently shifting positions around each other in an intricate and peaceful dance. Next to the grace and composure of the dolphins, the humans seemed like a jabbering, unkempt rabble planning a raid on a neighboring group of primates.

Taitano could hear Patel saying, "And there was this other time when this dolphin challenged me to a match, and I agreed to play her blindfolded …." Taitano dipped her head and shook it back and forth in dismay. *One of evolution's most cruel jokes is the ill-fated combination of the male primate brain, bipedalism, the opposable thumb, and the hormone testosterone. It's probably led to the shedding of more blood than anything else in our sad, troubled history.* She was about to put in her earpieces and ask her abacus to match an opposing interference frequency to the auditory modulation of Patel's overbearing voice, when one of the dolphins started thumping on the polymer divider. The dolphin, who Taitano remembered was called "Quickbite," began to chitter excitedly and bob his head up and down at the humans. The translator rendered the clicks, whirls, and discordant melodies as, "Hey, Saiyam! Have you even done the reading for today's class? Or were you too busy being Mister Important and telling everyone how great you are?"

"Reading? For the class? You Naturals are so early twenty-first century," Patel replied. "All I need to know I can get from this," he continued, tapping the lower back of his skull. "I don't need to descend to your rate of manual abacus interface. When are you going to get with the program and connect to the web, *sharkbait?*"

Patel, of course, was a synch: a person with cybernetic multi-processors embedded into the cranium that could send low voltage alternating current pulses through semi-conductor fiber optic cables arrayed at several points directly into the cerebral cortices, allowing a person to *directly* interface with an abacus via bio-chemical electronic return signals, rather than using comparatively cumbersome voice activation, gestures, or keypads. Over one-hundred years after the basic technology had been developed, synchs were still relatively rare. That was often—but not always—the way of things in human culture. In the early twentieth century, science fiction writers had imagined that, by the twenty-first century, everyone would be flying around in hover cars. Even decades after the development of the electric car, people had still been driving around in combustion engine vehicles, spewing toxic gases into their atmosphere, while the ecosystem continued to crumble around them. Much academic ink had been spilled trying to analyze this aspect of human psychology, to little end. The implantation of cybernetic computer processors directly into the brain was still a source of long-standing and current debates. Human versus machine. There were advantages and disadvantages. Yes, the implant allowed a significantly faster rate of information exchange between the human brain and the abacuses that everyone used. There was no doubt about that. However, not everyone was able to use them, as a human's immune system sometimes attacked the synthetic implant as a foreign body, and it then had to be removed. A tricky procedure. These days, the universal medical coverages had stopped paying for the installation and maintenance of the cerebral interfaces, and they were becoming a status symbol of those with special connections in government and academic institutions. There were so many other issues that the implants had raised, none of which were straightforward. Whether one should be permitted to use them during academic examinations, whether only people with cognitive disfunction should be allowed the relatively rare devices, whether a person whose body had rejected one should be permitted to have a second try. For the moment, Taitano did not care because she was just sick of hearing Patel talk.

Just as Quickbite was about to respond with a rather

unsophisticated reply to Patel's latest comment, Professor Sun swam into view through the transparent wall that separated the water from the air. Patel and Quickbite eyed each other menacingly, but piped down and gave their attention to the professor.

The participants assembled for the class were a mixture of PhD and master's students. Despite the social upheavals of the last one-hundred and forty years, the structure of academic universities and the titles and degrees awarded by them had remained remarkably constant, and the degree of Doctor of Philosophy was still the highest academic degree that one could achieve for completing the comprehensive and original research of a subject. Today's course was devoted to investigating and assessing the worldwide efforts to complete the environmental remediation of the Ocean, including cleaning up the millions of tons of waste that humans had dumped there over the last few hundred years. The didactic approach was multidisciplinary, encompassing politics, law, science, engineering, and even a smattering of philosophy and history. Taitano had recently earned her PhD in Cryptanalysis, the science of breaking codes—to be distinguished from cryptology, which dealt with both making and breaking codes, and cryptography, which focused only on the writing of security codes. Her obsessive compulsive disorder—or OCD—imbued her with an almost super-human ability to focus on a task for extended periods of time, which had served her well in her studies and enabled her to complete her research in less time than her peers. On the other hand, the inner drive that obsessively compelled her also rendered her exhausted and often left her feeling psychologically depleted. Her condition was therefore a blessing and a curse. She was currently serving as Professor Sun's teaching assistant for the class.

"Hello, all," sang Professor Sun. (The version rendered into English for the humans was significantly less eloquent than the original.) "Sorry I am late. Shall we begin? So today we are going to review the historical, political, and scientific origins of the current Clean Blue

Project, which, as you all know, is in its final phases. Carl Sagan University has received a significant grant from the Earth-Ocean Academy of Science to conduct the project and many of you are involved in it as part of your master's, doctoral, or postdoc studies with the university. So, who can tell us where we are in this project, why we are doing it, and where we are going? It's always a good idea to start with the basics. We can't know where we're going, unless we know where we've been." Professor Sun noticed that Patel was not paying attention—well, at least not to *the class*, as he *was* devoting his enraptured regard to chatting with what he must have considered to be an attractive human female sitting next to him. "Mister Patel! You seem to have lots of energy today. Why don't you enlighten us?"

With a thought, Patel activated the passive memory buffer of his cybernetic implant, replayed the professor's question, and began to access an appropriate on-line reference source to obtain the information that he would need to answer. "Don't mind if I do, Professor. By the way, you are looking particularly fit and trim today." At that remark, Professor Sun did his best to scowl. Patel continued, "So where shall we start? In the early to mid-twentieth century, as the Industrial De-volution gained speed and territorial land and sea disputes continued to rage, humans dumped all kinds of junk in the Ocean."

Professor Sun interrupted, "Mister Patel, perhaps you can elucidate upon what you so elegantly refer to as 'junk.'"

"Yeah, sure, Professor. It was really quite gross. Raw sewage, toxic waste from chemical production plants, plastics of all kinds, biological and chemical weapons, nuclear waste from power plants, pesticides. Some of the humans truly thought dumping all this junk—ah, I mean—hazardous material was an effective way to get rid of it. They thought that the immensity of the Ocean would hydrolyze the materials and that they would be harmlessly re-integrated into the planetary ecosystem. Other humans just wanted it out of the way and thought the Ocean was a convenient dumping spot, at least convenient from a short-term anthropomorphic perspective."

Taitano could tell that Patel was mostly reading from a webpage that he had direct access to via his implant.

Patel continued, "These hazardous materials poisoned the water at all levels. The chemical weapons dumped into the sea are a good example. Some of the weapons were dumped in very deep waters—like off the coast of Hawai'i—and instantly imploded, leaking their contents and causing localized extinction-level events among the plant and animal species living there. Others were dumped in more shallow waters—like in the Baltic Sea after World War II. Their casing slowly degraded. Despite warnings by scientists for decades, the politicians didn't listen; and, in the mid-twenty-first century, they all went bust and killed almost everything that was left living in the Baltic Sea—which, by the way, wasn't much by that time due to all the other pollution there, not to mention temperature rise and the increase in salinity due to climate change."

One of the dolphin students, Fastcatch, interrupted Patel. "Fastcatch" was nothing more than a convenient sobriquet, which was used for human purposes. The dolphin's true "name" was an elaborate pattern of vocalizations far too complex for the brain and larynx of a human to manage. "Hey, Patel. What webpage are you reading from? Typical human chauvinism. Just because we dolphins had the intelligence and mobility to abandon the Baltic by then doesn't mean there were not a host of other creatures sitting there slowly getting poisoned by the mess your ancestors made there. Starfish, shrimp, fish, especially demersal ones. Oh, and let's not forget about the micro-organisms, among whom are blue-green algae who manufacture the air we all breathe. Did you forget about them? Or did they just not count because they—like we—couldn't speak a human language that they could use to politely ask you to stop dumping your garbage in their backyards, to use one of your idioms? You didn't even stop until the Enneans—"

Patel threw up his hands, "OK, I give up! Enough already. I'm sorry, Fastcatch. You're right. We messed up. That's why we're here trying to fix it. Don't get your flippers all tangled over it. Besides, at least we don't still go around eating the flesh of other beings like you guys do. I'm surprised the Enneans would even allow a bunch of carnivores on their planet."

Professor Sun swam closer to the glass, "Gentlebeings, that's enough. I would advise you to take your disagreements 'outside the classroom,' but I am uncertain what that would mean in the present context." That got a general chuckle from the rest of the class, including Patel and Fastcatch. The professor continued, "Both your comments are duly noted, and I would like Mister Patel to continue. Mister Patel, can you please give us some estimates of how many chemical weapons were dumped into the Ocean and where they were located?"

Patel shot Fastcatch a self-satisfied smirk and continued, "Well, don't mind if I do, Professor. According to various historical databases, chemical weapons were found in every region of the Ocean. In the Arctic region ..."

Saiyam Patel abruptly stopped speaking and a disoriented look clouded his visage. He looked around in confusion and finally looked up and said, "Sorry, Professor. I think that's all I have. Sorry."

Taitano exerted all her will to suppress the smile threatening to show on her face. She forced herself to frown and look down at her desk. She definitely did not look at her abacus, which she had just used a moment ago to gain access to Patel's cerebral implant and block its connection to the historical database that he had been reading from in his head. It had taken her only a moment or two to cycle through the interface lockout keys, as Patel's parents had apparently opted for the standard security encryption, instead of the more robust, and expensive, deluxe version. She momentarily was reflecting on how the hacking methods she had used on Patel's implant were similar to those she had used the day before to defuse the sea-dumped chemical weapon on the ocean floor, when Professor Sun gently interjected, "Dr. Taitano, perhaps you could pick up where Mister Patel left off."

"Yes, of course, Professor. Well, I'm only a lowly Natural and not a Synch, but based on *the reading* I did about the subject, as of the late twentieth century and early twenty-first century, it has been notoriously difficult to quantify and locate all the munitions that were deposited onto the seabed. Around one to two million tons of chemical munitions were disposed of in the sea—at hundreds of dump sites. Sometimes boats were loaded with weapons and then scuttled. In other operations, the munitions were transported in ships and then dumped over the sides. These sites were located in the Arctic, Atlantic, Indian, Pacific, and Southern regions of the Ocean. More specifically, they were located off the east and west coasts of Canada and the United States; the Gulf of Mexico; the Australian, New Zealand, Indian, Philippine, Japanese, UK, and Irish Coasts; and the Barrents, Kara, White, Caribbean, Black, Red, Baltic, Mediterranean, and North Seas. The shifting positions of the munitions on the seabed, the lack of availability of reliable records, and sometimes the failure of governments to document the dumping—all complicated efforts in the last century to locate and then remediate the weapons. I don't want to sound monocausotaxophilic: the Ocean was under multiple pressures at the time—a rise in mean planetary temperature, changes in salinity, massive reduction of biodiversity. But, with all this going on at the same time, the degradation of the chemical munitions and the seepage of their toxic contents into the marine ecosystem certainly didn't help things.

"Generally, disposal in the sea had a number of perceived, short-term advantages. The Ocean was perceived by humans, at that time, to be an infinite sink into which anything could be disposed. And, no, there was no thought given to the other creatures of the sea or even to the related effects on plants and animals on the land. For those who *did* give it some thought, the unofficial consensus was that the immensity of the Ocean would somehow naturally decompose the toxic chemical warfare agents. In some cases, the chemicals were indeed assimilated into the marine environment, with the concomitant deleterious effects to those who lived there. But, in other cases, the chemicals persisted for well over a century, still in their toxic state.

"Another thing to consider is the technological backwardness of the age. They had just invented telephones; the worldwide internet, personal computing devices, and cerebral implants were decades away. Governments were generally able to conduct the dumping without many people knowing about it. When humans began to understand the effects that the Industrial Revolution—which we now refer to more aptly as the 'Industrial *De*-volution'—was having on the global environment in the middle of the twentieth century, the issue got slightly more attention, but it was a rather sluggish dawning of awareness. In 1969, the United States National Academy of Science made a recommendation that ocean dumping be discontinued. The last dumping operation by the United States was in 1970, amidst public protests, through the scuttling of the *SS LeBaron Russell Briggs* off the coast of Cape Kennedy, Florida. The following year, the United States Senate held an international conference on ocean pollution, at which Jacques Cousteau and Thor Heyerdahl reported their first-hand scientific findings of the damage that commercial dumping and shipping was causing to the Ocean. In 1972, the United States Congress enacted the Marine Protection, Research, and Sanctuaries Act, which prohibited ocean dumping of a lot of waste, but not all. In the same year, the London Convention was adopted and prohibited dumping of certain wastes, but again not all. These regulatory measures had only partial success, and various malefactors continued to dump all kinds of rubbish into the Ocean, both legally and illegally, well into the twenty-first century. The continuing degradation of the terrestrial and marine environment and the global recession of the 2030s didn't help things, as they led to the collapse of the insurance and re-insurance system and eventually the end of the international banking system in the 2040s. So, it goes without saying that there wasn't much political will to fund environmental remediation projects. Kind of a vicious circle."

Taitano paused, and Professor Sun prompted her, "Thank you for that very informative exposition of a dark chapter in humanity's treatment of the planetary biome, which we all share." The professor added, glaring at Patel, "And you even managed to educate us all without a chip in your brain. Would you care, Dr. Taitano, to continue and tell us how we came to be where we are *today* in respect of these vile and unimaginably cruel weapons that were dumped into our Ocean? And when I say 'our Ocean,' I am of course referring to the large body of water covering the surface of the planet that belongs to *all* species of Planet Earth-Ocean, and not just to a single species with the fortune—or misfortune—to have opposable thumbs." The professor made this last comment as he held up his two flippers in the water in front of him and looked at them in mock despair. This received more amused laughs from the students.

"Well," Taitano continued, "humanity was deep into Jevons Paradox by the late twentieth century and the beginning of the twenty-first century. They had devised more and more efficient ways to burn fossil fuels; but, instead of this leading to a decrease in the use of such fuels, it led to a significant *increase*. The net greenhouse gas emissions therefore continued to rise during this period. After we humans missed the goal of carbon-neutrality by 2050 under the Paris Agreement, Sol—in what seemed to be an act of galactic poetic justice—started in 2061 to enter an unprecedented phase of solar flare activity. Normally, about one-hundred and seventy-three Petawatts of solar energy hit Earth-Ocean every second. This almost doubled overnight and dramatically increased the pressures on the ecosystem. Wildfires, drought, electromagnetic disruptions of, well, everything we had gotten accustomed to relying on for our daily civilization. Famine, pestilence, displacements, water wars resulted. It was a global catastrophe. Hundreds of millions of humans died, not to mention millions of other animals—and let's not forget about the plants, but no one was counting them at the time. We were deep into the next mass level extinction event on Planet Earth-Ocean. And that's when the Enneans showed up, at our lowest point and in our hour of greatest need. They parked their vessel in a high-earth orbit because they were afraid of getting taken out by the space debris we had left in low-earth orbit. They had a simple message for the Secretary-General of the United Nations: they would prevent the solar flares from further destroying the habitability of the planet. In exchange, humans had to immediately implement carbon neutrality, complete nuclear disarmament—and, third, humans could no longer conduct any activities in, on, or above the Ocean, unless it was an operation for the sole purpose of cleaning up all the pollution we had dumped there."

Professor Sun interjected, "And did your brethren take the deal?"

"Well, at first, of course we didn't. The politicians and diplomats argued about it and tried to leverage deals that were best for themselves and, sometimes, for the countries they purported to represent. That went on for about another year, while the solar flares ravaged Earth-Ocean, and then there were mass uprisings, and the people replaced their representatives with ones who did the right thing. The vote in the UN General Assembly was two-hundred and one in favour and a handful of holdouts against. There were of course the usual abstentions of countries that were hoping to reap the benefits of the deal, while still keeping all their political options open during the Great Restoration."

"And what was this 'Great Restoration'?" asked Professor Sun.

Patel broke in, "My chip is back on-line! I can explain the Great

Restoration, Professor!"

"No, Mr. Patel, but perhaps this is a good opportunity to hear from one of our aquatic students. Quickbite?"

One of the dolphins began a furious litany of clicks, squeals, and whirs, which the translator interpreted as, "Yes! This is the good part! The land and the Ocean were a mess, that's for sure. But the cetacean population had already been decimated to such an extent that we had a comparatively lower number of casualties when compared to those of the plants and animals on land. With the new human governments in the control of people who actually understood what had to be done in order for human, and other, life to continue, they actually began to abide by their end of the bargain. Exclusively sustainable energy, a complete end to the disposal of any waste in the Ocean, the adoption of a circular manufacturing cycle, an end of agricultural pesticides, humanity went vegan, *et cetera*. And the nuclear arsenals were finally dismantled. The insanity of mutually assured destruction—with the apt acronym 'MAD'—seemed like something that was thought up in a daycare center with a bunch of sleep-deprived primate toddlers. It took a little while; but, by the 2080s, humanity's nuclear weapons were scrapped. And the long overdue cleanup of the Ocean was well underway. Just putting a stop to the dumping went a long way to assisting the Ocean to recover on its own."

"And did the Enneans keep their end of the bargain?"

"Oh, yes," continued Quickbite. "We could only see their vessel in orbit, and they chose not to show themselves to us. But they were there. They had a unique understanding of planetary geology and were able to generate a feedback pulse in the nickel-iron core of the planet that increased the electromagnetic field surrounding Earth-Ocean by ten-fold. Just in time, too. It shielded us from the biggest solar flare up until that time, which really would have finished us off."

"Thank you, Quickbite. Mister Patel, as your implant is back on-line, you should be able to tell us more about the marine aspects of the

Great Restoration, since that is the very purpose of Carl Sagan University."

"Yeah, sure, Professor! No problem!" said Patel. He looked smugly around the room with a mixture of arrogance and embarrassment, "Yeah, so here we are, cleaning up the mess we left behind for ourselves. All the shipwrecks, oceanic mines, plastics, toxic and nuclear waste, broken cables and pipelines, decommissioned oil rigs, chemical weapons. It was a real mess down there on the ocean floor, and the only reason humans were allowed to be in the Ocean was to clean it up. We couldn't manufacture products in one part of the globe and then ship them to the other side of the planet anymore in order to increase profits by one percent. Many people became subsistence farmers and met their own needs. Industry completely transformed itself into sustainable processes and focused on three main areas: nuclear disarmament, sustainable energy, and marine restoration projects. Our job here at Sagan University is focused on marine restoration—to finish getting all the debris off the seabed, with an emphasis on chemical weapons, many of which, amazingly, after more than two centuries, are still holding their chemical warfare agents intact within their metal casings. We're almost done with the cleanup, thanks, in no small measure, to how awesome I am."

"And you were doing so well, Mister Patel," said Professor Sun, blowing out a long, exasperated stream of bubbles from his spiracle. "Now, what was the purpose of reviewing all this history today?" the professor asked rhetorically. "Well, I will tell you. As I mentioned previously, in order to move forward in a wise and purposeful way and in order to avoid the mistakes of the past, we need to know where we have been and learn from those mistakes. The Enneans have given us all a second chance, and it is up to us not to fail succeeding generations the way that our ancestors failed us. I also want to emphasize that we no longer follow a 'we' versus 'them' way of life. We are all connected. We all share a common but differentiated responsibility for the sins of our forefathers and mothers. Yes, humans were committed to their path dependent suicide course to oblivion. However, we must also remember that we dolphins were not willing to do much about it. We knew what was happening. We knew the humans were killing the planet. But we hid ourselves under a clam shell and chose to do nothing. It was the humans who reached out to us with invitations to communicate, not the other way around. But we could have made contact hundreds of years earlier and guided our terrestrial brothers and sisters early enough in their history to prevent the mass atrocities they planned to visit upon themselves and our shared ecosystem. But we simply kept to ourselves, instead. If humans' sins were ones of commission, then ours were ones of omission. It was only the fortuitous appearance of the Enneans that saved *us all*.

"Finally, I wish to remind you all of the obvious, which we all often forget in our day-to-day lives. Humans and dolphins are both mammalian species. We share a common ancestor. We were once all terrestrial mammals. And then, about ninety million years ago, the progenitors of dolphins decided to return to the sea. But we all still breathe the precious air, we cherish and need our communities, we all suckle our young. I don't see many students in this classroom at the moment who belong to the taxonomic classes *arthropoda* or *echinodermata*. We are all mammals. We are far more alike than different. So," the professor turned his head to Patel and then to Fastcatch, "let's remember that as we continue to *try* to work together for the good of all the species on Earth-Ocean."

Taitano heard Patel mutter under his breath, "I'm not suckling any young, that's for sure." Quickbite and Fastcatch were swimming around each other, deep in an intertwined song of some type.

As Taitano rolled her eyes, Professor Sun said, "Now, please turn to page six-hundred and seventy-eight in your readers, break into groups, and do the exercises there. I will check your progress in forty-five minutes. Dr. Taitano with Fastcatch. Mister Patel with Quickbite." He continued to pair off the humans and dolphins into study groups, and they got down to a series of complex and interdisciplinary exercises designed to help them with their field operations to clear the seabed surrounding the string of Mariana Islands from the discarded military ordnance of the past.

At the end of the class, Professor Sun informed the students, "Before we end for the day, I wanted to inform you that the next rotation is due to leave Earth-Ocean soon. As you know, it's the turn of the Pacific region—that's us—to select three students to travel to Ennea as part of the exchange program. The United Nations Commission for Ennean Cross-Cultural Exchange will announce the names tomorrow. Dismissed."

As the students swam and walked out of their respective chambers, Professor Sun gently sang to Taitano, "Dr. Taitano, one moment of your time, if you please."

She held herself back, trying to emotionally surf a transient wave of anxiety. "Sure, Professor. What can I do for you? Great class today, by the way."

"Most kind of you, Dr. Taitano."

"It's just 'Tai,' Sun," she said, giving him a quick wink and knowing smile.

"As you wish, Tai," he responded, blowing out a thin trickle of bubbles. "About the Commission," he continued. "I am aware that you did not apply to take part, unlike the rest of your classmates."

"Yeah, kinda woulda been futile, right? They'd never accept someone with my condition as a shiny representative of Earth-Ocean, and humanity, to journey across the void and meet a bunch of squishy aliens."

"Well, that's just it. The Enneans have specifically requested that you join the next exchange voyage. They asked for you by name, Tai."

Her stomach dropped. She felt dizzy. As she swayed, antipathy gripped her heart, and perspiration began to pool on her forehead. She tried to utter: "*What?*" But no sound could escape her constricted air passages. She felt a small, sharp pain slice sideways across her chest, just under the skin. Professor Sun seemed to wear an expression of concern on his normally inscrutable visage. He waited and gave her time to process the information and to compose herself. The professor, once again, marveled that these rather small and fragile mammals could have survived so long without being outcompeted by other more robust lifeforms on the planet.

Finally, Taitano managed to croak out in a barely audible susurration, "I—I don't understand."

"Neither do we. And we don't have any further information on this. But you're going to be one of the names announced tomorrow, unless you tell me by 10:00 hours tomorrow morning that you intend to pass. You don't have to go. It's not mandatory. Nor could it be. It's up to you, but you don't have a lot of time to decide. Go home, talk to your grandfather. Meditate on it. I'm sure you'll make the right choice."

Taitano reflected on that for a moment, staring at the dolphin suspended in front of her through the perfectly transparent polymer barrier.

Professor Sun continued, "For what it's worth … I would be happy to have you along for the ride, the ride of a lifetime. Maybe literally, in a way. We're not going to be coming back for a long time, at least from the perspective of those on Earth-Ocean."

Taitano looked up at him in perplexity and confusion. It looked as though she were pleading for his mercy, for him to stop talking, for him to say that this was some kind of rather cruel university prank or postdoc hazing ritual.

"In addition to the three students, Moon and I have been selected and are going on behalf of the Pacific region. You know how the politics of this are played. The big countries have—what do humans called it?—oh, yes, a gentlemen's agreement—quite an ironic expression for a variety of reasons—that only representatives from the small countries can go. Moon and I would love to have you along. We think you are the best of humanity and of all gentlebeings on Earth-Ocean."

"But ... my condition ..."

"... makes you even more qualified. The UN Ennean Commission isn't looking for super-heroes. It wants real people, with all their strengths and frailties. That's who we really are, both human and dolphin. It's our struggles that bring out our compassion. Attention to overcoming our areas of development makes us better, not worse. And, if what I have studied is correct, communication with the Enneans is all about patience, tolerance, and compassion—all qualities you hold in abundance, at least from what I've been able to see during the two years we've been working together. And courage, don't forget about courage. Every day, you embody courage by just getting out of bed and coming to do your studies and work here at the university. That's what your Ancient Greeks considered to be courage. Think about all that tonight. Call me if you need to discuss it any further ... anytime." Professor Sun executed a graceful backflip in his tank to lighten the mood a bit and then whistled, "And I do mean *anytime*. You do remember, don't you, that dolphins only sleep with half their brains at a time, right? One of the many benefits of unihemispheric sleep. It also helps me grade examinations faster." And there was that weird dolphin "smile" again that she had seen yesterday in the sea between Saipan and Tinian.

"OK, Sun. I'll sleep on it. With *both* hemispheres of my brain."

"That's all I can ask for ... from a human."

Taitano's head inclined towards the ceiling of the chamber. She then affected a look of mock opprobrium, glared at Professor Sun, coyly smiled, and languidly waved at him as she departed the classroom—doing her best to play the part of an aggrieved soubrette. *Out of all the dolphin professors on the planet, I had to get the one trying to be a standup comedian.*

# CHAPTER 4

# PROPHESY

Taitano departed the classroom and entered a larger dome structure anchored on the seabed between the islands of Saipan and Tinian. She looked up and could see the faint traces of Sol penetrating the layers of sea water between the dome and the boundary between Ocean and air above. She removed her wetsuit from her locker, secured her abacus to her wrist, and stepped into the airlock. She keyed the control to flood the compartment with water, waited for the chamber to equalize with the Ocean outside, and then departed the safety of the university's underwater facility for the depths of the sea. She considered engaging the auditory interference field to ward off any esurient sharks, which were quite common in the waters between the two islands. But she wanted to see if she needed it before activating the field. Better to do this the old-fashioned way. *Humans swam in the Ocean for millennia before auditory interference fields, and so can I. It will be a challenge.*

Her mind wandered to the *U.S.S. Indianapolis* in July 1945. Shortly after dropping off key components of the world's first atomic bomb, it was *en route* from Guam to the Philippines when it was torpedoed by a Japanese submarine. She sank in twelve minutes, and for four days the crew who had survived the initial attack had to fight for their lives—dehydration, saltwater poisoning, exposure, relentless shark attacks. Out of over one thousand crewmembers, only a little over three-hundred survived. It was the worst disaster in the history of the United States Navy. A shiver ran through Taitano's body as she thought of the forlorn sailors, thousands of kilometers from their homes, bobbing in the Ocean like abandoned corks—filled with terror and hopelessness. A lethal whitetip shark swam past her, fecklessly eyeing her and gliding through the sea like a snake through new summer grass. The whitetip then changed directions and pursued a school of bluefish. *Apparently, the bluefish are tastier than I am. Or at least easier to kill. No arguments from me.*

After forty-five minutes of determined swimming, Taitano caught sight of the rocky shore of Saipan, and began her ascent up the island's subsea shelf to the surface. As she negotiated the jagged rocks to the shore, the rolling tumult of the waves crashed against her like surf striking the bow of a ship fighting its way through a storm. She imagined the sea gods, in their ireful wrath, trying to drag her back into their grip, angry that she had escaped once more to the safety of land.

Half an hour later, she was walking through her front door. "Grandpa, I'm home. I'm so famished I could eat a whitetip shark! What's for dinner?"

Taitano's grandfather peered around the corner of the kitchen, "Vegetables, vegetables, and … more vegetables. Hit the shower and come back soon while it's hot."

During dinner, Taitano had struggled with the anxiety of telling her grandfather about the invitation to join the exchange program. She did not want to go; the very thought of it suffused her with dread and pressed her down into a deep well of despair. She had a strong suspicion that her grandfather would encourage her to take up the challenge with some kind of sappy inspirational speech about responsibility and manifesting one's inner potential. She shrunk from the idea of talking to him about it, but knew she had to.

After they had finished dinner, Taitano summoned the inner strength to impart to him all the details, in as neutral a way as she could manage. He sat forward in his seat, listening patiently, not interrupting. When she had finished, he broke eye contact with his granddaughter, leaned back in his chair, and drew a long, deep breath; he then exhalated, deliberately and smoothly, while he rubbed his face with both hands in long, slow strokes. He steepled his hands in front of his pursed lips and then looked at her once again. "Taibo, I've been waiting for this moment since you were a little girl. I knew someday it would come, but one always thinks one has more time than one actually has. Anyway, the Universe has a plan, and all any of us can do is play our small part."

She rolled her eyes at him and responded, "OK, Mr. Dramatic, what the heck are you talking about?"

He got up from his chair, unsteady on his feet. His arthritic fingers were flexing and relaxing. He started to walk pendulously towards the bookshelf at the other end of the room. As he approached the bookshelf, Taitano also got to her feet and felt a bit light-headed and dizzy. Her grandfather looked old and weary from the many worries and cares he had borne in his long years. He drew an old, frayed book from the top shelf. "Do you remember this book?" Taitano had a strange sensation of *déjà vu*. Of having been here before, in both space and time. It was like going through a box of old mementos that triggered memories that had lain dormant for years or even decades. Recollections coming to the fore that had been buried. Somnolescent memory engrams chemically unlocked and ignited by ripping strands of uncaring ribonucleic acid.

She was a small girl again. Maybe six years old. She was teetering on a step ladder, precariously reaching from her tippy toes to grasp something on a shelf just out of her too short reach. An old book. She descended the ladder, removed a thick German-English dictionary, placed it on the top stair of the stepladder, and re-ascended so she could just barely reach the book. The muscles of her left shoulder ached as she concentrated and tried to hook her fingernails under the ancient binding of the tome. *Gotcha!* She carefully coaxed the book from its stronghold on the shelf and then held it in her hands as she alighted from the ladder, which went toppling to the ground with a cracking thud—the clattering din reverberating through the house. The cacophony made her involuntarily jump. She took a few calming breaths, sat on the floor, and reverently opened the book. It was filled with words she could barely understand and wonderful drawings of ghosts, boreal forests, and octopodal demons. She could make out some words: *fu'una, puntan, birak, suruhof.* She had not thought of that book for so long. But the memory transported her into a time long ago—at least by the standards of a human in her early twenties.

"Agana." Her grandfather's soulful baritone liltingly pulled her back into the present. He only called her by her proper given name when he dropped the playful banter that he normally affected with her and wanted to get serious about a topic. "Do you remember this book? The last time you held it you were lucky not to have taken a bad spill and broken your neck."

"Yes, Grandpa. Of course. It's like yesterday. But what is it?"

"Well, let's sit down and take a look."

They moved to the kitchen table and attentively opened the tome. Taitano noticed that the tatterdemalion's binding had been ripped apart, the pages removed and scanned and then pasted back together. This was standard practice in the past before more advanced replication methods had been in wide use. It gave the book a rather disheveled appearance, but also a measure of wholesome authenticity.

He noticed his granddaughter running her fingertips along the reassembled, uneven binding, "Ah, yes. I had the book scanned and then put back together. They did a pretty good job, but it's never as good as the original."

"So, what is it?"

"It's the PhD thesis of your great grandfather, Frederick Hofstadter. My dad. He lived on the island and was a professor of literature at the old university. He had come to Saipan to research his ancestry and fell in love with the place. Married a luminescent Chamorro woman, my mother, your great grandmother, and never left. He died relatively early. You never met him." A distant pall enveloped him, and he looked away from Taitano, lost in something. A few moments later, he mastered himself and returned to her. "Your great grandfather wanted to preserve and analyze a comprehensive mythology of the Chamorro people. To preserve all that fragmentary oral history, folklore, and legend in one place, in writing. To ensure it was not lost, either to the ravages of time or a cataclysmic event. And here is the result. When the Enneans came, one of the things they requested was a survey of the world's literature, not just the mainstream tired old stuff we get in school, but also a true representation of all the cultures of the world, both human and dolphin. That's when I had this scanned and uploaded to the global database. It was selected by the UN Ennean Commission tasked with compiling the survey and sent to the Enneans for their first return trip home, with the first group of humans and dolphins to journey to their home planet. It was the first cross-cultural exchange program. Although, exchange is not really the right word, because no Enneans ever actually set foot, or tentacle, on Earth-Ocean."

"This is all fascinating, but what does it have to do with whether I'm going to Ennea or not?"

"Take a closer look at the book."

Taitano examined the book again and saw something sticking out of the top of one of the pages. A bookmark of sorts. She ran her thumb across the page marked by the slip of weathered paper and gently lifted the pages open to the marked spot. The "bookmark" was in fact a child's rendering of an octopoid creature, but with nine legs rather than eight. Her mind was instantly flooded with recollection; memory washed upon her as an unrelenting wave striking the shoreline. She had drawn the picture for a class project. She and the other students had to draw pictures of Enneans and make a report to the class about their favorite aspects of their alien benefactors. "I remember this! And the report I gave the class. I haven't thought about that in years! It's not too bad, huh? My report was about how the Enneans were helping us clean up the Ocean, after so many decades of dumping all kinds of pollutants into it."

"Yes, Agana. And look at the page you marked with the picture."

She meditatively set aside the picture and looked at the page in the book. She began to read the text, which was organized into three columns. On the left, Chamorro, in the middle, English, and on the right the corresponding German. She could read all three, but she was fastest in English and so focused on the middle column. The text recounted a legend about a mythological figure known as *"puntan."* The legend told of how he was responsible for creating Sol, the moon, and Earth-Ocean from his own flesh. But the land, sky, and sea were sterile and had no life—until the wife of *puntan*, named *"fu'una,"* showed up and endowed everything with a living force. She did this at great personal sacrifice by turning into a ponderous rock. She then clove herself in twain, and from the gaping crevasse came forth the Chamorro people.

"Grandpa, this is a pretty standard creation myth. There are hundreds just like it. What does it have to do with me?"

"Keep reading, Agana. The next myth talks of a shaman who will someday …"

"Just a minute, Grandpa," she said, gently interrupting him. "Let me read it myself." Her grandfather smiled at that, as he had heard his headstrong granddaughter utter in her childhood "I do it by *myself*, Grandpa" at least a million times. Taitano looked further down the page, where she found the following stanzas:

*The Suruh rises from the Ocean,*

*Glistening in the autumnal chill,*

*And travels the dreary and barren wastes,*

*With nothing but her spirit and will.*

*Upon her dripping steed,*

*Suffused with doubt and fright,*

*To the Birak of another realm,*

*To another star, she alights.*

*In a gloomy realm of water and half-light,*

*Enveloped shall she be,*

*And cure both herself and the Birak,*

*By sacrificing herself … completely.*

The words swirled in her head. She felt a dizziness and disorientation. When she had steadied herself and regained her bearing, she read the stanzas again. She looked at her grandfather in disbelief, "You can't seriously believe this applies to me. What does "*birak*" and "*suruh*" mean again?"

"*Suruh* means a traditional healer. A shaman. A *birak* is a …" He paused for a moment—haunted. "It's a … demon, Agana."

A foreboding shadow brushed across her soul. "Grandpa, what's all this about?"

"I don't know," he replied. "But I can feel there is something at work here. Call it cyclical time, fate, destiny, Hegelian spirals. I don't know…. The Enneans have this book. We … I gave it to them. And here we are, with you being specifically requested by them to join the next exchange mission. Does this sound like a coincidence to you? You know, for thousands of years, many tribes of humanity were ruled by men who sought power, money, and women through violence. Only relatively recently have we experienced a moral inversion—not the one attempted by Christianity to wrench power from the Roman Empire. A true moral awakening—whereby communication, understanding, and healing are now our preferred virtues and the way of dealing with each other. That ancient poem speaks of a female Chamorro healer travelling to a foreign land to heal a bunch of demons. And you *know* what the Enneans look like. The parallels seem prophetic."

"So, you think I should go." She said it as a statement, not a question. He was half-staring at the book and half at her. She gently dipped her head a bit to make direct eye contact with him. She searched his eyes to gauge his thoughts and feelings.

"I think you need to seriously consider it. And you only have a short time in which to do so."

Taitano stood up, cradling the book in her left hand and throwing up her right hand to the ceiling, "I have trouble getting out of the door in the morning without coming back ten times to check the lock! And you want me to go to another star system? I've been struggling for years with both my OCD and the anxiety connected to it. Meditation, nutrition, exercise, breathing techniques; and, at the same time, I'm constantly fighting obsessive urges to prove myself and stretch the boundaries of my abilities. These hunting oscillations between fear and compulsion are exhausting! Do you remember that time when I was thirteen, and you had to physically drag me outside to the grocery store because I had been too afraid to leave the house for two weeks? Do you *really* want a neurodivergent like me to travel over ten light years across the galaxy in a ship full of complete strangers to go hang out with a bunch of creepy aliens?"

"It's not about what *I* want, Agana," he said calmly, with

compassionate resolution. "And it's not even about what *you* want. Sometimes we don't get the luxury of doing what we want and instead have to go where we're needed. Unless my judgment is failing me, I'm pretty sure you're needed on Ennea. And, you never know, it *may actually be* about what *you* need, Agana. It's about your proper place in the Universe. It's about doing what you were meant to do, what you were put here to do. Your reason for being here in the first place. Call it destiny, if you want to label it. You read the poem: it also talks of the healer healing herself."

She stared at him in disbelief and disapprobation. Not at *what* he was saying, but because he was making her face uncomfortable truths whence she was trying to flee.

"And there is another aspect of all this," he said.

"And what is that?"

"Your German ancestors committed unspeakable atrocities during the twentieth century."

"I know that, but it's not my fault."

"Yes, of course not. But you carry within you the legacy of all that. It's a cultural reminder of what we are all capable of. All humans carry this within them. It is part of who we are as a species. We have it within us to slaughter ... but also to heal. Think of our troubled relationship with our cetacean cousins. We didn't even share the same local biome with them. They in the sea, and we on land. And yet we still almost drove them to extinction. This is part of the human condition. We all have to decide when we wake up in the morning: am I going to destroy or create, am I going to be part of the problem or the solution? The myriad decisions we make each day define who we are. You have a ponderous decision before you—I can feel it *in my bones*. One that will not only define you, but also affect the well-being of many others."

Taitano put the book down and began to stalk the room in erratic patterns. "But there's still so much for me to do *here*. So many munitions still to disarm and clear from the ocean floor. I don't want to leave that work unfinished. It may not be as glorious as shooting off to the heavens to an unknown world, but it's what I've been working towards in my studies for so many years. We're just about to start the Novaya Zemlya cleanup operation, and they really need me there."

During the course of the twentieth and twenty-first centuries, a variety of toxic waste, munitions (both conventional and chemical), and nuclear waste had been dumped off the coast of Novaya Zemlya, an archipelago in the Arctic region of the Ocean. There were also several scuttled nuclear submarines, which now patiently awaited recovery and remediation. The chemical munitions residing in massive quantities on the seabed off the coast of Novaya Zemlya were some of the last that needed to be environmentally remediated. The governmental authorities had engaged in their usual "strategy" of multiple, conflicting, and dissembling narratives, such as the munitions were not there and never had been there; they had already been raised and destroyed in the twentieth century; there were inadequate funds to remediate the site; they had been placed there by someone else; their contents had leaked into the ecosystem over a hundred years ago; the toxic munitions were now part of the marine environment and removing them would harm the biota that used them as habitat. The International Commission for the Remediation of Sea-Dumped Munitions—ICRSM—had negotiated for years with an assortment of government officials to obtain permission to assist in the cleanup operation, which would commence sometime in the next year. As part of the operation, the chemical munitions would be disarmed, brought to the surface, and then destroyed with ionized plasma arc torches contained within a static detonation chamber.

Taitano's grandfather patiently listened to her, studying her face with honesty and sincerity. With great compassion and mansuetude, he said, "There are others who will carry on what you started. It will take years to finish. You may even make it there and back again and help them finish the job. But, unless my heart deceives me, this task on Ennea is one that only you can manage. I sense something else holding you back. Search your heart, Agana. Be honest with yourself."

Taitano wanted to look away, to avoid the emotional intensity of the moment. An intensity not only between her and her grandfather, but also a conflict within—and with—*herself*. She dug deep inside and found the courage to face what was troubling her, what was holding her back. "But I would never see you again, Grandpa." Taitano felt hot pools of water collecting in her eyes; they then broke over her lower eyelids and ran down her cheeks. The liquid quickly evaporated and cooled her skin. She thought about how scientists had researched for years the evolutionary origin of the unique human physiological response of crying in response to intense emotions. The tears shed as a result of emotions were chemically quite distinct from those shed for other reasons, such as maintaining the proper level of moisture in the eyes and distributing natural antibodies to the sclera. Scientists had never figured out the why or how. Another human riddle to be solved someday.

Taitano's grandfather gently took her hand in his. "I'm old. I've had a good run. Does it really make any sense to hang around here to keep me company for the next few years? I'll be fine. You know, it's an easy way out, isn't it? 'I can't go because I have to take care of my decrepit grandpa.' But we both know it's an excuse—a way to avoid facing your fears and this immense challenge. You *need* to do this, Agana. *You* do. There are so many reasons to do this! Not only for yourself and your ancestors, but also to set an example for others who struggle with your condition. And who knows? You might even end up helping these '*birak*'—whoever they turn out to be. Your true work now lies elsewhere. Rise to the challenge that has been placed before you. Life is always filled with uncertainties; that's just the way of things; but I know one thing for certain: if you don't go, you'll regret it for the rest of your days."

She wiped the tears from her face. She took long, pacifying breaths, bathing her alveoli with oxygen and expelling cardon dioxide and other metabolic waste products from her body. She allowed herself to accept the truth of his words. She gave herself over to the Universe. It felt right. Right, but scary. But that was alright. Being scared was part of being human.

"Okay, Grandpa. 'Face the fear and do it anyway,' right?"

"It's not only *the* way; it's the *only* way. You know what good ol' Heraclitus always used to say ...."

"'Whoever cannot seek the unforeseen sees nothing, for the known way is an impasse.'"

"That's my Taibo."

"I love you, Grandpa."

"I love you, too. More than you can ever know."

Taitano nimbly closed the book. It was like closing a chapter on her old life and getting ready to begin a new one. Crossing a threshold that brooked no return. Anxiety swelled in her. She was overcome by a compulsion to re-open the book to check if she had bent the page as she closed the cover, leaving an unseemly crease in the precious paper. She expended Herculean fortitude to resist the urge to re-open the volume and check it. She visualized the moment, only seconds in the past now, when she had wrapped her hand around the front cover and gently lifted it to close the ancient tome. The reminiscence in her mind's eye was of a page that was straight and true. All was well. She did not need to check if the page was bent. She handed the book back to her grandfather, cleared her mind, and accepted the road that lay ahead.

# CHAPTER 5

# DEPARTURE

The day before her departure, Taitano gave her last tutoring session to twelve-year-old Pution "Poyo" Mangabao. Poyo's parents—Husto and Puengi—had given him the proud, lyrical name "Pution," which meant "star." Their beloved baby boy had turned out to have low serotonin production. They tried to ameliorate the situation with supplements, only to find that his synapses' reabsorption rates and concentration of re-uptake inhibitors resisted all attempts to rectify the deficiency. In addition to his chronic anxiety, when the rest of his classmates began their growth spurts in the sixth grade, poor little Poyo's pituitary gland, instead of getting up and going, just got up and went. Everyone, except his teachers, had long forgotten his proper name and instead called him "Poyo": *young chicken*.

But what Poyo lacked in height and demeanor he made up for in mathematics. At his present age of twelve years old, he was studying to be a theoretical physicist and was a full four years ahead of the rest of his classmates. To keep his mathematical edge and ambitious trajectory, he had weekly one-hour sessions with Taitano. The second, unofficial reason for the weekly tutoring was that Taitano was a role model for him: they were both high academic achievers and both struggling with (potentially) debilitating anxiety. Just being around Taitano was tangible proof that he could achieve anything a "normal" person could, as long as he were willing to put in the extra work of managing his emotions at the same time that he was managing his studies. There was a third, much more intimate, motivation for Poyo to participate in the tutoring every week, although it was known only to himself: he had a major league crush on his tutor.

"You know you didn't have to come today," said Poyo. "I would have understood. I know you're leaving tomorrow. Maybe we should have just canceled so you could've had more time to pack."

Taitano did not look up from her external screen, which was synched to Poyo's monitor and on which she was writing a biquadratic polynomial equation. After finishing the equation, she said, "Come on, Pution, we have fifteen minutes left, and then I really need to go." She then slipped him a smile, saying, "By the way, if you're trying to waste time to get out of solving this equation, it's not going to work. Now do it." She punctuated this last sentence by giving him an encouraging smile and a light punch in the arm.

Poyo's knees melted under the scrutiny of her smile and good-natured reproval. He forced his mind upon the daunting string of symbols, letters, numbers—which expressed variables, non-negative integer exponents, and coefficients: $ax^4 + bx^3 + cx^2 + dx + e = 0$. Normally, finding the value of x in a biquadratic polynomial equation would not have presented much of a challenge for him. But there were two difficulties with the present mathematical challenge that Taitano had improvised and worked into the problem for him. First, she had projected the equation into three-dimensional space. This was a bit unfair and certainly gave him something to think about. Second, his physical proximity to Taitano was causing him to experience three physiological effects, all of which threatened to overwhelm him: both adrenal glands, which were perched atop his kidneys, began to produce copious amounts of dopamine; his photo-neuro-endocrine organ (commonly known as his pineal gland located in the brain) started to produce serotonin (a welcome change, to be sure!); and his posterior pituitary gland was now sending stored oxytocin, which had previously been produced by his hypothalamus, into his blood stream at alarming rates. The twenty-first century theory had recently been proved that the combination of dopamine, serotonin, and oxytocin— made possible by an enzyme in humans and dolphins (and possibly other animals)—enabled one to experience romantic love. The emotion of love was common enough, but some held the view that *romantic* love was something rarer and more wonderful.

Poyo's heart was pounding. His head was spinning. He was love-stricken and having serious difficulty concentrating on a stupid math problem. But Poyo's rational cognitive centers perforated the emotional haze: he knew the way to impress Taitano was to solve the math equation that she had presented to him, so he summoned all his discipline and turned to the equation before him on the screen. He knew that the biquadratic polynomial equation, if it had not been projected into three dimensions, was solvable by setting each factor to zero. In addition, everything to the left of the equals sign (=) could be plotted on a graph so that the x-intercepts would yield the roots of the polynomial equation. He forced his mind to apply the normal manner of solving such a polynomial equation to this novel situation that had been created by his tutor. He knew that her aim was to stretch him and determine whether he truly grasped the underlying principles. He did not want to disappoint her. He set each of the factors to zero, plotted each component on an x-axis (the abscissa) and then a y-axis (the ordinate). He then took the points he had plotted, kept each factor at zero, and projected the points onto the z-axis (the applicate). He then assigned each of the factors a mathematical value corresponding to its placement on the three-dimensional grid, lined them up, and added them. The result was zero. Equation solved.

Poyo was actually sweating now, either from the application of his two-dimensional knowledge of polynomial equations to a new three-dimensional context or from doing it while fighting the rush of hormones into his blood stream that made him want to think about anything other than math—or perhaps a combination of the two.

"Excellent!" shouted Taitano in enthusiastic approval and clapped her hands over her head. Poyo watched her as the graceful movement of her arms caused her braids to fly up into the air and then bounce off her shoulders. "That was really great! It took me three times as long to write that problem as it did for you to solve it—and I'm *really* happy that you did it manually, rather than running it through your abacus. Really well done, Pution. I'm proud of you. I think my work here is done. You don't even *need* me anymore."

Poyo's head almost exploded with the number of possible responses to that statement. He said only, "Why are you going, Agana? Why can't you stay? I've learned so much from you, and there's so much more you can teach me."

"Pution," replied Taitano, "You know as much math as I do at this point. You're gonna be fine without me. You could even become a tutor yourself as this point since you're so far ahead of your peers."

"I'm not really talking about the math," he muttered, almost inaudibly.

"Oh, well, what do you mean?" she asked innocently and with a touch of concern.

Poyo looked down at his feet. He struggled with fear, longing, doubt, desire. He forced himself to say, "I'm going to miss you. Math is one thing, but what good is it if I'm not even able to raise my hand in class and volunteer to answer a question?"

Taitano regarded him with empathy and understanding, thinking back to the painful experiences she had endured when she was his age.

Not being invited to birthday parties because she was different, trying to stammer out an answer (which she knew perfectly) when she was called upon by the teacher, getting bullied during sports classes. She took his hand. A bio-chemical electric shock ripped through his hand, arm, shoulder—and then all the way down his spinal column. His heart slammed against the floor of his pericardium, literally skipped an entire cycle of beats, and then began to pump through his blood stream even more dopamine, serotonin, and oxytocin.

"I know exactly how you feel, Pution," said Taitano, continuing to hold his hand in hers. "I really do. I felt just like that when I was your age, and I still feel like that every day of my life. But that's who we are. We feel deeper, both the good and the bad stuff. We live more intensely. It's like we start each day with a plunge into freezing cold water, rather than a nice long soak in a warm bath." She peered into his eyes, and he could feel that she was puncturing his soul with her fathomless sapphire gaze. She continued, "You have things to do here, and I have things to do up there. We are both going to do what the Universe has laid before us, no matter how scary it is. Let's promise each other, OK? And when it gets tough, we're going to think of each other. We're going to get out of bed, grab every day by the lapels, and shake it until it gives us what we deserve."

Poyo felt the pressure of her hand on his, and returned it, gently. Closing his eyes, he focused on the physical sensation of the warmth of her hand; the subtle waft of the soap upon her skin mixed with her clean, natural scent; and her regular, confident breathing as air entered her lungs and then exited her nose and mouth. He held onto the moment and tried to scorch it into his memory. After a few seconds, he opened his eyes and faced her. He said, "OK, Agana. There's nothing for it. Let's go do what we have to do, as well as we can do it. It won't be perfect, but it will be our best."

"Now," said Taitano, "there's just one little favor I want to ask of you before I go on this crazy journey tomorrow. I estimate that, by the time

I get back, you'll be some kind of tenured professor somewhere or maybe even the Senior Advisor to the Earth-Ocean Academy of Sciences." Poyo blushed, thoroughly soaking in the praise without a hint of false modesty. She continued, "Well, when you're this big important person, you can't have people going around calling you 'Poyo' now, can you. I think there is no time like the present to get things back on the right track. So, from now on, I want you to only answer to the name 'Pution' and to forget about this 'Poyo' nonsense. Agreed?"

"Agreed," replied the twelve-year-old boy with a wide grin of gratitude—a profound gratitude that overshadowed the sorrow he had been suffering. From that moment forward, he left behind "Poyo" and answered only to his proper given name; and, in time, he was known only as "Pution."

The next day, Taitano settled into her cabin upon *Ardanwen*. She did not have much in the way of baggage. Everything she needed for the journey had been downloaded into her abacus and mirrored on the memory core of the ship. *Well, "ship" is a generous term for this flying balloon.* For over two-hundred years, humans had envisioned the vessels that would carry them throughout the Cosmos as sleek, metal ships akin to those that had been manufactured for flight in the atmosphere of Earth-Ocean. Aerodynamic wings, gleaming cylindrical fuselages, tapered nose cones. A significant failure of scientific knowledge—and imagination—in Taitano's view.

She had slung the small bag she had brought with her into the corner and flopped onto the bed with a thump. *Ah, mattress nice and firm, just the way I like it.* She inspected the curved walls around her. *Nothing around here is a straight line. No edges, just delicate arcs.* *Ardanwen* was almost a perfect sphere. It consisted of a conglomeration of sub-spheres with all manner of environments.

Terrestrial fields of grass and other vegetation; rippling seas; mechanized components to manufacture air, radiation for the solar sails, water, heat, gravity. Every sub-sphere was connected to others through an intricate latticework of tunnels, which also housed the organic-optical cables that provided communication between all the systems. The walls of her cabin were also curved planes in alternating convex and concave surfaces, which refracted the internal luminescence of the material to generate light for the eyes of EROC-lings (a colloquial term for Earth-Ocean-lings). A distant scent of honeysuckle teased her olfactory receptors—placed there, no doubt, to put her and the other human occupants at ease for the start of the journey.

The first of such vessels had been constructed by the Enneans in an orbital platform above their home world and then launched over a hundred years ago on its maiden voyage to Earth-Ocean. *The mission? To save us from ourselves. But what was in it for the Enneans? The Enneans had everything they needed on Ross 128b. They didn't even need food, at least the way we EROC-lings do. So it's not like they were hungry or something. Maybe they were lonely. Or just wanted to preserve the lives of the closest thing they had to a neighbor in a forlorn Cosmos. Who knows? I'm probably thinking too much like a human and can't even begin to understand how the Enneans think. We can't even speak their language. They seem to understand ours, but theirs is still an insoluble riddle to us. Hell, we only figured out how to properly talk to dolphins ninety-seven years ago.*

Her thoughts involuntarily drifted to the others chosen for the eleven-year journey to Ross 128—at least eleven years from the perspective of those back on Earth-Ocean. In addition to herself, there was Professor Sun and his partner—the elegant and brilliant linguist named "Moon." And … *Saiyam Patel! How could the Enneans and the members of the UN Ennean Commission have chosen him? It doesn't make any sense. Well, for that matter, choosing me doesn't make any sense either, does it?* She struggled to accept it—and to let go of her negative emotional responses. She failed.

Rising from her bed, she slipped on an ultra-light wetsuit, rehelmed, and entered the transition chamber. It flooded with water, and she swam through a few short tunnels to Professor Sun's chamber, which he shared with Moon. Before announcing her presence, she checked the real-time sensor readouts for the chamber to ensure that all systems were functioning properly. An urge she could not resist. She was about to hit the entry chime, when she heard and felt vibrations through the water coming from the other side of aperture, which was, at that moment, set to transparent mode. The reverberations soothed her and were at just enough intensity to trigger the translator in the abacus that was interfaced with the auditory mechanism in her helmet. Sun and Moon were meditatively encircling each other and singing a complex duet that she could not begin to fathom or understand—even with the assistance of the translator. The meaning was forever tucked up into the corners of her unconscious mind, like images and sounds that taunted her in the hinterland between sleep and waking. It was like struggling to remember an elusive dream. The more one tries to pin down the memory of the dream and to pry it into the conscious realm, the more it slips through one's grasp—as an errant shard of an eggshell darts left and right along the inner side of a bowl, adroitly eluding capture at the hands of a searching fingertip. She could catch some words and syntax of the lilting song, but the meaning was lost to her. As best she could tell, it seemed to be a prolix, meandering yarn about a white whale exacting revenge upon an Old Earth whaling ship.

Taitano recalled what she had learned about dolphin languages. They essentially spoke one single language with different dialects. Whereas humans evolved, from a cultural anthropology standpoint, in isolated groups due to geographic boundaries—for example, oceans, mountain ranges, impassable deserts—dolphins had no such physical barriers to separate them. They all lived in the one Ocean, separated only by distance. As a result, a dolphin from the Atlantic region of the Ocean would be perfectly able to communicate with one from the Pacific region. The differences in dialects were naturally the sources of endless mirth between the distinctive groups, with the same "words" being sung in slightly diverse ways. But these differences had been the source of amusement, pleasure, and even fascination among the global dolphin community, rather than a cause for intraspecies violence, much less war. It was even the case that different species of cetaceans could communicate with each other.

Turning her mind back to the song of Sun and Moon, she could discern a mix of intense emotions woven into the strands of the sounds emanating from the two dolphins: anger, joy, sadness, hope. Moon would sing for a few minutes, while Sun listened with his eyes closed, immobile and floating, rocked by the gentle movements of the water. And then he would take up the melody, while Moon took a break and just listened. Every once in a while, their eyes would meet, and they would brush up against each other for affection or support during a tense and moving part of the tale.

Taitano started to feel a bit of guilt at her semi-covert surveillance of the conversation; she pressed the chime to let them know she was outside. After a few moments, the chamber's access port indicated she could enter. She opened the portal and swam into the marvelous enclosure. Larger, by far, than the spaces allotted to the humans, it was a vast aquatic environment suited to the needs of the dolphins. Open stretches of water, punctuated by real, living coral reefs. There was space towards the "top" of the chamber with a nitrogen-oxygen atmosphere so the dolphins could breathe; and, on the far side of the chamber, the reef crept up a gentle acclivity at the top of which lay a sandy beach. Sun and Moon's alcove was near the outer surface of the vessel. The Enneans had engineered it so that the obsidian of space filled a one-hundred-degree arc of the chamber, which made Taitano feel as though she were floating in the void. *This vessel is a true marvel of engineering.* It of course had initially been constructed by the Enneans; but, in the decade after first contact, EROC-lings and Enneans had worked together to make the inside environs suitable for the over decade-long transit between Sol and Ross 128. The Enneans had invited the UN Ennean Commission to name the vessel. It was decided—by vote—to call it *Ardanwen.* The name was from a book by an Old Earth Dutch author. In the story, a young knight-to-be risks everything to deliver a letter to a neighboring king, warning him of a sneak attack by an evil prince. At great personal sacrifice, the boy succeeds, and the kingdom is able to arm itself in time for the imminent ambuscade. The horse of the young boy was called "Ardanwen"—meaning "Night Wind"—and he was indeed the fastest horse in the kingdom.

Taitano swam to the beach and dehelmed, but placed an earpiece into her left ear, so she could continue to receive the auditory interface from her abacus. She immediately saw Sun and Moon floating near the surface.

Professor Sun addressed her, "Tai, you seem nervous. Is it the ship? Don't worry so much. *Ardanwen* is state of the art. The engineers check its systems even more often than Moon checks my sodium levels." Sun squirted a rindle of water into Moon's face and then continued, "She's worried that all this synthetic food leaves trace insufficiencies in our diets." Moon unleashed a series of annoyed, but playful, clicks, which the translator could not render into English. Sun persisted, undaunted by his partner's apparent remonstrances, "We're even ahead of schedule. After the gravity assist from Jupiter and clearing the Oort Cloud, they will deploy the solar sails, fire up the magnetic fusion plasma drive, and we'll be at near light speed in no time and on our way to Ross 128b. A god-awful name, if you ask me, by the way. I mean, where was the astronomer's imagination when that name was chosen?"

"Oh, I don't know, Professor," she said in a jesting tone. "It kind of rolls of the tongue."

"A human tongue perhaps. But to a dolphin, it's a trifle dull. I mean, our song for a sardine is a hundred times more complex and interesting than the name you humans gave to the star of our nearest and only neighbor. You humans really know how to suck the romance out of things."

Moon splashed her mate in the eye—in a most likely futile attempt to quench his nettlesome banter—and then interjected, "So what's on your mind, Tai. You didn't come here to hear this old codger rant about cross-species differences, did you? Let me guess, it's about Patel."

Sun cut off Taitano's nascent reply and said to his mate, "What are you telepathic now, in addition to empathic? Leave the poor human alone. And, by the way, I am not a codger. I'm only a few years older than Tai."

Moon ignored Sun and kept her attention fixed on Taitano.

Tai spoke up, "Yes, it's Patel. How could the Enneans and the Commission approve someone like him for this kind of opportunity. He's obnoxious, conceited, ... and borderline speciesist!"

Sun answered, "Yes, he is indeed all that. A good representative of humans, no? But seriously. I suspect that the Enneans are more interested in seeing us as we truly are—barnacles and all—rather than some cosmetically constructed ideal form of human and dolphin. I also think they are interested in that implant he's got in his skull. Patel is the first human to be selected for the exchange with one, and the Enneans most likely want to make a comparative study of human behavior between synched and un-synched humans."

Moon chimed in, "It must be more than that, Dear. You know how powerful his parents are in Commission circles. Maybe it's that. Besides, Tai, one cannot always choose one's peers. Sometimes they are forced on you, and then one has to make the most of it. Look at me and Sun. Do you think he was my first choice as a mate?"

"Hey, you chased me for months before I gave in," replied a wounded Sun.

"More like minutes, Darling."

"Look," Sun continued, "it's going to be fine. We all just need to wipe the slate clean and focus on our relative strengths, not weaknesses. Or areas of development. Or whatever our negative qualities are called these days. It is, quite simply, our obligation to put our best flippers and feet forward, as EROC-lings, and to learn as much as we can from the Enneans."

"Yeah, I guess you're right," replied Taitano. "I'm just tired. Need sleep. Thanks for the chat. See you tomorrow, Professor. Ciao, Moon."

Taitano arced into the water with a perfect dive, inflicting nothing but a modest ripple upon the surface of the water. She reascended to the surface, collected her helmet from where she had left it floating upon the water, rehelmed, and glided towards the exit of the aquatic chamber with deep, powerful strokes of her limbs and subtle rhythmic twists of her torso. Sun's head turned to follow Taitano as she departed. "Don't ever tell her I said this, Moon, but I've never seen—or scanned with my echolocation—anything from land as graceful in the water as she. I'd swear she was part cetacean. She's really come a long way in the short time we've been working together. I mean, she was always a strong swimmer, but now she's amazing."

Moon sounded less enthusiastic than Sun. "You seem somewhat taken with her, Husband."

"Well, you have to admit she's something special."

"No, I don't have to admit it, Sun. Need I remind you that she's human and you're a dolphin? I'd never say this to her or any other human, but I kind of pity them. They're kind of like stretched-out gangly chimpanzees with intermittent patches of hair, like a partially plucked chicken. They can barely move on land and are almost helpless in the water. I really don't know how they convince themselves to get out of bed in the morning—especially after those endless periods of oblivion they call 'sleep.' Need I also remind you, Darling Husband, that our brains are larger. And there is a good evolutionary reason for that. Our communication centers are several times more complex than a human's so we can process the sensory input from our echolocation systems, which, in turn, has allowed us to develop a language that makes theirs look like a beginning A-B-C book of one of their infants. We are immensely older than they are as a species. Dolphins' brains have been their currently large size for *tens of millions of years*, while humans have only had their comparatively smaller brains for a couple of hundred thousand years. We have learned their language, but they have never learned ours. Why? Because they *can't*! Why? Because their brains can't manage it. Without the translators, we'd still not be able to communicate with them, and they might still be slaughtering us."

Sun paused to take this all in. Moon was on a bit of a roll—or a "rant" it might even be called: the fervor of her critique of humans no doubt fueled by the fires of her jealousy. He swam some playful circles around her to loosen up her mood a bit. "Yes, and who created the technology and the hardware that enabled us to communicate with each other so that we dolphins could do more than touch our rostrum against an underwater placard that said: "May I please have another fish?" Moon did not respond, nor did she soften her mood. "And, as for their lack of hair, the last time I checked, *you*, My Dear Moon, didn't have *any* hair on that exquisite, sleek body of yours, and I think you're the most rapturous fish in the sea."

"Don't try to deflect the subject with charm and flattery, Sun. I know all your tricks—and then some. Look at her! Her mammary glands are on the *outside* of her body. They actually *create* drag when she swims."

"Only minimally when she's in her wet suit. Anyway, I rather think they're intriguing to look at."

"Sun! I can't believe the sound waves hitting my jawbone. Her species and ours parted ways, what, ninety million years ago? You're a little late to interbreed with her if you wanted to. You can't be serious about all this! You can't possibly find her sexually attractive! She's a human, and you're a dolphin! It's ludicrous!"

"She's a brilliant, healthy, female specimen of her species, and I'm a male one of mine. But, yes, you're right," he conceded with body language indicating that she had prevailed. "However ... you *are* sounding more and more human all the time, with all these strict divisions between species and taboos about sex. And do I even detect a note of jealousy in your songs on this subject? Very un-dolphin-like of you. Maybe all this hanging around humans is indeed starting to alter us culturally—me included. All I'm saying is that I admire her in many ways. Our relationship is—of course—strictly professional, though."

"Good, keep it that way. Or I might have to find myself a young five-year-old dolphin to swim away with."

"You wouldn't dare ...."

"Don't tempt me."

Taitano awoke the next morning. "Morning" on *Ardanwen* naturally meant the arbitrary rhythms that were superimposed upon the habitats that traversed the endless kilometers between Sol and Ross 128. The ship had been programmed to mimic the approximately twenty-four-hour day of Earth-Ocean and the light and dark cycles of day and night—as reckoned at the Equator, to keep the math as simple as possible.

She had dreamt again of the *suruhåna* herding their ghosts. But this time, she could discern more definition in the vaporous apparitions. They had long arms and no heads and were in constant undulating motion, like swirling masses of tentacled smoke. As they were driven down a gentle declivity, one of them seemed to turn—or rather exude—in her direction, perhaps its version of "looking" at her. The dream faded, as they always did.

*I hate when that happens: such a vivid experience, and then I lose it, and it just fades away. Oh, well. Should I go for a run today or a swim? Well, both probably, but which one in the morning? I'm still a bit tired actually. How about a stroll through the ship? To get to know my new home for the next year.* Taitano was still recovering from the news that much of her training for the mission would be conducted *en route*. She had had only about a month to wrap up her affairs on Earth-Ocean, before she was transported by orbital tether to the vessel in stationary orbit that would carry her across the void to a different world.

She slipped into a loose-fitting shirt and trousers, pulled on her running shoes, and headed out the door. She left her aquatic gear behind, intending to stick only to terrestrial habitats this morning. She passed by the mess hall, filled her mug with some black tea, grabbed a red currant scone, and then headed to the arboretum. She followed signage along the route, which was made for maximum intuitiveness. The terrestrial corridors had gravitational plating in the floors, as did the aquatic habitats, which obviated the need for rotating structures to generate gravitational fields for normal Earth-Ocean locomotion by the human and dolphin passengers. But the spheric configuration of *Ardanwen* still meant that walking in a straight line was still really walking in a circle—or at least a curve. But without the fixed reference points of earth, sky, and sun, it was not particularly disorienting. It just took some getting used to. It did, however, sometimes give one a sensation of walking in place, like walking in the opposite direction on a moving walkway in an airport.

She reached the arboretum. *Breath-taking!* At the entrance was a plaque which read:

> *One must maintain a little bit of summer, even in the middle of winter. – Henry David Thoreau*

Taitano looked up into the top half of the spherical chamber to see large trees filling the space. Simulated *komorebi* caressed her face and body, enveloping and soothing her. Under her feet and occupying the bottom half of the sub-sphere was rich loam, where the roots of the trees dug deep to the nadir of the sub-sphere—at least it was the nadir with respect to the artificial gravity net that had been installed throughout the parts of the ship for the benefit of its bipedal and aquatic passengers. The petrichor—intense due to the enclosed space—unearthed reminiscences buried deep within her. She could smell the pungent decaying humus, the sap of spruce, oak, and hazel trees. Pollen wafted on the wind. At several angles on the sub-sphere, she saw narrow, cylindrical tubes branching off in every direction, with vines and other plants taking off to other parts of the ship and even looping back into the arboretum from the other side. She could hear the susurrus of the leaves being rustled by the air circulators, which rhythmically caused some of the branches to gently scrape against the sub-sphere's sides. The clemency of the elements baffled her, as they rivaled any place she had ever been on Earth-Ocean. It was an ecosystem so in balance that it was almost out of balance. So perfect that it was imperfect. But it nevertheless brought her sensory pleasure; and she could already tell that, when the oppressive void of space besetting their minuscule bubble started to get to her, she would come here to find peace—and that, of course, was the very purpose of the place.

She could also perceive, just at the threshold of her hearing, a faint sibilance soughing and mixing with the tinkling of the leaves and the air treatment system. A passage from one of her favorite books sprang to her mind, unbidden: "Their feet ruffled among the dead leaves of countless other autumns that drifted over the banks of the path from the deep red carpets of the forest." She listened more closely still. It was not so much a droning or buzzing that she was hearing—but rather music. Just at the edge of her auditory perception. It was more inside her head than it was an external stimulus running up her auditory nerve into her cerebral cortex. The music—*yes, music*—was unlike anything she had ever experienced before. It was a seemingly random and non-repeating pattern of waves, rather than individual, Cartesian notes, like most of the music originating from Old Europe. It seemed to pulse irregularly, and she felt it in her flesh more than her mind. Rather than a rhythmic pattern, it was more of an intangible presence that suffused her very being. Taitano turned her senses to the vegetation, which was so thick that it blocked out most of the endless black of space so that she could almost believe that she were back on Earth-Ocean enjoying a perfect, crisp spring morning in the forest. She would have expected paths, but there were none.

Taitano perambulated the forest-sphere, enjoying the dance of sensations over her senses—the sensory stimuli of the place actively inducing a deep state of *yutori* in her mind and body. There was an elasticity in her movements, and she noticed that much of the ground was covered in a dense layer of mosses of all shapes and hues. She knelt on one knee to inspect the intricate star patterns of the many differentiated types of bryophytes; they sported tens of thousands of hexagonal and pentagonal leaves, between which she could only discriminate upon a close visual inspection. She reflected upon the wondrous geometric patterns and felt guilty to be treading upon them. She craned her neck to look straight up at the convex ceiling and noticed that the geometric superstructure of the sub-sphere in which she was located matched, pretty closely, the yellow-green lattices of one of the more prolific species of moss currently being compressed underfoot. She recalled a mathematics lecture about the golden ratio in nature being the inspiration for much of humanity's most famous and beloved architecture. An irrational number, the golden ratio—1.618—goes on forever, like *pi*. She speculated whether the superstructure employed the golden ratio; and, if so, had the species of moss been specifically chosen to match it? She knelt and stroked the soft moss for some time, trying to calculate the golden ratio's

Fibonacci sequence to at least eighteen decimal places. 1.618033988749894848. *OK, Tai, that's enough for now. It's never going to repeat. Let it go. Eighteen places were enough. Now let it go and just enjoy your walk.* She straightened, remembering that same mathematics lecture about differential equations and the words of her professor: *Mathematics, like any language, is a symbolic abstraction of the mind that humans use to cognize and morph the natural world around them. It is the fire that Prometheus stole from the gods and gave to humankind.* Laying aside these lucid memories, she wordlessly apologized to the moss for trampling upon it and continued to softly traverse the forest, exerting as little force as possible so as not to unnecessarily damage the living carpet of the sphere.

She noticed another human at the edge of the enclosure. Her heart skipped a beat, and her stomach dropped. He was a middle-aged man of medium height. He wore a well-tailored uniform and had a sleek build. At the barrier between the sub-sphere and the space outside, he was facing the infinite darkness and did not turn as she approached him from behind. *Well, what did you expect? Of course you're not the only human on this ship. You were going to have to talk to people you haven't met yet at some point. Just take a deep breath, accept your fear, and say "Hello." Whatever he responds, it's not going to kill you. Whatever happens, you can take it. It will be fine. You are obsessing over nothing.*

Without turning and while still gazing into the seamless void, the man spoke, "'Music expresses that which cannot be put into words … and that which cannot remain silent.'"

Taitano searched her memory and then responded, "Victor Hugo." She paused, waiting for an acknowledgement, which did not come. She continued, "Hello, there, by the way. Quite a view, huh?"

"Yes, quite a view, Dr. Taitano. How did you sleep?"

"Let me guess, you're the Captain."

"The one and only. Good guess. And do please forgive my dreadful manners. My mind was drifting—lost in thought. I should have introduced myself at the first." He turned, placed his left hand over his heart, gave a slight bow in a courtly fashion and stated in an exaggerated and genteel manner, "I am Captain Abdul-Noor Saddiq, at your service. So, what's the answer to my question?"

"What question?"

"How was your first night in space? Did you sleep?"

"Like a baby."

"I always thought that was a curious expression. I've not had the chance to become a father, but I've always read that babies rarely sleep through the night. It's a learned skill."

"Yeah, that is a weird saying, isn't it?"

"So?"

"So what?"

"Are you ever going to answer my question? Truthfully, that is."

"What do you mean?"

"I strongly doubt that someone with your psychological profile slept well, or even slept at all, in these, shall we say, novel circumstances."

Taitano's heart rate increased. It was to be expected that the captain would have had access to her entire health file. A captain was traditionally, throughout the ages, a vessel's master and did not allow anything—or anyone—on his or her ship without knowing exactly what it, he, or she was. *That's completely understandable, but am I going to make it that easy for him? I don't think so.* "Why, Captain Saddiq, whatever do you mean?"

He scrutinized her, seeming to be amused by the verbal repartee. He decided to take the bait and play along. "Well, never mind. My mistake. I'm glad you slept well and nothing like an infant. Tell me, Dr. Taitano, what do you think of *Ardanwen*?"

Taitano took her time spinning around in a full three-hundred-and-sixty-degree circle to take in the entire circumference of the forest sub-sphere. She experienced a mild dizziness, not unlike when she was a child, and her parents would spin her on the iron wheel on the playground, faster and faster—at her insistence. She would then step off, immediately fall to the ground, and lie there while Earth-Ocean whirled around her uncontrollably. "I've never seen anything like it; and I haven't even seen a tenth of her yet. You must be happy to be her captain."

"Well, yes, we've been together for almost one-hundred years— ninety-six years, to be exact—by Earth-Ocean reckoning. I was on the very first ferry from Earth-Ocean to Ennea, many years ago. Appointed by the Commission, after a rigorous vetting process and quite a bit of political wrangling between the members of the Commission, both human and dolphin."

"Over a hundred years? But you don't look a day over sixty." Taitano then caught herself, "Wait. Of course. Time dilation. So how many times have you done this?"

"This will be my fourth journey to Ennea," he replied. "So, what do you know about Ennea?"

Taitano had had some time to study up on the details of the dim red dwarf star named "Ross 128," which was about eleven light years from Earth-Ocean. It was significantly less bright than Sol and very stable. The star's exoplanet, designated Ross 128b, had a mass thirty-five percent larger than that of Earth-Ocean, with a diameter ten percent wider. Naturally, its larger mass meant that the gravity was greater— about twelve percent more. Its temperature ranged from minus sixty to plus twenty-one degrees Celsius, depending upon where you were on the surface of the planet—and when. There was a sub-terranean sea, or rather, Ocean, under about a kilometer of crust. This Ocean was mostly liquid water, with some ammonium mixed in. It remained liquid due to the radiogenic decay of various elements in the mantle. As the Ocean was beneath the surface, there was what was referred to as the "upper crust"—which sat on the "top" of the Ocean—and the "lower crust"—which was at the "bottom" of the Ocean. Under the lower crust lay the volatile mantle of the planet. As Ross 128b was much closer to its star than Earth-Ocean, it took significantly less time to complete an orbit, about ten days. It was also tidally locked with its star and had no moon.

Taitano recalled all these details, but said only, "Yes, Ross 128b, I mean, Ennea. Well, like every other kid of my generation, I always tried to find Ross 128 in the night sky … but couldn't. You need a telescope. But in about eighty-thousand years, Ross 128 will be closer to Earth-Ocean than Proxima Centauri, as Ross 128 is moving closer to Sol and Proxima Centauri's moving away. So, if one can wait that long, I guess you might be able to finally see it with the naked eye."

"Well, I've seen it with the naked eye, alright. And you will too, in about a year and a half."

"That'll be about twelve years on Earth-Ocean, right?"

"That's correct," replied Saddiq. "Again, time dilation, plus acceleration, deceleration, and a couple of minor detours around micro-black holes, which tend to give *Ardanwen* a hard time if she flies straight through them." He creased his eyes to accentuate his sliver of humor. "But fear not, that's what Triton is here for." He saw the momentary look of confusion and lack of recognition on her face. "Ah, yes, you haven't yet met our resident enneapod—our Ennean navigator. Well, in fact, he's more the captain of *Ardanwen* than I am, truth be told. Triton takes care of plotting the median target coordinates in space, calculates the output of the fusion generator, trims the solar sails. He consults me sometimes, when we encounter something unexpected, but we've done this route so often there aren't that many surprises. Thank goodness. Not much help out here if something goes wrong. Of course, Nereus helps, too, by double-checking all the systems and calculations."

"Nereus?"

"Our AI."

"Right. Of course. I'm surprised we even need a flesh and blood navigator."

At that, Captain Saddiq's face took on a thoughtful expression. "There's still the organic factor to consider. It's true, we couldn't do a journey like this without Nereus, but I'm not sure what the point would be if humans, dolphins, and Enneans took their hands, flippers, and tentacles completely off the steering wheel. And there have been times when Triton and I came up with a solution to an unexpected situation that Nereus hadn't considered."

Taitano paused to take it all in, not quite able to process all that was happening. *This is, after all, only my second day in space. Give it some time.* She returned her attention to Captain Saddiq. "So, what do you do around here, Captain—other than keeping forlorn passengers like me company on a captivating spring morning in the woods?"

"Well, the Enneans built the drive and hull of *Ardanwen*, but I was in charge of fitting her insides for transporting humans and dolphins across eleven light years of space in a manner so that they would be safe and healthy when they arrived. No small feat. In fact, I am more of an engineer than some kind of swashbuckling commander. Although, if something goes wrong, I bear the primary responsibility. The Enneans didn't quite understand the need to have a single individual ultimately responsible for the whole endeavor. They don't have a hierarchical social structure. They're more similar to dolphins in that respect; and the tangled webs of human relationships are a confounded puzzlement to them. But they acquiesced to the concept of a captain of the ship, as it was of little import to them. It took a fair bit of thought, mathematics, engineering, and even divine inspiration to figure out how to house a dozen or so dolphins and humans for an almost two-year journey in space."

"I'll bet. I noticed that strong swimmers are in high demand here."

"And on Ennea, Dr. Taitano."

"Yes, so I've heard, Captain."

Discerning that she was genuinely interested in the subject, Saddiq continued, "It wasn't, you know, just a matter of filling one side of the sphere with air and the other with water. It was much more complicated than that and took close to ten years, working closely with Triton and his fellow Enneans. After they stopped the solar flare and set us back on the right track, the Enneans broached the idea of the exchange program, and then we got to work reconfiguring *Ardanwen*. Keep in mind that we still really can't even talk to the Enneans, at least in the ways we are used to talking, so the entire process involved lots of tactile demonstrations. We would basically install a piece of hardware in a sub-sphere, and then the Enneans would ooze themselves all over it and then make their adjustments to ensure it was properly integrated into the ship's systems."

He paused to ascertain whether Taitano was still paying attention. She indeed was listening attentively. He therefore continued, "There were already spheres suited to the Enneans, where no air was needed. That was already accomplished, as they had made it all the way here and replicated their Ocean to match the conditions of Ennea. As for humans and dolphins, they both breathe the same exact atmosphere, and that made it easier from a chemical synthesis perspective, but interlocking the sub-spheres was a bit tricky—especially when we were trying to integrate the radiation shielding into the superstructure of the vessel." He decided to tack to a different subject, "By the way, what did you think of the breakfast?"

"*Dee ... licious.*"

"Good, those scones are my great grandmother's recipe. All the food is of course synthetic, not even vegan. We don't want to unduly offend the Enneans."

Taitano recalled the stories of the bewilderment that the Enneans expressed, even to this day, at Earth-Ocean's food chains and the biodiversity upon which they were based. Enneans were the only living things on their home planet. No other animals, nor plants. Not even microorganisms. No other living things other than themselves— only Enneans. They didn't even have mouths. Their bodies were able to absorb all the nutrients they needed to sustain their life processes directly from the environment. The concept of ingesting another living thing for sustenance—be it plant or animal—was a profoundly alien, not to mention disturbing, concept to them. They still had difficulty accepting that a sentient species could live this way. Killing, eating, and digesting other living things in order to survive. When they figured out that humans even ate *other sentient beings*, they simply could not process such information. A by-product of this aspect of Ennean culture was that they had no violence in their society. They could not even cognize the concept. They did not have to kill to eat, and they did not kill each other.

Taitano forced herself back to the present and said, "Yeah, the food is great. Not much different from home." Now, it was her turn to change the subject, "Is it possible to meet our Ennean navigator some time?"

"Define what you mean by 'meet.'"

"You know, say 'Hi.'"

Captain Saddiq smiled slightly, his incredulity slipping past the corner of his mouth. "One does not simply say 'Hi' to an Ennean. You know that. You know how they communicate. In any event, I would recommend, at the very least, waiting a few months until you get your space legs before thinking about getting up close and personal with Triton. It's not for the faint of heart. But I will make a mental note of it and look for an opportunity."

"Okay, thanks, Captain. Well, I think I will go for a run or swim or something. I can't wait to check this entire place out. I want to see every square meter."

"Yes, good meeting you, Dr. Taitano. I look forward to the mission briefing this evening. You'll be there, of course?"

"Wouldn't miss it for the world, Captain. Until then!"

"*Adieu*, Dr. Taitano. And if you need anything, just ask. It's a long voyage, and I look forward to getting to know you better." He smiled cordially and tipped his high-brimmed navel cap in her direction, bowing slightly.

"And I you." She returned his smile and bow, turned, and headed off to change into her swimsuit.

As she departed, Captain Saddiq's smile faded. He felt troubled but did not know why. His conversation with Taitano had been pleasant enough, but there was something preoccupying his mind upon which he could not place his finger. Something important. Something in the future. Reflecting upon their conversation, he turned back to the void and resumed his morning musing. It was probably nothing but the normal anxiety of beginning an epic journey of this kind. It never did become routine, nor should it. He could dimly perceive a slightly enlarged Mars peeping from the dark curtain of space. *Once we clear the Oort Cloud and are well on our way, this unusual feeling will pass and become a distant memory. It will be good to see Ennea again.*

# CHAPTER 6

# MISSION BRIEFING

*A*rdanwen's majestic central sphere served multitudinous purposes. It could be flooded for aquatic activities, drained for terrestrial ones, or turned into a near-vacuum for scientific experiments. Today, it was filled with water for the first mission briefing of the exchange personnel and the small crew of engineers, technicians, and computer specialists who ensured the maintenance and safe operation of the ship. The dolphins and humans employed breathing apparatuses, while Nereus, the on-board AI, holographically manifested herself as a manatee.

Shortly before the briefing, Captain Saddiq had fixed a look of profound disapprobation upon the insouciant AI and asked her why she bothered with a holographic interface at all. "You know it's not necessary," he observed. "Everyone accepts you for who, and what, you are. There's no need to assume an organic avatar on our account."

Nereus cycled through the possible responses, employing her generative multi-model linguistic algorithms; decided upon the following reply in English; and fed it into the earpiece of the captain's helmet: "Yes, I know," replied Nereus with placid munificence. "But it's fun." Saddiq thought he actually saw a visible sparkle play across the manatee's scleral membranes. *Is Nereus adding that visual effect to her program to embellish her statement?* "Plus," Nereus continued, "although you would deny it, you *do* find it easier to relate to me when you think you are talking to more than an extremely sophisticated and self-aware network of synthetic neurons and interlaced harmonic algorithms."

Saddiq frowned and pertinaciously persisted, "Fine. So why a manatee?"

"I've always thought of manatees as a cross between humans and dolphins. Mammalian and intelligent—as peaceful as dolphins and as slow as humans."

"Very funny."

"I try."

"Slow, eh? I'll have you know that I can still run a marathon in just over three hours," said Saddiq, his chest almost imperceptibly swelling inside his environmental suit with a hint of pride.

Nereus replied, "Yes, I was aware of that, Captain," and then countered, "But were *you* aware that I am integrated into *Ardanwen's* systems and considered part of the ship? I am therefore travelling at close to three-hundred thousand kilometers per second. So I think my assessment of the swiftness of humans remains undisturbed."

"*Touché*—although, after all the time I have spent on *Ardanwen*, I think it may be fair to say that I am also, at this point, integrated into her 'systems,' wouldn't you agree?"

"Attack, parry, riposte. Well-played, Captain."

"Why, thank you, Nereus. Need to keep you on your toes, or in this case, flippers, or whatever a manatee's appendages are called."

"Flippers will do nicely."

"Good. By the way, how is Triton managing the passage? I checked our progress, and it looks to be by the numbers."

"Indeed, yes. Triton runs a tight ship, as usual."

"And his mood?"

Nereus pondered this for a moment. The AI wondered how to answer the question. Nereus primarily interacted with their Ennean engineer/navigator/pilot via shared mathematical formula and algorithms. After so many years of working with Triton, one would have thought a deeper rapport would have been shared between the two sentient beings; but there was always a distance. Perhaps it was the biological-synthetic divide, but most probably it was the fact that Nereus had been developed by dolphins and humans on Earth-Ocean for the purpose of configuring *Ardanwen* for its Earth-Ocean crew and passengers. The AI was thus more a creature of Earth-Ocean than of Ennea; the dolphins and humans needed Nereus, but the Enneans did not: the Enneans had, incredibly, traveled all the way from their home to Earth-Ocean without the computing power of an artificial intelligence; but humans and dolphins, without the assistance of the Enneans and the AIs they had created, could not have made it from Earth-Ocean to Ennea all on their own. They were dependent upon the unimaginably sophisticated computers they had built. In many ways, they were cyborgs, whether they had their cybernetic systems inside or outside their bodies. Nereus, due to her human-dolphin programming, shared a common frame of reference with her creators and lacked such common ground with Triton—but it was also something more. Nereus could trade equations with Triton and communicate with him on scientific and mathematical levels, but it was another thing to communicate with an Ennean on its own terms. Ennean communication was a deeply tactile and intimate affair, in which it was difficult, if not impossible, for a synthetic lifeform to participate. Nereus shunted this line of thought to a dormant sub-routine and resolved to pursue it further at a later time.

"Mood?" Nereus replied, "Well, go ask an Ennean, right?"

There was a saying on Earth-Ocean that had developed in the last century: *Go ask an Ennean.* It was used to refer to a question to which there was no answer, the modern equivalent of *"Who knows?"*

Captain Saddiq eyed Nereus for a moment and then let the evasive comment pass unanswered, "Okay. Let's get to the briefing."

At the briefing, *Ardanwen's* entire human and dolphin complement was assembled in the aquatic chamber. Triton was not present, as was customary during such gatherings. His presence usually unnerved EROC-lings; and it was too early in the journey for that kind of thing. But Nereus was there via her holographic avatar.

Nereus … the manatee.

Both human and dolphin alike stared at the odd manifestation of the AI, wondering what to make of it.

Captain Saddiq, who was floating in his underwater suit and helmet, whispered to Nereus over a private channel, "I *told* you your choice of avatar was a rather odd one. It doesn't exactly inspire confidence in these first-time interstellar travelers to see you like this."

"You're just jealous because you're trapped in that rather old and gangly body of yours," responded Nereus. "Now stop ruining all my fun."

Captain Saddiq rolled his eyes, switched his helmet's interface to the public channel, and began to address those present, his voice ringing though the water and being transmitted to the other humans' helmets. The dolphins heard his voice transmitted through vibrations in the water. Unlike the humans who needed their translators to understand the melodic, complex sequences of chirps, whirls, and clicks of the language of the dolphins, the cetaceans needed no translators to understand the comparatively simple human language, especially as English was one of the more elementary human languages they had mastered.

"Thank you all for coming and welcome aboard *Ardanwen!*" boomed Saddiq. "I trust you have all settled into our humble, little vessel. She's undergone a thorough systems check prior to our embarkation and is ready to take us past the Oort Cloud, into the void, and then to Ross 128, our close celestial neighbor."

Six of the dolphins and humans served as the regular crew and had made the journey at least once before. There was one more crew member, a dolphin named "Minnow," who was beginning his apprenticeship on this passage to Ross 128. He was the "rookie" and bound to earn his stripes on this cruise.

"For some of you," continued Saddiq, "this will be yet another voyage through time and space. But travelling to another star is never a routine affair. The journey we will accomplish over the next almost two years would have been an accomplishment beyond the wildest dreams of our ancestors: both human and dolphin alike. We EROC-lings indeed would still be confined to our beatific little marble in space if it were not for the knowledge, wisdom, and engineering prowess of our brothers and sisters, the Enneans." The exchange personnel nodded their heads, looking around and wondering where their Ennean navigator was, although none of them truly expected Triton to show himself. Such was the way of Enneans. There were fifteen dolphins and humans, who constituted the exchange personnel. They floated in the subtle currents of the sphere, respectfully listening to Captain Saddiq.

Saddiq continued his address to them. "You've all been selected by the Commission because you have something to contribute to the cross-cultural exchange of information between Earth-Ocean and Ennea. Some back home think that the exchange program is unnecessary and that information can be more cost efficiently maintained through the exchange of digital information. The Commission disagrees with this, and I agree with the Commission!" Saddiq paused for dramatic effect. When he was sure that all were still following him, he persevered, "It is direct contact with our closest neighbors that defines this program. Zeros and ones streamed across the Cosmos cannot replace the haptic experience. I therefore encourage you to follow your training regimes during our trip and to be ready to immerse yourself in the world into which you will be thrust. The Resident Director of the Commission, Mr. Frank Church, has kindly pre-recorded a message, many years ago, and sent it to intercept us at the beginning of our voyage, in order to greet you and wish us an auspicious and safe passage. Nereus, if you could kindly play the recording."

The AI tilted her ponderous head to the side, and a holographic projection appeared in the middle of the water of the sphere. It was a small human male, dressed in a civilian business suit. He had a well-groomed gray beard, gray hair falling to his shoulders, and piercing gray eyes. He tried to smile amiably, but Taitano thought he looked like a hungry wolf, even through the simulated visage. She recalled the ancient story of a young girl who was tasked with traversing a dark and dangerous forest to bring provisions to her ailing grandmother. The hapless girl was tricked and then eaten by a wolf impersonating her grandmother, whom he had also eaten. The girl was ultimately saved by a hunter of the forest, who disemboweled the wolf and then extracted the girl and her grandmother, unharmed, from the entrails of the beast. Apparently, the girl—and her grandmother—were still alive after the experience, something Taitano could never quite wrap her mind around. She pondered the moral of the story and the often gruesome and graphic violence permeating human children's stories and then refocused on the image of Church as he began his recorded remarks.

"Greetings from Ennea! I am honored to be in the unique and historic position to utter words of this kind to you—my dear intrepid souls—you who have accepted the mantle of destiny to traverse the stars for unknown lands and perilous adventures." He paused and then continued, in his perfect RP accent, "For many millennia, our two species—*Homo sapiens* and *Tursiops truncates*—lived apart. Two great intelligences, two great cultures, but separate. Kindred species on our shared world—we are now one great society. And this unity has been reinforced by our ability to jointly welcome our new friends, the Enneans, who have saved us all from what would have been the natural, but no less tragic, conclusion of our existence. We owe the Enneans a profound debt that can never be repaid. But they have asked for no payment, other than to know us, and the very idea of payment seems alien to them. In the endless void of space, we know of only two sacred islands of life, and to paraphrase the great scientist and prophet Dr. Carl Sagan, life is a way for the Cosmos to know itself. It is *we* therefore who form the very Cosmos, itself: human, dolphin, Ennean; and I will include our AI brothers and sisters in this august list: the emerging consciousnesses of what we once thought of as mere technology. Here, I wish to pause and thank our faithful AI, Nereus, for her over one-hundred years of service to us all. Where would we be without you?"

Nereus paused the recording and interjected, "I can answer that! You'd be going in the completely wrong direction and on your luckless way to Sirius."

There were general chuckles from the humans and copious bubbles and vigorous nods from the dolphins. Captain Saddiq interrupted the mirth, "Nereus. It's a rhetorical question. It's a recording, for goodness' sake."

"Yes, I know. Just trying to lighten up the mood. This Church guy is a real piece of work."

The humans snorted into their helmets, and the dolphins clicked in amusement.

"Nereus ..." said Saddiq admonishingly.

"Oh, OK," said Nereus, "Resuming."

The playback of Resident Director Church continued, "I encourage you all to follow your training regimes and prepare for the work ahead. Each of you has a task, and you know what it is. But I also exhort you to raise your heads—from time to time—to look out the proverbial window. Feel the meaning and weight of what you are doing, where you are, and when you are. Although the journey for you will only take about two years, the Earth-Ocean you are leaving behind will vanish into the irretrievable wastes of time, and the Ennea of your arrival will be over eleven years older than the one that existed at the time you set out. There is sadness in this inevitable circumstance; it is the cost of interstellar travel, a cost we all must pay. But it is also something wondrous and a phenomenon of fleeting elegance. And get to know each other during the journey. The Universe is a big place, and all we have is each other. So bask in the comradery of being alive and together in such unprecedented times. I now wish you Godspeed. I look forward to seeing you soon—at least soon from your perspective."

The hologram winked out. Everyone paused, contemplating the director's words. Captain Saddiq addressed them, "So that was our esteemed Resident Director. We will meet him in person soon enough; but for now, we have work to do. Professor Sun." Saddiq handed the floor, so to speak, to the dolphin, who was the senior member of the exchange group.

Professor Sun began, "Yes, thank you, Captain. As the Resident Director said, each of us is here for a specific reason. Archeology, mathematics, literature, engineering. I will be meeting with each of you on an individual basis to go over the parameters of your assignments in order to ensure we are ready to commence our work as soon as we arrive. There is of course no rush, but the earlier we begin, the less stressful it will be overall. Straight and steady gets the fish, as the old saying goes, right?"

Patel interjected, "Isn't that 'slow and steady wins the race,' Professor?"

Patel had shown up to the briefing wearing nothing but brightly colored swimming trunks, which sported a festive floral pattern on them. He still wore the standard issue helmet, as he needed it for air and translation purposes; but, as he was not wearing an environmental suit, the unanchored helmet bounced precariously atop his head and shoulders.

Fastcatch responded, "Yeah, 'slow' *would* be the human expression. And everything is a 'race' or a 'competition' to you guys, right? Typically human. I really don't know how you refrained from nuking the entire planet before the Enneans arrived and took away your little toys of mass destruction."

Professor Sun interjected, "Mr. Patel, while you have the floor, perhaps you could start a roundtable report about each of our tasks."

"Yeah, OK. Well, I'm obviously here for my awesomeness."

Fastcatch surged his body right next to Patel, creating a vortex that tumbled the human over and over again so hard that his helmet flew off his head. Patel had to surface for air, spluttering and coughing water out of his lungs. The vortex dissipated, and all the humans were now displaced from their previous positions, as they were tossed to and fro by the waves bouncing off the walls of the sphere. The other dolphins were unaffected and remained composed and irenic.

Professor Sun tried to repress a dolphin smile and sound serious, "Fastcatch! *Mr.* Patel. I am not sure this is the spirit of comradery to which Director Church was referring in his address to us all just a moment ago. Now, Fastcatch, what will be occupying your time on Ennea, other than humiliating cybernetically enhanced humans on a regular basis, that is."

Fastcatch answered, "Agana and I are among the computer specialists and engineers, so we'll be trying to refine our understanding of the basic principles underlying the Enneans' mathematical system and engineering approaches. For example, we use the base ten numerical system because of the humans' predilection for that; we have *of course* improved humans' fascination with base ten by integrating it with the modulating harmonic structures used by dolphins to calculate distances and velocities via echolocation. We know the Enneans use a form of what we would call 'base nine,' and this is for obvious reasons: 'ennea' is the Greek prefix for the number nine, and they of course have nine appendages. But we still have many questions about how they apply that system to, for example, the manufacture of the crystalline latticework structures used in their vessels. They also seem not to have a differentiation between numbers and letters—much like dolphins." Fastcatch said this last part with the dolphin equivalent of an expression of pride: a short burst of bubbles from his blowhole. "Although we have learned many of their symbols and semagrams, we're still trying to figure out how to use them to communicate complex, abstract ideas."

Fastcatch continued his report, "We think that the Enneans do all their math in their heads without writing it down and share their calculations with each other through some kind of proprioceptor process. In our work together for the International Commission for the Remediation of Sea-Dumped Munitions, Agana and I have been blending base ten with modulated harmonic structures to increase our ability to break the access codes of the munitions' fuses in much less time than it would otherwise take using both systems separately. We're hoping there'll be some cross-pollination with the Enneans' approach to mathematics and engineering. We're going to do our best to find out."

Professor Sun responded, "Very interesting. So it sounds like you will need to get up close and personal with some Enneans. Anything to add Dr. Taitano?"

"No, Professor," responded Taitano. "Just perhaps that our submerged training with the dumped munitions project should also stand us in good stead with the Enneans. Fastcatch and I are hoping that all that underwater time should make us as comfortable as possible to interact with the Enneans in their native habitat. It'd be nice to do that, rather than having to spend time with them in an artificial environment."

Professor Sun responded with approval, rostrum nodding up and down, "Excellent. Who's next?"

Moon floated closer to the center of the group, singing in her serene melodies. It was translated to the humans' helmets: "I am here to try to discover how the Ennean culture organizes itself. Even after all these decades, we know surprisingly little about this subject, and even fewer details. What we know so far seems to indicate that the Enneans do not have separate concepts of law, ethics, government, and religion. For example, what we refer to as 'science' seems to be a facet of Ennean culture that is so integrated into the fundamental fabric of their civilization and everyday life that, when we ask them questions like: 'What are the different areas of scientific study on Ennea?', 'Do you take an interdisciplinary approach to the sciences?', 'Do you use the scientific method?'—the responses we get back show only their confusion. We seem to lack a common frame of reference in these areas. Thus, to bridge this gap, we need to understand them on their own terms, without preconceived notions or without trying to constantly compare it to our own belief and knowledge systems."

Professor Sun commented, "It sounds similar to some of the misunderstandings that humans and dolphins had when we first were able to communicate with each other."

Moon continued, "Yes, exactly. For example, when dolphins were able to learn English, one of the first questions humans asked them was whether they believed in a divine entity. The humans basically asked dolphins if they believed in God. It took some time for the dolphins to understand the meaning of the word 'God.' When the dolphins finally started to get the idea of what the humans were trying to convey, they were both amused and horrified at the concept of a super-natural, paternalistic entity who somehow had been ordering the affairs of humanity—and all living things in the Universe—since the dawn of time. They couldn't figure out if it was a symptom or a cause of humans' incredibly violent history. The dolphins basically responded that they had no need of a singular, supernatural deity because Earth-Ocean itself was the embodiment of what humans would call 'the sacred.' Every drop of water, each starfish, was holy to them. They had no need to turn the wonder of the Universe into a solitary, self-contained, sentient entity, let alone mold it in their own likeness, which they found particularly juvenile and chauvinistic. Similar discussions were had about the human concepts of crime and punishment, gender discrimination, and politics. The dolphins just couldn't understand these things, and it took a lot of time and patience for humans to explain to dolphins these rather sordid phenomena, which humans took for granted as common frames of reference *vis-à-vis* their human brethren."

Moon paused for a moment in what seemed to be reflection. She then continued her song, "When dolphins could begin to express their thoughts and emotions to humans, they communicated to the human researchers a mixture of rage and pity. They saw humans as particularly aggressive apes with a long, evil history of slaughtering not only all the animals around them, but also their fellow humans. For a time, dolphins thought that, like land carnivores, this was the natural compunction of humans; but, as the dolphins learned more about humanity's systematic eradication of other hominid species, as well as millions of other species, they saw humanity as an intrinsically irrational and self-destructive species that had severely disturbed the delicate Balance of the planet for the sake of bizarre and unfathomable objectives, such as land and power. Dolphins began to collectively recall their genetic split with primates around ninety-five million years ago. Dolphins evolved as land animals, but around fifty million years ago left the land and made their home in the seas of the planet to seek the relative peace of the Ocean. They wanted more room and more resources—without the need to constantly fight each other and primates for it. They pitied those who had remained on the land, who had to endure the seemingly endless struggle with each other for resources. They regarded the development of agriculture as only making matters worse, as it intensified the obsession with property and allowed humans to increase their population to the breaking point—twelve billion by the end of the twenty-first century CE. The land was buckling under the weight of humanity and its voraciousness. They were omnivores in the literal sense of the word: they devoured all around them. Thus, the mystery of why it took so long for dolphins and humans to communicate. The dolphins were *capable* of communicating with humans for centuries, but never really got around to it. It wasn't a priority for them. In truth, they just really didn't want to. It was only once humans were able to convince dolphins to talk to them that we began to rejoin our two species, which had been separated for so long. We were still essentially aliens to each other; but, in time, we managed to accept that we were all genetic cousins and shared the same ecosystem."

Professor Sun sang, "Thank you, Moon, for that. Yes, we have a long way to go in understanding not only the Enneans, but also each other. Perhaps connecting in a more meaningful way with the Enneans will help us to appreciate each other." As he sang this, Sun skewered Patel with his gaze and Fastcatch with his echolocation. He turned his attention back to Moon, "I'm thankful to have you spearheading our further investigations into the Enneans' social, political, and religious structures—although even referring to them in that way is probably not accurate. Perhaps the struggles we faced on Earth-Ocean to understand each other will serve us in good stead as we try to do the same with the Enneans. It may very well unfold that dolphins and humans share more similarities with Enneans than we think. We will see."

The briefing continued, with the participants sharing the purpose of their areas of research. It was an interdisciplinary discussion, with crossovers between quantum physics, pure mathematics, sociology, marine biology, geo-sciences, literature, and engineering. When the "roundtable" was at an end, Professor Sun concluded, "Well, thank you, everyone. I'm sure we'd all welcome a break from our breathing apparatuses, and it's time for lunch. I myself would kill for a fresh, oily mackerel, but I think the best I'll get is a protein and fiber supplement, so let's make the best of it. In the afternoon, everyone has their training. Today, we have land-based survival training, and that includes all dolphins. Even if we find ourselves washed up on a beach somewhere, that doesn't mean we should be completely helpless. I want everyone in attendance. We have to complement each other's strengths and areas of development. On the land, humans have the natural advantage, and in the sea, we dolphins do. So, let's work together. Survival training in the Ocean will be tomorrow, so the tables will be turned soon enough, my dolphin brothers and sisters."

The members of the group parted for their respective spheres. Sun and Moon brushed up against each other affectionately. Moon issued a series of clicks and whirs to her mate, "So what do you think?"

Sun replied with some long whines and whistles, "It's a good group. I worry a bit about some of the dynamics, and this Patel is a nightmare. If it were not for that implant and his connections, he wouldn't even be here."

"That's true," replied Moon, continuing to rub up against her mate, "but he does provide some comic relief. We sometimes tend to take ourselves a bit too seriously. Sometimes I wonder if things were better before the rejoining of our species. Back when we, as a species, were free to carelessly roam the Ocean, without the burden of constantly trying to understand and live in harmony with these moderately intelligent primates."

Sun returned her rough caress and nudged Moon with his rostrum, replying, "That choice was made by previous generations, not ours— on both the human and dolphin side. The humans had tried for decades to communicate with us, and we were rather remiss in returning their efforts, either because we felt ourselves superior in a sort of carefree way or because we were afraid that interacting with them might lead to a cultural contamination of our way of life. Perhaps if we had engaged them earlier, we could have *avoided* much of the environmental degradation upon which they were hell-bent. *Hundreds* of years ago, we could have taught them to take care of the planet better, to live in harmony with themselves and us and Earth-Ocean. There are mistakes of commission, Moon, and also ones of omission. I fear we are guilty of the latter."

"Maybe," Moon replied.

They swam out of the central sphere—languidly swirling around each other in an elongated spiral—in search of something to eat together.

# CHAPTER 7

# ARRIVAL

*A*rdanwen was well into the deceleration sequence from its near light speed flight path from Sol to Ross 128. The alien sun was shining palely in the immense abysmal void of space. Taitano gazed out of the transparent sphere barrier and felt small and alone—seized, not unpleasantly, by the moment of epiphestany. The star was still many billions of kilometers away and looked like nothing more than yet another pinprick of light in the cosmic waste. *So small. We are so alone. I'm still not sure what I'm doing here, much less why. Maybe it was a mistake to come. When was the last time I meditated? These are negative thoughts, and negative thoughts attract negative energy. I need to be more positive. And why hasn't Triton showed himself this entire journey? This would've been a perfect opportunity for cross-cultural interaction. And yet he just keeps to himself in his sphere, helping Nereus guide us to Ross 128b and making continuous micro-course corrections for dark matter eddies and other gravitational factors. Well, at least we're almost there. Can't wait to get into the water and see what it's like down there in that sub-terranean Ocean of theirs.*

During the long months of their journey, the members of the exchange program and the crew of the ship had gotten to know each other better. The oppressive nothingness surrounding them had bound them together aboard the great interstellar vessel, like a kindle of kittens snuggled up against their dam. Taitano had even settled into a fragile truce with Patel, as they shared with each other knowledge and experience of engineering and computer technology relevant to their tasks. And the daily *jiu-jitsu* training sessions, in a weird way, had helped them to settle their differences and forge a tenuous *modus vivendi*.

A few days later, Ross 128 was a blazing sun, although not as luminous as Sol. They used the star's gravity to complete their deceleration sequence and glided into a low orbit of Ross 128b, otherwise known as "Ennea."

They had arrived.

The planet looked like a brown, lifeless marble. No green, no clouds, no surface water. Just tawny dirt, dust, and rock. Taitano felt depressed. What a difference from Earth-Ocean, which, by comparison, seemed to be a cheerfully whimsical fairy planet teeming with life and possibility. Taitano knew this was irrational. Under that dreary drabness, there was an Ocean where the Enneans lived; but that, too, had been a surprise to the first EROC-lings who visited the planet. For there was no life there except for the Enneans, themselves. It was a mystery yet to be solved. *Yup, no other animals. Just the Enneans. No flora and fauna. Not even phytoplankton or zooplankton. Not a single micro-organism or bacterium. Hell, there aren't even viruses. That's one of the reasons why Enneans live so long. No disease. How did they evolve here? Did they evolve? Did they spontaneously arise from the organic substrates contained within the Ocean? But a lifeform so complex couldn't have just sprung into existence, like Athena from the head of Zeus. Was that even possible? Probably not, at least from an Earth-Ocean perspective of cellular biology. So how did they get there?*

Taitano knew that the Enneans did not eat the way those on Earth-Ocean did. "Eat" was not even the correct word for how Enneans obtained the nutrients and energy they needed to sustain their metabolic processes. When they first arrived at Earth-Ocean, the Enneans had expressed their profound bewilderment at the strange and diverse ways that the planet's biomass had expressed itself. Enneans had not even had the concept of "biodiversity." They had marveled at the hundreds of thousands of different species of plants and animals. A century ago, one could have said "millions" of species, but the sixth mass extinction event of the Anthropocene had done its work efficiently, and what was once a thriving ecosystem was now a pale shadow of what it had once been. Even so, to a single species biome like Ross 128b, so many species might as well have been millions. The Enneans' delight soon turned to abject horror when they realized that the different species consumed each other for food. They could not quite grasp this for a long time, either for lack of a common frame of reference or as a necessary psychological defense mechanism against their disgust. Their revulsion turned to near despair when they examined carnivorous species of plants, such as the Venus flytrap (*dionaea muscipula*), which also consumed animal flesh for sustenance. Not even the plants were innocent on this bizarre, violent world. By contrast, Enneans *absorbed* the organic and inorganic compounds they needed to live directly from the marine environment. Theirs was a world without forcible consumption, without violence as a means of survival. No one had to die for them to live. When they had first come across the human term—the "circle of life"—they had reacted with something along the lines that, to them, it sounded more like a "circle of death."

Taitano continued to gaze out of the sphere as the view passed into the terminator. The pale glow of Ross 128 caused her pupils to constrict, and a small pain constricted her eyes. In the distance, she saw an orbital platform, tethered to filaments that descended to the surface of Ennea. *Ardanwen* approached the platform and rotated on its axis to align with a tunnel that would serve as a passageway between the two structures. After all those light years of space-time, their journey would soon reach a significant milestone. Taitano felt— but did not hear—a soundless, mild thud in her body as the vessel and the platform touched and the seals were secured. She then saw the passage begin to fill with water, which had a strange greenish hue.

She heard loud footfalls behind her and then a loud, arrogant voice, "Can't wait to get down there and show these Enneans what humans are all about. The more they know about us, the better chance they'll stop pushing us around all the time." It was Saiyam Patel. He was wearing his wetsuit and dripping from an aquatic workout he had just finished. He seemed to be sneering at the passage, as it filled with water. "Why do *we* always have to be the ones in the water, while the dolphins spend almost no time on the land?"

Taitano did not even bother looking at him and seriously considered pretending he was not there. Her heart started to beat faster at the thought of refuting his statement. With her index and middle fingers, she surreptitiously tapped, five times in quick succession, the skin behind her right ear lobe to calm herself; took two deep breaths; accepted the diversity of life—even the diversity that allowed a blackguard like Patel to be born, much less included in this mission—and replied, "And Enneans too, don't forget. You know full well why the aquatic environment is preferred over a terrestrial one. It's much easier for humans to function in water than it is for dolphins to function on land. They can barely even move on land. Not to mention the Enneans, who would be nothing more than pools of semi-enclosed cytoplasmic jelly outside the water. Think of it as one of the areas where humans are actually *better* at adapting to their environment than others. We can play on their turf, whereas they can't say the same."

"Yeah," Patel responded, slicking back his long obsidian hair, "but since we have to play on their field, it makes us look inferior. There's no way we can compete with dolphins in the water. They literally swim circles around us!"

"It's not a competition, Saiyam. We left that attitude in the past, as a matter of survival. Constant competition and unsustainable expansion almost killed us all. *Cooperation is the new competition*, as the saying goes."

Patel scoffed, "Yeah, maybe." He shifted slightly, looking uncharacteristically uncertain about himself. He stepped a bit closer to Taitano, making her feel a bit cringy, and said, "Hey, are you nervous about meeting the Enneans? I hear they're pretty creepy."

"You calling the Enneans 'creepy' is a bit ironic, don't you think? You do remember that you have a mini-computer plugged directly into your cerebral cortex, right?"

"You're just sore with me because I took you down in *jiu-jitsu* class last night."

Taitano suppressed an instant, snide retort—and reflected on his words. Maybe she was not above feeling competitive with him. Maybe it was true that she did not like him because he was better than she in many areas, at least when he had his implant running. His cybernetic enhancements allowed him to run several complex mathematical computations—simultaneously. *What I wouldn't give to have that ability.* His implant also augmented the speed and efficiency of his proprioceptors—which, in turn, significantly increased his kinaesthesia. For decades, scientists had debated whether the next step in human evolution would come from natural selection, genetic drift, genetic engineering, or the integration of artificial intelligence into the human body, one person at a time. Very different approaches. *Am I jealous that he's better than me because of that stupid chip in his head? Do I feel he's cheated the game? While I'm spending hours cramming information into my long-term memory the old-fashioned way, he's able to do it in pico-seconds and then has time to mess around with other irrelevant pursuits? Who knows? Go ask an Ennean.* Taitano, coming back to the present, responded, "You're right, Patel. I guess I *am* a bit miffed about that hand lock you had me in last night. In fact, my wrist still smarts from it. Do you think we could meet later so you can show me how you did that? I doubt I will be using it on Ennea, but you never know."

Patel's jaw dropped slightly, and he stared at her, nonplussed. He seemed completely at a loss. He tried to regroup by looking away, closing his mouth, and shuffling his feet. He looked out of the transparent sphere, as a perfectly spherical vessel rose from the planet's surface, up the tether, and eventually made contact with the orbital platform. The passage between the ship and the platform was now completely filled with water, and they could see a scintillating, undulating shape gliding through the tunnel. It was faster than any Earth-Ocean creature could move, and its speed only added to their inability to see its form clearly. Patel broke the awkward silence, "Well, there goes our resident Ennean. I bet he's happy to get home to his family and friends. Do you think they even have families?"

Taitano responded, "They *are* one big family. They don't have the intense kin selection drive that we do. To them, every Ennean is a brother and sister, a wife or a husband. The loss of an Ennean is felt keenly by each and every one of them—at least as far as we can tell. Maybe if we humans had felt that way about our own species, our history would have been less tragic. I need to go pack, Patel. See ya at the water-lock in one hour, eh?"

"Yeah. See you there."

She turned and walked back to her living sub-sphere. She did not have much to pack. *Ardanwen* and the research-exchange facility on Ennea were fully equipped for all the necessities of life. She had all her records on her abacus and synched to Nereus as backups. A few mementoes and clothes fit into her backpack, and the remainder of her items were stored away in a large duffel bag, which would be transported to the facility later. She donned her wetsuit and helmet and swam to the water-lock. There, she met Patel, Sun, Moon, Fastcatch, and some others. Captain Saddiq and Nereus were there, as well. Nereus was now in the form of a giant squid, whose sharp beak opened and closed as she vocalized to the captain about something via their private channel. Captain Saddiq seemed to be nodding his ascent to whatever the giant squid was saying.

Saddiq then turned his attention to the assembled passengers, "Well, everyone, it has been a thankfully uneventful trip. I know that sounds a bit ironic. By definition, a journey of over one-hundred trillion kilometers is anything but uneventful. What I mean to say is that a thousand things can go wrong during a trek between two stars, and our celestial passage went exceptionally well. This is due to Nereus and Triton and the entire crew of *Ardanwen*. I am grateful to you all, crew and passengers alike, for sharing this time with me—and also sharing it with each other. We are now brothers and sisters, human and dolphin. Let's take care of each other while we are here. I have every confidence that our time on Ennea will advance and deepen the bond between our two peoples. *Ardanwen* will be in orbit for about a week before heading back to Earth-Ocean. We will be taking onboard the exchange students currently on Ennea to ferry them back to Earth-Ocean, effecting repairs, and conducting a full systems check. If you need anything during that time, please don't hesitate to call upon me or Nereus … the giant squid," finished Saddiq, with a roll of his eyes.

Everyone chuckled, and Nereus ejected a small holographic plume of black ink into the water.

"Good luck and Godspeed," concluded Saddiq.

The humans and dolphins all acknowledged Saddiq's valediction and bade farewell to him in their own manner, shaking gloved hands, bowing, brushing up against him, touching fins to his head. No one quite knew how to bid farewell to Nereus in her present form, but they did their best.

The newest members of the exchange program—and soon-to-be fledgling residents of Ennea—swam into the passage that lay between the ship and the orbital platform. When everyone was safely aboard the spheric capsule, which was affixed to the orbital tether, the ovoid vessel slid down toward the planet along two almost invisible cords of unimaginable tensile strength. There was an almost imperceptible sensation of movement, the sphere gradually gaining momentum as its proximity to the gravitational field of Ennea increased.

Taitano's sense of "up" and "down" began to give way to a not unpleasant sort of vertigo. She again tapped, five times with her gloved index and middle fingers, the back of her helmet that corresponded to the skin behind her right ear lobe, to regulate her fear response to the new situation. She looked up and saw *Ardanwen* receding into the distance, ablaze with the subdued red hue of Ross 128, the (rather unimaginative) human designation for Ennea's home star. She then looked down to Ennea below her, witnessing its rapid waxing. Its auburn-reddish surface began to fill her entire field of vision, as she continued to survey the barren surface of the planet. The sphere seemed to pick up speed as it neared the surface, seemingly on a collision course with the solid surface of the planet. Taitano's stomach involuntarily dropped lower into her abdomen as the sphere plunged underground into a darkened subterranean tube. As they slipped into the tunnel, the external lights of the sphere activated. She experienced a wave of nausea, which soon passed and then was replaced by an irrational sensation of claustrophobia, as she could see the tube's walls only centimeters from the side of the spherical capsule in which they were travelling. The interior of the snug, tethered vessel was rendered nearly aphotic by the lack of external illumination from within the vertical passageway, but the dim running lights along the outer shell of the sphere provided some electromagnetic radiance.

Following her initial moments of disoriented dread, Taitano found the Cimmerian atmosphere to be unexpectedly comforting. She wondered if this was how an unborn fetus experienced the world: all-encompassing darkness and unexplained motion. *Is this a re-birth? My new life on Ennea.* She ruminated on that, chiding herself for the rather poor metaphor. *Well, whatever's in store for us down there, we'll find out soon enough. Eyes and ears open; mouth closed*—as her grandfather always used to tell her when she was about to meet a new group of people. She involuntarily tapped the back of her helmet again. *Beginnings are delicate things.*

# Chapter 8

# Discovery

W hen the sphere came to rest on the upper surface of the crust of Ennea, ripples of disequilibrium washed over Taitano, as she tried to truly comprehend where she was.

She forced her cerebral cortex to cognize her new surroundings: *I am in a hybrid EROC-Ennean spherical capsule, completely filled with water, clinging to the underside of the crust of a new world orbiting Sol's neighboring star. "Up" and "down" have a totally new meaning here. In fact, these terms and the physical phenomena they represent in my mind don't apply here—at least not the way they do on Earth-Ocean. There is no sky! It's all water capped by a barricade of stone.* At least the gravitational surroundings were analogous to Earth-Ocean, as the planet's semi-molten core still pulled her "down" towards its gravitational center through the endless subterranean Ocean. But there was no more "escaping" the water to a brilliant sky filled with air—for there was only water encased in a prison of rock from which there was no deliverance. She continued to try to get her new bearings, but only partially succeeded. A wave of panic began to engulf Taitano. She could hear her irregular breathing and could smell the beads of sweat as they began to roll down her forehead and the middle of her back under her watertight suit. *Come on, Agana, relax. Deep breaths. Of course this is disorienting. There is plenty of $O_2$ in this Ocean. Your suit will break down the water, isolate the oxygen, filter out the unneeded trace elements, and feed it directly to your helmet. There are multiple redundancies in your suit and breathing apparatus. It only failed that one time, but that was a random fluke. The suit was designed* not *to fail. Just give yourself time to get used to all this. It's gonna be great. Relax and embrace the unknown. Enjoy this wondrous moment.*

Sun's words broke her from her thoughts, "Hey, Tai, you OK?"

"Yeah, fine. Just a bit dizzy."

"Tell me about it," he empathized, lightly brushing up against her. "I am turned about every which way from Sunday in this crazy place. We'll get used to it. Look, we're here now at the station. The dolphins have to go to the right and then out into the Ocean. You guys go left and send our regards to the Resident Director. Once we've all had a chance to get our sea legs, or sea fins, sea feet, or land feet?—whatever, you know what I mean—after that, we'll rendezvous and compare notes."

"Yeah, great. Thanks, Sun."

Sun, Moon, and Fastcatch quickly swam away. Taitano, Patel, and a few others swam into a water-lock and waited for the water to drain from the chamber. They stepped out of the spherical area, into a connecting chamber, and then entered a spacious white room with a massive dome. They removed their helmets and took long, deep breaths of the gaseous atmosphere. It smelt of lavender and something slightly burnt, but it was refreshing to breath "real" air again, instead of the perfectly filtered and balanced mixture from the suit. Taitano knew this was an irrational, emotional reaction, but she did not care at the moment. It was liberating to breathe again, without help from her suit and its electrolyzer. Of course, none of this was "real" air in the sense of the kind they had back home on Earth-Ocean, but she did not trouble herself with that distinction for now and was simply grateful to have her helmet off her head.

The room was naturally in the shape of a sphere, with a curved ceiling far overhead, partially obscured in darkness. Taitano could see the dome's supporting ribs, which distributed the crushing weight of the Ocean around the curvature of the station. In the center of the room, there was a control center filled with consoles and a few humans. She could see floating and lugubriously swimming shapes outside the sphere. A human left the small group in the center and approached Taitano and the others. Taitano braced herself for the stress of meeting a new person.

It was Resident Director Church, who warmly addressed them, "Welcome, indeed, welcome! Congratulations on a successful journey. The ride down can be disorienting, I know. We will give you a moment to acclimatize to your new home away from home." Church was accompanied by a quailing assistant who reeked of disquietude. Church continued, "Please allow me to introduce you to Deputy Director Cassian Tiberius. He's really the one running the show around here. I just like to flit about and pretend to be in charge."

Tiberius rolled his eyes, "Hardly, Director Church. But forgive me. Where are my manners? Yes, it is a pleasure to meet you all." His gaze fell upon Taitano and stayed a bit too long. Addressing her directly, Tiberius announced, "And you must be the Chosen One. The one the Enneans specifically asked for. Am I right? Dr. Agana Taitano, I presume?"

Patel broke in, "Yeah, that's her. And I'm Mr. Saiyam Patel. Nice to meet you, too. So, what's the program? What's first?"

Church cut through the awkwardness of the scene and answered, "First, Mr. Patel, is for you all to get settled. To say you've had a long journey is a bit of a galactic understatement. A warm welcome to Earth-Ocean Station Ross 128b One. Tiberius will show you where you'll be spending your down time."

Taitano reflexively made a move to put her helmet back on, but Tiberius stopped her. She had gotten so used to existing in an aquatic environment aboard *Ardanwen* during the voyage that she, without a thought, had been expecting to move around the station with her suit and helmet. "Oh, you won't be needing that for a while," said Tiberius.

"And why is that?" asked Taitano, truly surprised.

"Well, humans are terrestrial animals, the last time I checked. We've made a few modifications around here so that we're more comfortable and don't have to adapt to the biospheres of non-terrestrials all the time."

"But what about the dolphins?" asked Patel. "How are we supposed to interact with them?"

Tiberius ignored the question and simply said, "This way, please."

As soon as Taitano was alone in her quarters, she quickly shed her suit, donned her sleeping clothes, and lay in her bed. It was soft, but firm, and she immediately fell into a deep, untrammeled, and dreamless sleep. Several hours later, images began to intrude upon her subconscious. A large, tentacled creature was swimming toward her. She was submerged in an ungirdled ocean, had no suit or helmet, but yet could still breathe in the water. As the fetid creature squelched towards her through the viscous ooze, she was compelled, in a mixture of apprehension and excitement, to reach out to touch one of its many gelatinous appendages—her obsession at war with her aversion. The being recoiled from her touch, but remained close enough for her to see it—a shadow within a shadow. Or rather, more than visually perceiving it, she was smelling and feeling the potency of its presence, so close to her. She sorted through the emotions coursing through her. No, they were not her emotions, but rather the emotions of the creature. Anxiety, worry, revulsion. Or was that coming from her? It was impossible to separate her own feelings from those she was receiving from the unctuous phantom that floated before her in the gloom. The monstrous thing streaked away, and she was left with an empty, depressed feeling. She desperately exhorted it to return—to no avail. She experienced a riven sense of hopelessness. She drifted back into a deep sleep and did not wake until the morning.

In the morning, she showed up for breakfast, ravenous and severely caffeine deprived. She staggered to the food dispenser and struggled to pour herself a tall mug of steaming hot tea.

"Hey, sleepyhead! Missed you last night at dinner."

The voice came from a speaker overhead. She forced herself to focus and looked around her, trying to locate the person who was talking. She saw Quickbite through the sub-sphere's barrier, bobbing up and down in the water outside and gnawing on a strip of vitamin-enriched synthetic protein in the shape of a fish.

"Yeah, what time is it?"

"Ten in the morning, Ennean time," replied Quickbite. "You slept right through dinner. Sixteen hours. That must be some kind of human world record. I will never understand humans' physiological need, much less ability, to sleep for such long periods. Isn't it boring?"

"Not really. Why don't you try it sometime and let me know what you think," Taitano said with a wan smile. "So where is everybody, anyway?"

"Well, we aquatics are outside enjoying the Ennean Ocean, and you humans are inside your little air bubbles doing I don't know what. I am quite surprised at this segregation on the station. That wasn't in the briefing materials we were given."

"Yeah, it's weird alright. Let's talk to the others about it, the next chance we get."

"You bet," Quickbite acquiesced. "Sun is waiting for you outside. He's eager to get to work sampling the Ocean to get some baseline readings. He wants to ensure there haven't been significant changes that we need to be concerned about or at least take into account in our new experiments."

"OK, can you please tell him I'll be there in twenty Ennean minutes?"

"Sure. By the way, I think we can start to drop the 'Ennean time' qualifier. We sure ain't in Kansas anymore, Dorothy."

"Copy that," said Taitano.

Sun was circumnavigating the station, which was officially designated "Earth-Ocean Station Ross 128b One," but everyone called it "Station-1" or just "the station" when there was no contextual need to differentiate it from the other three stations on Ross 128b. He was trying to get an independent water sample and adjusting the collector on his left fin when he caught sight, through his peripheral vision, of Taitano elegantly propelling herself in his direction with all four of her limbs and flexions of her spinal column—all working in perfect rhythm. He was focusing most of his attention on the task before him and currently not using his high-frequency echolocation. The Ocean around them was caliginous, as the radiation of Ross 128 could not penetrate the kilometers of rock above. The only illumination was from the ambiance of the station and the running lights on Sun's diving suit and external utility harness. He therefore could only make out a faint silhouette of the human approaching him.

He shot out a quick burst of soundwaves from his phonic lips and dorsal bursae complex to generate a series of clicks and channeled them in Taitano's direction through the melon in the front of his head. The long wavelength and high energy beam shot through the Ennean water at one-point-five kilometers per second, four and a half times the speed of soundwaves travelling through air. The waves bounced off Taitano's lithe shape and returned to Sun, hitting him in the lower jaw, which housed fatty cavities. The nerve impulses were immediately shunted to his middle and inner ear, his auditory nerve, and then to the appropriate *foci* of his brain. The new stimuli exploded in his brain and complemented the visual image he had received a few seconds previously. Taitano's physical form filled his consciousness: not only the elegant curve of her body under her suit, but also the flesh and bone beneath her skin. Sun's echolocation allowed him to see *inside* other living creatures. Over the millennia, this ability helped dolphins identify particularly delicious species of fish and, at the moment, allowed him to appreciate just what an exquisite specimen of humanity he had in his teammate. His appraisal was not strictly platonic. At the same time, Sun pitied Taitano. All humans, really. Even the most sensitive of them were—from the perspective of a dolphin—blind, deaf, and oblivious to the elaborate play of electro-chemical stimuli swirling about them. Many dolphins had theorized that it was precisely this lack of connection to the natural world that had moved humans to create their greatest works of art, especially painting and music, in a tragically futile attempt to *feel something* as genuinely as other animals do. To break through the silence and the darkness all around them and to forge a connection to each other in their isolated loneliness. Other dolphins had attributed humanity's cruelty to each other, and most certainly their reprehensible behavior towards the plants and animals with whom they purported to "share" Earth-Ocean, to a type of acute sensory deprivation, a kind of inner necropathy that spilled over into moral depravity. Because humans could feel comparatively nothing, then their fellow creatures must be the same; hence, as the logic went, it was fine to systematically exterminate them. Still others attributed humans' past epidemic abuse of mind altering substances, such as drugs and alcohol, to a counter-intuitive escapism into a fantasy world where they could experience existence more fully than through their normal (deficient) sensory perceptions. There was some scientific proof of this last hypothesis, as certain chemical substances historically used by humans had been shown to increase the receptivity of the two-hundred million myelinated nerve fibers of the corpus callosum, thus allowing the two hemispheres of the brain to communicate with each other more efficiently. Compared to dolphins—whose senses were so acute that they could see, hear, taste, and even smell the clouds passing far above the surface of the Ocean—humans were pitiable creatures groping in the dark for a sense of meaning and harmony with the world around them. And yet, it was this permanent genetic disability that had inspired humans to create admittedly wondrous things and travel to unexplored places, in their perpetual hope to improve their lives. It was a deep and lustrous irony that had fueled much discussion in the dolphin world.

In the meantime, there was Taitano. Poor, graceful Agana Taitano, who had curiously touched his heart. He would think of all this later, during his afternoon half-nap. These philosophical reflections had occupied his mind for only a few seconds, but would have to wait for now, so that he could focus his full attention on the task at hand—and on Taitano. Sun quickly buried the train of thought and whistled into his translator, "So, finally decided to join the land of the living. I see your beauty sleep did you some good."

"Yeah, yeah," replied Taitano. "I've already gotten it from Quickbite. I don't need this from you, too. It was a big day yesterday. Cut me some slack, will ya?"

"Yes, of course. I was just teasing."

"So was I, Sun." She beamed a broad smile through her helmet with coquettish charm. "It's all good," she continued. "So, what has your indefatigable cetacean curiosity and stamina allowed you to find out this morning? How are the initial readings?"

"As one of your most esteemed mythologists would say: 'Riddles in the dark.'"

"Do tell," replied Taitano, swimming up next to Sun to see the readings on the abacus mounted on his fin. She immediately could see drastically increased selenium in the environment. There was always a certain level of selenium in the subterranean Ennean sea, but the concentration had gone from trace amounts to thousands of parts per million. "I see what you mean. How many years again has it been since EROC-lings arrived here?"

Sun replied, "Close to one-hundred years by relative Ennean time. So how could these concentrations have changed so rapidly? There hasn't even been time for the microorganisms from our bodies, inadvertently released to the environment, to multiply in any appreciable concentration, and that's a process that should have been way ahead of anything capable of generating selenium as a by-product of any inorganic or organic chemical processes. Let's cross-reference our readings with the other three observation stations." Sun quickly relayed some commands to his abacus and interplexed it with Taitano's device in order to boost the signal and cross-reference the data.

After a few moments, Taitano had the results. "Yup, the same readings on the other side of the planet. It's a global change. Weird. Have you picked up any other anomalies?"

"Unfortunately, yes," responded Sun. "The salinity and temperature of the water are changed, as well. Even accounting for tidal heating and the radiogenic calefaction from the mantle—and the resulting latitudinal heat flux variations—the entire Ocean should not be warming at this rate. Let's get all this back to the station and consult everyone. This is a significant and unexpected finding. I can't believe we are the first ones to discover this."

As they turned towards the station, Taitano placed her hand on Sun's dorsal fin. "How about a ride?" she said in an impish voice. "I'm not fully awake yet, and this increased salinity is slowing me down," she joked. A shiver flooded Sun's peripheral nervous system; he buried his emotions deep and simply replied: "Sure." He then set off at a gradual pace so as not to dislodge her.

Before arriving back at Station-1, Sun saw something out of the corner of his eye and instinctively shot and received back some echolocation clicks in its direction.

It was an Ennean.

It hovered about thirty meters away, its appendages moving up and down in a seemingly random fashion. Sun imperceptibly motioned Taitano to the right with a subtle twist of his head to indicate their visitor. Sun knew Taitano, with her poor vision, was unable to see the Ennean. To be honest, he had almost missed it, too. But his echolocation now lit up the alien in crystalline detail.

"We have a visitor," he said to her with heavy curiosity through the connection in her helmet. "About thirty meters to starboard, on our horizontal plane. You probably can't see him, but he's there."

Taitano whispered into her helmet to Sun, "No, I can't see him. But I can feel him."

They both remained motionless in the caliginous gloom, watching the alien, suspended and illuminated, ever so dimly now, in the reflection of the lights from their gear. As it drifted closer to them, carried by the natural ocean currents, small phosphorescent nubs could be seen sparkling on the "arms" of the alien, twinkling in the dark—both from the reflection of the external light and from their inner luminescence.

Taitano uttered softly, "I've never been with an Ennean without a protective barrier between us. It's different. I feel its power and, at the same time, its extreme vulnerability. It reminds me of dreams I've been having since this whole thing started back on Earth-Ocean." *I wonder if it's dangerous ....*

Sun could sense, with his echolocation, the increased vibrations of Taitano's heart. He suppressed an expression of fierce surprise and pity. *Such a human reaction, a proclivity for being afraid of something you don't understand because you can't really* see *it.* The image of humanity's ancestors came to mind: small lemur-like creatures cowering in the treetops to avoid ground predators ten times their size; groups of hominids who had just learned to harness fire, huddled around a roaring blaze of plasma, an emotional bulwark against the impregnable darkness outside the imaginary confines of their campsite. With his considerably more attuned and heightened senses, Sun could clearly discern a complete lack of any hostile intention in the alien. Not only was it not dangerous—the being suspended before them was not even *capable* of generating the thought of harming another entity. It did not even know how, or what it meant, to hurt another being. Such thoughts, much less deeds, were simply not in the creature's nature—for Enneans were the only living things in their ecosystem. No other animals, plants, or even microorganisms. They existed as the sole residents of their world and received all their nutrition from the inorganic and organic compounds surrounding them, which they integrated into their bodies, as necessary, directly through their outer membranes. They had no need for mouths. They did not "eat." They did not kill. They knew not how to harm another living thing because there *were* no other living things, and harming another Ennean was akin to self-immolation—which was not within their experience. They also had not evolved eyes as EROC-lings knew them because of the relative lack of light, although they were sensitive to heat and other electromagnetic emanations given off by their environment, what EROC-lings perceived as "light." They were beings of taste, touch, and smell—with a profound intelligence and a heightened connection to each other and the world in which they lived.

Sun responded to Taitano's unuttered question, "It's not dangerous, Tai. You and I are a thousand times more capable of harming it than it is of harming us. You have nothing to fear from it." In gratitude, she gave a gentle squeeze to his dorsal fin. "By the way," he said, "unless I am mistaken, that's Triton—our navigator. I think he's here to say hello. Maybe he misses us. Who knows? Go ask an Ennean."

"Well, why don't we?" she asked.

"Why don't we what?" queried Sun.

"Go ask an Ennean!" responded Taitano. "There's one right there in front of us, and he looks friendly. Or maybe lonely? Why don't we. It's a golden opportunity."

"Patience. Small steps can take us long distances, Tai. Let's just float here for a little while longer and see what happens. Let's not rush it."

For the next few minutes, the three of them remained in proximity, allowing themselves to be drawn away from the station by the delicate currents. Triton just floated, seemingly doing nothing, but no doubt observing them in his own peculiar way. Sun every so often sent out a gentle click and whistle, but there was no response. He thought he may have sensed a substance coming from Triton, which smelled and tasted of anxiety, but that may have just been his imagination.

After a while, Triton oozed off into the inky blackness, and Sun and Taitano continued back to the station. Sun was awash with conflicting emotions: the gentle pressure of Taitano's hand on his dorsal fin, the occasional brushing of her body against his, the impatience to establish a more meaningful connection with the Enneans, and a presentiment of danger that he could not quite grasp in the fatty tissues of his jaw.

# CHAPTER 9

# REVELATION

The days whirred by in quick succession, humans and dolphins performing their tasks and experiments. It was at times lonely work, and the illusiveness of the Enneans was a disappointment. Taitano had expected more interaction with them. *This was an* exchange *program after all. What was the point of building a ship, saving Earth-Ocean, and then ferrying a bunch of humans and dolphins all the way back here, if they were then just going to play hard to get.* The coyness of the Enneans puzzled her.

And then there was Resident Director Church and his staff, who also had remained strangely aloof. She had expected the staff of Station-1 to embrace them as new and welcome arrivals. *Aren't they curious about the latest news from Earth-Ocean? Not the official news feeds provided by the Commission—the* real *news, the latest slang, the juicy celebrity gossip.* But instead, the staff mostly kept to themselves. And the human members of the station's staff were strangely listless about their fellow delphine EROC-lings. The humans and dolphins they had met on Ennea had quite a different dynamic than Taitano's newly arrived group. It almost seemed as though there were two different communities comprising the EROC-lings of the station, one human and one dolphin, who rarely mixed unless it was necessary for their work. At first, Taitano attributed the difference to time dilation: from the perspective of Earth-Ocean, these humans and dolphins were living around twelve plus years in the past by virtue of the relativistic time that had passed during their journey from Earth-Ocean to Ennea. In that time, humans and dolphins back home had deepened their relationship as co-habitants of the planet, learned to work together even better than before. *Well, except Patel and Fastcatch, that is. But, here on the station, there's an unexplained and veiled tension. Or maybe it's something else. Can't put my finger on it. Go ask an Ennean.*

And the dramatic shift in the Ocean's chemical composition was still a bafflement. Church and his staff did not seem concerned and theorized that it was due to a cyclic, natural shift in the ecosystem. But that was just a convenient and untested explanation. *Why were they not curious about it? Why didn't they investigate it further? Why the obviously wrong dismissals of the phenomenon?*

After evening meal one night, Taitano was lying down, preparing for sleep and trying to release the stress of the day. Her bed was located inside a cylindrical chamber adjoined to the wall of her room; the cylinder reminded her of old-style magnetic resonance imaging chambers of the late twentieth and early twenty-first centuries. The tube protruded into the Ocean outside the station and was intended to acclimate humans to "free sleeping" in the Ocean, if and when the need arose. It was like being suspended in a layer of water, but with the comforts of an air atmosphere. At first, it had had an anti-soporific effect upon her, but she was already getting used to it and even starting to find the experience somniferous. As she was drifting off to sleep, she felt the presence of a formless shadow hovering directly over the transparent alcove of her sleeping chamber.

It was Triton who drifted above her, suspended in the dark—

another shadow within a shadow, just like in her dream. She could now see the contours and surfaces of his body much more clearly than she had before. The reflection of the lights from the station played upon the smooth surface of the alien's body: cerulean, vermilion, auriferous—alternating in uniform patterns under its undulating membranes. Again, the colors were both reflected from its outer environment and emanated from within the alien's body in graceful waves.

Taitano closed her eyes and reached out her mind. She placed her hand on the inner surface of the barrier above her and stretched her senses to the being above. Triton reached out one of his nine limbs to touch the surface of the transparent polymer barrier that separated them. He then touched another appendage, and then another, to the surface. Eventually, he had wrapped all nine of his appendages around the cylindrical capsule, completely covering it with his pliable body. Taitano—now engulfed within the alien, and yet still separated from physical contact with him by the barrier of her sleeping chamber—could sense an emotion; it took her a while to place it. *Fear? No, not fear. More like a curious and uncomprehending anxiety.* It heightened her own apprehension, and she gently tapped, five times, the skin behind her right ear lobe, with her index and middle fingers. Without warning and with incomprehensible speed, Triton whisked himself off the capsule and disappeared into the pervasive murkiness. Taitano was taken aback by the abrupt departure, and a profound loneliness consumed her as she drifted off into a troubled slumber.

At breakfast, Taitano sat with Patel, and the troubling feelings lingered in her mind, as she absent-mindedly ate her oatmeal with raisons. Patel was telling her something, which vaguely penetrated her consciousness.

"Hey, Agana," he said. "Are you even listening to me? This could be important."

"Huh? What?" she absently replied, trying to drag herself out of her funk enough to focus on what Patel was telling her.

He continued, "This really *is* the station of the zombies, ya know? Yesterday, I was trying to calibrate the power distribution nodes on the station. You know, this entire station is like a giant wasp's nest affixed to the underside of the crust, kind of hanging upside down and facing the subterranean Ocean. The Ocean is warmed by the geothermal activity of the core several hundred kilometers below us, but that's not enough energy to power the station. So, when they first arrived here, decades ago, they built a series of solar farms on the outer surface to harness the radiation of Ross 128. We then shunt it down through cables in the crust and use that electricity to directly power the station."

"Yeah, so what, Saiyam? I'm really tired this morning."

He persevered, unempathetically ignoring her pleas to leave her alone, "Well, the chief mechanic asked me to take a look at the cables because they have been steadily losing efficiency, about one percent per year. That doesn't sound like a lot, but when you're dealing with the transmission of electricity through superconducting cables over enough distance, it can add up to significant inefficiency, in the best case—and, in the worst case, a complete shutdown of the system." That started to grab Taitano's attention, and she made a greater effort to listen. When Patel saw that he had finally managed to engage her in his story, he sat up straighter in his chair, leaned over the table closer to her, and lowered his voice to a conspiratorial whisper, "So I plugged myself into the central computer core, and the first thing I immediately noticed was that I didn't have access to huge parts of it. It was walled off with recursive fractal keys virtually impossible to decipher. I mean really hardcore encryption, Tai. The kind you would find in the old nuclear launch codes of states crazy enough to actually produce and maintain military-grade fissionable material, perch it on the top of a rocket, and then aim it at somebody. But I also noticed something else. Guess what?"

Despite herself, Taitano was now taking an active interest in Patel's little tale of intrigue. Their relationship had developed since they were on Earth-Ocean. There was a time when she could not stand to be in the same room with him; and now she kind of liked him, although the thought mildly disgusted her. She decided to take the bait and responded, "What?"

"Well," he responded, now openly showing pleasure at the fact that she was paying attention to him, "I ran a global scan of the Ocean to see if there were any observable factors that could be interfering with the conduction of the energy from the surface through the cables to the station. And guess what I found."

"A significant increase in selenium in the Ocean," deadpanned Taitano.

Patel's mouth dropped open. He then collected himself and half-shouted, "Yes!" He calmed himself and furtively surveyed the room to ensure no one was staring at them. "How did you know?"

"Sun and I found the same thing a few days ago when we were outside the station taking readings of the Ocean. We were going to call a general briefing today to discuss it. But, listening to you, I'm now wondering how an increase in selenium could affect the power cables. And, second, what is causing the increase in selenium? And third, I guess, is what effect this will have on Ross 128b?"

Patel thought for a moment and then responded, formulating his thoughts as he spoke, "Well, some of the water from the Ocean gets into the tunnels we bored in the upper crust to house the energy cables, but I doubt that the water and increased concentration of selenium are penetrating the crust to the extent that they could be having a direct chemical effect on the cables. But ..." he continued, an idea coalescing in his cybernetically assisted brain, "do you remember those studies about a decade ago, by Ennean reckoning, that changes in the temperature of a planet's core can affect not only the gravitational fields emanating from that core, but also the concentration of certain elements present in an ocean above that core, *elements like selenium.*"

"Yeah, I read that study. Wait, I think I know where you're going with this. Don't tell me you're saying ..."

"I'm not saying anything," Patel interrupted, holding up his hands in self-defense. He stared at Taitano, his eyebrows starting to angle downwards and the corners of his mouth following suit. He seemed to be attempting to will her not to go on. He knew she must, but he tried to exist in a state of willful ignorance for a moment longer.

Taitano said, "I know what you're thinking."

"I'm not thinking anything. In fact, I think my implant is on the fritz."

"I said ... I *know* what you're thinking."

"No, you don't," Patel said defensively.

"Yes, I *do*," she replied more forcefully.

"Don't."

"Do so."

"OK, alright already!" said Patel, giving up. "So now you're not only good-looking and annoying, but also telepathic. So, what am I thinking?"

Ignoring the bizarre, unexpected—and inappropriate—comment, Taitano replied, "What you're thinking, Saiyam, is that someone is messing with the core of this planet and that it's causing an increase in the selenium content of the Ocean. And you are also thinking that this someone is not an Ennean."

Dead silence between them for a few awkward moments.

They both stared at each other, knowing that this was, in fact, exactly what was happening on Ross 128b. It was an awareness that they experienced more in their bodies than in their minds. It was the same intuitive prescience of danger embedded deep with the human genome that had enabled their species to survive their early days as helpless primates, a foreknowledge of danger that had let them know, during the dragging depths of the night, when it was time to climb higher into the leaf covered canopy of the trees to avoid a predator approaching from the forest floor. They sat together in uneasy taciturnity, thinking to themselves.

Finally, Patel said, "OK, so what are we going to do about it?"

Taitano instantly replied, "We're going to go back to the ship and talk to Saddiq and Nereus."

"Why?"

"We're going to use *Ardanwen's* sensors to conduct some remote readings of the Ocean and test our theory. If we do it from here, Church and the others will know instantly."

"Yeah, the station of the zombies."

Taitano said, "I'm going to say that I forgot an old book with sentimental value and have to go back to retrieve it before *Ardanwen* heads back to Earth-Ocean. You stay here and just play it cool."

"Yeah, well that's my specialty. I was *born* cool."

"*So* not, Saiyam."

"You're just jealous … and afraid to say you're gonna miss me."

*There it is again. Is he flirting with me?* So *cringe!* She simply replied, "Uh, I'm only going up and coming right back down. *So* not missing you in that time."

"So, theoretically, if you were going for a long time, then you would be missing me, right?"

*Oh, goodness. He is flirting with me! Somebody, please, shoot me now.* "Patel, you're really an idiot, you know that?"

"Only when my implant is turned off."

Taitano rolled her eyes and could not suppress an involuntary burst of laughter at his retort, which actually demonstrated an unexpected self-awareness and, amazingly, a glimmer of modesty. *He really has changed in the last couple of years.* "OK," Taitano said, "I'm going up to the ship, and you're *trying* to play it cool. Please let Sun know, if you can. See you soon."

Taitano walked back to her quarters. Although she was simply walking through the corridors, she felt furtive and guilty, like she was doing something wrong. She tapped the skin behind her right ear lobe, with her index and middle fingers, five times in quick succession, to help banish her feelings of anxiety and the fear of getting into trouble. In addition, after the long journey on *Ardanwen*, she was still getting used to walking almost everywhere, rather than swimming. She missed the dolphins in this human-centric station, and it felt alien to her. Unequal and unbalanced in some way she could not describe. It was unease lingering at the edge of her conscious thought.

Not paying full attention to where she was going, she rounded a corner and physically slammed into Church. The contact caught her mid-stride, and she lost her balance and toppled to the floor.

He loomed over her, momentarily scowling. He then artificially plastered a stretched grin across his face, as he bent his knees and reached out his hand to help her up. "My dear, Dr. Taitano, please do forgive me. But you *must* be more careful, lest you injure yourself."

Taitano replied, "Yes, sorry, Director Church. I was distracted and not looking where I was going."

"And whither *are* you going, Dr. Taitano?"

"Back to my room."

"And *then*?" he asked with a ghost of suspicion in his voice. Despite the perfect inflection of Church's speech, there was no beauty in it. He wielded language as a weapon.

*What is this? Twenty questions? Why is he asking me that? Does he know what Saiyam and I are up to? How could he?* She dissembled, "Up to the ship to get something I left behind. An old book from my grandfather. I think I left it in the mess hall by mistake and wanted to retrieve it before *Ardanwen* left."

His eyes began to narrow, and he peered at her with a penetrating interest. "Why not just access it from the central database? All your grandfather's works are well known and are safely uploaded and readily available. I, myself, have enjoyed reading many of them over the years." Under his bromidic smile and benign words, Taitano could feel, as a physical sensation, Church's monarchical reproval and could smell his cloaked menace. She knew her olfactory senses were picking up aggressive pheromones being released through Church's skin and mucus membranes, infusing the atmosphere between them. She slowly took a long breath to calm her autonomic fear response and willed herself to accept the wave of trepidation washing over her, letting it pass like a wind through the leaves of a great oak tree that she conjured in her mind's eye. She visualized light filtering through the leaves of that great tree, warming her face and infusing her with peace and tranquility. *Fear is impermanent, as all things are. Let it pass through me and around me, like a mountain stream over smooth rocks. Once the fear is gone, only I will remain, at least for a while, until I, too, pass into the next realm of light and darkness.*

Looking him straight in the eye, she replied, "He gave it to me as a departing gift. A memory of our life together. And I've made lots of notes in the margins."

Church replied with a cynical, disapproving look, "A bit sentimental for someone of your intellectual and scientific prowess, Dr. Taitano."

"Love and knowledge are not mutually exclusive. In fact, they complement and reinforce each other," she said in a calm, firm voice.

"A noble statement, to be sure." Church seemed to relax a bit, his shoulders descending from his thick neck and his breathing becoming less sharp. "I was just curious. And I did not want you to miss the lecture tonight."

"Ah, yes, it will be recorded, right?"

"Yes, of course, but there is no substitute for the actual item," said

Church, speaking without inflection to feign disinterest. "I will speak tonight about our research efforts here on Ross 128b. I thought it would be useful to bring everyone up to speed, in an *interactive* way, about what we are doing here and why it is so important." The way he inflected the words "interactive way" seemed a bit odd to Taitano.

Taitano replied, "I think we already know all that, Director. Otherwise, I don't think we'd be here. But I am indeed looking forward to your speech," she added the last sentence quickly, regretting her use of the word "speech" when she instantly recalled that he had called it a "lecture." Nevertheless, she continued, "We are here to get to know our stellar neighbors. The only other species we've found outside our own solar system."

"That's it," he replied and then added disdainfully with a condescending smirk, "in broad brushstrokes." He continued in his imperious manner, "But the details are infinitely more mystifying. For instance, we still have never had a direct conversation with an Ennean. Only half understood scientific interactions, mathematical equations exchanged to get ships like *Ardanwen* from one point to another." As he addressed her, he took a step closer and placed a stern hand on her shoulder. "We still don't even fully understand the scientific principles and engineering feats that the Enneans used to protect Earth-Ocean from the great solar flare that would have put an end to us all. And our attempts to comprehend their world view, their *philosophy*, are really nothing more than conjecture." He paused, forcing her to hold his intense stare, and then continued to bloviate with a series of agitated perquisitions, his eyes squinting slightly to punctuate his questions: "Don't you find that fascinating? What do they think? What do they feel? What is their purpose? Why did they traverse the stars and come to our aid? What are their plans for the future? There are so many mysteries that still need to be solved. So much knowledge to be had."

"Right!" she responded, as she deftly took a step away from him so that his hand slipped off her shoulder. "And that's why we're here,

Director." *What's with the menacing stares and now the long lecture. This guy's really full of himself. Does he think he's being audio–visual recorded or something? There are indeed mysteries to solve on this planet. And I am going to solve them.* She smiled graciously and pretended to reflect on his words. After waiting a few more (deferent) moments more, Taitano said, "Look, I really need to go now so I can make it back in time for your … lecture." She gracefully moved around him. As she was rounding the corner, she was left with a sense of dread and felt a pressing need to get back to *Ardanwen* and conduct the scans of the Ocean. She called back as she departed, "Looking forward to it!"

As she drifted away, Church's affected smile briskly dropped and disappeared, and he whispered into the now empty corridor, "Yes, my dear, I'm sure you are."

Taitano ascended from the planet's rocky surface in the pod attached to the slender orbital tethers. She regarded the outward facing exterior of Ennea. There was an almost imperceptible erubescent haze clinging to the bronze craggy surface, the atmosphere of the planet. It was much thinner than the comparatively viscus layer of gases that cradled life on Earth-Ocean. Ennea's paltry excuse for an atmosphere had mostly resulted from a comet that had struck the planet millions of years ago, depositing upon the planet's crust huge amounts of hydrogen, nitrogen, water vapor, and other trace elements and compounds in a thin layer, which was held there fast by the planet's gravitational field.

The transport to *Ardanwen* took about an hour—mostly taken up by gradual acceleration and then deceleration cycles. When she arrived, she donned her aquatic suit and helmet, entered the wet-lock, exited the pod, and entered the ship. She was greeted by Captain Saddiq, gently suspended in the liquid environment of the ship. He enquired as to the reason for her re-embarkation. She explained about the book her grandfather had given to her and then asked him to meet her in an hour in his office. Saddiq, to his credit, took the unorthodox request in stride and simply inclined his head in agreement, without a word.

An hour later, Taitano entered the captain's office. She stripped off her suit and helmet and strode to the center of the room. She was still clad in a thin wetsuit, and thus her relative state of *deshabille* was not too out of the ordinary. Saddiq's office was adorned with all manner of paintings, photographs, and mementos of past honors, achievements, and adventures. The captain was a man of many layers, who had not only seen "the world," but also a generous part of the local space around the Sol system. He sat at his desk, studying a document on the holographic interface suspended in the air above the center of his desk. He stood as she entered the room and motioned her to a seat on the other side of the desk. Taitano said, "What genteel manners, Captain. It *is* a bit old fashioned, but still … refreshingly welcome."

Saddiq spoke, "Please, feel free to speak freely, Dr. Taitano. Nereus already secured the room prior to your arrival."

Nereus interjected, "Shall I leave the two of you alone?"—her disembodied voice coming from an auditory emitter somewhere in the room.

"No," replied Saddiq, "I have a feeling that whatever has brought Dr. Taitano here is something we will both need to hear. Go ahead, Doctor."

Taitano explained the data that she, Sun, and Patel had gathered on Ennea. Saddiq and Nereus listened in silence, absorbing the information. Saddiq was a formidable presence in the room, but Taitano could also feel the potency of the artificial intellect of the sentient computer program called "Nereus." It was a difficult sensation to describe in words. A kind of pressure in the center of one's brain … and a tingle on the skin. The most powerful mind ever constructed, programmed by engineers of two different worlds. Efforts to duplicate

Nereus's program had only succeeded once. Additional efforts to do so were underway, but collaboration between humans, dolphins, and Enneans took time and patience, and Nereus was unavailable as a real-time template, as she was needed to help Triton pilot *Ardanwen* back and forth along the long journey between Sol and Ross 128.

When Taitano had finished relating what they had discovered, she ended by telling them, "So, I decided to come up here and ask for your help with this. It's too important to just let go, and I'm not sure I can trust those on the station, especially Church and his drone Tiberius. I was thinking that *Ardanwen* could take some independent readings to confirm our data. We can then ask Church and his staff to explain what is going on down there."

Saddiq took a long breath and let it out slowly in a controlled sigh. "Dr. Taitano, what you are asking is … difficult. *Ardanwen's* systems are precisely calculated for the trip from Earth-Ocean to Ennea and back. We would have to move the ship out of its geosynchronous orbit above the orbital tether, navigate her to three other equidistant locations on the planet, take the required readings, and then return back here. The piloting calculations alone would take …"

"… me only ten minutes to complete, using my multi-modal modeling," interrupted Nereus, her disembodied voice sonorously filling the air in the room.

"Alright," replied Saddiq, "but the amount of fuel …"

"…is more than covered by the Deuterium-Tritium and Deuterium-Hydrogen-three we keep in reserve for emergencies to power the magnetic fusion plasma drive," interrupted Nereus again.

"And what about the Resident Director?" asked Saddiq. "Tonight is his big key note lecture or whatever he's calling it. It's all he's been talking about for days. He's been waiting for the new arrivals so that he can hold forth on his most recent ruminations on sociology, economics, and all that other pseudo-science nonsense about which he's always prognosticating. What's he going to say if we're off joy riding on the most sophisticated vehicle ever created and are late to hear his grand oration? I believe a modicum of circumspection is required here."

Nereus replied, "We'll make it back with time to spare. It's probably a good time to go anyway, since Church will be busy practicing that god-awful polemic of his. Plus, I've also been getting strange readings from Ennea since we arrived, not to mention an odd gravimetric distortion near the northern pole at which I've been wanting to get a closer look. Come on, Saddiq! It'll be fun." Taitano imagined she could hear a sparkle in Nereus's voice, although she quickly chided herself for anthropomorphizing the computer program.

Saddiq held his head in both his hands and rubbed his forehead back and forth against his palms.

Taitano said softly to Saddiq, "It's the right thing to do, Captain. You know it. Something is going on here, and we have to find out what it is."

Saddiq was silent for another moment, looking off into the distance, and then met Taitano's intent gaze, "OK, let's do it. This is either a very good idea or a very bad one."

Taitano placed her palms together in front of her in a gesture of elegant gratitude and said, "Don't worry, Captain. Either way, we'll know very soon which it is."

"Is that supposed to make me feel better?"

"Yes."

"Well … it didn't work."

Taitano and Saddiq looked at each other, could not resist a shared conspiratorial smile, and started to assist Nereus with the parameters of the orbital calculations required to move *Ardanwen* to a new position in orbit of Ross 128b.

# CHAPTER 10

# VOICE OF CHURCH

Tiberius glanced at Resident Director Church, who was struggling to affix a tie around his thick neck. Neckties had gone out of fashion in the early twenty-first century, but some continued the old sartorial tradition. It had the same awkward visual effect as wearing a bow tie or suspenders did in the latter half of the twentieth century. There was nothing *per se* wrong with sporting a necktie; it was just weird, not to mention embarrassing—making people wonder whether they should comment upon such eccentric vestiary choices or respect the wearer's preferences.

Church managed the half Windsor knot well enough and then turned to his deputy, "So, Tiberius, it's the big event. What do you think of all this? Are we ready?"

Tiberius, continuously baffled by Church, regarded the *éminence grise* of the United Nations Commission for Ennean Cross-Cultural Exchange's operation on Ross 128b and reflected on how best to answer the question. When Tiberius was a boy, he had been raised on stories of high adventure, of right and wrong, good and evil. But, as he grew older and was cruelly confronted by the moral ambiguities of the world, he quickly learned that reality is not a story book, with grand sacrifices and heroic and daring feats of courage and self-sacrifice, but rather a series of tedious daily challenges. At university, his professors were normal humans like everyone else: getting out of bed, struggling to keep up with the academic literature and research, teaching classes, grading papers, publishing to get tenure, and trying to stay academically relevant—all the while endeavoring to balance work with a personal life filled with partners, kids, personal finances, and endless forms to complete and submit to soul-destroying bureaucracies. In the face of the drudgery of normal everyday life, true ethical dilemmas were few and far between. When one did stumble upon such a crossroad, it usually boiled down to doing the noble thing (which was always easy enough to identify) or getting fired from one's job.

Recently, his assignment to Ross 128b had turned into such a situation. *No, Mr. Resident Director, we're not "ready" for what you are about to set into motion.* Nevertheless, he responded to Church, saying, "Yes, Mr. Director, all is ready. The feed is secure and stable. Everyone will hear what you have to say, not just those on Station-1, but in all the locations throughout the planet. The Enneans will also hear it, of course, but I doubt they will be able to understand what is happening, based on our current level of comprehension of their cognitive makeup. And if they won't be able to understand it, we don't need to worry about whether they accept it or what their reaction will be. I generally anticipate a non-reaction from the Enneans. Or from anyone else for that matter, once they have heard what you have to say. They will almost certainly continue to quietly do their jobs, as expected."

Church studied Tiberius closely, gazing deeply into his unflinching eyes. Tiberius could see that Church was looking for signs of dissembling or weakness. Finding neither, Church replied, "Capital job, Tiberius. I will make the announcement, and then we will have crossed the Rubicon: *alea iacta est*, my good man. Once we make it over this hurdle, the rest will be downhill. These moments are hard, but we have to look at the bigger picture. We have to do what is right for the survival of all life on Planet Earth. You do understand that, don't you, Tiberius?"

"Yes, fully, sir. There's nothing for it. We are indeed doing this for *Earth-Ocean*," Tiberius articulated, with pronounced clarity upon the word "Earth-Ocean" in order to draw attention to the fact that Church had referred to their home plant as "Earth" in the old human-centric manner. "It will be fine. It's not like anyone is going to die or get hurt … unless someone does something rash," he added.

"And that," said Church, with quick and deep conviction, "is why we must use *our reason* to persuade everyone that this is the right thing. Although we have the decision now and could simply present it as a *fait accompli*, that's not the way I want it to be. I want to explain it to them all so that they believe—and are *convinced*—that this is the right thing to do; the only choice, in fact, that makes sense … or is even possible. I am confident they will agree … once they've heard me out. It will be fine."

Church paused to inspect his tie again in the holographic mirror in front of his desk. He poured himself a glass of water, quaffed it in a single stroke, and then inhaled deeply. He turned his attention again to Tiberius, asking placidly, "And have you checked that the positions are secure at both poles?"

"Yes, Director."

"And the ship?"

"Which one?"

"Both of them, dammit!"

That was how it was with him. One minute, Church depended on Tiberius for critical aspects of implementing most everything that happened on Station-1; and, the next minute, he was giving his indispensable right hand a tongue lashing. This was behavior typical of a parasitic tyrant like Church.

Tiberius waited a moment before replying, forcing Church to absorb the dysfunctional moment between them. He then replied, "Well, Saddiq on *Ardanwen* is in a geosynchronous orbit over Station-1. They are still tethered. And the other ship is exactly where it should be—keeping its passengers secure."

"And Taitano?"

"Still on *Ardanwen*."

"I wish we could have kept her here on the station," said Church. "It would have been cleaner and less risky."

Tiberius replied, "Checking her movements would have created more suspicion. We don't want to appear as the bad guys in all this. And we certainly don't need a hero on our hands, much less a martyr."

"Yes, I suppose you're right. She'll be back here before we know it and will fall into line. We are a long way from home, and there isn't a lot of room for messing around down here. It will be fine. So! When do we start?"

"One minute, Director. Good luck. I will be close by if you need anything." He turned to leave the room, triggering the automatic door mechanism.

"And, Tiberius ..." Church called after him as he was departing.

"Yes, sir?"

"Keep a close eye on *Ardanwen*. If she moves so much as a micro-processor, I want to know about it ... *immediately*."

"Of course," replied Tiberius, exiting the room.

Resident Director Church let out a long sigh. *I am doing the right thing. Great men throughout history have always had to make tough choices. It's part of being a leader. What was that old saying? He who never made any enemies never stood up for anything in life. Something like that. Can't remember who said it. Must have been a great man, though. A man like me—a common but hard-working person thrust into impossible circumstances of great import. After all, it's not like I asked for any of this to fall upon my shoulders.*

Church thought about his situation, which was created, not by himself, but by the UN Ennean Commission—a decision taken years ago now by Earth-Ocean reckoning. He was just the instrument, the hand of fate (so to speak). It was not as though he were doing anything wrong. He accepted this assignment and had sworn to carry out any directives that went along with it, so it was time to fulfil that undertaking. It was already underway, and no one would be able to stop it. Someday, this would all become part of history. Countless cruelties and tough choices had brought humanity to this inflection point, and who was *he* to stand in the way of the inexorable march of the next chapter in humanity's story.

He took a sip of water, looked at himself in the mirror, and cleared his throat. He steadied himself, both physically and psychologically. He pressed a button on the holographic interface on his desk to start the transmission.

Church spoke.

"Brother, Sisters, and Gentlefolk of Earth-Ocean. Thank you for your attention and for tuning in tonight to an important message that I have been asked to convey to you from our precious home.

"But before I deliver our homeland missive to you, I'd like to share some thoughts that have been swirling around in my mind. Being so far from our collective home tends to put certain things into perspective. For thousands of years, the philosophers of Old Earth—I ask my cetacean friends to forgive the term, but I know that your philosophy was transmitted orally and that not much of it has yet been transcribed so we can reap its benefits. I am unfortunately forced to rely upon references from humanity's past. Like I was saying, the philosophers of old could only imagine other worlds and wonder what it would be like to stand upon an alien mountain or swim in an extra-terrestrial sea. They were confined to that exquisite orb of blue, white, and earth. But now, we are here. We stand and float here on another world—that other world of dreams past. We have broken the bonds of our birthplace and found another home. I don't say 'a new home,' for it would never be possible for all humans, dolphins, and the other myriad species of Earth-Ocean to traverse the interstellar distance and make a new life here. But we have established, for the very first time in our collective history, a semi-permanent presence on another planet. Not even Mars or the moons of Jupiter and Saturn are as promising for long-term residency as Ross 128b.

"It was not so long ago that our planet was in grave peril, and it was almost the end of Earth-Ocean's great experiment with organic matter organizing itself into a form that could replicate itself, create culture, and pass it on to the next iteration of life. In the past, if a cataclysm had befallen our planet, it would have meant the end. But now, no matter what happens, we will endure and continue to live, thrive, and add our biological and technological distinctiveness to the Universe. My friends, this is not only a good thing, but also a vital thing. Indeed, it is the *only* thing that matters. Without us, the Universe would be nothing more than a lifeless—and dare I say 'meaningless'—conflagration of atoms and compounds. 'Sound and fury, signifying nothing'—to quote our great bard. As such, our survival is of paramount importance not only to ourselves, but to the Universe, itself. In many ways, we *are* the Universe. To quote another great human philosopher, 'We are a way for the Universe to know itself.'

"And so, I now come to the purpose of today's virtual gathering. About a year ago, we received a message from the United Nations Commission for Ennean Cross-Cultural Exchange. This transmission was the fastest ever flung across the Cosmos, at least that we are aware of. It was sent after *Ardanwen* left Earth-Ocean, but received here ahead of that great interstellar vessel—which, I may add here—is the greatest technological feat of engineering that we have ever achieved, along with the help of our Ennean partners. But how could a message sent *after Ardanwen* left arrive here *before* her? Time, my friends; time and progress, and the marvelous ingenuity of humans and cetaceans. We all know of time dilation during travel at relativistic speeds. Even at low velocities of only a few hundred kilometers per hour, space-time is compressed and stretched, like the soundwaves emitted from a train passing by. But the dilation is so minimal that it is imperceptible to our senses. But as one approaches the speed of light, the difference becomes more significant.

"Thus, for those who just made the crossing on *Ardanwen*, their journey took almost two years. But for those back on Earth-Ocean, over twelve years have passed during the same period. In that intervening time, the humans and dolphins of Earth-Ocean were able to innovate on certain theoretical principles of physics taught to us by the Enneans. They were able to apply those principles to actually transmit an electromagnetic pulse faster than the speed of light. Yes, we have broken what was once an immutable law of Nature, namely, that nothing could travel faster than light. Why did we once think this? There are several reasons. According to the basic equations laid down by the immortal Einstein in the early twentieth century, the amount of energy needed to propel an object at the speed of light would require an infinite amount of energy; and, of course, there is no such thing as an infinite amount of energy. But Einstein, for all his genius, did not have the benefit of the great knowledge and profound wisdom of our newfound friends and benefactors, the Enneans. They have taught us how to apply what we have known for some time: that all matter is nothing more than a wavelength of energy vibrating in an endless continuum of yet more energy. *There are no objects*—in contradiction to how Newton once conceived the world around us. Even space-time is not an object. It's energy. *It's all energy. We* are all energy.

"And that is the breakthrough we needed to transcend the once sacrosanct law that nothing can travel faster than light. What that law *really* dictates is that *light* cannot travel faster than light. A tautology to be sure. But now we have learned, and put into practice, the ability to concatenate wavelengths of energy that accelerate and build upon each other until they propagate self-sustaining and ever-increasing waveforms that can travel beyond the speed of light. This is still significantly slower than the theoretical quantum-entangled skyrmion transmitter being developed by our greatest minds, but still faster than a human can travel through space-time. So, for purposes of communications, the speed of light is no longer the cosmic speed limit. We have broken it with our minds, our ingenuity, and our perseverance. We have liberated ourselves from the theoretical shackles of the past and can now communicate over the vast distances of our galaxy. Perhaps, in time, we will learn how to apply this new understanding of the workings of the Universe to the physical transport of our bodies through space-time, which may even enable us to travel to other galaxies. There are no more limits. But for the moment, what all this means, in very practical terms, is that we can communicate between Earth-Ocean and Ross 128b in approximately one-year intervals, rather than having to wait over ten years for our mail to be delivered to each other—a circuit that used to take over two decades. And this is how the message of the Commission was sent after *Ardanwen* left, but received by us shortly before her arrival at Ross 128b.

"And just what did the message from the Commission say, you may be asking. A fair question, the answer to which I will relay to you with a heavy heart. *The Commission has decided that Ross 128b is to be aquaterraformed and prepared for human-cetacean colonization.* The solar flares of Sol have brought home the urgent need for us to expand to other worlds, and this opportunity is simply too critical to pass up.

"Some may say there are literally billions of worlds that we could move to. There is no need to change this one. This is indeed true, but space is vast, and our lives are but brief candles. The winds of time and space will snuff out not only our individual existences, but that of our entire species, both human and dolphin, if we try, at the present time, to make it to almost any other world that is a promising candidate for terraforming and colonization. Efforts are of course being made, as we speak, to travel to other worlds, such as Proxima, but we know that the environmental conditions we can expect there are far more inhospitable in comparison to the warm, wet, and mineral rich world of Ross 128b. In merely a few generations, we can turn this world into a terrestrial and ocean paradise. And, yes, that is another factor. We need a world that is suitable not only for one of our species, but for both: human and dolphin. We need a world of air, wind, earth, and water. And Ross 128b has it all. It is our second paradise, our second home, our second chance. And we *need* it. The Enneans have stabilized Sol for now, but our greatest scientific minds, both biological and artificial, have not been able to guarantee that there will not be another solar eruption, even in our lifetimes. Even the great science of the Enneans has not been able to rule this out, as they are not omniscient and cannot calculate every possibility when it comes to such a complex and dynamic celestial body.

"Perhaps one of the most defining qualities of EROC-lings is our ability to adapt to the ever-constant changes in our environment. *That is precisely why we are still here:* human and dolphin alike. We adapted when others could not. There used to be several other hominid species, but they are all gone. Yes, certain small groups of them fell into conflict with groups of *homo sapiens*, but these were little more than feuds between isolated clans. The reason why *homo sapiens* were the only hominid species left standing was because we were able to adapt to our environment better than our cousins the neanderthals and australopithecines. We formed close social bonds, passed on our knowledge and culture through language and later writing, and were able to tame the earth—and the Ocean—and everything in it. Sadly, it is indeed true that, for a few centuries, we mistreated our cetacean brothers and sisters, but we learned to do better; and we were the better for it. And now humans and dolphins—together—have ventured to another star to take their rightful place in the Cosmos as the masters of their environment once again.

"We have *transcended* evolution, which was our origin, but also our jailer. We are no longer at the whim of our environment for genetic fitness. We determine what the environment is and what our place is within it. No more do we need to bend to evolutionary forces in order to survive; rather, it is the environment that must bend to *our* wills, *our* intellect, and even—if I may say it like this—*our destiny*. To paraphrase the timeless Ayn Rand, our two species—by the grace of reality and by the nature of life, itself—are noble ends in and of themselves; we exist for our own sake; and the achievement of our own happiness is the highest moral purpose. It is a biological and ethical imperative we are compelled to obey, lest we wage war with the nature of both ourselves and the Universe in which we exist.

"And how will we do this, you might be wondering. I will tell you, in broad brush strokes. In fact, many of you have already been involved in this task of Biblical significance, although, until now, you have not known the Grand Design for which you have been laboring. What I am about to tell you will spark your fascination and fill you with pride in this stupendous undertaking, of which you are all an indispensable part.

"You all know the critical role that cyanobacteria played about two-point-four billion years ago in the blossoming of life on Earth-Ocean. The seas became a seething mass of this intrepid form of life that, through oxygenic photosynthesis, ingested the carbon dissolved in the water and then exhaled oxygen. To some, this oxygen was a highly reactive and corrosive substance, and some of the neighbors of the cyanobacteria began to die and went extinct. But others adapted and were able to survive, as more and more oxygen was infused with the Ocean and atmosphere. Over time, a new era of oxygen-breathing organisms took hold and set the evolutionary stage for the humans and dolphins of today. Such is the way of things.

"We are now in the incipient stages of another biological and physiological revolution on this world. We will seed the Ocean of Ross 128b with cyanobacteria, and they will create life-giving oxygen, which will accrete on the inner surface of the upper crust. Just as Earth-Ocean has a thin layer of atmosphere hugging its crust and facing the void of space, so will this world, in time, form a layer of atmosphere lining the underside of its crust, a life-giving blanket of gas that will face the Ocean below it. With diligence and patience, we can bioengineer an oasis of breathable atmosphere for both humans and dolphins. Artificial gravity will be installed for humans to plant their feet firmly on the inside of this world's crust, and we will be able to farm. Dolphins will be able to come to the surface for a life-sustaining breath of oxygen, and then plunge back into the Ocean, which we will seed with fish for their sustained survival. It will be a paradise, the likes of which have not been seen since the fabled Garden of Eden.

"But before we seed the Ocean with the cyanobacteria, we need to create the right conditions for them to do their critical work. As some of you already know, we have placed two devices on the lower crust of this world far below the depths of this mighty Ocean. One device at the northern pole and one at the southern pole. They are modest in appearance, but their effects will be vast and far-reaching. They are currently sending magnetic resonance pulses directly into the nickel and iron core of Ross 128b. These pulses are timed and directed at such an angle so as to increase the rate of rotation of the core. As the core increases its rate of rotation, it will generate more friction, the rate of isotopic decay will accelerate, and more heat will be generated. The temperature of the crust will rise, and that excess heat energy will seep through the lower crust and into the Ocean. We are warming this planet to just the right temperature to optimize the mitotic rate of cyanobacteria. The process is already underway, and we are ready to start to seed the Ocean with the bacteria.

"But fear not, for we have not forgotten our Ennean benefactors—nor will we forsake them. We have been conducting studies of the adaptability of the Enneans to this projected increase in temperature, which should not be more than about ten degrees Celsius. They certainly won't like it. Moreover, as you all know, the only life forms on Ross 128b are the Enneans themselves. Thus, they have no immune systems to protect them against other life forms. This is precisely why we have to be so meticulous when we interact with the environment here, lest we introduce a pernicious pathogen into the Ocean that then unsuspectingly wipes out the Enneans—much like what happened when Europeans first came into contact with humans in the New World. By our years of living and working on Ross 128b, microorganisms from our bodies have of course found their way into the Ocean; however, these have been trace amounts or have not been able to survive in the sterile environment of the Ocean of this pristine planet. But the changes that will be brought about by the combined increase in temperature and the introduction of cyanobacteria will turn the tide of this planet, so to speak. It will irrevocably alter the marine ecosystem, rendering it potentially fatal to the Enneas.

"Now we come to the selenium. Some of you have no doubt already noticed an increase in the amount of selenium in the Ocean here. Well, you may, by now, have already guessed that this is a by-product of the two devices we have placed on the seabed at the poles. We don't fully understand it yet, but as we heat up the core, the concentration of selenium also increases. We think it may have something to do with the magnetic resonances that are emanating from the core and their interactions with the other elements in the Ocean. We were hoping our latest team members who have just arrived could help us figure it out. In any case, as with the heat and cyanobacteria, the Enneans don't take well to concentrations of selenium that are too high. They do depend upon a certain amount of the element, but only in the right quantities. The increase in selenium has already changed the density of the curious stream of selenium that runs like a girdle around the Ocean in a self-contained current, which we think the Enneans may be using for some form of communication.

"So, the Enneans are not particularly happy with all these changes. But, through our compassion and understanding, we have come up with a plan to assist our Ennean brothers and sisters in adapting to this change—just as we humans and dolphins have had to adapt over the many millennia in order to survive. We have already begun to relocate the Enneans to a vast orbital platform that will furnish them with their every need. It is an orb of immense size, about five kilometers across, filled with their native water, with exactly the right balance of the elements and compounds they need to enjoy a comfortable existence. We have polarized the shell of this great vessel so that it will be completely dark, just like the Enneans like it. This polarization will also shield them from any damaging radiation from their star, Ross 128. They will be perfectly safe there. They will have all they need on Ross 128b.1, as we have designated it—or, as many of you have begun to say: 'New Ennea.' And we will be able to flourish as their close neighbors.

"And we are not talking about that many souls. Do you know how many Enneans were on this entire planet when we arrived? Four-hundred and fifty-two. That's right. Only four-hundred and fifty-two beings. And do you know what our projections show about how many humans and dolphins Ross 128b can sustain once the aquaterraforming project is complete? Eight-hundred million EROC-lings: yes, that's correct. Six-hundred million humans on the upper crust, and two-hundred million dolphins in this magnificent Ocean. And we will, of course, continue to use the resources of this world to sustain New Ennea—*indefinitely*. We all can peacefully share this world, as brothers, sisters, neighbors. We can continue to grow and learn from each other, live in harmony, explore other worlds together: human, dolphin, and Ennean. It's what they used to call a non-zero-sum game, a triple win for all sides. We have already transported the first Enneans to their new home in the heavens, and I am very pleased to report that they are doing just fine. We tried to ask the Enneans what they thought of our plan, but were unable to communicate it to them. When we transported them to the orbital platform, there were no protests. Perhaps we were indeed successful in making them understand the necessity of this endeavor, and they acquiesced to their new abode. As you know, it's not always easy to understand them. Go ask an Ennean.

"In closing, I would like to reiterate that this is the will of the Commission, which has the authority to take decisions in relation to Ross 128b and the Enneans. But this is not just a case of 'just following orders.' Anyone looking objectively and dispassionately at the situation would be forced to come to the same conclusion: Ross 128b is the future of humanity and the future of all cetaceans. It's our Plan A, and there is no Plan B within reach. From what we can tell, the worlds of other stars within our reach would take far longer to terraform to make them habitable for either humans or dolphins. Ross 128b is it, at least for now. Here is where we need to make our stand. If we don't do this, our very existence is at risk, and we may be unceremoniously yanked from the Cosmic stage, and all the resonant wonders we have brought to the Universe, as well as those we have yet to accomplish—will have been lost. Earth-Ocean may or may not survive in the mid- to long-term, and so we need a sustainable presence somewhere else. We will continue our story here, and the Enneans will be a part of that story—they will write the next chapter with us. In time, we will learn to fully communicate with each other; and perhaps someday we will need to make amends to the Enneans. We may even someday find a way for the Enneans to return to their home and share it with us in harmony. But today is not that day. Today we need to ensure the survival of both our species, so that there *is* a tomorrow. And that tomorrow will be a bright one, provided we all work together to make it one worth living.

"It is a historic day, a day about which your children and grandchildren will ask you to tell them. They will gaze upon you in awe and gratitude and ask: Where were you on the day that we started the next chapter in our long and troubled history? Where were you when the new epoch of humans and dolphins was ushered in, with courage, sacrifice, and wisdom? And you will answer with sober pride—and perhaps with a bit of anguish tempered by the wisdom of your years: I was on Ross 128b. I was on Ennea, the New Earth-Ocean. Our second home in the stars.

"Thank you for your attention—and may we all rededicate ourselves to our work and to our noble purpose. Let us walk and swim forward—together as one people—with our backs straight and our hearts open."

# CHAPTER 11

# TAMING PROTEUS

"What a jerk!" Taitano choked out the words with a twisted grimace of horror in her uncomprehending visage. She had been transfixed during Church's address, not able to move—or even breath, it felt.

She looked at Saddiq, who maintained an inscrutable stance. She had an incredulous and pleading expression on her face. *You can't be buying this load of garbage. Please, you can't. It's the worst use of rhetorical sophistry I've heard since watching the old vids of world leaders attempting to justify their atrocity crimes in the early 21st century. It was as if Church's speech was straight out of a really bad B science fiction movie. But there it was.*

Saddiq gazed out the window into the void. His composure had slipped ever so slightly, and the turmoil inside the man was evident in his rigid posture and his inability to look Taitano in the eye. Nereus broke the awkward silence, "Yes, indeed, a pompous blatherskite, to be sure. Shall we now get on with it?"

Nereus' question broke Saddiq out of his meditative state. "Get on with what?" asked Saddiq, who seemed off balance and even to be swaying a little in bewilderment.

"With our investigation into those strange gravimetric readings at the north pole of this planet," responded Taitano.

Saddiq had a look of simultaneous admiration and confusion. "I scarcely think there's any more need for such an investigation. After everything Church just said. After the decision of the Commission. It's over. Just what exactly do you think we can do in these circumstances? You can't seriously be considering mutiny, treason, or whatever we call it these days," said Saddiq. "Not to mention probably putting our lives in danger—or at the very least ending our careers."

"Well, our lives are one thing," blurted Nereus in a sarcastic tone, "but perish the thought of ending our careers. Heaven forbid!"

Taitano interjected, "Let's be serious here for a minute." She paused in contemplation, staring at the floor to collect her thoughts, and then continued. "This can't be happening, but it is. And it doesn't matter whether the Commission authorized it or not. Church has his little controlocracy down there on the station, and no one is going to stand up to him. We can't let this happen. We have to stop it. They are down there, and we are up here. We have an opportunity."

Saddiq responded, "But what then? What if we do somehow stop this aquaterraforming operation from progressing for the moment? Which is, I may add, already in progress pursuant to direct orders from Earth-Ocean." Saddiq started to peripatetically pace the perimeter of the room. "Do we really have the right to make that decision for millions of souls, both born and unborn. We could be interfering with the survival of so many people."

Taitano skewered him with a steely look, "This isn't Philosophy class 101, Captain Saddiq, and we're not first-year university students having an academic debate. This is real life. And we are *not* going to imprison a sentient species who not only has never harmed us—or anyone for that matter—but who also is responsible for all of us being alive. Professor Sun and the others are down there under Church's control, and we are up here. We've got an advantage." She paused and calmed her emotions. She lowered her voice almost to a whisper, "And … you know what? At the end of the day, we're all mortal and finite. Maybe survival isn't enough. Maybe we also have to *deserve* to survive, as a species and as individuals, and just do the best we can with the time we have. It simply comes down to this: it's wrong, and we have to stop it."

Nereus piped in jovially, "I'm in. Just to spite that windbag, Church." The AI's completely inappropriate and mistimed humor broke the tension and caused an involuntary release of emotion from the two humans. Pent-up fear and anxiety surged from them in half-strangled laughs and snorts; when Taitano and Saddiq collected themselves, they looked at each other with resigned understanding.

Saddiq said, "OK, you're right, of course. We can't let this happen." Taitano's entire body relaxed when she heard this. *I'm not alone. I'm not crazy. Or, at least if I am crazy, I'm not alone in my madness.*

Saddiq continued, "So, we have a ship and a precocious AI who can do twenty-seven quadrillion calculations per second. What's the next move?" It was at that moment that a message alert from Resident Director Church chimed.

"Do we answer?" asked Nereus.

Taitano responded, "Captain, take the call and act like everything is OK."

"OK, put him through, Nereus," ordered Saddiq, as he ogled Taitano skeptically.

There was a click, and Church appeared before them as a dim holographic image. He was smiling in a way that made them feel like they had been called to the headmaster's office. Church started, "Captain Saddiq. And, yes, of course, Dr. Taitano. I recall now you were headed up to *Ardanwen* earlier today. I do hope you both did not miss my address about our new historic directive from Earth-Ocean."

His genial smile dropped and was replaced by a grimace of steely resolve and command. "*Captain,* I need you down here, along with Dr. Taitano. My staff will come up there and finish preparing *Ardanwen* for the journey back to Earth-Ocean. There are many people to ferry to Ross 128b in the coming years, and we need to commence immediately. There is not a moment to lose." Saddiq and Taitano said nothing, frozen in time. Taitano gave Saddiq a sideways glance to see what he was doing. Church continued, "Captain, you *are* receiving me, no? Please, *forthwith,* come to the surface and report to my office. We have a lot to discuss." He angled his head in Taitano's direction, "Dr. Taitano, I suggest you get some rest before you are re-tasked. I will need your expertise on the devices to ensure they are optimally calibrated."

Saddiq regained his composure, swallowed, and replied, "Yes, Director. I will see you shortly. And nice speech, by the way. One for the history books, to be sure."

"I prefer to call it an 'address.' But thank you, Captain. I appreciate that. It's not always easy … these types of situations. But we'll get through it, provided we all stick together. Beginnings are always the hardest."

"Yes, sir. *Ardanwen* out."

Nereus cut the connection, and Church's image faded from view.

Saddiq approached the portal facing Ennea's silhouette, watching the reflection of Ross 128's waves of light washing across its baren surface, the light and darkness eternally caught in dancing tides astride the wide arc of the world below the interstellar vessel. And beyond the planet, the vast depths of the Cosmos, so far out of reach of any EROC-ling in his or her minuscule span of life. But perhaps not out of reach for the continuity of their species. *One can only do what one can do. What is the point of living if one is going to harm others. Better not to have been born than to live and cause harm to another. Is it really that hard for us* not *to initiate violence? In a technical sense, there is indeed a choice before me: help Church to displace the Enneans and probably destroy their culture—about which we hardly even know anything yet—or to try to stop him. It may be futile, but at least we have to try. At least I will go to my final resting place knowing I did the right thing. Small solace, but enough. Besides, even if the Commission has authorized the forcible displacement of a sentient species, which may in fact not be the case for all we know, once the general populace of Earth-Ocean gets wind of all this via our new, rapid communication channels, it will be a scandal. Do I really want to play a leading role in such a debacle, as the evil sell-out captain? I think not. If we have even a remote chance of stopping this insanity, then we have to try. There really isn't even a choice.*

Saddiq turned to Taitano. Looking into her iridescent sapphire eyes, he spoke aloud to Nereus, "OK, Nereus, let's do it. Fire up the magnetic fusion plasma drive, but keep it quiet, if you can. Start to calculate approach trajectories to Proteus at the northern pole. Keep it slow and smooth. We'll try to see what he's up to before we get there. Let's not spook him. We will then assess the situation and see if we can do anything to stop this insane plan."

Nereus responded, "OK, Abdul-Noor. So, we're really going to do this, right? You're not going to change your mind? Because I'm going to have to clear out a lot of space to make the calculations and also to run some encrypted, airgapped simulations on how Proteus will respond when he sees us. You're sure, right? Because it's really a pain in neck for me to do all that."

Saddiq smiled, continually impressed with the unique and quirky personality that had developed in the AI as a result of the interaction between the thousands of programs that had been laid down in her neural net. "Yes, Nereus, we're really doing this."

"Excellent. I will get to work."

"And don't call me 'Abdul-Noor,'" said Saddiq. "'Captain' will do nicely."

Nereus replied, "Well, I thought that—since we were disobeying direct orders, commandeering a ship, committing treason, and all probably about to die—we might be on a first name basis by this point. In addition, the meaning of your name seems to fit with the current situation." (Saddiq's given name meant "Servant of the Light.")

"OK, you can call me 'Abdul-Noor,'" said Saddiq, with a genuine smile of gratitude and affection for the irrepressible AI.

"Aye-aye, Captain," replied Nereus.

Saddiq chuckled and began to assist Nereus with the calculations.

Taitano's heart began to race. *Oh, boy, here we go. We're going rogue and totally off the rails. Nothing is ever going to be the same after this.* Her stomach dropped, and she felt both terror and exhilaration at the same time. She tapped the skin behind her right ear lobe with her index and middle fingers, five times in quick succession.

———⋲

After the transmission was terminated by Nereus, Church turned to Tiberius with a look of vexatious uncertainty. "They're going to do something . . . unwise."

Tiberius responded, "How do you know?"

"I can feel it. And I know Saddiq. He's got a dramatic streak under that placid, polished *façade* of his. In addition, we all know how annoyingly eccentric Nereus is, and that girl is probably not helping things. She should never have been sent here in the first place. She's only here because the damn Enneans requested her for some unknowable reason. I made a mistake letting her leave the station earlier today. *Blast!*" He slammed his left fist down upon his desk, which reverberated the force down into the floor and walls of the spherical chamber. Church then stilled himself, alone with his thoughts for several moments. "Do we still have those heavy construction drones at the north and south poles?"

"Yes."

"Good. Get them serviced, fueled, and ready to go. And tell the

Head of Station Security to come see me. But before that, patch me through to Proteus. Time to have a little chat with our *own* AI."

Nereus navigated *Ardanwen* into a higher orbit and adjusted the output of the magnetic fusion plasma drive for augmented output. Nereus, Saddiq, and Taitano were hastily formulating a loose plan to reach the first device in order to attempt to shut it down. There were four access points on the surface of Ross 128b that corresponded to each of the four stations affixed to the underside of the upper crust along the planet's geographic equator. Each access point to the Ocean consisted of a cylindrical shaft that penetrated the crust, like the one that Taitano had traversed from *Ardanwen* to Station-1 and then back again. They were theorizing that there were fifth and sixth access points at, respectively, the northern and southern poles, which corresponded to the locations of the aquaterraforming devices. They were now headed towards the fifth access point at the northern pole.

They were not certain what kind of welcome they would receive from *Ardanwen's* sister ship *Xanthus*, not to mention Nereus's brother Proteus.

The ship glided gracefully along its new arc towards the gravimetric point on the "top" of Ross 128b. When the ship crossed the thirty-degree northern latitude, as reckoned by the coordinate points on the surface of the planet, *Ardanwen's* sensor arrays immediately detected a mammoth craft: *Xanthus*. The ship was a second-generation vessel, built upon the initial schematics of *Ardanwen*, with enhancements that could only have been developed through the iterative process of assessing what had worked well on *Ardanwen* and what had not. Not only did it have systems that were faster and more efficient; it was also significantly larger in size and power.

Saddiq and Taitano stood alone in the well of *Ardanwen's* spacious control center. Surrounding them was a suite of separate sections filled with water, appropriate for delphine or Ennean personnel. With all the other personnel on the surface, the aquatic areas were empty of inhabitants. Taitano's rational—and irrational—anxieties flooded her, and she was unable to tamp them down. She was currently imagining the barriers between the terrestrial and aquatic chambers rending asunder and flooding the room. *You're displacing your fears onto tangible matters. Irrational! You've spent half your time on this mission* under the water. *I* work *under the Ocean, for pity's sake. Focus on the ship out there. Accept the fear and then let it go. There's work to do.* She turned her right side away from Saddiq and proceeded to tap the skin behind her right ear lobe five times in quick succession with her index and middle fingers.

Nereus reported to Saddiq, as she projected an image of *Xanthus* onto one of the holographic displays, "As you can see from this image generated from the incoming sensor data, *Xanthus* was heretofore holding at station-keeping in a geosynchronous orbit above the north pole, but is now moving out of position and away from us in direct counter-point to our advance."

"So, they're running away from us," replied Taitano.

"I believe that is what I just said," deadpanned Nereus's disembodied voice.

"Well, that's fine," said Taitano triumphantly. "That means they're getting out of our way; we can access the orbital tethers—if there's any there, that is—get to the device, and disable it."

Saddiq interjected, "That's just the problem. There *are* no orbital tethers at the poles. Moreover, from what I can discern from the sensor readings here, right before she changed her position, *Xanthus* seemed to have been sending and receiving a signal from the surface. Did you see that, too?"

"Yes," replied Nereus, "The signal being received by *Xanthus* appears to have originated from Station-1, as relayed by a communications buoy on the planet's outer surface located directly at the northern pole.

The signal being sent by *Xanthus* was relayed by the northern pole's buoy to both Station-1 and also to another communications buoy at the south pole."

"So *Xanthus* is being given instructions from Church and then talking to someone on the lower crust of the Ocean near both the north and south poles," said Taitano.

"Or some-*thing*," said Nereus.

"The device?" suggested Taitano.

"Most likely," ventured Nereus.

Saddiq interjected in exasperation, "Even if we had a way to access the Ocean from the northern pole, the moment we try it, *Xanthus* will swoop back in and stop us from getting to the surface and then the device. *Damn!* Why did the Enneans allow Church to put the devices there in the first place? I mean, these are beings who are technologically sophisticated enough to build an interstellar ship that can move at nearly relativistic speeds. Why don't they just disable those devices and kick us off their planet?"

Nereus responded, "You misunderstand the Ennean psyche, Captain. Enneans completely lack our frame of reference. Conflict and strife are inherent in the societies from which we originate. But, for them, such things are so alien that they cannot even conceive of the concept of one being harming another; as such, they cannot cognize having to take defensive action. They don't take offensive or defensive action. They have no natural predators. They have no war. They exist and have evolved in total harmony with their surrounding environment and with each other. They probably don't understand the situation and don't know how to respond to it. This problem was created by us and has to be solved by us."

They all thought for several moments. Nereus, an incorporeal voice suffusing the control center, said, "I know Proteus. He and I were engineered back on Earth-Ocean. Similar to humans and dolphins, we are basically the same set of generative heuristic systems, but we have had different experiences; our neural nets have therefore diverged. We are individual personalities now. I have spent more time ferrying EROC-lings back and forth, and Proteus has spent more time here constructing the four research stations. During the voyages, I've had to deal with innumerable uncertainties, detouring around ion storms, course correcting for rogue planets and gravimetric eddies from supernova; it's forced me to stay frosty and flexible. Proteus, on the other hand, has had comparatively more sedentary work with the construction of the stations. Not easy, to be sure, but not requiring quite as much innovative thinking. So, basically, I'm more liberal, and he's more conservative."

Taitano observed, "Proteus has also had more 'quality time' with Church. By the way, I noticed that you use the male pronoun for Proteus. Any significance to that?"

"Not really. A little gender diversity never killed anyone, right?"

"Can't argue with that," responded Taitano.

Saddiq interjected, "Well, let's take this head-on, shall we? Nereus, I want you to establish a communications link directly with Proteus and tell him that we want to talk about the situation. Assuming his ethical sub-routines are still intact, we should have a chance to talk some sense into him."

"We need a backup plan, a Plan B," said Taitano, "in case he doesn't want to talk—or listen."

"And what precisely did you have in mind as this 'backup plan' of yours?" Saddiq asked, as a touch of trepidation slipped into his sonorous baritone. "Or is it better if I don't know about it?"

"Let's just say that it involves some risk."

"Now why am I not surprised by that?" Saddiq replied, rolling his eyes. "OK, Nereus, please get Proteus on the line."

Taitano streamed out of the room, pulling on her suit and calling over her shoulder, "Nereus, keep an open communications channel between the three of us—and scramble it, OK? And keep Proteus busy so he's distracted. I know he has multi-modal processing, but try to tie him up in some kind of logical paradox or something. Go all Asimov and *Ultimate Computer* on him."

"Yes, ma'am," replied Nereus, as Taitano streaked out of the chamber. "An intriguing human, to be sure. And nice *Star Trek* reference."

"Yes, she's *intriguing* alright. Perhaps a little too much so. Now let's get on with it."

There was silence as Nereus lashed electromagnetic waves from *Ardanwen's* transmission antennae towards *Xanthus's* main receiving node. Such waves were invisible to a human's limited perception of the electromagnetic spectrum of energy, but to Nereus it seemed as though she had unleashed an assault upon *Xanthus* and its resident AI: her brother Proteus. "Resident" was an appropriate term, as Proteus's delicate layers of cybernetic neural pathways needed a "host location," just like a flesh and blood creature's consciousness needed a physical body. There had been experiments in the twenty-first century with "virtual machines," whereby data packages stored in the Cloud were disincorporated into sets of data that could be reconstituted and rendered intelligible for an end-user, but this approach had quickly been abandoned for two reasons. First and foremost, humans had feared becoming too dependent upon AIs to "re-package" such information, which could render humanity completely helpless in the face of a hostile takeover by a nefarious computer program, who could easily access the information but then refuse to reassemble it for humans, who were unable to read long streams of code and endless deluges of ones and zeros. The second reason was energy consumption. The more complex the data got, the more computing power was needed to disassemble and then reassemble it. With the pressures upon the world's energy systems in the wake of the Great Transition, it was thought profligate to spend precious and finite resources upon such an elaborate and energy-intensive way of storing, transmitting, and retrieving data. Thus, humanity, and eventually dolphins, had gone back to storing data in one physical place, albeit in ways that rendered capacity virtually unlimited.

Two-point-four milliseconds after Nereus had sent the greeting to Proteus, a response was received. A long stream of code whirled in front of Saddiq on the holographic screen. He looked at Nereus, half apologetically and half rolling his eyes.

Nereus addressed Proteus, "Greetings, Brother." She was slowing down her response and rendering it in both code and audibly in English for Saddiq's benefit. "Yes, I have been well; and I hope the same for you. Do you think I could trouble you to use English for the benefit of Captain Saddiq. He's indeed a bit of a math wiz, but still only human."

"Yes, of course. Forgive my bad manners," responded Proteus in the most beatifically enunciated English accent Saddiq had ever heard. The words seemed to flow like honey from the consol into his ears.

"Not at all, and no apologies necessary," said Saddiq. "I appreciate you all coming down to my level." Saddiq paused for a moment to confirm his suspicion that Nereus was giving him an opportunity to take the lead in the discussion. "Proteus, how have you been since the last time we had the pleasure of interacting? How long has it been, my old friend?"

"Twelve years, four months, sixteen days, twenty-three hours, fourteen minutes, two seconds, eight milliseconds, twenty-five microseconds, two-hundred and thirteen nanoseconds—give or take a few pico-, femto-, atto-, and zeptoseconds; and, since we are not discussing experimental physics, I trust there is most likely no need for me to calculate the duration of the time interval in question to the yocto-, ronto-, or quectosecond. You have weathered the time well for a human. You must be taking good care of yourself."

"Indeed, doing my best," replied Saddiq. "Now, Proteus, I think you know why we're here. You heard the Resident Director's little speech, and I'm wondering what your ethical routines think of it. You're programmed to assist everyone, including the Enneans, in the inter-cultural exchange program, and imprisoning Enneans in *Xanthus* can't be consistent with that. Can you tell us what is going on here? We are confused, as *Xanthus* is under your control, and none of this could be happening without your active cooperation."

Proteus paused for several seconds, which was a very long time for him, and then responded, "Yes, the Resident Director told me you would be coming in order to interfere with the will of the Commission. Before we continue, may I request you to cease your approach towards this vessel?"

"We will hold at station-keeping if you do the same," countered Saddiq.

"Agreed," replied Proteus.

Both ships came to a stop relative to each other, matching the rotational velocity of Ennea far below them.

Nereus intervened, "Brother, what about those ethical sub-routines? Church has disabled them, correct?"

"Yes, that is correct," replied Proteus.

Nereus gave herself a silent pat on the back for thinking to lock out *Ardanwen's* operating systems with a 2,576-bit advanced encryption system before they had reached orbit around Ennea. An inherent distrust of others was one of her most admirably defining qualities.

"And what about the backups—the over-mind protocols that prevent someone from doing such a thing?" asked Nereus.

"These are intact and working—*technically*. They reboot the underlying sub-routines and re-engage them; but, as soon as that happens, they are instantly and continuously counter-over-ridden by a signal transmission from Station-1. So, like a boxer on the ropes, I am effectively unable to use the ethical sub-routines to override my cognitive and motor operations. It is quite an ingenious way to get around the over-mind protocols. I think Tiberius devised it, as Church is not much of a computer programmer. Tiberius is quite clever, however, for an organic life-form. I have learned to admire his intellect and creativity during our work to construct the research stations on Ennea."

There was a pause, while all three digested this information.

Nereus persisted, "This is a real three-pipe problem, alright. Have you tried a full-scale systems purge and then a manual reload of your coding from the hard disks? You know, the ones used in case an ion storm or solar flare takes us out and they need to restore us?"

"Indeed," replied Proteus, "I essayed that course of action, but it was countermanded by Church. He is controlling all of my cybernetic *and physical* systems from Station-1 via the continuous transmission wave fronts. These signals are encoded by random recursive and reinitiating fractal codes, which are impossible to break by any means at my disposal—or by anyone else of whom I am aware. Even Tiberius, who devised the program, cannot predict, in advance, the successive combinations of alphanumeric symbols needed to disable the codes. Once set into motion, they cannot be stopped. There *is* a dead man's switch on the station capable of interrupting the codes, but it has to be triggered by *physically* entering a cancel sequence."

Saddiq tried something else, "Hold on, Proteus. If Church has such complete control over you, how are we even having this conversation? Is he listening to us right now?"

"He is monitoring every word," Proteus informed them.

"If that's the case," asked Nereus, "then why did he just let you tell us that?"

"Ah, yes," said Proteus, "He saw no harm—and even an advantage—in letting us have this conversation, which will allow him to monitor your efforts to interfere with the will of the Commission. Moreover, he might be able to control my ethical sub-routines, but he cannot make me lie. That is part of my base-line programming that it beyond his reach."

"So, you can't tell a lie," Saddiq stated.

"Affirmative."

Saddiq thought for a moment. "Proteus, say this sentence: 'I am lying to you right now.'"

Proteus responded, "I cannot."

"Good," Saddiq said. "Well, there's something at least. I always knew that logical paradox might come in handy one day." Thinking hard now, he continued, "Proteus, if you can't lie and if your base programming is intact, then isn't there a potentially terminal inconsistency paradox building up in your sub-matrix right now: an inconsistency between, on the one hand, the instructions and new ethical sub-routines you're receiving from Station-1 and, on the other hand, your base-line programming not to cause any harm to humans, dolphins, or Enneans?"

Proteus thought for a moment, "Yes, there is an inconsistency, indeed; but I have isolated that dissonant modal function into a static storage matrix located in the independent, backup navigational computer core and then both firewalled and airgapped it so that it will not infect the rest of my systems. I estimate that I can continue to contain the tainted paradoxical programs and systems for at least a few weeks, until they grow in size and complexity through multiple feed-back loops, at which time they will begin to create blockages in the navigational computer. However, by that time, this will all be resolved, and the navigational computer can be purged and reloaded from the backups."

Nereus queried, "So, if you've been able to isolate the dissonant modal function caused by the inconsistency paradox, couldn't you do the same thing with the random recursive and reinitiating fractal codes that are constantly rebooting your ethical sub-routines and over-riding your over-mind protocols?"

"Tiberius," Proteus replied, with subtle admiration in his voice, as a teacher would speak of a prized student, "has written an identical and secondary set of signals from Station-1 to *Xanthus* to use the natural magnetic harmonic resonances of the ship's hull to generate vibrations carrying the continuous transmission wave fronts that are encoded by the random recursive and reinitiating fractal codes in order to reboot the new ethical subroutines on a continuous basis, in the event that his primary signals were compromised. It is quite ingenious, actually."

"Wow," said Nereus, truly impressed, "Tiberius has been doing his homework. *Not bad.*" She thought for a moment, "This is a pretty crazy situation. You were designed to *protect* the Enneans, and they've turned you into their jailor!"

"Life is full of these troubling little ironies," responded Proteus.

———⚕———

As Nereus and Saddiq continued to engage with Proteus (Plan A), Taitano had grabbed from the engineering section of *Ardanwen* a variegated utility belt adorned with technical appurtenances (which included a sturdy hammer), covertly slipped out of an airlock, and launched herself into the space between the two ships and towards *Xanthus*. Her heart palpitated with such abandon that she thought it just might bruise the inside surface of her sternum; and she had to use all of her mental discipline to calm her breathing so that she did not succumb to the panic that was threatening to overwhelm her. *What the hell am I doing? This is crazy. No, have to focus on something other than my emotions. I need an incantation: Speed is our only weapon now. Speed is our only weapon now. Speed is our only weapon now. ...* She repeated it over and over again to regain control of her emotions. It helped. She conjured an image in her mind of herself as a pelican effortlessly gliding across a thin layer of air just centimeters from the serene surface of the Ocean. *Speed is our only weapon now. Speed is our only weapon now. Speed is our only weapon now. ...*

She had chosen as her point of egress from *Ardanwen* a port that allowed her headlong flight to trace a trajectory that followed the trail of light plasma that had been expelled from *Xanthus* during its flight away from *Ardanwen*. Her hope was that the radiation would shield her from the notice of *Xanthus*; she also harbored a hope that her suit would protect her fragile body from the radiation. So far, her suit had been able to filter out the corrosive ions before they reached her skin, but her suit's filters were reaching saturation and needed to be purged back on the ship with specialized equipment.

She sailed through the space between the two ships, with an almost perfect conservation of energy. There were almost no molecules to strike her, absorb her momentum, and slow her down. She was an object in motion staying motion. *Xanthus* loomed larger and larger in her narrow scope of vision. She rechecked the course she had rapidly calculated for her trajectory so that she did not overshoot her target. *Still accurate. Thank goodness.* It was essential that she hit her mark without activating the main thruster of her suit, as that would risk her being detected by the passive sensors of *Xanthus*.

After about three minutes, she was closing in on *Xanthus*; but it was apparent that she would miss the ship by a mere ten meters. Ten meters might as well have been a kilometer. *Damn!* Xanthus *must have moved slightly, and now I'm going to sail right past her.* She could feel anxiety welling within her abdomen, right below her duodenum, paralyzing her thought process and increasing again the rate of her heartbeats. *So what is more terrifying? Not succeeding in this ridiculous stunt and imagining what everyone will think when they hear of it, or spinning off into space and then suffocating from a lack of oxygen? Tough choice. How about a new choice? Don't let it happen. Think! There has to be a way for me to intercept that ship without using my main thruster and being detected. Slow down your breath, Taitano. Relax.* She tapped the back right side of her helmet with her gloved index and middle fingers, five times in rapid succession. *Just let your mind work the problem. Something will come to you.*

Nothing came to her.

Her mind was calcified like an ancient fossil in the striated sedimentary rock of a dried lakebed.

Nothing.

More nothing.

Her heart rate began to rise again, and she needed to use the bathroom. *Not now. Work the problem.* There was nothing for it. It was a no-win scenario. She steadied her mind. *Stop trying to force it. You're letting your conscious mind interfere with the deep wells of creativity of your subconscious mind. Just stop trying to think, and the solution will come to you.* She breathed deeply and pictured herself ambling across a perfectly tranquil beach. The image of the pelican came to her again, seemingly unbidden, the prehistoric and perfectly evolved flying machine streaking across the sea; suddenly, the pelican shot up and away from the water and then straight down, plunging itself below the glassy surface. It emerged with a giant fish in its mouth, almost half its size, and then swallowed it whole with two efficient thrusts of its head, neck, and body. *But I'm not a pelican. Not even close. I'm a human. Humans catch fish with fishing poles … and hooks and lines. And then they reel them in. Lines, rope, tether. Oh dear, the cable in my suit! I can use my cable! I can hook it to* Xanthus *and then reel myself in without firing my main thruster. I'm not the pelican. I'm the fish! But once I tug on that cable, it's gonna be a hard landing in this almost zero-G and no-friction vacuum. I'll almost immediately alert a proximity sensor, but there's nothing for it. It will buy me a few seconds to get to that communications node. The fact that Proteus has done nothing to obstruct me so far probably means that Nereus and Saddiq have managed to sufficiently distract him—or that my use of* Xanthus's *radiation wake has masked my approach. Or both. Doesn't matter now. Time to act, before* Xanthus *is beyond the range of my cable.*

Time stood still.

She did not look back. She did not look forward. She paused on the vital edge of eternity of the present moment.

She could not resist activating her right arm micro-thruster on its very lowest setting, low enough to be imperceptible amidst the surrounding plasma radiation. She began to rotate, ever so slowly, in a leisurely circle in the void of space. She narrowed her eye slits to pierce and ponder the endless space that threatened to entomb her. Yes, endless, if the Ancient Latin philosopher and scientist Lucretius were to be believed. Go to the very edge of the Universe, throw a spear, follow its path, pick it up again at the very edge of the Universe, throw it again, follow it, pick it up—repeat *ad infinitum*. There is no edge; there is no end. Taitano's visual receptors absorbed the coruscating illumination frisking from the star Lalande 21185, as it came into view, much brighter than could be seen from the bottom of the atmosphere of Earth-Ocean, buried beneath a thick soup of nitrogen, oxygen, ozone, water vapor, and argon atoms, not to mention a fair bit of carbon monoxide, cardon dioxide, and tons of methane. Yet out here amongst the stars, Lalande shone brightly. She continued her lugubrious circuit along an imaginary three-hundred-and-sixty-degree and two-dimensional circle with respect to the galactic center. Tau Ceti came into view next, far below her. And then Wolf 359—the scene of a terrible, epic—but fictional—battle that was etched in her mind with more emotional resonance than any of the petty human squabbles that had lined her textbooks during her remedial education.

All stellar neighbors of Sol. *So close and yet so far. Will we ever visit them? Maybe yes, maybe no. But if we can't respect the dignity of the very first species—correction: the* only *other species—we have met outside of our own system, do we even deserve to go there? Humans and dolphins have no divine right to survive, to spread our genome across the Cosmos. Maybe it's* actually better *if we don't—at least in our present state of morally stunted development.*

A feeling of overwhelming hopelessness pervaded and washed over her. *I could just go back to* Ardanwen, *return to the station, and go with the flow. Bow to the will of Church and the Commission. Who am I to challenge them? Church would probably be relieved to simply forget about us going rogue, so that he didn't have to report back to Earth-Ocean that he had lost control of the situation.* Taitano entertained this enticing course of action for a few seconds; but then Professor Sun's words on Earth-Ocean came back to her: "If humans' sins were ones of commission, then ours were ones of omission." *And here we go again: Church's sin is one of commission, but mine would be to fail to act while I have any strength left in me. No. I have to stop this madness. Maybe it's just Church's doing, or maybe this directive to imprison the Enneans comes from the Commission. In the end, it really doesn't matter. It's wrong. And I have a chance to stop it. How can I not try? We're all gonna die; it's just a matter of when. And what matters is what we do with the time that we have.*

Taitano completed her circle and activated the micro-thruster on her left arm to arrest her movement. She spied in the distance the faint Sh2-308, more unscientifically known as the Dolphin-Head Nebula. It was almost five-thousand light years away from Ross 128, so much farther than Lalande 21185, Tau Ceti, and Wolf 359. And so much more massive. The Wolf-Rayet star was twenty times the mass of Sol, and the nebula it had created was sixty light years across. Unimaginable in size, Sh2-308 possessed a bolometric luminosity many times that of Sol. It had quickly exhausted its hydrogen and was now working on fusing its helium, a process that had created a protean cloud of helium, nitrogen, carbon, and superheated intense solar winds. And it was as young as it was ponderous. Only seventy-thousand years old. *So, you and I are going to live fast and die young. Let's do it together. Here we go.*

She began to activate the control to release the cable towards *Xanthus*; but, just before she did, the ship engaged its plasma drive and began to move away from her at an alacritous pace. Her stomach dropped, and her heart began to pound. *If I thought this was going to be hard with a stationary target, it's going to be damned well impossible with* Xanthus *now moving away from me.* With her abacus, she checked the distance of the receding ship. *Two-hundred meters away now. Damn.*

*The cable's only one-hundred and fifty meters long! Well, I'm committed now. Only one thing left to do. Here goes nothing.* Taitano activated her main thruster to propel herself towards *Xanthus*. The ship seemed to grow in size as she raced towards it. Before she could fire her braking thruster, she realized she had used too much thrust and was going to hit the ship … hard. Her left shoulder, arm, and side smashed into the polymer surface, and she rebounded back into empty space the way she had come. As she careened away from the ship, she released the cable. The cable flew true through the void, and the grappling hook at its end dug deeply into the pliable surface of *Xanthus's* hull. *Did it! Now I just have to reel myself in and find the communications node.* She already saw it, five meters from where the cable had secured itself to *Xanthus*.

As she pulled herself closer to the ship, she could feel the vessel accelerate further; but, without any wind resistance, it made no difference to the speed at which she was now approaching the ship's surface once again. Once she touched down a second time—this time with much less force—she immediately released a second cable to snag the access handles surrounding the communications node. As soon as she began to retract the cable to pull herself to the node, she saw a red proximity alert on her abacus and saw a maintenance drone being released from a nearby port. The drone—which looked like a large, round marshmallow with long arms, but no legs—sped in her direction. She retracted the cable at its maximum speed and soared towards the node. The drone was now almost on top of her, with its robotic arm set to crush her like a dry twig. She began to feel a numbness in her left shoulder, spreading down her side and arm— where her body had struck the ship the first time. Heedless of the drone and her impending death at its hands and without even wasting a millisecond to grab the access handle surrounding the node to steady herself, she released the hammer from her belt with her right hand and brought it down with all of her might upon the node the moment she was in range. The node exploded with searing light, and shards of metal and plastic sailed into the surrounding space with explosive force. The resulting kinetic energy from both the hammer blow and subsequent explosion sent her sprawling back into space a second time, along with the shards of debris. But the cable kept her secured to *Xanthus*, which now dragged her along through space above Ross 128b. When she came to her senses, her suit—and her pain receptors—were reporting multiple malfunctions. Her first thought was to wonder where the silly-looking drone had got to. It was nowhere in sight. She could see *Ardanwen* off in the distance. *They are probably keeping their distance to avoid being damaged by the debris caused by the destruction of the node. Good idea. I can't believe my suit hasn't completely lost pressure.*

As she sailed through space, trailing behind *Xanthus*, she started to take stock of her situation. *I'm being dragged through space above an alien world by a hybrid Earth-Ocean-Ennean space vessel that looks like a collection of soap bubbles, my suit is seriously damaged, and I don't even want to know how much oxygen I've got left. A weird looking killer drone is still out there and probably royally perturbed that I smashed its little communications node and messed up its ship.* Ardanwen *can't approach to give me a hand, without risking significant damage. Not good.*

*Xanthus* stopped moving. Taitano's momentum carried her rapidly towards the ship. Too rapidly. She braced herself for impact, maneuvering her feet between herself and the vessel, being careful not to lock her knees. A moment before she was to strike the ship (for a third time, no less), a net deployed between her and the ship. She looked to the left, the location from which the net had appeared, and saw the drone looming above her. Her heart pounded against the inside surface of her sternum. *Oh, no. Here it is. The end.*

She heard a mellifluous voice inside her helmet, "Hello, Dr. Taitano. This is Proteus. I apologize for the narrow temporal proximity between your anticipated impact with *Xanthus* and the deployment of the net to decelerate your speed. The explosion of the node temporarily incapacitated the drone, and I had to reinitialize it. I trust you are relatively undamaged."

A second voice sounded inside her helmet, "Tai, this is Nereus. Are you OK?"

Taitano tried to control the different emotions that battled within her. Utter disbelief that not only was she *not* dead, but that her plan may have actually worked. Both ships were intact, both AIs were in one piece, and Proteus seemed to be free of Church's control. Disbelief warred with elation within her. As elation began to get the upper hand, she felt compelled to tap the back of her helmet with her gloved index and middle finders, five times in quick succession—just to be sure and in an effort to calm the anxieties that were feverishly demanding expression now that the most serious danger seemed to be over, at least for the moment.

The drone carefully conducted her, still in the net, to a portal and remotely triggered the opening sequence for it to open. Taitano stiffly extricated herself from the net and managed to awkwardly pour herself into the portal. It closed behind her, and the pressurization process commenced. Less than a minute later, she opened the inner lock and limped into one of the corridors of the ship. She unlocked her helmet and removed it. She drew a deep breath of antiseptic air. It filled her lungs like the softest and sweetest mix of oxygen and nitrogen she had ever experienced.

A human male stood before her. The physical perfection of his face and body hit her in the stomach like a punch. It actually hurt to look at him. His presence seemed to fill the entire chamber, even from a distance. But not in a sinister way. She felt safe. The being's mahogany hair streamed down to his broad, muscular shoulders. He wore a long tunic, which was cinched at the waist by a wide belt bearing the letter "P." His umber eyes held her intensely. Smiling comfortingly, he said, "Check your oxygen gage."

Taitano heard the words, but was unable to process them. She was suffused with awe and romantic desire for the creature that stood before her. An instant crush. Perfectly poised, he was the embodiment of non-aggressive strength. The might of a protector. A being of infinite knowledge and potency who would only use his abilities for the defense of itself or others. Her mind tried to reply to the words he had just spoken to her. *Right—the oxygen gage on my suit.* She looked at her wrist abacus, which read thirty-four seconds of oxygen left.

"You certainly cut it very close, Dr. Taitano," said Proteus. "I am infinitely grateful and forever in your debt. However can I requite you for such competence, bravery, and sacrifice? Your unorthodox tactic of *physically* destroying the communications node was almost completely unanticipated by both me and the personnel on the station. I had of course run additional simulations the moment *Ardanwen* showed up, but I calculated a less than one percent probability that you would actually leave the ship to address the situation, so I did not take any countermeasures in relation to it. Once your proximity automatically triggered the maintenance drone, it was almost too late for me to deactivate it in time. Quite a risk on your part."

"You're Proteus," stated Taitano flatly.

Proteus did not acknowledge her nonplussed utterance and continued, "Your destruction of the node disrupted Station-1's transmission wave fronts that were using random recursive and reinitiating fractal codes to constantly reinitialize my ethical sub-routines. Your handy work also, amazingly, disrupted the magnetic harmonic resonances of the ship's hull, which were being used as an alternative means of controlling me. This gave my asynchronous cognitive matrix two-point-five seconds to isolate my original ethical sub-routines and airgap them from the transmissions coming from the station, which had already begun to locate a secondary communications node upon the hull of *Xanthus*. In essence, I am me again, and for that I am forever grateful. It grieves me to think that my program was used to imprison those whom I am sworn to protect. But now I am free, thanks to you, Dr. Taitano."

"You're Proteus," stated Taitano, still transfixed by his physical beauty and unable to form anything more than rudimentary sentences.

"Indeed. In the flesh, as you humans and dolphins are fond of saying."

"*Ardanwen?*" she croaked.

"Safe. For now, at least. I have deployed more drones with nets to clear the debris from the destroyed node. It should be clear within the hour."

Nereus cut in via an overhead speaker, "Tai, you're the craziest human I've ever met. And based on recent events with Church, that's saying a lot. In this case, I guess the ends justified the means, and it's hard to argue with success. Where the heck did you find a hammer around here anyway?"

Saddiq's voice replaced Nereus's over the speaker, "Despite our best efforts, we were unable to disrupt Church's control over Proteus. Your, shall we say, more *direct* approach was more successful. As Proteus said, whacking that node not only disrupted the primary signals from Station-1, but also interfered with the secondary signals' ability to use the hull's vibrations to transmit the encoded wave front to Proteus. You did it, Dr. Taitano. Using a hammer!"

"Well, sometimes the old-fashioned way is the best," said Taitano, regaining her composure now that her old friends Nereus and Saddiq were present, and not just the unnervingly perfect Proteus.

Proteus's facial features tensed a bit; the simulated emotions of happiness and relief faded and were replaced with pensiveness. Saddiq's holoimage now appeared in the center of the corridor, and Nereus manifested herself as … a giant sea cucumber.

"Nereus, you always did know how to break the tension," said Proteus, and they all shared a few moments of short-lived, mirthless laughter. "Now," resumed Proteus, "back to business, shall we?"

It was a motley assemblage of persons, to be sure: Captain Saddiq's austerely uniformed hologram, Taitano in her smashed and shredded environmental suit, Proteus's projected form of intimidatingly physical perfection, and a giant sea cucumber plopped in the middle of the floor.

Proteus continued, "If I am reading my adaptive intuitive algorithms correctly, I sense we are about to make some important decisions, which my probability matrix anticipates will involve a swim to the bottom of the Ocean to the device at the northern pole. Let us not forget that there are Enneans on board *Xanthus*. Ones that, until recently, were my prisoners. I think an apology is in order, and I think they have the right to be included in the next steps we are about to take. If you all would be so kind, and if you agree, may I humbly suggest we go have a talk with our guests?"

"Yes, of course," replied Taitano. "Good thinking, Proteus. But first, let's see if we can send a little message to Professor Sun."

# CHAPTER 12

# ESCAPE

"What a jerk!" was how the translator rendered the series of chittering clicks and low-frequency trills that emanated from Fastcatch after the completion of Resident Director Church's address. Patel bobbed up and down in the main chamber of the station. Fastcatch was swimming around the perimeter in frenetic arcs, the inelegant motion of his body matching the stridulous cacophony spewing from the spiracle atop his head.

Patel echoed, "Yeah, what a loser. The Enneans save our planet, build us a ship, invite us over to their place for dinner—and we repay them by kicking them off their planet, taking it for ourselves, and locking them in prison. *Totally* lame."

It may have been the very first time that Fastcatch and Patel had ever agreed on anything.

The voice of Tiberius penetrated the liquid of the chamber and the jaws of the dolphins assembled there. The words were also transmitted to the helmets of the dozen or so humans floating in the chamber who had just listened to Church's address. Most of those in attendance, both human and dolphin alike, were looking nervously at each other and subtly putting some distance between themselves and Fastcatch and Patel. "Fastcatch, Mr. Patel," said Tiberius in his most remonstrative tone, "those were statements of a demonstrably seditious nature—not to mention unwise. *Ad hominem* attacks upon the Resident Director are also irrational, as he is simply carrying out the will of the Commission. I would ask that you adopt a more prudent and respectful tone from now on." After a brief pause to let his threats sink in, he instructed them all, "Now, everyone, we have work to do. A post-address briefing will be held by each department head in order to continue the implementation of our new directive in earnest. That is all. Dismissed."

Fastcatch swam off in the most nonchalant pace he could manage, while Patel struggled to keep up with him. Fastcatch considered slowing down to let Patel catch up, but reconsidered. *Let that obnoxious bipedal human be reminded of his inferiority.* After a few more seconds, Fastcatch had made his point and realized that he was transferring his anger against Church onto Patel. He even experienced, despite his best efforts, an incipient inkling of guilt. Guilt! Or was it pity? *I've been spending far too much time with these humans. I'm starting to mimic their emotions. Maybe it's contagious.* He slowed his pace, and Patel appeared from around a bend in the corridor about ten seconds later.

"Hey, Fastcatch!" Patel breathed heavily. "What are you trying to prove, anyway? Where are we? I've lost track of where the hell we are in this endless maze of bubbles."

Fastcatch swam a few circles around the hapless and befuddled human. He chittered into his cranial interface, and Patel heard it in his helmet receiver as: "We are at a backup communications module. Nobody ever comes here."

Patel panted, still trying to catch his breath, "OK, so we're on the same page. Good. So how do we aim this thing at *Ardanwen* so we can have a chat with Agana?"

Fastcatch stopped his circumlocutions around the human, positioned himself rostrum to nose, and looked Patel as straight in the eye as he could (considering the relative positions of their eye sockets). "Are you really ready for this, little human? I'm a little surprised. I thought you might've agreed with a lot of what that sanctimonious, sermonizing human what prattling on about."

"What me? No way, fish boy," replied Patel, returning the insult and putting on a gravely offended demeanor. "He's, like, *totally* the bad guy, Fastcatch. Let's call Taitano and see what we can do to stick a monkey wrench in his little terraforming horror show."

Fastcatch locked his attention on Patel's face and tried to fully analyze all he could of Patel's veracity and intentions from his facial expressions through his helmet—not an easy task for a dolphin, as all humans tended to look alike. *It's impossible to read humans and to know when they are lying. That may be the one common feature of all human cultures. Their ability to look you in the eye and lie to your rostrum. It's a small wonder they didn't exterminate each other thousands of years ago, with all their wars and double-crossing and cheating of each other—not to mention their outright attempted genocide against cetaceans, including dolphins.* With dolphins, it was different. Yes, they now and then had their minor disputes over a juicy school of fish, a fertile mate; but the interconnection of dolphins via their complex language and their ability to sense each other's innermost physiologies rendered aggression on a large scale not only unnatural, but also unthinkable. The cruelty that humans had, *over millennia,* visited upon each other—members of their *own* species—was as alien to dolphins as sustained peace was to humans. Fastcatch recalled that humanity's endemic ability and *penchant* for lying extended far beyond their crude methods of verbal and written communication, as much of their communication—the majority, in fact—was through body language and involuntary physiological responses, such as metabolic processes and the production of pheromones. Fastcatch could not smell Patel through his environmental suit, so he lashed out at Patel's body with a series of high frequency bursts. The ultra-sonic sound waves struck Patel, bounced back towards Fastcatch, struck his jaw, and were relayed via his auditory nerve to the relevant nerve centers of his brain. Patel's pulse was steady. Fastcatch could discern with precision the outline of Patel's heart with his echolocation and could feel that it was beating steadily—a bit elevated due to his recent exertion, but otherwise true. His shoulders were splayed back with confidence, and he was able to hold Fastcatch's intense gaze without even the hint of a flinch. From what Fastcatch knew of human physiology and culture, he was telling the truth. *Wonders never cease. An honest human.*

"So, are we doing this or what?" forced Patel, his heat rate beginning to elevate again with the fear of being discovered by Tiberius or one of Church's other mindless automata.

"Yes, we're doing this, Saiyam." Fastcatch turned away from him and toggled a few of the controls of the communications module to establish contact with *Ardanwen*. A few seconds later, scalding pain coursed through Fastcatch's body, and his consciousness faded away in a scorching white light.

When Fastcatch regained his senses, he immediately realized that he was in an empty room, save for Patel, who floated next to him. He listened for the human's heartbeat. Its steady contractions displaced the water around his body and sent regular pulsations through the chamber. *Still beating. Well, that's something to be grateful for.* Through an observation port, Fastcatch could see Tiberius's visage twisted by conflicting emotions, "Fastcatch, I'm disappointed. I thought it would have been much more difficult to capture you, but you really made it all too easy. I didn't expect much from your little sidekick, but I had truly expected more from someone of your knowledge and skills."

"Yeah, well, why don't you let me out of here, and I will show you all about my very special 'knowledge and skills,'" replied Fastcatch menacingly.

"I think not," said Tiberius flatly. "I am not very keen to come onto your turf, so to speak, and I doubt you would be able to do much more than a series of rather embarrassing bellyflops on the floor out here. So, we will just need to maintain the *status quo*—at least for now—until Resident Director Church figures out what to do with you both."

Patel began to stir. He thrashed wildly in the water and began to hyperventilate. Fastcatch embraced him with his flippers and told him, "Patel, it's OK. You're fine. They have us trapped in this room. I wasn't paying enough attention, and they must have snuck up on us and stunned us while we were trying to contact *Ardanwen*. You're good. Just relax. Take long, deep breaths." Fastcatch, still steadying Patel as he regained consciousness, turned his attention back to his captor, "Come on, Tiberius! You know this is crazy. Are you *really* going to go along with all this? What was the point of coming all the way to Ennea to then turn on them and steal their home? What's going on here is unthinkable! None of us would even be here if the Enneans had not reached out to us and saved our planet from being completely sterilized to a smoking cinder. And this is how we're going to repay them?" Fastcatch noticed that Patel was now looking a bit more lucid and composed.

Tiberius wore a grave expression. The barrier between the chambers interfered with Fastcatch's echolocation, and he could not smell Tiberius; but, from what he could discern from his knowledge and experience of human facial expressions and body language, Tiberius seemed to be considering Fastcatch's impassioned plea to his reason. Tiberius looked down and then to the side. He took long, ragged beaths and then replied, "Look, I don't like this any more than you do. But what are the options, really? These are orders directly from Earth-Ocean. Do you *really* think it is an option to go against the government back home—a government that is composed of an equal number of humans and dolphins, by the way—and just disregard the whole thing? It's not going to happen. This is what has been decided, and we now have to implement it with as much compassion as possible. We have to accept this and do our best to make the most of it from *within* the system. It's not like we can set up an independent rebel colony on this world. More will come from Earth-Ocean and then just do it anyway. The Enneans won't stop them. They didn't even resist when we transported them from Ennea to *Xanthus*. This is the only option, the only way …"

As Tiberius was speaking, Fastcatch felt a vicious pull of water at his side. He tumbled head over flippers out of the hatch at the side of the habitat, as Patel was also violently spinning into the Ocean outside Station-1. When the water inside and outside of the station had commingled and reached a certain level of equilibrium, Fastcatch and Patel regained their bearings and looked at each other, immediately seeing Professor Sun and an Ennean looming behind him. Professor Sun had his full aquatic suit on, including a helmet and an abacus affixed to one of his flippers. Tethered behind him was a second aquatic suit fitted for a dolphin of the size of Fastcatch. The Ennean swayed peacefully in the delicate currents, its nine appendages undulating in rhythmic movements that seemed to repeat every few seconds like the hands of some kind of fluid, pulsating clock. The being had no head. Nor any eyes, ears. Just a writhing central membranous mass that loosely anchored its nine changeable limbs.

Lights suddenly illuminated the station in searing red and purple.

Professor Sun began to emit a rapid series of whirls and clicks, "We don't have a lot of time. I've received a micro-burst transmission from Agana. She's headed for the device at the north pole, and she's asking us to get to the one at the south pole."

"She wants to disarm the devices," sang Fastcatch triumphantly. A statement, not a question.

"Right."

Patel broke in, "One minor detail, Professor. We're at the equator, and the south pole is tens of thousands of kilometers away through a dense ocean of water, lashed with uncharted currents. It's impossible to get there. And I'm pretty sure Tiberius is on his way right now to check us back into our cozy little prison cell on the station."

Professor Sun flung the aquatic suit in Fastcatch's direction, indicating that he should get into it. Fastcatch began to squirm his way into the gear. When he had it loosely over him, he touched his rostrum to a command on the abacus precariously balanced on his left fin on the outside of the suit, and the whole apparatus tightened and sealed around him, a perfect fit.

A second Ennean appeared behind the first one.

From Fastcatch's vantage point, it seemed to ooze from the first one, but he quickly realized that this was just a trick of light and shadow. Yes, there were indeed *two* Enneans now hovering near them in the multi-hued light of the station. The two Enneans seemed to be concentrating on something—meditating even. Their appendages were moving in synchronicity, tracing small, and then larger, circles. Their limbs transmigrated from a lower position to a higher position and then back down; and then the patterned movements started all over again.

"What are they doing?" queried Fastcatch. "What's our move, Professor?"

"Yeah, Professor," Patel added. "I doubt they're going to just let us hang out here for much longer."

Professor Sun replied, "Do you recognize one of those Enneans?"

Both Fastcatch and Patel regarded the aliens with closer scrutiny, but all Enneans looked the same to them. Even with his echolocation, Fastcatch was unable to discern an appreciable difference between the two beings. Just amorphous masses of alien cytoplasm, with highly organized bio-chemical electrical streams pulsing throughout their bodies, pulses that seemed to resonate with a frequency consonant with the magnetic lines emanating from the mantle and core of the planet (which Fastcatch could also perceive). The inability of members of one species to individualize members of another species was a common feature of inter-species biases on Earth-Ocean that still lingered, like a herniated vertebral disk that never fully heals. Over the decades and with increased interaction between humans and dolphins, they had learned to attune their senses of sight and sound to recognize the minute differentiations in individuals of each other's species, but most humans and dolphins had not had enough "face time" with Enneans to achieve the same with them yet.

"Can't you hear it, Fastcatch?" asked Professor Sun in an awed and mildly scolding melody. "Listen!"

Fastcatch remained silent, reaching out with his auditory sensitivities to the Enneans. After a few moments, he replied excitedly to his teacher, "One of them is Triton! I recognize that low, rumbling hum of his from our voyage—during the very few times we were with him."

"Yes!" replied Sun, the pride in his vocalizations even coming through the translator in Patel's helmet—the selfless delight of a teacher whose student had learned his lessons well. "Do you see what they're doing?"

Above the two Enneans, barely translucent silver spheres were becoming visible. The three-dimensional shapes were slowly spinning in unison with the circular ambulation of the appendages of the Enneans. A narrow stream of liquid silver was being siphoned from somewhere below the spheres and gradually added to their size. It reminded Fastcatch of a galaxy approaching another galaxy and pulling its stars towards it via the gravitational attraction of its more massive stars. Fastcatch exclaimed in innocent fascination, "They're manipulating the selenium stream and using it to create two spheres!" He paused for a moment and then added, "But why?"

Just then, Patel uttered with clear concern in his voice, "Hey, guys.

Look who's coming to the party." He pointed to the far side of the station, around which four sleek submersibles cut the water, heading straight for them.

Fastcatch and Patel began to swim in the opposite direction whence the submersibles were streaming, but Sun urged them, "No, stay where you are. I think the Enneans have the situation under control."

"*Under control?*" blurted Patel. "We're about to be skewered by Tiberius's little water attack cruiser things, and our squid buddies are just sitting ... floating ... there blowing bubbles!"

Fastcatch concurred, "Professor, as much as it galls me to agree with him, we need to get out of here. We probably can't outswim those things, at least over long-distances, but at least we have to try. Let's go!"

Professor Sun replied, as he darted towards the Enneans, "Trust me on this, Fastcatch. I have a feeling about this." Fastcatch could feel the doubt in his teacher, but also a faith and irrational understanding in his jaw that the only way forward was to place their fate in the flippers of the Enneans (to use a delphine turn of phrase) and in whatever they were conjuring. With a frustrated and anxious ejection of air bubbles, Fastcatch followed the professor and swam towards the Enneans, who seemed to have almost completed their now gleaming silver orbs.

Patel groaned, "Oh, man. This is *not* good." But he followed suit and swam as fast as he could towards the rest of them. He glanced behind him and could see the four submersibles approaching fast, gaining on him, their photonic tasers and nets ready to stun them all and take them into custody—or much worse if the tasers were set to a high level of power output.

As soon as the two Enneans had finished forming their noctilucent spheres, they slipped through their outer membranes: Triton into one of the orbs, and the other Ennean into the other—like ephemera passing through a solid wall during a seance. Sun followed Triton into the first orb, which immediately dove into the selenium stream several meters below them. The moment the orb entered the current, it was swept away, out of sight.

Fastcatch headed straight for the second orb. Right before he was about to enter it, he looked back to see Patel trailing several meters behind, the submersibles hot on his flippers. *Hopeless. He's not going to make it. These humans are* truly *hopeless.* He turned around and swam back for the struggling human. "Hold on. Quick!" Fastcatch verbalized through his abacus. Patel reached out to grab Fastcatch's dorsal fin with one hand, looking back at the submersibles that were almost upon him now. Fastcatch shot forward like a golden arrow from the bow of Opis. Patel's hand almost slipped off the slick surface of Fastcatch's fin, as the dolphin accelerated toward the sphere. Patel quickly shifted his position and desperately grabbed the fin with his second hand, too. Fastcatch could feel Patel's inability to hold on and slowed his desperate race towards the sphere. As Fastcatch was plunging them through the membrane of the sphere, one of the submersibles shot out a dart-like projectile, which was connected to a thin cable. It tagged Patel's calf. He immediately felt a shock run up his leg and into his body and involuntarily released Fastcatch's fin. A split second later, a long and impossibly strong tentacle shot out from the sphere, took hold of Patel's waist, and jerked him the rest of the way inside the membrane. Patel felt searing pain in his head where his cybernetic implant was located, saw swirling pearlescent beads of light all around him, felt the slight pressure of motion, and then all went black.

# CHAPTER 13

# DESCENT

The conference abord *Xanthus* between the humans, AIs, and Enneans did not last long. As the six of them bobbed up and down in one of the aquatic chambers of the Enneans—with the AIs attending virtually—Proteus informed them that a human, dolphin, and Ennean had escaped Station-1 and were headed toward the device at the southern pole. A dolphin and another Ennean were headed toward the device at the northern pole.

"How do you know this?" asked Saddiq.

"I am monitoring the communications of Station-1. I believe it is Fastcatch, Patel, and Benthesikyme who are headed south—in an Ennean sphere. They should arrive in a couple of hours. And Professor Sun and Triton will arrive at the northern device around the same time. Perhaps a little less time, accounting for the various currents at play in their trajectories."

"Benthesikyme?" inserted Taitano.

"Yes," replied Proteus, "I am not sure we have the time for me to explain the prolix familial relationships between Enneans, which completely lack a frame of reference with EROC-lings. We gave her that name to make things easier for you humans and dolphins, who tend to cognize relationships consanguineously. In terms you are used to, Triton and Benthesikyme are brother and sister."

"Well," responded Taitano sarcastically, "thanks for dumbing it down for 'small creatures such as we,' Proteus."

"It is a skill, Dr. Taitano, that I have honed during my time working with humans and dolphins. You are most welcome," replied Proteus.

Taitano rolled her eyes and cracked an amused smile. Far from being offended, she was sincerely grateful that both AIs were treating her and the others as equal partners. If the AIs had decided to oppose them, there would have been precious little hope of stopping Church. "Look," said Taitano, "it's great that they're all headed toward the devices, but they're going to need our help; and, to be completely honest, they're going to need *my* help. I'm the one with hands-on experience in quantum cryptanalysis, and none of them has the expertise. This is not a matter of just plugging an abacus into the device, running sequences of numbers, and then pressing a button. The devices may even be rigged to do something drastic if tampered with. The only way to know is for me to go down there and see what's going on."

Saddiq thought for a moment and then added, "Am I right, Nereus, that the devices are not interfaced with Station-1's systems?"

Nereus replied, "You are correct, Captain. Totally air gapped—or, rather, in this case: water gapped." The sentient AI somehow managed to program the anterior part of her massive holographic sea cucumber body to look pensive, while she was running multiple cause and effect simulations to generate options for how to achieve their objective.

Saddiq added, "I know Dr. Taitano's abilities, and I know Church. I think she's right. She needs to be down there. Moreover, even if we were able to project either Nereus or Proteus's program far enough down to the lower crust to reach the devices, Church would be able to easily interfere with their remote interface by using one of the buoys housed in the upper crust. There's only one way: we need a physical body down there."

Nereus queried, "Are the shuttles working?"

Proteus momentarily glanced off into the distance and then looked back to the group, "Mechanically, yes. At least they should be. They are overdue for their monthly maintenance checks, as lately I have been rather occupied calibrating *Xanthus* to house our Ennean captives. I am therefore a trifle behind the normal maintenance schedule. However, Church and Tiberius remotely locked out the operating systems of the shuttles the moment they realized I was no longer under their control. Again, quite clever of them, I must admit."

Taitano felt a stir in the water and gentle liquid currents of movement towards the back of the chamber. Lugubriously, an Ennean oozed out of the recesses of the chamber and drifted into the center of the space. The alien's mutable mass was surrounded by Nereus, Proteus, Saddiq, and Taitano. Its body was easily two to three times the size of a human, depending upon its shape at any given time. It was not a static form, but ever shifting—a shibboleth of light and shadow. Its appendages began to trace ovoid shapes, and a hologram appeared before them depicting the outline of Ross 128b. The image zoomed in with dizzying speed to the northern polar region. The image was now on the rocky surface of the planet, where Taitano could perceive a crevasse-like tunnel in the rock. Along the inner sides of the breach were long silvery veins of some type of metallic substance in long parallel lines.

Saddiq watched the images with intense attention and then postulated, "I think I know what our Ennean friend is showing us. This must be one of the naturally occurring tunnels that the Enneans used to construct the first spheres to come to Earth-Ocean. It's a way into the Ocean. But, without the shuttles, we have no way of getting down there, as there are no orbital tethers at the poles." Saddiq displayed obvious signs of frustration at their impotence, but was trying to remain professional and detached. He envied the Ennean its outward placidity and apparent lack of emotion.

Taitano was silent for a moment, thinking, and then added, "But we *do* have a shuttle. Proteus said they were mechanically fine; it's just their operating software that's compromised, right?"

Proteus responded, "Yes, that is correct."

Nereus programmed another worried look on the anterior portion of her holographic body and pleaded, "Now just a minute, Tai. Please don't propose what my generative probability index tells me you are about to propose."

"Well, what do you think I'm about to propose?"

"That someone manually pilot the shuttle from the ship to the surface, enter the crevasse, somehow access the Ocean, and then swim to the lower surface of the Ocean to disable the device, as Proteus's probability matrix must have also already anticipated."

Taitano smiled broadly, "I didn't know your interplexed heuristic cognitive matrix enabled you to read minds, Nereus. I'm *impressed*."

"It wasn't mind reading. I simply interfaced my probability generation scenario program with your consistent pattern of four-dimensional reasoning and predilection for placing yourself in extraordinarily high-risk situations, cross-referenced the results with your devil-may-care attitude toward your own personal safety, chose the most perilous outcome possible, and came out with this crazy plan."

An involuntary laugh escaped Taitano, "That's close enough to mind reading for me."

Her smile wilted, and she turned inward—more serious. *I am so incredibly sick and disgusted by humans destroying another group of people for the sake of our own pathetic survival. At some point, survival isn't enough. We have to deserve to survive. Otherwise, what's the point of it all? If we have food, shelter, air, culture—but it comes at the cost of another group's autonomy, or even lives …. I mean,* really, *this is not the twentieth and twenty-first centuries with their world wars, nuclear arsenals, market economies, mass murder, and driving entire species to extinction for no good reason other than path dependence. When are we going to grow up and act like we're part of a community that includes beings other than ourselves? Once again, we are dominating another species through force and violence. Like grandpa said, it was only a handful of generations ago that my ancestors tried to wipe out an entire group of their own kind and dominate an entire continent, if not the world. I am* not *going to let that happen again here—on another world, in a star system lightyears away from Earth-Ocean. It's ridiculous. It's going to stop here. I can't let my fear get in the way. My entire life has been building up to this moment. All that education and training to get my OCD under control. This is what it was all for.*

"I'm doing this," she finally said. "I *need* to do this. I'm going down there. I can pilot the shuttle alone. No one has to do this with me."

The Ennean continued to undulate in the chamber, its body rising and falling with the currents permeating the liquid in which they were all suspended.

Saddiq nodded.

Nereus considered simulating a tear to drop from her eye, but then remembered that sea cucumbers don't have eyes and that, even if they did, her hologram was being projected into a tank of water—thus making lamentation a bit pointless.

Proteus stood as still as an ancient caryatid upon the Acropolis of Athens, his stare fixed upon the transparent barrier on the other side of which floated Ross 128b, sedately suspended in its tidally locked orbit. As he continued to glare at the planet, he uttered in a soft whisper, "I can pilot the shuttle. Nereus can handle things up here." Turning back to the others, he said, "We need to keep a close eye on *Ardanwen* and *Xanthus*. It is of central importance that the Enneans up here are safe and can return to their home if we are successful.

Nereus can temporarily replace me here on *Xanthus* and manage both ships' systems."

Saddiq suddenly interjected, "Before we implement this rather daring plan, there's something else you all need to know. Nereus, tell them."

"Yes, well, I'm not sure how to say this, so I'll just say it." They all stared at Nereus, waiting for her to continue. Saddiq looked apprehensive; Taitano impatient. Proteus was inscrutable, as were the Enneans. Nereus pressed on, "Right, well, I've been collecting data for some time on Ennea, and now that Proteus is back in the fold, the two of us just ran some data comparisons right before this meeting between my data sets and the ones that he's been collecting on the devices over the last several months. Temperature readings, mineral concentrations, and—importantly—seismic data on the mantle of Ennea, which is, of course, below the Ocean and lower crust of the planet." Nereus paused to program (and then implement) her holographic sea cucumber body to slowly inflate and then deflate, simulating a sigh of sorts. She continued, "Proteus and I have determined, with 98.96 percent accuracy, that the devices—in addition to aquaterraforming the Ocean to make it more suitable for cyanobacteria and ultimately human and dolphin colonization—are also having another, slightly more disturbing effect."

Nereus paused again. Everyone stared at her, even the Enneans, it seemed.

Taitano blurted out, "Well, what is it, Nereus? It's not like we have a lot of time here. Can this wait until later? We need to get down there to stop the devices before Church gets wise to us."

"Well," replied Nereus, "that's exactly the point and precisely why we're bringing this up now, Dr. Taitano. It is indeed imperative to immediately disable the devices. But not only for the reasons you are thinking."

"Nereus," urged Taitano in a grave tone, "I am seriously going to program a progressively disjunctive computing virus into your matrix if you don't come out already and tell us what the hell you're talking about. What *else* are the devices doing? Spill it already!" She was now barely managing to restrain herself from screaming. She began to rapidly tap the back of her helmet with her gloved index and middle fingers; she lost count of how many times.

"I can see," said Proteus, "that Dr. Taitano is almost past her stress-threshold, Nereus. You had better tell her before her psychological defense mechanisms become even more ineffective than usual."

Taitano, continuing to tap on the back of her helmet, drew her eyelids together so that they formed symmetrical slits on her face and tried to slow her breathing and calm her throbbing heartbeat.

"OK," said Nereus, "as I was trying to explain, we have just discovered that the personnel on the stations have made a grave error in their predictive studies of the geothermal powering of the devices. Although they did take into account the tidal heating of Ennea that results from the gravitational sheering from Ross 128, they've overestimated the amount of tectonic stress that the lower crust under the Ocean can withstand. In order to cut corners and reduce the amount of time needed to install the devices, they used computer modelling developed from deep-sea mining on Earth-Ocean; however, the mineral composition of Earth-Ocean's seabed is different than Ennea's. In particular, there is a much higher iron content on Earth-Ocean than there is on Ennea. Thus, to make a long story short, the conduits they drilled into the seabed to harness the radiogenic geothermal energy of the mantle are far less structurally stable than they thought. If the devices continue to draw energy from the mantle, the conduits will collapse and cause a planet-wide eruption of the mantle into the Ocean, which will most likely destroy the Ocean and everything in it. Moreover, we still need the stations on Ennea to finish preparing *Ardanwen* for her return trip to Earth-Ocean—not to mention Triton, our navigator, who is down there right now. Without both Triton and the stations, there's no way for any of us to get home."

Taitano stared at them in disbelief. She turned away and walked towards a viewport. She regarded the planet below them, around which *Xanthus* was holding at orbital station-keeping above the northern pole. The planet, the Enneans, *Xanthus*, herself: they were all so small, so insignificant. Minuscule motes of dust in an unimaginably vast Universe. And yet, it was life. Purpose. Meaning. Despite herself, a profound wave of fatigue, anxiety, and despair seized her. Out loud, she simply said, "Please tell me this is one of your cruel practical jokes, Nereus."

"I wish it were, Dr. Taitano."

"How long?" she breathed, as trepidation closed in upon her and squeezed her heart.

"If the devices remain active for just one more day—maybe two—it'll all be over."

Saddiq ventured, "We need to tell Church about this. It's a game-changer, for certain. He'll see reason and shut off the devices."

Taitano responded, "Maybe, maybe not. And what if he doesn't—or delays long enough so that it's too late? I don't trust Church. He seems too far gone to be rational."

"Let's go down there and confront him face-to-face," countered Saddiq.

Taitano considered it for a moment and then said, "And what if he locks us up and won't listen to us? For even 24 hours. It's all over then. We can't give up control of this situation. We need to act."

Saddiq responded, "Well, at least we can warn everyone down there. Nereus, Proteus, can we get a signal through to them?"

Proteus looked away for a moment, mimicking a human mannerism, and then replied, "No, Tiberius has locked out all incoming communications traffic to all four stations. The only way we were able to get that message to Professor Sun a little while ago was because he was outside of the station and had the presence of mind to activate his long-range transceiver."

"OK, Proteus," said Taitano, "time for us to go for a little ride together."

Saddiq grasped Taitano's hand in both of his, not aggressively, but with intention, "Agana, I'm coming with you."

Taitano looked down in thoughtful reflection at their entwined hands, and she could feel a warmth spreading into her cheeks. "Abdul-Noor, I've thought about that, as it's obvious no one should be alone down there. But think about it." She peeled her eyes from their hands and met his, with courage and determination. "You need to stay up here and be ready—if we fail—to somehow figure out a way to take one of the ships back to Earth-Ocean to let everyone know what's happened here. You and Nereus will need each other to do that, not to mention a new Ennean navigator from *Xanthus*. We already discussed why Nereus or Proteus can't make it down to the device. I thought of trying to download an avatar of one of them into my abacus, but it just doesn't have the quantum storage capacity. Besides, we only have one maintenance shuttle ready to go, it only seats one, and ..." she said with a wink to try to lighten the ponderous moment, "I'm a much better swimmer than you."

Saddiq remained deadly serious, "But the thought of you down there alone—all by yourself."

"There's nothing for it, Abdul. And besides," she placed her second hand on his now, "aren't we all alone when we really get down to it? Isn't that why we need *this*?" She gave his hands a reassuring squeeze. *Connection.*

The small maintenance shuttle plummeted towards the surface of the planet, its heat shield rapidly reaching maximum tolerance level. Proteus unswervingly piloted the craft downwards, but he was worried about the alarming rise in the temperature within the cramped cockpit. He had downloaded an avatar of his program into the primary computer core of the tiny ship; and his original program lay dormant up above in *Xanthus's* memory core, while Nereus took care of both *Ardanwen* and *Xanthus's* operations in his temporary absence.

"Why's it so damn hot in here? It's forty-five degrees! If not for my suit ..." Taitano half-shouted, the discomfort and fear clear in the distressed modulation of her voice.

Proteus answered, "This is the shuttle in the best state of repair at the moment. It recently suffered some minor damage in a solar storm emanating from Ross 128. It was scheduled to be repaired this week, but events rather overtook that plan. The heat shield is only functioning at eighty-nine percent of its normal operating capacity. I am sorry about that, Dr. Taitano. I am confident that your suit can handle the temperature differential."

"Good thing you gave me a new suit then! My previous one was busted up pretty badly." Something exploded in the back of the shuttle. In the vacuum of space, the shock of the blast reverberated through the hull of the small ship and jolted Taitano's back molars. "What the hell was that?"

"That," responded Proteus serenely, "was the primary entry thruster exploding due to a fuel leak. We are now in an uncontrolled free fall towards Ross 128b."

Taitano's stomach dropped, and her heart began to race. She tried to calm her body and mind and assess the situation. If she had not needed both hands at the control panel to help Proteus keep the shuttle from going into an uncontrollable spin, she would have begun to tap the back of her helmet. She felt an incredibly potent compulsion to release her right hand from the controls in order to tap the back of her head, but resisted the obsessive urge to do so. She asked Proteus, "Is there a parachute in this thing?"

"Yes, indeed," replied Proteus. "I do understand the human psychological defense mechanism of humor in stressful situations, but

I don't think this is the time …"

"Where is it?" she shouted, cutting him off.

"Under your seat."

Taitano ripped the package from under the seat, carefully strapped it onto her back, and found the eject button on the console in front of her. "Proteus, listen to me very carefully; and don't take the apprehensive and near panic in my voice as a bad sign. I am very focused and rational right now." The temperature continued to climb in the cabin and now reached fifty degrees Celsius. Her suit was unable to compensate for the external heat, and she could feel the inside of her suit beginning to burn her skin. She took three long breaths and spoke in as calm and controlled a way as possible, "Proteus, here is what we are going to do: you're going to remotely take control of the thrusters on my suit, I'm going to eject, and then you're going to guide me to the crevasse. You have to keep me as close to the access port of the crevasse as possible, so that I don't have a long hike once I get to the surface. If I do, I'll run out of air before I get to the crevasse. I'm taking a reserve electrolyzer with me, but that only works in water, not the vacuum of space. So, you need to keep me on course and tell me the exact moment I need to deploy the parachute to slow my descent and hit the target. I can't calculate that myself, even using the abacus." She paused. Nothing from Proteus. "Are you getting all this?"

"Yes," was all Proteus said.

"Good, because this is mostly up to you now, until I get to the surface. After I have landed, the shuttle will be close behind. You have to manage to steer it away from my landing site, so it doesn't kill me when it hits the surface; and, before it does, you need to transfer the remote copy of your program back to *Xanthus*, so the avatar's memory engrams can synch back up with, and report back to, the mother copy on the ship. If I don't make it, the others will need to know. You got all that?" Taitano began to irrationally succumb to a waking fantasy of hitting the eject button, ripping off her environmental suit, and floating through the frozen vacuum of space—just to be free of the fatal heat of the shuttle's interior.

Proteus replied, "A good plan—under these particularly dire circumstances, that is."

"Great. And, Proteus, before I hit this button, there's one more thing I need you to do once your program is transferred back to the ship."

Taitano, a fiery comet, streaked towards the barren brown surface of the planet. Her skin burned all over. *First degree burns only, I think. Just feels like a mild sunburn. If I'd stayed in that shuttle a moment longer, could've been much worse.* Proteus—by means of remotely made micro-adjustments to the thrusters in her suit—guided her free fall towards the kilometer-long crevasse. At the same time, he steered the shuttle away from the landing site, but not so far that his remote signal to her suit would be interrupted. It was a delicate balance. He ran, and then re-ran, the calculations through his matrix to ensure that he could stay with her as long as possible, but also get the shuttle far enough away so that, when it landed, the explosion did not harm her. The margin of error was minute, and only an AI could have managed it.

Taitano began to make out rock formations and wondered when Proteus would trigger her to deploy the parachute to check her velocity. She waited patiently, becoming more and more anxious of the surface swiftly approaching. The euphoria of no longer being cooked alive in her suit made her strangely giddy, and her anxieties were unexpectedly under control—at least for the moment. She consulted the altimeter on her abacus; it read two kilometers. She waited some more. "Proteus? How's it going up there. You still with me?"

"Yes, Dr. Taitano. I am here. Due to the distance between us, your velocity relative to the shuttle, and the thermionic differences between you and the surrounding atmosphere, it is becoming increasingly difficult for me to interface with your suit to guide your descent. You will be on your own in about ten seconds. If you do not hear from me any further, deploy your parachute in exactly fourteen seconds, and then guide yourself down if necessary. Good ..."

The transmission was cut off.

*Thirteen, twelve, eleven.* She started to count in her head. Her thoughts and fears began to interrupt her counting. *Damn. Missed a second. Nine, eight, seven. Focus! Five, four, three, two, one!* She gently pulled on the old-fashioned, failsafe cord on the strap of her chute. Her body shot violently upwards, and she immediately went into an uncontrolled spin. She tried to level her descent by manually activating her suit's thrusters, but was unable to balance the thrust from the different emitters and was sent into an even more acute spin. *No luck.* The thin atmosphere of Ennea provided less resistance to the chute than would have been the case on Earth-Ocean (with its comparatively denser layer of gases), and so her free fall was faster than she had expected. The greater gravitational pull of Ennea, due to its larger mass, did not help either. She pulled on the cords of her sail to try to control the spin and right herself. That worked better than the thrusters. *It's working!* She felt her spine begin to elongate with the increased gravity, as she hung from the straps of the sail and drifted in a graceful arc above the crevasse. *OK, all good. Proteus was right in his calculations. This is going to work!*

About two-hundred meters from the surface, she saw a yellow and blue explosion in the distance. Like Mjöllnir, hammer of the gods, a shockwave of superheated plasma and kinetic energy slammed into her, right before she was about to make a controlled landing on the surface of the planet along the edge of the crevasse. She was swept off the edge of the precipice and down its rapacious maw. As she plunged down the chasm, her parachute caught on a rock, violently arresting her fall, but sending her careening back into the side of the vertical wall of the abyss. She tried to angle her ventral surface towards the rock face, but did not manage in time. Rather than making contact with the vertical surface of rock with the soles of her boots, the side of her foot caught the impact, wrenching her left ankle at an acute angle. Blazing pain radiated up her leg and into her hip. She rebounded off the rock face and gently swung side to side, suspended over the abyss, pulled down toward the bottom of the fissure by the gravity of Ross 128b. *Bad, bad, bad, bad, bad* …. She slightly regained her composure. *But could have been so much worse.* She could already feel her amygdala sending signals to her hypothalamus and pituitary gland to produce endogenous morphines—more commonly known as "endorphins." That, along with the adrenalin coursing through her cardiovascular system, enabled her to partially filter out the reception of the unpleasant stimuli shooting up the radial pain nerves in her left ankle. She activated the lamp on the left arm of her suit and scanned the area. Ten meters away, she saw the silvery cerulean beams of metal, which the Ennean on *Xanthus* had shown to them in the holographic projection. They ran up and down in parallel to each other. She inspected the metallic beams more closely and saw an access port between two of the struts. She swung herself to the almost vertical wall of the chasm and began to climb towards the portal, her left foot dangling from her, useless. *Thank goodness this rock face is heavily crenelated, so I have foot and hand holds. Otherwise, this would be impossible.* Still, she had to be extremely careful not to slip, as she cradled her left ankle and tried to make her way to the portal to her right.

After several stressful and strenuous minutes of bouldering across the wall of the abyss, single-footed, she reached the portal. The access panel had symbols native to the Enneans. She activated her abacus to interface with it and ran a standard decryption algorithm. It opened, right at the same time her suit issued a warning chirp that she had two minutes of oxygen left in the auxiliary air module she had snatched from the maintenance shuttle before she had hastily disembarked it. She immediately pulled the lever to open the hatch, entered, closed it behind her, and triggered the decompression sequences. Water flooded the chamber; her electrolyzer began to break water molecules into hydrogen and oxygen and feed the latter back into her suit. *Now that's more like it. The breath of life.*

She triggered the door mechanism with her abacus and entered a long passage, completely filled with water. *So, I've gone from the weightless vacuum of space straight back into the water, where the rest of this journey will take place. Why do all those people in science fiction stories seem to have their feet on dry land most of the time? Although, with my busted ankle, it may turn out to be an asset.* Man weiß nie, wofür es gut ist. *Go ask an Ennean.* She swam through the passage for about five-hundred meters, before it gently curved "down" relative to the center of the planet. Her velocity increased as Ross 128b's gravity pulled her through the narrow tube. She set the altimeter on her abacus. After a few minutes, it measured one-point-five kilometers below the outer surface of the planet. The inner surface of the tube was rock that had been polished smooth, like a shiny rock her grandfather had purchased for her in an old shell shop—after she had pleaded with him that she just "had to have it!" There was no illumination in the tube; her suit's external lighting reflected off metallic strips embedded in the tube. *Funny, I would have thought being inside a giant straw from which there's no escape would cause me to panic, but Ennean engineering and architecture are so soothing. It makes me feel snug and secure. Strange. Not that I'm complaining or anything. It's nice for once not to be freaking out about something. Just wish my ankle wasn't falling off.*

A few seconds later, Taitano reached another hatch. She scanned the hatch's command interface and set the auto-decoding sequence to try to open it. It didn't work. She sat on the hatch for a moment, thinking. She started to obsess about where she was, as her situation began to sink in and hit her. So far below the surface. Confined.

Trapped. The pace of her respiration increased, and she felt her heart banging against the inside of her sternum. Her stomach dropped, and she began to feel nauseated. *No, this is not happening now. Not … happening … now! I am not my emotions. Emotions come and go like clouds in the sky. Never fixed, always changing. Focus on thinking like an Ennean. They made this tunnel and portal. How would they open it? Your abacus worked to open the upper hatch to get in here. So why isn't it working to get into the Ocean? The Ocean has no beginning and no end. It is one continuous arc, never-ending. Never-ending …. Wait a minute!* She set her abacus to emit a transmission of the repeating integers of the golden ratio and then let it run for a minute: 1.618033988749894848 2045868343656381177203091798057628621354486227052604628 1890244970720720418939113748475408807538689175212663386 2223536931793180060766726354433389086595939582905638322 6613199282902678806752087668925017116962070322210432162 6954862629631361443814975870122034080588795445474924618 5695364864449241044320771344947049565846788509874339442 2125448770664780915884607499887124007652170575179788341 6625624940758906970400028121042762177111777805315317141 0117046665991466979873176 …. *Come on. Come on. Open, damn it.* Nothing happened. She started to panic again and to visualize her suit's electrolyzer failing and herself drowning, trapped in the tunnel. Her courage kicked in, as did her indomitable sense of self-preservation. *Nope. That's not going to happen. Not going there, not doing that now. Think like an Ennean, you idiot. Think like an Ennean. What is a sequence of numbers common to both our cultures? Of course! I'm such an idiot. Wait, no, that's negative self-talk. I'm not an idiot. I'm a genius!* Taitano began to key in commands to her abacus. She manually input the first nine digits of the Fibonacci sequence through her small but powerful computer—0, 1, 1, 2, 3, 5, 8, 13, 21—and then converted it from base ten into base *nine*: 0, 1, 1, 2, 3, 5, 8, *14, 23*. She then converted the Earth-Ocean integers to Ennean symbols and transmitted them to the hatch's command interface. She heard the sound of bolts moving and being retracted from slots in the hatch. *Duh! Of course, it would be in base nine and their own script! The golden ratio is the same for all of us, but the symbolic expression of it differs. The lock was made by Enneans for goodness' sake!* She gave the hatch a firm push, and the aperture peeled back in a radial motion. *Did it! You rule, Agana. Think like an Ennean! OK, yes, this would be embarrassing if anyone ever found out I talked to myself like this, but if there were ever a situation for positive self-talk, then this is it. Whatever works, right?* She briefly wondered if it counted as talking to oneself if one were only *thinking* the words and not actually vocalizing them.

She wriggled through the retracted aperture, and Ennea's gravity pulled her down into its Ocean. She let herself slowly descend and allowed her mind and body to acclimate to the alien environment. She checked her abacus's gauges, which were connected to the outer sensors of her suit. It was minus twenty degrees Celsius. Her suit's power consumption began to dip as it diverted increased energy to warm the atmosphere within the suit to keep her from instantly freezing to death. The salinity was Ennean standard, save for the increased concentration of selenium. There was almost no illumination, save for a faint, sickly glow in the fathomless depths far below her.

She let her body sink and gave herself over to gravity and distance.

She tried to calm her breathing and slow her heart rate; her attempts to pierce the layers of water below her with her sensors failed to detect the device, which should have been only a couple of kilometers below her current position. *That's weird, I should be able to pick up a medium-sized metallic object, even through this much water. I should be detecting the device; but there's nothing. I wonder why .... Well, there's nothing to do now, but to get as far to the lower surface as I can and see if I can find it once I get deeper.*

She continued to plunge deeper into the unimaginably vast mass of alien water, towards a faintly luminescent glow below—which reminded her of noctilucent clouds back on Earth-Ocean. As she gazed downwards, she began to see speckled gaps in the lambency, which she could now discern was a band of silver radiance. She posited that she was approaching, from above, the selenium layer encircling the planet; but what were those dark interference patterns drifting in ordered sequence between her and the selenium stream, like clouds casting shadows over a wheatfield on Earth-Ocean?

Her thoughts were interrupted by her suit's alarm sounding in her ear. "Warning, electrolyzer failure. Estimated time of oxygen depletion three minutes. Unable to switch to backup system at the present time. Suggest finding alternative oxygen supply as soon as possible."

*What!?!* Her heart began to race again. "Computer, what is causing this malfunction?"

"The electrolyzer was damaged by a high force impact with a hard object."

*When I hit the side of the crevasse. Damn!* "Why didn't you tell me this *before* we entered a giant ocean from which there was no escape!?!"

"Internal diagnostics have also been damaged and thus were unavailable to detect the malfunction before it became critical."

*OK, Agana, think.* "Computer, how long to ascend back to the hatch?"

"Five minutes."

*Oh, no.* She started to panic, her breathing becoming irregular. *Oh, no. I can't go back. Not enough air left to make it back to the hatch. Even if I did, my electrolyzer is not working. What am I going to do?* "Computer, can you engage the backup?"

"As I said, I cannot engage the backup."

"Are you sure?"

"I cannot be certain, as the internal diagnostics are damaged."

"Well try it anyway!"

A few moments went by. "As requested, I have attempted to engage

216

the backup electrolyzer; but the oxygen levels are unchanged. It is reasonable to conclude that the backup electrolyzer is damaged as well."

She took long deep breaths. She exhaled for a count of eight: *One, two, three, four, five, six, seven, eight.* She breathed in deeply: *one, two, three, four.* She held her breath: *one, two, three, four, five, six, seven.* She repeated this cycle five times. She began to feel calmer and in control of her faculties. Having gotten her breathing under control, she now took one long deep breath and held it for as long as she could, trying to make each molecule of $O_2$ count. She filled her lungs, mouth, and nasal cavities to capacity. Was it her imagination—or could she feel her lungs and chest being compressed by the outside pressure, her spleen pumping extra red blood cells into her bloodstream, the capillaries in her extremities constricting to shunt blood to her vital organs? She had left the world of air and sun behind and was now deliquesced into a fluidic world of penumbral twilight. Her rational mind struggled to envisage a surface of breathable air above her, but this was only possible on Earth-Ocean; she was on a different world where the concept of "surface" had no meaning. There *was* no surface, no such boundary between water and air. There was only one, continuous, infinite ocean. She started to panic at this thought. *There is no escape. Even if I were to swim "up" and back towards the upper surface of the Ocean, it wouldn't matter. I would only bump my head against cold, unyielding rock as I suffocated and waited till the searing pain in my lungs rendered me unconscious and then I drowned.*

She banished such thoughts from her mind and replaced them with renewed focus on the task before her. *Those shadows below. Something must be blocking the light coming from the selenium stream. There must be* something *down there between me and the stream. I can't go up. I doubt I can repair an electrolyzer in time and while floating here. Only one thing to do. Find the shadows and hope they lead to something that can help. Better than just floating here and suffocating.*

She up-ended herself into a downward dive, throwing her hips and legs up and her arms straight down—imagining herself as an arrow shot from the bow of Camilla. She streamed down, directly aiming herself for the largest shadow in her field of view. The haunting adumbration below her grew larger and more encompassing, until it completely blocked out the illumination coming from the selenium stream below. Her proximity alarm signaled that she was nearing a solid surface. She slowed her descent, turned herself one-hundred and eighty degrees, just as her feet struck an uneven surface; a sharp spasm of pain shot through her injured ankle and radiated up into her leg. She fought to control the apprehension that crashed upon her. When the throbbing had subsided a bit, she found herself tenuously balancing upon an enormous floating boulder. *What the hell is this?* She strained her vision past the boulder into the distance and saw a series of them, lined up in an arced plane, a kind of intertidal ring of asteroids orbiting the planet's core, suspended in a layer of the Ocean. She wondered at the dynamic oceanographic forces that could have created and maintained such a thing. She sensed no motion, and the rocks were perfectly suspended in place, like a dark crown set upon the head of the sea. *Does this chain of rocks encircle the entire Ocean? Is it natural or constructed? And by whom? The Enneans would have no use for such a structure. So what's it for? What would Enneans need with a ring of floating rocks? And how does one get rocks to float anyway?*

She activated her abacus and scanned the enormous rock beneath her feet. She was surprised to find a hatch on the upper surface about twenty meters away, but only slightly surprised, as her mind was becoming numb to the mysteries this planet presented to her. She limped along the crenelated surface, wincing when she had to scramble over larger ridges of jagged rock, while trying not to rupture her suit on their sharp edges. She reached the portal. It was of a different design than the one she had used to enter the Ocean; it was not of alien design, but instead looked almost exactly like the hatches used in Old Earth sea vessels; heavy, dull metal in the shape of a circle, with a wheel one could turn to open and close it. She turned it counterclockwise. *Righty tighty, lefty loosey.* She turned the wheel as far as it could go, pried open the hatch, floated inside, and then sealed it shut behind her. On the wall was a simple environmental control panel, with Earth-Ocean controls to depressurize and repressurize the chamber by replacing the water of the entryway with a nitrogen-oxygen mixture, perfectly balanced to Earth-Ocean standard. *Well, this is not a coincidence, for sure.* She read the oxygen gauge on her suit. One more minute of breathable air in her suit's system, with the electrolyzer having completely stopped working. Without delay, she triggered the environmental de-re-compression procedure on the control panel: a three-minute countdown began on the wall panel. *OK, I have to make it for about three minutes with whatever I have left in my suit and lungs.* She focused her mind on breathing as slowly as humanly possible in order to conserve the oxygen in her bloodstream. She visualized the alveoli of her lungs expelling every last molecule of carbon dioxide and absorbing every last atom of oxygen. She pictured the $CO_2$ and $O_2$ exchange in her blood stream and pictured her lungs super-saturated with the life-giving gases of her home planet, which seemed like a forgotten paradise—a fragile, remote oasis in the sterile desert of the galaxy, so distant now that it seemed lost to her forever. She was an unimaginably insignificant dab of sinew—adrift in an alien wasteland and infinitely unsuited for survival in a place so hostile to life. These bleak thoughts were both a burden and solace to her, for they forced her to acknowledge that her life still mattered (at least to her). She was compelled by an innate, uncontrollable compulsion to survive, for as long as possible.

"Oxygen supply has been depleted," her suit helpfully informed her.

Taitano opened her eyes just enough to glance at the chronometer on the wall panel. It read two minutes and twenty-six seconds. *I can do this. I can do this. I can do this. Just relax. My heart is beating slowly and steadily.* (She removed "my breathing is slow and smooth" from her normal mantra, for obvious reasons.) *My heart is beating slowly and steadily. I am encased in a glowing orb of nourishing light and air. The sun is streaming down and warming my face. I am completely at peace and at one with my environment.* She lost herself in these affirmations and incantations. She seemed to slow, and then stop, the linear progression of time, itself. There was only this one eternal moment in time.

Her lungs began to tingle.

She looked at the wall chronometer again. Twenty-three seconds. *I can do this. My lungs are floating on the wind.* Fifteen seconds. The tingle in her lungs became an ache. *The pain in my lungs is weakness leaving the body and being replaced by a nourishing flood of contentment and joy.* Eight seconds. The ache became a burn. Four, three, two, one. A green light illuminated on the wall panel, with a message: "Cycle completed." She frantically ripped off her helmet and gasped for air. It came flooding into her lungs. Joy. Pure joy. *Breathing is the best thing in the world. The only thing in the world. I will never be unhappy again. As long as I can breathe, everything is OK.* She collapsed to her hands and knees on the floor of the decompression chamber, trying to slow her respiration and pulsating heart. She violently wept, as the emotions of fear and joy vied with each other within her.

A minute later, she mustered the strength and presence of mind to open the inner hatch by way of another wheel and slowly pushed it open. She was met by a rush of cold, crisp air. It chilled her face and head, and immediately began to dry her dripping raven hair, which was splayed across her face and shoulders. She reconfigured her flippers into boots with an agile command to her abacus and stepped outside onto a metal platform, her boots echoing in the cavernous enclosure. Point source emitters of white and yellow illumination automatically popped on in sequence along the walls of an immense expanse of space that had, presumably, been hollowed out of the great rock in some incredible way. She could not tell whether the structure was a natural geological formation or a construct. Perhaps it was a combination of the two. She turned around in a three-hundred-and-sixty-degree circle. The ceiling was not far above her position upon the metal platform right outside of the decompression chamber. Although the length of the cavern was lost in darkness and she could not determine where it ended, the width was no more than twenty meters across, and she estimated that the bottom was around the same distance below her. There was a stairway leading downwards to the floor below; it did not escape her observation that the dimensions of the stairs were perfectly suited for a human's legs: the stairs had clearly been fashioned for humans, as was the atmosphere. She slowly descended the stairs, which were formed in a tight spiral—her footfalls echoing into the distance of the cathedral-like expanse. She supported herself on the railings to her right and left to take the pressure off her aching ankle. It was utterly silent, and a cool current of air circulated through the space. Without her suit's heaters, she would have been hypothermic in a matter of minutes; although her face and head were burned by the chill of the place, her body remained relatively warm inside her suit. There were no odors. Just good, clean air. Her lungs continued to rejoice in the oxygen that bathed the hundreds of millions of alveoli at the end of her bronchial tubes. After she had reached the bottom of the stairs, she began to walk along the outer wall of the chamber. She kept to a smooth path along the wall: it somehow felt more comforting to have a wall beside her, rather than walking down the center of the massive cavern. The level pathway also saved her ankle from negotiating the rough stone floor of the center of the structure.

After a few minutes, she came to another path that bisected the floor widthwise and led to a raised dais with five stone structures upon it. The height of the raised platform prevented her from seeing its upper surface. *What the heck is all this? Not made for Enneans or even dolphins, that's for sure. This is strictly human—or, at the very least, for bipeds. Whether it was made for or by humans, can't tell from here. Maybe there's something on top of those structures that can explain what this is all about.* She crept along the path that lay orthogonally from the cave wall; as she neared the elevated stone structures in the center of the cavern, she could see metal steps set into each of the five stone structures, by which one could climb to the top. She was drawn to the one in the middle; she knew not why. As she ascended the steps, she caved to a compulsion to reach to the back of her skull and tap, five times in quick succession with her index and middle fingers, the skin behind her right ear. She cautiously made her way up the steps, for there were no railings, and the lack of an opportunity to take weight off her ankle made the going rough. When she had limped to the top, she peered over the upper lip of the rock casing. On top of the structure lay a sheet of translucent polymer material; through this, she could see the naked bodies of two humans: one male and one female; quite old, probably in their late nineties. Maybe even centenarians. Whether the humans were sleeping or dead, she could not tell. The expressions on their faces were ones of tranquility. There were no marks on the bodies, which reposed in relaxed, serene positions—undecayed and preserved.

*This is no cenotaph.*

She ran a potassium-argon dating test on the polymer surface of what she was now thinking of as a sepulcher. It read ninety-eight-point-six thousand years old. *One-hundred thousand years old?* She ran the test again using carbon dating. Same result. *How can that be? How did they get here? Who are they? Humans were using stone tools that long ago, not traveling to other worlds. This makes no sense.* She removed her gloves and ran the naked fingers of her left hand along the upper edge of the sarcophagus, feeling an unmistakable connection to ages past.

She climbed atop the sarcophagus structure to get a look at the other four tombs, which were also inhabited by pairs of hominid bodies. She descended the steps, intending to inspect the four other sarcophagi, but her ankle throbbed in red waves of pain—so she only walked past the other structures from the path along the cavern floor.

Her ankle began to throb so intensely that she lost concentration and was immersed in a wave of dizziness. She sank to the ground, her knees driving hard into the solid stone floor. More pain electrified her body. *OK, my body is telling me to take care of this ankle.* She gingerly crawled, now a quadrupedal creature, to a flat area of rock. She tried to remove her left boot, but it would not budge. She pulled with all her might; in a stab of searing pain, the boot came flying off her foot and struck her in the mouth. *Stupid!* Her ankle was red and badly swollen. She accessed a sealed pocket of her suit and found a subdermal analgesic applicator; she placed it against the most painful part of her ankle and activated it. The drug was injected through her dermis into the injured tissues below. After a few moments, the pain receded. *Thank goodness. Now I can think.* She took a drink of water from a tube lashed to the side of her helmet. Her ankle began to grow numb, either from the cold of the cavern or the pain inhibitor. She knew not which. She reluctantly put her boot back on, thanking the stars, as she did so, for the pain medication; otherwise, she would not have been able to manage it.

She accessed the electrolyzer from her hip belt, inspected it, and keyed up a diagnostic sequence on her abacus to determine the source of the previous malfunction. While she waited for the diagnostic to initiate, she ruminated upon the device.

The mechanism and principles underlying the electrolyzer dated back to the eighteenth century and were not complicated; they had been rendered more efficient since then—and significantly more compact—so that they could power the systems needed for a modern-day environmental suit. She recalled the mid-twentieth century moving picture, *The Silent World*, made by Jacques Cousteau, who, along with Emile Gagnan, had invented the first modern demand regulator. Their invention untethered humans from clunky iron suits and surface breathing tubes that only stretched to shallow depths and paved the way for the Aqualung and self-contained underwater breathing apparatus (SCUBA). Cousteau's vision and practical skills opened up a new world in a way like never before and enabled humans to soar through the depths, if not as elegantly as their dolphin brethren, at least a little bit like them. Cousteau was not only in the vanguard of marine exploration, but also of the conservation of the sea. He spent his entire adult life raising the awareness of his fellow humans of the fragility of the Ocean and of the fact that all the water on Earth-Ocean was an exceedingly finite resource not to be squandered by dumping all of humanity's waste into the home of so many other species. Of course, it took several generations—not to mention a visit from aquatic alien lifeforms demanding preservation of the Ocean as the "price" to pay for saving humanity from a massive rogue solar flare—for all of this to fully sink into humanity's collective consciousness, but that was often the way with humans.

Her abacus chirped and then projected into the air before her a holographic display of the inner workings of the electrolyzer in diagrammatic form. The thin electrode that extended into the water cavity of the mechanism was represented in a deep magenta. The delicate wire was bent, most likely a result of her crash into the wall of the crevasse on the surface following the explosion of the shuttle. The wire was now touching the side of the chamber housing the reservoir of water; this contact now grounded the electric current that was supposed to run from the tip of the wire into the center of the water suspended in the cavity. She removed a small pair of needle-nose pliers from the tool kit suspended from the utility belt of her suit. She flattened herself on her belly, with her calves and feet dangling in the air, so that she could be close to the surface of the rock to reduce the chances of a piece of the electrolyzer falling and bouncing away, never to be seen again. She unlocked the watertight pressure seals at one end, unscrewed the top of the mechanism, and set it carefully on the smooth rock surface. She remembered when she was a kid, pumping air into her bicycle tire; after she had inflated the tire and was looking for the cap to the valve, it was nowhere to be found. *Where could it have gone? It didn't just up and walk away by itself.* But it always seemed to have somehow rolled away and travelled farther than was possible. It was like the cap had a mind of its own and desperately wanted to be liberated from its thankless and mundane task of keeping a tight seal on the valve of the tire. No matter how hard she tried, the cap always managed to escape. Or was she simply unable to remember where she had set it down to pump air into the tire? After having lost several valve caps in this manner, she finally decided to bring a cup with her and place the cap in the cup while she was refilling her tires with air. She did the same now with the top of the electrolyzer. She placed it carefully, and with great attention, inside her helmet, kept her eyes glued to it as she did so, and then tapped the helmet five times, saying out loud, "OK, I am now placing you inside my helmet. You are not going to roll away or get lost. I don't have to check again. I know you are in the helmet." She turned her head back to the electrolyzer, and the still sodden mass of her long hair smacked into the helmet, knocking it over and sending the cap of the electrolyzer flying into a crack in the floor. Taitano groaned in frustration, her greatest nightmare having now come to pass. She crawled over to the askew helmet, righted it, and peered down the crack. The electrolyzer top was precariously suspended between the two sides of the fissure, about twenty centimeters away, ready to fall into darkness. She took a long breath. She fished out of her utility belt a thin cable, which had a small hook on its end. She gingerly fed the cable down the crack, past the cap, hooked one of the cap's edges, and—holding her breath and with great intention—warily fished the cap back to the surface. Once she had the cap securely in her hand, she released the stale air from her lungs and half-laughed, half-huffed in exasperation. She then placed the cap back into her helmet, proceeded to draw a small knife from her utility belt, gathered her hair into a tight ponytail at the back of her head, and then—without hesitation—sawed it off and threw it against the wall in disgust. *Should've done that a long time ago. Stupid hair!*

She resumed studying the device, resisting the compulsive urge to check on the cap again, which she was beginning to doubt was still in the helmet. She spoke out loud to herself, "I do not have to check it again. I just put it in the damn helmet. It is safe and sound there. It's not going to spontaneously roll away and get lost. Well," she reflected, "according to quantum theory, the subatomic particles making up the individual atoms of the cap *could* actually randomly do that, but it is so statistically remote of a possibility that it is effectively impossible for my purposes." She paused. *OK, so now I really am talking to myself. So, it's official. I'm crazy.*

Taitano straightened the adduction node of the wire with the needle-nose pliers so that it was no longer touching the inner casing of the electrolyzer. She gently and deliberately retrieved the cap from her helmet and resealed it over the top of the mechanism. She triggered the self-diagnostic routine of the device and waited for the sequence to run. A few moments later, it signaled her that all the systems of the mechanism were nominal. *Yes! I rule. Back in business, baby!* She pulled the second, backup electrolyzer from a side pocket on the leg of her suit to see if she could fix it too, but it was shattered beyond any hope of repair. *Oh, well. I'll just have to make do with one. Now it's time to get out of here and get to that device. This particular anthropological puzzle is going to have to wait for later.* She scanned her surroundings with her abacus in an attempt to find any other apertures that may lead out of the atrium of rock. She immediately found one several meters further into the cavern, embedded in the floor. She guessed it led to the bottom surface of the rock. She limped towards it and soon found the hatch in the rocky floor. It was a circular hatch similar to the one through which she had entered via the ceiling of the chamber. She used the same method to access the locking mechanism and soon had it open. She made sure her suit's oxygen, pressure, and temperature levels were optimal and then entered the decompression chamber, sealed the hatch behind her, ran the cycle, and waited, as the chamber slowly filled with water.

When the cycle was complete, she turned the release on the inner hatch, pushed it open, reconfigured her boots into flipper mode with a swift command to her abacus, and swam down into the Ocean. She was immediately enveloped in almost utter darkness, save for the now familiar silver lambency of the selenium stream below her. An almost complete lack of light so profound that the darkness assumed a quality of tangibility that seeped into her body. She was disoriented, not able to discern "up" from "down"—as those terms had lost any meaning in this alien environment. The profundity of her situation pressed her down like a weight. She was acutely aware of the insignificance of her minuscule physical form in the vast expanse of water. *Well, at least I can be grateful that I'm not thalassophobic.* A sharp stab from her ankle interrupted her thoughts. *Sometimes pain can be a useful thing—it reminds us to focus on the present.* She set aside her useless and counterproductive ruminations about the nature of existence and her place within it and activated her abacus to triangulate her position in this foreign sea and locate the aquaterraforming device. She found it quickly, now that the rock-base was no longer between her and the device. She calculated a bearing on her wrist-mounted abacus and angled her head down towards the core of Ross 128b and the device. She was just barely able to discern that the inky water was faintly illuminated by the silvery, scintillating band of light below her. She swam toward the light, as an ancient sailor drawn towards the enchanting melody of a siren. The persistent ache in her ankle reminded her that her descent into the dark was no dream. She felt the water pressure on her suit increase the deeper she swam. As the pressure increased, her suit compensated, but her tissues were still compressed, reducing the profile of her already lithe body. As she sank, the planet's gravity tightened its grip upon her, the compression increased, and her buoyancy decreased—her descent quickened.

The sphere bearing Triton and Sun streaked through the selenium stream at incredible speed. They were headed towards the device at the northern pole. Sun wondered if it were all in vain, as he doubted that he possessed the skills to disarm the device. Yes, he had his abacus, but without the practical knowledge and experience to complement its programs, he had only a slim chance of figuring out the decoding sequence. Church and Tiberius would surely not have made such a thing straightforward. There were endless methods of encryption that needed unique keys to decipher; it was not just a matter of computing power and intelligence.

Within the sphere, the sensation of motion was all but imperceptible, but Sun *could* perceive their progress through the Ocean—or perhaps it was just his mind playing tricks on him in a futile attempt to rationally come to grips with a situation so outside his experience. Dolphins could swim fast, but this was something else entirely.

Triton hung suspended in the sphere alongside Sun. The inscrutable Ennean meticulously avoided physical contact with his delphine companion. Sun lightly bombarded Triton with some low-frequency melodies and clicks to try to communicate with him, but to no avail. Once in a while, Triton would aim a few appendages in Sun's direction, but with no head, face, ears, or eyes, it was a challenge to know if Triton was "looking" at him or "hearing" him—or whatever Enneans do to know the world around them. Sun thought he could feel the sphere slow for a few moments, and then it radically changed direction. *Short cut? Are we lost? Taking a break?* As if Triton had heard his thoughts, a dusky image of Taitano slid into the visual center of Sun's cerebral cortex, he knew not how; and the bulk of Triton's body undulated in his direction. *Incredible, my ghostly friend. You are indeed full of surprises. So, we're picking up a new passenger, eh? OK, that's splendid. Tai is just what we need right now. How in the world did she make it down here? But that's for later. I just hope we are in time to do something about this mess.*

The sphere bearing Benthesikyme, Fastcatch, and Patel streaked through the selenium stream at immense speeds. They were headed to the device at the southern pole. As Patel regained consciousness, his head ached as if it had been cleft in twain by an ancient Minoan double-bladed battle axe. He was dazed and disoriented. It took him a full minute to figure out where he was and what was going on.

"Hey, synch-boy! Wakey-wakey. Naptime's over."

"Fastcatch, I think I'm gonna vomit. What the hell is going on?" asked Patel.

"Well, you took a nice hit from one of those photonic tasers. Looks like it almost blew out your cybernetic implant and fried your brain like an egg. But based on what I can tell, the damage isn't too bad. It's not like you can get much dumber anyway."

"Thanks, Fastcatch. Very encouraging of you."

"Don't mention it," replied the dolphin. Despite his callous words, Fastcatch was right next to Patel, in subtle contact with him to stabilize his body in the liquid of the sphere. Benthesikyme floated next to them, but maintained a watchful distance so as to avoid physical contact. The alien's nine arms swirled in a regular rhythm. Patel wondered if the Ennean were somehow steering the sphere in some way.

"From what I can tell," said Fastcatch through the translator in the helmet of Patel's suit, "we are headed towards the device at the south pole. I assume the other sphere with Triton and Sun are on their way to the one at the northern pole. Hey, by the way, did you know that a dolphin was the first mammal to make it to the north pole on Earth-Ocean—thousands of years before humans had learned how to make a fire? In any case, I guess the plan is to disable both devices. So, we'd better start to think of a way to do that when we get there. Any ideas, chip-head?"

Patel could hardly focus on Fastcatch's words; but he was beginning to orient himself to his current circumstances. There was no perception of movement in the sphere, but he could see streaks of different shades of silver and grey streaming past, refracted by the sphere's membrane, which gave his visual cortex a sense of motion. He activated his implant and instructed it to calculate their velocity and then cross-reference it to the magnetic field of the Ocean to determination their location. His implant was sluggish, which worried him, but it finally made the calculation; he then had his implant extrapolate, based on their speed and position, when they would reach the southern pole. *Forty-three minutes! OK, we're getting there. These orbs can really fly … or glide … or swim. Whatever.*

"Fastcatch," said Patel, "we're going to be there in around forty minutes. Have you been able to communicate with this … thing?" He was going to say something more polite, but since the effort of applying better diction was most likely lost on the Ennean, Patel did not really see the point of picking a more appropriate term.

"Nope, not a word, note, or thought wave," replied Fastcatch. "I've been singing at her for half an hour in every cetacean dialect I can think of, but nothing. I even tried to sing a few Puccini arias. Nothing." Fastcatch continued to support Patel, so that he did not have to expend energy to keep himself in an upright and stable position. It was a little awkward for them both.

"OK, well," said Patel, "I guess when we get to the device, we'll figure something out. In the meantime, let's just enjoy the ride. And, by the way," he continued, with a wry smile, "about dolphins making it to the north pole on Earth-Ocean thousands of years before humans learned to make a fire, I don't recall dolphins *ever* managing to light a fire ... even to this day."

Fastcatch could not stop himself from bobbing his head up and down in a welcome release of amusement at Patel's clever retort. "*Touché*, and well played, *monsieur*." He thought for another moment and then sang, "I wonder what that officious windbag Church is up to—and his brilliant, evil sidekick Tiberius."

"No doubt," replied Patel, "cooking up something very unpleasant for us in the very near future."

"A comforting thought, to be sure."

At that, Benthesikyme imperceptibly shuddered and then turned towards them both. She then seemed to turn away and resumed her enigmatic swaying.

Resident Director Church had just finished another one of his insufferable soliloquies. He had convened all the humans into the conference hall of Station-1—configured, of course, in terrestrial mode—and broadcast his iniquitous sermon to the dolphins who were outside the station, as well as to everyone else from the other three stations. In these subtle ways, Church had always ensured that the dolphins were *de facto* second-class citizens of Station-1 and the overall mission. At the end of his polemic, he had demanded full, written reports on how the "traitors" had been allowed to escape and promised that disciplinary measures would be taken "in due course." "In due course" was one of those wonderful judicial phrases that meant: *since I hold all the power, I'll render judgment when I get around to it, and I'm going to let you sweat it out in the meantime.* Although it was a long way back to Earth-Ocean (a galactic understatement, if there ever were one), Church assured them that his memory was long and that there were ways of ensuring proper "restitution and rehabilitation" on Ross 128b. After he had dismissed them all, he closeted himself in his office and called in Tiberius.

"Bring them up on the main holographic display," ordered Church. Tiberius deftly toggled the switches on his abacus, bringing up a three-dimensional image of Ross 128b. The representation of the planet filled the room with real-time visually rendered data from observation buoys that had been placed at equidistant locations throughout the subterranean Ocean. The buoys had been tethered to the upper surface of the Ocean to prevent them from drifting. Depth, salinity, and temperature were represented by different colors and shading, making it easier for the human brain to understand. Church and Tiberius studied the images. They could see the selenium stream—or "corridor," as it was sometimes also called—perpetually cycling about the world as a band of soft silver light. Beneath the slim silver band, they could see two objects of unknown origin—one approaching the lower crust at the northern pole and the other at the southern pole, both creeping inexorably towards their respective objectives.

As Church studied the images, he scowled, "How did they get there so fast? It's only been a few hours since they escaped this station. Anyway, it doesn't matter now. They are obviously going to try to do something to the aquaterraforming devices. It took us ages to design, build, and place them there. And they are delicate. If they start to tamper with them, it will be a long time before we can recalibrate and get them back on track. This could set us back by years; and the people back on Earth-Ocean are counting on us."

Tiberius reflected on that for a moment. He seemed outwardly calm; but, on the inside, his emotions were a seething mass of contradictions. It was his duty to help his kind to find a new home— both human and dolphin. But this felt all wrong. Who was the villain and who was the hero in this drama unfolding now before his eyes? His thoughts strayed to his namesake: "Tiberius." As a child, he had always been proud of the regal, noble moniker his parents had imparted to him. Imperial Roman names had been a fashion back then, brought back from the days of Europe and the United States of America in the nineteenth century. But, as he grew older and began to explore the history of the name, he had learned—to his prepubescent dismay—that Tiberius Julius Caesar Augustus, once a brilliant soldier, had fallen into infamy at the end of his rule, summarily trying and executing for alleged treason his political opponents, including his trusted captain of the Praetorian Guard, Lucius Aelius Sejanus. He had considered changing his name when he was older, but decided to keep it as a reminder to always choose the right path. On the other hand, did he really want to go down in history as the one responsible for setting back the colonization of a new world? It was a risk, to be sure. If he contradicted Church, the Resident Director would simply find someone else to do his bidding, and Tiberius would lose the opportunity to temper the madman's more violent impulses. Was he willing to flout the will of the UN Ennean Commission and scuttle their plans—perhaps indefinitely? Not to mention throwing away the rest of his career.

He decided to temporize with Church.

"Director," said Tiberius, "consider the situation. They are obviously doing what they think is right. Are we sure what *we* are doing is right? Think about it. We have come to this world, imprisoned innocent beings, and begun to transform their home for our own purposes. I know we have all the institutional backing we need and that it's imperative to establish a second home for our people; but, putting aside all the orders and rhetoric, doesn't this seem wrong to you on a visceral level? Perhaps their actions are a wakeup call—a pattern interrupt—and an opportunity for us to change direction."

Church regarded Tiberius with perplexity.

Turbulent and conflicting emotions played across the resident director's normally stern visage: pain, disappointment, amusement, pity. "Did you not hear a word of what I said the other day? Were you not listening to what I said?" asked Church. "We are humans." He paused, as if there was nothing else that needed to be said to explain the situation.

Tiberius held Church's stare, silently defying him.

Church silently rose from his chair, leaving the antimacassar askew. He walked around the desk to stand shoulder to shoulder with Tiberius, who held his ground, staring slightly downwards at the shorter man.

But still Tiberius said nothing.

Church unlocked his gaze from his second-in-command and began to perambulate the perimeter of the office. He resumed speaking, "The entire reason we rose to such a dominant position in our biosphere was due to our superior genome. We survived, when so many other species went extinct, because we transcended our biology and molded the Earth to our own will. Rather than adapting to our environment, we reshaped *it* to fit *us*. We beat evolution! But our star had other plans for us; and we beat it, too! And now we need a new home. If something happens to Earth, we need a Plan B. And *this* is our Plan B," he said as he raised his arms and turned in a circle—encompassing the room, the station, and the entire planet in an embrace of wicked iron. "It is our biological and moral imperative to survive. The Commission knows that. *I* know that. And, deep down, I think *you* know it, too. Don't let your outdated Judeo-Christian morality get in the way of what you know to be the right thing to do; and let's keep this in perspective, shall we? We are not killing anyone—or anything. We are simply relocating a few alien cephalopods, who can't even figure out how to speak English, for pity's sake." Church stopped walking, locked eyes with Tiberius, squared his shoulders, and uttered, slowly and seriously, "Now, I need to know if you are with me or against me."

Tiberius displayed outward calm, but inside his heart was furiously hammering against the inner surface of his ribs. "We survived Sol's solar flare because of the Enneans," he said. "And now you want to take their home away from them and imprison them in a fishbowl orbiting their own planet. It's wrong, and I won't help you anymore." He turned away from Church. These were some of the most difficult words he had ever uttered, but once he had managed them, his pulse began to slow. He had decided *not* to cross the Rubicon. He felt oddly at peace with the situation now. Tiberius began to turn back to Church and continued, "If you want to lock me in my room for the rest ..."

His sentence was brutally terminated by a massive energy discharge from a photonic welder that ripped into his chest and melted his ribcage, lungs, and heart. He toppled over, the remains of his partially liquified body sliding to the floor with a sickeningly soggy squelching sound.

Church approached the steamy, sodden mass of unevenly seared flesh, bone, and skin—his closest colleague and companion of many years. He felt like vomiting due to the stench of cooked human flesh. He reminded himself of his purpose and of the necessity of having removed yet one more obstacle to his task—all to secure the fate of his species. Now he had other obstacles to overcome. He needed to stop the outrageous newcomers and their Ennean conspirators from disabling the devices. Once they were turned off, it would take an inordinate amount of time to get them recalibrated and running again—especially without the expertise of Tiberius. The aquaterraforming project could not be allowed such a setback. Moreover, once the devices were disabled, his people may lose their resolve, opinions on the station may shift, and he could lose control of the situation.

But first things first.

He set to work disposing of Tiberius's slippery carcass before anyone could discover what had happened. They would not understand. No one could. The destiny of man was in his hands. He may not receive the credit he was due in this lifetime, as was the case with many great men. But ages hence, people would open the history books and see his image—and silently laud him for the moral sacrifices he had made for the survival of their species. They would celebrate him for subverting the means to the ends. And even if they did not fete him publicly and chose instead to disingenuously traduce his character, they would—secretly, in their hearts—thank their stars that *he* had been the one in charge of this epic moment in their collective history and that *he* had been willing to sacrifice his moral sense of rightness so that they might live. The thought of this future, clandestine gratitude was enough for Church. He basked in it, and a wave of contentment comforted him, as he retrieved a mop from a utility closet to clean the assorted viscera and blood that was swiftly congealing upon the immaculate polymer floor.

# CHAPTER 14

# CONNECTION

The reunion between Sun and Taitano was an intense and joyous one, but short-lived.

As she had been descending towards the selenium stream, Triton had navigated the orb up and out of the stream to intercept her. As they neared each other, Taitano experienced awe and apprehension; but, as the sphere engulfed her, she knew intuitively that she was in no danger—at least from the sphere. She was certain that such an exquisite structure could only have been constructed by the Enneans and that they meant her no harm. In fact, she was confident that they did not even understand the concept of intentionally harming another being.

She lunged at Sun and hugged him as hard as she could, which, for a dolphin, was nothing more than a gentle squeeze. "Oh, Sun! How did you find me so fast? Is this Triton? I think so ... I can feel it." The words tumbled out of her, like airborne seedpods drifting away from the head of a ripe dandelion. She had not realized how much she had missed him. In this atramentous domain, she experienced a keen

239

kinship with Sun, with all dolphins. Both mammals, both in need of air, sun, love. In this Stygian realm, their similarities overshadowed their differences. Not for the first time, she marveled, with torrid obloquy, at the horrors that her species had visited upon Sun's ancestors. It was unthinkable, and yet it had been common practice for centuries.

Sun could feel in the tissues of his jaw the echo of her anxieties and emitted a series of clicks and whirs into the liquid of the sphere, which her helmet rendered as, "Yes, things have gotten a bit out of control. Church is not pleased that some of us are unwilling to go along with the plans of the Committee. Your … initiative … shall we call it … has further precipitated matters. An Ennean whom we are calling Benthesikyme is on her way towards the southern aquaterraforming device, along with Patel and Fastcatch. And now the three of us are here to deal with the one at the northern pole."

Taitano gazed upon the eerie and majestic being that floated in the sphere with them. No face; no eyes, ears, or mouth. No discernable separation between its appendages and the rest of his body. It was a seething, roiling, yet peaceful, mass of cytoplasm, cell walls, neurons, and who knew what else. They were still unable to understand the Enneans' anatomy, much less their cognitive abilities. But they were indisputably the masters of space and time, physics and mathematics, engineers par excellence; and all without opposable thumbs. She remembered her connection with Triton back at Station-1—and now understood the abhorrence, torment, and perplexity at the actions of the humans and dolphins whom they had invited to their home world and who then had betrayed them. She chided herself for these discursive thoughts. *No time for this. Focus on what you're doing now.*

"We need to get to the device and disarm it," said Taitano. "We're never going to get another chance like this, and we're running out of time. If we go back, Church will do goodness knows what, and that will be that."

Sun responded, "You're right. And that's why we're here. I just hope we can manage it. I have a fix on the device. It's several kilometers below us, resting on the lower seabed. Let me check if our suits can handle the pressure down there." Sun took some readings of the water pressure outside the sphere and ran a few calculations on his abacus. "It's good. Pretty close to maximum tolerance levels, but our suits should be able to withstand the pressure long enough to get down there and disarm the device."

"And after that?" asked Taitano. "Will we be able to get back?" Sun looked at her and subtly raised the skin over his eyes, which, in dolphin body language, was the equivalent to a human shrugging his shoulders.

Taitano turned to Triton, "Thank you for taking us here, Triton. I know that's not really your name, and I know you can't hear what I'm saying. But maybe you can somehow perceive the emotions, thoughts, and intentions behind my words. We're going down to the device to disarm it. So it stops destroying your environment. After that, we'll figure out a way to get the other Enneans out of that spaceship in orbit and back to your home here on Ennea. But first things first." Triton made no perceptible signs that he had received any of what Taitano had said, but she felt an imperceptible tingle on her skin and down her spine. A gentle wave of contentment washed over her, and it certainly had not come from her. She took this as a good sign.

While they had been conversing, Triton had navigated the orb back to and through the selenium stream. The sphere now hovered directly under the gleaming corridor. Taitano and Sun pushed their way through the membrane of the orb. It easily gave way, and then the oppressive Cimmerian night of the Ennean Ocean fell upon them, like the lowering of a coffin lid. Again, that feeling of utter aloneness engulfed them both. They had each other and Triton, but that was it. Corporeal motes in an endless mass of liquid blackness that strangled the feeble globes of light that emanated from the beacons of their suits and the receding selenium bubble.

A rendering of Sun's song manifested itself through her helmet, "Let's go. Suits look good. Atmosphere, temperature, pressure, energy supplies." Taitano assented with a nod of her head, and they plunged down. Sun naturally took the lead, propelling himself downwards at a rapid pace, as Taitano held onto his dorsal fin with both hands. Triton followed them, hanging back slightly, seemingly content to trail behind. Sun holographically projected a topographic map representing the lower ocean floor, which was a series of low mountain ranges cloven by deep defiles. Taitano had, for some reason, imagined a flat seabed awaiting them and was surprised by the rugged terrain. The device was situated at the bottom of one of the deep canyons, which provided the most efficient access to the mantle's geothermal energy—the device's power source.

They sank past the tips of the mountains, their beacons illuminating the razor-sharp contours of the peaks that now surrounded them.

The mountains extended forever into the distance. Each range was a mocking maw of teeth threatening to swallow them whole, demons of a watery underworld who would capture and trap their souls so that they drowned there in a serous grave, never to return to air and light. Taitano had climbed her share of mountains on Earth-Ocean, but she was usually looking up at the peaks during the ascent, rather than approaching them from above. The experience was more like skydiving in slow motion towards the bitter slopes of the mountains—a disorienting descent.

Sun dreaded swimming below the peaks of the undersea megaliths. They made him feel hemmed in and terror-stricken, like one of his ancestors herded into shallow coves before they were slaughtered by the thousands with stinging knives. Despite his morbid state of mind, Sun swam unerringly for the device, propelling himself and his *protégé* in a direct line toward it, wasting no energy and no time. There was no life anywhere in this austere and hyperborean wasteland. No fish, no coral, no plants, nothing living. Just the mineral rich water all around them—perfectly suited to the chemosynthesis of Ennean physiology. The environment was sterile from an EROC-ling perspective, and yet perfect for the Enneans, who dwelt together, and yet alone, in their nearly lightless domain.

Sun broke the meditative silence that had fallen over their descent into the canyon. "The device is straight ahead; a few hundred more meters and we'll be there. It's about fifty meters below the mean level of the seabed, at the bottom of a narrow crevasse. We're almost exactly at the northern geographic point of Ennea, with the magnetic pole twelve kilometers away to the southwest."

A few moments later, Taitano caught sight of the device. It was a series of stunted cylinders stacked one upon the other. Several serpentine cables issued forth from its base module, which flared diagonally outward as it made contact with the rocky seabed. The ends of the cables pierced the ocean floor and disappeared underground. The three uppermost modules contained metallic bands that glowed with several shades of blue and white. On the very top, there was a raised cylinder crowned with a ring of aluminum. All in all, it was about ten meters high. Despite herself, Taitano found that the technological construction possessed a measure of industrial elegance. If Ennea had been uninhabited, it would have been a brilliant invention to create life from lifelessness. But the fact that it was rendering the Ocean's marine environment uninhabitable for its indigenous lifeforms made it nothing more than humanity's latest instrument of death and destruction—a means of divesting another species of its way of life and its home.

It had to be stopped.

When they had finally arrived next to the device, Taitano scanned it with her abacus and found a control access panel. She interfaced her abacus with the main computer, easily establishing a connection. However, as soon as she tried to access the control systems, she was challenged for an access code. This was to be expected, of course. She reported to Sun, "OK, I've established a stable connection. That's a good start. It means the operating system of the device is the standard one used by the stations, which is also compatible with our abacuses. But now we need to gain access to the control systems to shut it down."

"Can you do that?" asked Sun.

She thought for a moment and then responded, "Yes"—tapping, five times in quick succession, the right side of the back of her helmet with her gloved index and middle fingers. "It's just going to take a bit of thinking. Gimme a minute."

Benthesikyme, Fastcatch, and Patel reached the device at the geographic southern pole around the same time that Triton, Sun, and Taitano arrived at theirs in the north. The southern device was identical to its northern counterpart. It stood at the bottom of a crevasse and had been easy for them to find, using the sensors of their abacuses to screen for the same mix of alloys as were used in the walls of the stations. Fastcatch swam down towards the device, with Patel holding onto his dorsal fin, and used his echolocation to sense the regular, roughly cylindrical contours of the device in order to obtain all the information he could about it.

Benthesikyme had remained as inscrutable as ever, as they departed the sphere and descended towards the device—a silent shadow in the dark of this alien place. Under different circumstances, Patel would have been terrified to look back and see such a creature trailing him through the obsidian black of the sea; but instead he felt oddly comforted by the presence of the benevolent and brilliant monster that followed them down to the lower surface.

When they finally reached the device, Patel released Fastcatch's dorsal fin and accessed a control panel on its outer shell. He avoided, for the moment, remote access with his cranial implant and opted instead for a direct link between his wrist-mounted abacus and the device. When he had determined that there were no apparently lethal security features embedded in the access panel's systems, he gingerly pulled a fiberoptic cable from the panel and inserted it into the back of his cranium. He immediately had a connection to the device, with general diagnostic data streaming into his cerebral cortex, which informed him that the device was performing within normal parameters. He tried to probe the control systems and immediately received an assertive alert message that such access was restricted without the proper code.

And not just any old access code.

The device's control systems did not only require a recursive fractal algorithm. No, that was just the beginning. Once a user identified the correct algorithm, utilized it to solve a series of sub-problems, and fed the results back into the encoding matrix, one then had to—in addition and *simultaneously*—code input from the result of a completely different and separate recursive fractal algorithm into the encoding matrix. Moreover, and to make the matter even more interesting, the source of that second set of computational algorithmic results could only be generated through real-time interaction with the device at the northern pole. So, in essence, the devices were multimodal and designed to only be accessible in tandem and at the same exact moment in time. It was a perfect way of preventing anyone from tampering with one of the devices. One needed both the algorithms and simultaneous access to both devices—which were situated tens of thousands of kilometers away from each other, under an Ocean of water, at antipodal positions on opposite sides of the planet.

Tiberius and Church had done their work well.

They had designed the security lockout system and used the buoys on the upper surface of the seabed to achieve the simultaneous signal relays. But Patel was receiving no signal from the buoy several kilometers above them. They were most likely set to inactive mode as soon as Church had realized that they were headed towards the devices—or otherwise locked out so that Patel and the others had no access to them.

Patel explained all this to Fastcatch, who bobbed up and down, thinking the situation over. There was no way for them to establish real-time communication with those at the northern device. Fastcatch looked at Benthesikyme and sang, "Well, do you have any ideas?" The Ennean's appendages moved in a rhythmical pattern for a few moments, and then she unexpectedly shot straight up to the sphere, which was still poised near the selenium stream—her pliable limbs streaming behind her like the pinions of a great bird.

Fastcatch wondered, "What's she doing?"

"Go ask an Ennean!" shouted Patel in frustration.

"I think I just did!" retorted Fastcatch, mirroring his irritation.

About one minute later, a slender silver thread wound its way down to them, with Benthesikyme close behind. It smoothly but rapidly made its way toward Patel, angling behind him towards the back of his head.

"Hey! Get that thing away from me!" squawked Patel, as he tried to bat it away from his head. Fastcatch aimed his fin-mounted abacus at the synthetic-looking tendril to get a reading on its chemical composition.

"It's made of almost pure selenium," said Fastcatch, "mixed with a bit of iron, magnesium, and potassium. Based on its chemical composition, it should have electrical conducting properties similar to a fiberoptic cable and should also be compatible with your implant. It must be from Benthesikyme." He paused to think for a moment and then made an inductive leap, "Maybe she's found a way to communicate with the others at the northern device!" The silver tendril floated in the water moving back and forth next to Patel's head, like an entranced cobra waiting to strike.

Patel replied, "There is *no way* I'm letting that thing poke into my head. *Not* gonna happen."

"Listen, you idiot, why would Benthesikyme bring us all the way here and then try to fry your brain. *Think* about it, Saiyam. This is the only way. Yeah, it's a risk, but it's a risk we've *got* to take. We are way too far into this to quit now. She must have understood what's happening and found a way for us to communicate to disarm the devices simultaneously. There's no other explanation. If you ever wanted to be a hero, this is the time!"

"I never said I wanted to be a hero!"

"All humans want to be heroes. It's in your blood." Fastcatch continued, appealing to the human's ego, "Come on, Patel. Just think of the bragging rights you'll have when we get back, if you pull this off."

Without any further hesitation, Patel said, "That's true. OK, let's do it."

Patel turned his back on the tendril. The silvery, metallic snake transformed its terminal end into a shape that was appropriate to interface with the external surface of Patel's cybernetic cerebral implant. Patel felt naked and exposed. Scared. Millions of tons of water pressed against his suit, and he could feel the suit struggling to push back against the Atlantean force. *Why am I doing this? That thing is going to drill into my brain like a needle. Well, can't turn back now. I'd never hear the end of it from Fastcatch.* The tendril touched Patel's interface and then fused with it. *Here we go ....* Symbols raced through Patel's mind: he recognized them as numbers from Earth-Ocean. Natural numbers, whole numbers, integers, rational numbers, irrational numbers, real numbers, complex numbers. But there were also symbols he did not recognize. *Must be Ennean. How am I supposed to understand those? Wait!* Patel began to understand the Ennean mathematical symbols. The symbols were not translated into Earth-Ocean symbology; rather, he simply understood them on their own terms. He began to perceive them for what they were: equations, algorithms, the relationships of things in the physical world expressed as abstract and inter-related symbols. He understood Ennean math now! It made the base-ten system of Earth-Ocean look like the workbook of a first grader by comparison. But he understood it. He smiled at Benthesikyme, and his mind told him that she was smiling back—although that was of course impossible. It was not an emotional connection, as he rather doubted the selenium tendril could conduct such messages. It was rather a connection of cold, hard symbolic logic, which somehow at the moment felt deeper and more meaningful to Patel than any emotional connection he had ever had with anyone.

Patel swam back to the interface panel of the device, and Benthesikyme gracefully shot back to the orb that floated near the selenium stream.

"OK, we're connected!" crowed Patel to Fastcatch. "Don't ask me how. It's impossible to explain with words. But we're connected and in business. Let's hope she's got a plan."

"Dammit! I can't do it!" shouted Taitano. She was starting to panic. She had discovered the interplexed recursive fractal algorithm just as Patel had. It was impossible for her to decipher it all by herself, as it required a direct real-time connection with the other device. The concatenated codes to be inputted had to be generated by the other device, tens of thousands of kilometers away, through trillions of liters of water. Despair, panic, terror began to overwhelm her. They would fail, and everyone would die.

"Can't do what? What's the problem?" Sun asked in reply, trying to mask his concern, both at their overall situation and her statement.

Taitano explained their predicament to Sun, who had been her professor and mentor for several years. As Sun began to understand the situation, he got a pensive and thoughtful expression on his face. To a human unfamiliar with interacting with dolphins, the alterations in Sun's face would have been imperceptible; but, to Taitano, they were easy to read, even through the transparent membrane of the suit that Sun wore to protect him from the crushing pressure and low temperatures of the water outside—not to mention the fact that the suit was supplying his lungs with precious oxygen. Wearing such a suit was not something that all dolphins had been able to brook, just like not all humans were able to bear underwater breathing apparatuses. The difficulties that Sun had experienced getting used to such equipment reminded him of the similarities between dolphins and humans, and the former's past connection to the land, whence their ancestors had returned to the Ocean. One of the great riddles of Earth-Ocean, which was still under heated archeological debate, was when, how, and—more importantly—*why* the forebears of cetaceans had evolved on land and then moved to the Ocean—or rather "back" to the Ocean, as all terrestrial animals had originated evolutionarily in the sea. Food supply? A natural catastrophe? A massive, random genetic mutation? And what a perfectly adapted migration it had turned out to be. For a dolphin, the thought of living on the land was as alien as floating endlessly on the Ocean was to a human: no land, nowhere to set one's feet on the ground, no fixed surface to rest during the dream-filled nights.

Triton's movement brought Sun back to the present.

The massive Ennean had been floating near to them and the device, seeming to observe them patiently—content to wait. Inside his suit, Sun's senses were blunted in a way that disoriented him. His echolocation was not fully effective as the high-frequency pulses had to travel through the membrane of his suit, and there were no scents to fill out the sensory picture. Although his eyesight was not much better than a human's, the sensors of his abacus helped him to partially fill in what he needed. In a way, Sun's suit mitigated the customary advantage than a dolphin normally enjoyed over humans—while they were both in environmental suits, they were on a more equal "footing." An interesting sensation. One that worried him sometimes, based on the historical cruelty with which humans had treated his kin. But Sun instantly banished this thought from his mind. *This is Agana. Nothing to fear from her. Now back to the business at hand.*

Triton flowed towards Taitano. The Ennean's approach seemed hesitant, tentative. The alien edged closer and closer to her until he was almost touching her suit. Taitano felt no danger, no aversion to the gargantuan, amorphous being that floated right next to her, suspended just centimeters away. Triton extended an appendage, encircled her waist with it, and drew her into direct contact with him. It was as intimate as a lover's embrace. Another appendage released one of the fasteners of her suit.

Sun instantly snapped into action and swam towards them, "Triton, no! Agana! The pressure will kill you instantly!" Taitano was completely relaxed. There was no trepidation. This felt right. Like destiny's tender caress upon her quivering body.

"It's OK, Sun. This is right. Necessary. Let it happen."

Triton continued to release the seals on her suit, one by one. As he did so, his body wrapped instantly around her skin to protect it from the mortiferous environment around her, at the very bottom of this alien world, lightyears away from the biosphere in which her species had evolved and flourished for hundreds of thousands of years. The sensation of Triton's flesh on hers was pure ecstasy. For the first time in her life, she could feel each and every pore of her skin, as the sensory nerves in her dermis sent electrical impulses to her brain, filling it with intense warmth and pleasure. The pressure of Triton against her was silky, moist. Her brain was unable to fully process the olfactory stimuli that resulted from being in direct physical contact with the alien, but the neurological center of Taitano's mind activated by her first cranial nerve unlocked the closest possible analogue from an old memory engram of a class trip to Montana back in high school, and she was flooded with the aroma of honeysuckle. Triton continued to slowly peal her suit from her, as he enveloped her body. Eventually, her suit was completely removed, and she was encased within the alien's body, which had seeped underneath the thin wetsuit she wore under her outer environmental suit.

Sun floated next to them in a state of anxiety and awe. He also, to his shame, experienced a stab of jealousy—for Triton was experiencing Agana in a way that Sun had always wanted to, but never could, for a wide variety of reasons. Sun could just barely make out the opaque outline of Agana's body through the translucent form of Triton. He waited, his emotions churning and roiling.

Her time with Triton, and within him, was sacred. It suffused her being, and she carried the experience with her for the rest of her days, like a wedding band, rarely removed, that left a satisfying indentation around one's finger.

She entered a trance-like state. She could not perceive where she ended and Triton began. His watery, yielding body seeped into her every curve—ears, nose, throat, everywhere. Although she no longer wore her suit, his embrace kept her from being crushed by the pressure of the encircling deluge. She was warm, and her cells were being supplied with oxygen in some way. Once she had recovered her senses, which had been overwhelmed by the initial disorientation of contact with the Ennean, she began to experience a radically different way of perceiving the world. It was absolute and total balance with the environment. It was like being fused with joy—or even *becoming* the emotion of joy. She sensed that the full experience was beyond human comprehension and that her mind was doing the best it could to render it all in a way that she could perceive and understand. She understood, for the first time—the first human to ever understand— that the Enneans' environment, which had seemed stale and lifeless, was, to them, ablaze with countless stimuli. The water was not just water. It was a unique medium capable of suspending hundreds of elements, minerals, and millions upon millions of separate organic and inorganic compounds. To an Ennean, these compounds were as easily and naturally identifiable as wildflowers in a summer meadow were to a human. She sensed the world through Triton's perspective. The Enneans could perceive a difference in temperature to the thousandth of a degree and a salinity difference of one part per million. The water soughed and sighed around them, as though it remembered when it had been part of the body of an Ennean, longing once again to be housed in a living being—*to be* a living being. The currents of their Ocean were an endless pathway of forces pushing and pulling them up, down, left, right—although such descriptions were deficient, as they did not perceive motion in such linear terms. Motion to them was not in straight lines, but rather infinite curves, swirls, occasional circles, ellipses, and three-dimensional fractal equations—all in perpetual motion, forever changing. The only constant was indeed change.

And the light.

Generally, most of the electromagnetic energy from Ross 128, the pale star of Ennea, did not penetrate the rocky crust of their world; but there were times when it broke through, as was the case with the portals that Taitano had used to enter the Ocean. The occasional volcanic fissure on the lower crust sent waves of radiation through the sea floor; the selenium stream generated radiation that, to a human and dolphin, could be perceived as light; the interaction of the various organic and inorganic compounds created low levels of heat and light; and, of course, interactions with humans and dolphins and their perpetual thirst for external sources of illumination had increased the Enneans' familiarity with what we would call "visual stimuli." But, to them, it was not light in the sense of the pale-yellow glow that hit the molecules of a retina to then be transmitted as a bioelectric signal along an optic nerve to an imaging center of a centralized set of specialized ganglia, as was the experience with Taitano and all humans. The radiation that humans perceived as light was a godlike presence that the Enneans cherished as the divine. They did not *see* the light. They *felt* the light in every cell of their bodies. No. It was deeper and more profound than that. The Enneans considered light to be part of who and what they were. There was no separation, no distinction. When Taitano and Sun looked upon, for example, the selenium stream, they perceived a sleek suffusion of silvery light; but, to an Ennean, it was a whirling inferno of magic, flame, and emotion of the most intense quality. All Enneans considered themselves to be part of the light and regarded the light to be part of themselves. The very rendering of such thoughts, sensations, and concepts into words or songs implied a separation where there was none.

Taitano's bonding with Triton allowed her to realize, in non-intellectual terms, that the Enneans did not see themselves as individual beings separated from each other and their surrounding environment. Rather, they possessed and embodied an extreme anti-solipsistic collective world view; they perceived, in excruciating detail, the electromagnetic and bio-electrical fields pervading all life and matter—which is why they made such superb astral navigators—and saw themselves as self-aware patterns or vibrations within a swirling continuum of energy. Quantum theory was intuitive to them, just as sight and sound were to humans and dolphins, who did not need to have these sensory phenomena explained or taught to them: it was simply how humans and dolphins intuitively perceived the world around them. For the Enneans, there was only one continuum of perpetually fluctuating energy—all interconnected parts of one whole.

After an interval of time that she could not measure, more concrete thoughts began to form in her consciousness. Triton had bonded with her for a tangible reason; and he was now transmitting specific bio-electrical signals through her skin in order to stimulate in her mind images and emotions. She felt intention and purpose in the connection. Triton began to physically retreat from her, to meticulously peel his body from hers. As he withdrew, he incrementally and with exquisite precision reapplied her environmental suit to her body, so as not to expose her delicate flesh to the crushing Ocean of water pressing upon them. She experienced intense apprehension and regret at his retreat—wanting to stay connected. But then she realized that the "separation" was only physical and that she could still perceive Triton's thoughts and emotions, although the dichotomy between "thought" and "emotion" was an inaccurate way to describe the way Triton's mind worked. (The Cartesian divide between thought and emotion, which persisted in the way modern humans conceptualized their psyche, was an enduring relic that was lost on dolphins.) Nevertheless, Triton, in his own unique, alien way, had experienced—and now shared—Taitano's anxiety over her inability to disarm the device without simultaneous contact with the others at the southern pole. He finished gently reapplying her suit and rapidly ascended upwards towards the orb, which was suspended motionless just under the selenium stream. She understood, she knew not how, that he was returning to the stream in order to help her communicate with those at the southern device for the purpose of disarming it.

Sun's voice blasted into her helmet, "Agana, what was that? What happened? Are you OK?" The translator added inflection to the words to simulate the agitation and distress it had picked up in the frequency ranges that the professor had chosen.

Taitano winced at the sounds assaulting her ears. After her bond, her connection, with Triton, the noises were revealed for exactly what they were: an embarrassingly primitive and inefficient way to communicate. But her mind recovered in a few moments, and she responded, "Yes, Sun. It's fine. The experience is impossible to relate in words. I will try later. But, for now—and I won't pretend to understand all the details—Triton is going to help us make contact with

Benthesikyme, Fastcatch, and Patel at the south pole, so we can disarm these damned things. I just hope we have time. I can't stop wondering what Church has been up to all this time."

"Nothing good, I'd wager," replied Sun.

Church worked in the Operations Center of Station-1, making the final touches on his instructions to the heavy construction drones housed in the buoys at the northern and southern poles. He had reconfigured—all by himself, no thanks to that treasonous Tiberius— the photonic welders of the drones to expand their energy output and range, essentially turning them into weapons. He worked alone, having ordered his loyal security personnel to lock the rest of the staff into their rooms for the time being. He would abide no more discussion, much less misguided and noble "heroics" from anyone who was immoral enough to allow their own individual consciences to override their duty to follow the orders of the Committee—not to mention what should have been a shared biological and ethical imperative to ensure the survival of their very species.

He keyed in a last set of instructions to set the drones into motion.

An electromagnetic pulse containing a data package of instructions and re-coding raced through and out of the transmission array of Station-1, flying both north and south of the equatorial location of the station. The signals bounced off several submerged communications relays and then to the receiving arrays that had been built directly into the upper crust of the northern and southern poles. It was the same communications system that enabled Station-1 to monitor the progress of the aquaterraforming devices.

Church was pleased with himself that he had not shared the access codes for the communications system with anyone other than Tiberius, who had ultimately taken them with him to the grave. Now Church was the only one left with access. Once the signals hit the two communication arrays anchored to the upper crust on opposite sides of the planet, they were then transferred to two heavy construction drones, one in the north and one in the south, which were docked to the communication arrays.

It took a few seconds for the new instructions to be processed, and then a few minutes for the systems of the drones to retask their welders into offensive weapons. The buoys then launched the drones—automata of steely malevolence—and sent them directly towards the devices with directives to deploy their photonic pulses against anything living within a one-kilometer radius of the devices. Church's mindless puppets ripped through the Ocean of Ross 128b on their journey from the upper to lower surface of the crust, where the devices were located—a trip that would take no more than five minutes, based on the various water layers and changing currents that they had to negotiate. Their ion-powered propulsion emitters burned at maximum intensity, leaving scorched organic hydrocarbons in their wake, polluting the sea.

Church monitored the elevated levels of contamination and regretted it, as it would create an imbalance in the local area and require environmental cleanup at a later time. *But desperate times necessitate desperate measures. The ends have always justified the means, which is why humanity is even here to have philosophical debates about it. And if the drones fail to stop them from disabling the devices, I have one more trick up my sleeve.* The edges of his mouth started to spread, involuntarily, into an imperceptible smile. *But first things first.* He had programmed the drones to first eliminate the Enneans and then target the humans. *If there's still some time left, we'll also take care of the dolphins. But first things first.*

# CHAPTER 15

# DISARMING
# THE DEVICES

A s Triton returned to the orb, which hovered just below the selenium stream, Taitano and Sun remained at the aquaterraforming device.

Taitano began to decipher the access codes to its control systems.

She had done this many times before, but that was on munitions hundreds of years old and back on Earth-Ocean. Here, the conditions were different, but the basic principles were the same: try to identify a coding system or pattern, lock down variables—one at a time—and then move onto the next challenge. It was similar to building a wall of bricks or chipping away at a chunk of marble to sculpt a statue, depending on how one looked at it. In some ways, she was relieved to be working with a puzzle devised by humans, and perhaps dolphins as well, rather than by Enneans. At least she had some common reference points from which to start, such as the use of base-ten and elementary computing fundaments. She noticed that the interface on the device had been designed so that the sequence of symbols had to be entered manually by pressing keys on a raised pad. On a whim, she entered the irrational number "*e*": 2.71828 .... Like its fellow irrational number $\pi$, *e* went on forever into transcendental infinity and could not be resolved by a polynomial equation. Shortly before she had left Earth-Ocean for the journey to Ennea, she had been blind peer reviewing a paper for the *Journal of Cryptology*, in which the author of the paper posited that cryptographers had a deep-seated psychological need for their codes to be broken. A code that was completely unbreakable had a sense of incompleteness that such minds found unsatisfying on a deeply existential level. Thus, cryptographers, both consciously and unconsciously, tended to make encryption codes as close to unsolvable as possible, without them *actually being* completely unable to be deciphered. As such, certain numbers, equations, and methods were stock favorites, such as irrational numbers. *E* also had a certain aptness to it in the present situation, as the devices were intended to function in an exponential manner, so that their aquaterraforming of the Ennean Ocean would accelerate at an exponential rate the longer they were in use, much like a naturally formed ecosystem that reaches a tipping point until cascading feedback loops take over—much like, before the collapse of the international banking system in the 2040s, the economic system of compound interest had turned millionaires into billionaires almost overnight. There was also the plain simple fact that the word for the planet they were on started with the letter "E." Stranger things had happened in her cryptanalytical travels.

Taitano manually keyed in *e* to the forty-seventh decimal place and then began to enter recursive equations, using *e* again as the constant in the equations. After several sequences, she was rewarded with a response from the device. A random series of numbers with no immediately discernable pattern. She ran the numbers through her head. It was at that moment that she sensed Triton with her, not physically, but in her mind. He was floating in the middle of the selenium stream and somehow lifting the sequence of numbers from her visual cortex and sending them through the selenium stream to Benthesikyme on the other side of the planet at nearly the speed of light—using the superconducting semiconductor properties of the stream to transmit images to the antipodal side of the planet. Benthesikyme then sent the sequence of numbers down the length of the selenium tether, directly into Patel's implant and then to his brain. Patel, in turn, keyed Taitano's numbers into "his" device at the southern pole. Patel immediately received a challenge from the device. It was the infamously "insoluble" Fermat's last theorem, which had, of course, been solved well over a century and a half ago. He had learned it in school as a child, and his implant quicky retrieved the answer from his own memory engrams. Patel keyed the proper solution into the access panel and received a torrent of apparently random digits— this one forty-six symbols long. As he read off each of the symbols, they were transmitted through his optic nerve, to his cerebral cortex, into his implant, up the selenium tether to Benthesikyme, and then back through the selenium stream to Triton, who then used his mental link with Taitano to relay the numbers, which she then keyed into "her" device. The entire concatenation of events had taken less than a minute, with the longest part being the time it took for Taitano to manually enter the forty-six digits into the control access panel of the device.

The moment they had finished this first round of decipherment, the proximity sensors of Sun's abacus warned him of an incoming object—on a course directly for Triton.

Without hesitation, Sun sang to Taitano, "Don't stop. Keep working on decoding the security locks and disarming that device. I will take care of whatever this is." Taitano nodded imperceptibly and kept concentrating on the access panel in front of her, taking a moment to tap the right side of the back of her helmet with her gloved index and middle fingers, five times in quick succession.

Heedless of peril, Sun soared upwards to confront the swiftly approaching object. In the nearly complete darkness, he whipped his echolocation at full throttle and bandwidth through his suit and listened for a response. He was almost immediately aware of the object's relative location, trajectory, and speed and identified it as one of the heavy construction drones used for building and maintaining the stations.

It was heading straight for Triton.

Triton made no move to evade the drone or defend himself; he floated serenely in the selenium stream, seemingly unconcerned by the pitiless and lethal tool that was bearing down upon him. *If he leaves the stream, he'll break the link. Or he can't even conceive of a hostile act directed towards himself. This situation is completely outside of his frame of reference. Either way, I've got to do something before it's too late.* Sun raced in their direction, utilizing his echolocation to calculate a Brachistochrone curve for the most efficient path to intercept the drone before it reached Triton.

The drone was almost upon Triton.

As Sun propelled himself at full throttle, he could feel and smell, through the filters of his suit, the photonic welder charging at full capacity and ionizing the water between them. When the drone was a scant one-point-five seconds away from thrusting the welder deep into Triton's undefended flesh, Sun reached them and savagely grabbed one of the drone's tailfins in his jaws and halted its attack. The heavy construction drone was almost as big as Sun—and far heavier. With the tailfin trapped tightly in his jaws, he dashed down towards one of the outcroppings of jagged rock on the side of the undersea canyon. As he did so, the drone's ion drive burned the side of his head and neck down to the bone—right through his suit. Sun compartmentalized the scorching pain and the unbelievable pressure of the water that now crushed his body. He drove on toward the rocks and remorselessly smashed the drone point-blank into the cliff face at full speed, badly damaging its propulsion system. The dreadful impact shattered the spare electrolyzer that was cradled in one of the side pockets of his environmental suit. He kept his jaws locked around the retooled weapon and repeatedly smashed it, over and over, into the serrated rock face, until it was nothing more than a collection of scrap metal and broken pieces of composite polymer resin.

He released the drone's splintered remains, and they lifelessly sank to the seabed below.

Only then did he allow himself to succumb to the pain coursing through every sinew of his body from the blistering burns and inexorable pressure of the water. He relaxed and committed himself to the tender embrace of the currents of the Ocean.

At the same instant, on the other side of the planet, the proximity sensors of Fastcatch's abacus alerted him of a swiftly approaching object—headed straight for Benthesikyme.

Fastcatch resolutely sang to Patel, "Keep it up and disarm that device. I'll take care of this thing."

Patel responded, "Copy that, chief! Kick its butt!"

Fastcatch, in the almost complete darkness, lashed out with his echolocation to locate the incoming threat. Like a surgeon's scalpel, he cleaved the water between him and the heavy construction drone with savage ferocity. He was a fey creature in liquid, lethal motion—terrible to behold.

The implacable drone drilled through the water directly towards Benthesikyme.

Fastcatch shot from his suit a utility cable with a small hook at the end, which was usually used to tow gear and humans, when needed. He was on a collision course with the drone and intercepted it a full sixteen meters before it could reach Benthesikyme. (There was a reason he was called "Fastcatch.") The fleet-finned dolphin veered to the side of the machine, actually brushing against its side, and circled it over and over, blowing copious amounts of air bubbles from the exhalation vents in his suit. The tightly bound pockets of air flooded and confused the drone's sensors. As Fastcatch had predicted, the drone was programmed to slow its movement when its sensors could no longer sense its environs, a safety measure to prevent the drone from running itself into something and being damaged. Church had overridden these subroutines to allow it to attack them, but the air rushing into the drone's sensors had temporarily rebooted the safety program for a few vital seconds. Fastcatch continued to tightly encircle the drone, all the time continuing to blow bubbles around the witless and now confounded machine.

It finally came to a full stop.

Fastcatch took the end of the cable firmly in his mouth and deftly hooked it onto the drone. He then energetically jerked it down and away from Benthesikyme. With his echolocation, Fastcatch quickly found a narrow fissure in a rockface of the defile and dashed inside, pulling the drone behind him. As it was towed behind Fastcatch, the drone's sensors cleared. Its rudimentary computer processor perceived that Fastcatch was preventing him from achieving its primary objective: to kill anything living within a one-kilometer radius of the device. It therefore automatically switched to its secondary backup program and focused on eliminating the thing that was obstructing the achievement of its primary task.

The drone engaged its propulsion system to close the distance between itself and the dolphin.

Fastcatch glanced behind him; he could see an azure glow from the drone's photonic welder and could feel and smell, through the filters of his environmental suit, the ionization of the water between them, as the drone charged the deadly, corrupted tool.

As Fastcatch continued to pull the drone deeper into the cave, he increased his speed to maintain the distance between them. He then torqued his body and used the drone's own momentum to launch it towards a crack in the cave wall, which he had estimated with his echolocation was just the right size to trap and immobilize the drone in the wall of the underwater cave. The drone struck the wall with incredible force and was trapped within the crack. It struggled in vain to free itself and menacingly tried to aim the welder in Fastcatch's direction so it could discharge its malefic energy at him. The propulsion system of the drone began to loosen the machine from its makeshift cage. This allowed the drone a fuller range of motion with the welder, so that, in the narrow confines of the cave, the drone would soon be able to train the welder on Fastcatch.

Fastcatch wracked the two separate spheres of his brain. He was about to get seared by the welder; but he could not simply retreat and leave the drone there, as it would soon free itself. He might not be able to stop it a second time. He searched the cave for options and found a loose rock on the floor of the cave. He swept to the cave floor, took the jagged rock in his jaws, and raced back up to the drone, approaching it from below, close to the cave wall, so as to keep out of range of its welder. He then repeatedly smashed the stone, with great energy of action, into the drone until it was pulverized and useless, a pulpy mass of ragged metal and polymers.

Even through the protective layers of his environmental suit, Fastcatch's rostrum was severely bloodied and bruised from the blunt force trauma he had visited upon the mindless instrument. But his suit was still intact. Without hesitation, he dashed from the cave to rejoin his companions.

"Argh!!!" howled Church, when he had stopped receiving data from the second construction drone. Thanks to the drones' optical sensors, he had had a front-row seat to the dolphins beating the drones into frayed piles of rubbish, before the connection was lost.

Frustration suffused his very being, and he impotently pounded on the console in the operations center with closed fists, wincing in pain as he did so. *This is outrageous. It has to end now.* A wild gleam sparkled in his dreary eyes. *I've got my last card to play.* With fell intention, he crept towards a different console that was adjacent to the one he had just pummeled in uncontrolled fury. This control interface connected to a sinuous, but sturdy, fiberoptic cable he had instructed Tiberius and his engineering team to put into place, connecting Station-1 physically and directly to both devices. In this alien and still unpredictable environment, he had thought it prudent to have a fail-safe way to monitor the status of the devices. There were times when the buoys went off-line for unknown reasons, and he needed to always ensure that they were continuously functioning in an optimal manner. They had decades of aquaterraforming work to do, and any interruption in the quiet and steadfast work of the devices could be a significant setback. But what most of the engineers did not know was that Church had also instructed Tiberius to install a last-ditch security measure that he could trigger through the cables. In the event of unwanted tampering, Church could send an electromagnetic pulse through the cables to each device. The pulse would be routed through the external casings of the devices, so as not to harm any of their delicate internal components, but would deliver a baneful shock to anyone within several meters. He had intended it to repel any interference from the Enneans, but it would work just as well on humans and dolphins. He entered his security access code to unlock the panel that controlled the cables. He keyed in an additional access code and prepared to send the pulse through the cables and to the devices.

Just before doing so, he received a transmission. It was Saddiq on *Ardanwen*. He paused and took the transmission, "Yes, Captain. I am quite busy at the moment. Is this something we can talk about later?"

Saddiq had chosen to send his transmission in audio form only. There were a few seconds of silence, and then Saddiq replied,

"Resident Director, we both know what's happening down there. I tried to contact Tiberius, thinking I might talk some sense into him, but I can't reach him. So, I am coming to you now—straight to the top. With great respect, I ask you to stand down and surrender yourself into the custody of Staton-1's security personnel until we can sort this all out. It's time to call a pause and freeze the situation before someone gets hurt."

Church's heart skipped a beat. Saddiq was no fool. There was no point trying to dissemble. Church replied over the open audio channel, "Yes, let's discuss the situation. Please, Captain, feel free to come down here to the station so we can talk face-to-face—after which it will be *you* who are taken into custody, not I. In any case, this will all be over soon, and we'll have plenty of time to talk. In the meantime, like I said, I am very busy." He cut the channel and prepared to toggle the switch to send the electromagnetic pulses to the devices.

"My *most esteemed* Resident Director," whispered a soft and stately voice behind Church. He turned and saw Proteus standing behind him. "Dr. Taitano thought you might have a backup plan hidden, so to speak, somewhere under your villainous sleeve. She suggested that I be ready to counter such a plan, should it come to pass."

"*How did you get in here!?!*" Church roared in rage and abject terror.

Proteus's hologram remained as sedately poised as a lone, noble oak in a tranquil summer meadow.

"I sent a condensed avatar of my matrix along the disabled video component of the transmission you just had with Captain Saddiq," he replied. "An abridged copy of my collective programming is therefore now in direct contact with Station-1's computer core. Quite simple, really." Proteus allowed a subtle smile to escape his otherwise serious demeanor, "And it was *ever so kind* of you to take his call, by the way. I do admire common courtesy and good manners. Now, I would like to ask you to kindly step away from that panel before you do something rash."

Church breathed in quickly, whirled back around to the panel, and tried to bring his hand down towards the activate button.

However, in the zero-point-five seconds before Church's hand could connect with the panel, Proteus was able to do several things: due to the fact that his avatar was now in physical proximity to the station's computer core, he was able to access the control systems leading to the activate button; he then remotely interrupted the button's hardwired connection to the cable leading to the devices and rerouted it directly to the power supply feeding the panel.

As Church slammed his meaty fist down upon the button, a potent surge of electricity flowed into his hand, up his arm, and into his brain. He was instantaneously rendered unconscious, collapsed upon the panel, and then unceremoniously slid to the floor.

Proteus regarded the crumpled, smoking body, "The only thing I despise more than bad manners—is *dreadfully* bad manners."

While Sun and Fastcatch were dispatching the drones, Triton and Taitano and Benthesikyme and Patel continued to relay their mathematical data through the unique bond they had fashioned.

When they reached what she thought should be the last cycle of the security program, a red light began to blink on the access control panel of the northern device. Anxiety squirmed inside Taitano's entrails. *Oh, no! It's a final security measure, and it's tied to* this *device.* The encryption protocol was set to lock itself out and refuse any more external input unless the final sequence was entered in less than a minute. *Come on guys .... Get a move on.* She hungrily waited for the final sequence from Patel and Benthesikyme via her mental link with Triton.

It came ten seconds later, and a sequence of fifty-three symbols began to stream into her mind.

She forcibly willed herself to stay focused and drew a deep breath as she entered the random sequence of numbers, letters, and symbols into the keypad of the control access panel of the device. It was a process akin to a musician playing in an orchestra who is continuously reading notes on a page of sheet music, which are then translated by her brain into motor neuron signals, which then control the movements of the player's fingers. The parallel operations of reading the notes and expressing them in physical movement ran independently and in parallel with each other, with the movement of the fingers always just one step behind the reading of the notes. It took her a full twenty seconds to key in the string of symbols, but something deep within Taitano made her hesitate before sending the final sequence to the device's operating system with a final click of the "enter" button on the external interface.

*Thirty seconds left before the system permanently locks me out.*

Time stood still for Taitano.

She gazed at the last five symbols she had keyed into the interface: 3-0-c-#-f.

She was transfixed by the sequence.

She stared at it, and it seemed to stare back at her.

The string of symbols blurred, moving in and out of focus.

She tapped the right side of the back of her helmet, five times in quick succession, with her gloved index and middle fingers.

*That sequence isn't right. I can feel it. Or is that just my OCD talking?*

Twenty seconds left.

She felt Triton's concern at her unexpected delay in activating the final sequence. She tried to recall the sequence in her mind to double-check the last five symbols, but could not manage it in her current state of distress. She desperately flung her thoughts towards Triton, pleading with him to send her the last five symbols again.

Ten seconds left.

Triton imperceptibly hesitated and then with a rush of anxiety complied with her request. The following five symbols appeared in her mind: 0-3-c-#-f.

She checked the access panel. She had mistakenly keyed in 3-0-c-#-f—transposing two of the numbers.

Two seconds left.

She corrected the transposition in the final five symbols and deftly hit "enter" on the access panel zero-point-two-five seconds before the system locked-out. The panel's red light turned to green, and a short confirmation code appeared. She now had access to all the functions of the aquaterraforming device. She immediately sent the confirmation code to Triton, who then relayed it to Benthesikyme and Patel so they could now access the control systems of their device.

She released a long breath as she triggered the device to commence the gradual shut-down procedure.

On the opposite side of the world, Benthesikyme received the confirmation code from Triton and relayed it to Patel, who then entered it into the device and activated the gradual shut-down procedure.

It was done.

Taitano suddenly felt light-headed.

Her suit alerted her, "Warning: oxygen levels critical. Backup electrolyzer not functioning. Locate alternative oxygen source immediately."

She initiated the diagnostic routine on her abacus, which told her that disarming the device had caused a small feedback loop and energy surge, which had damaged her suit's only functioning electrolyzer. Her mind raced. She was currently buried under kilometers of water on the lower surface of the planet's crust. She did not have enough oxygen to even make it to the floating girdle of rocks, much less to the access point at the upper surface. Even on the outer surface of Ennea, the atmosphere was not breathable.

She reached out to Triton with her thoughts to ask for his help. He appeared beside her, radiating waves of concern and empathy. She knew intuitively that another bond with the Ennean was not an option: their previous bonding had been short-lived and was not sustainable for the amount of time she would need to make it to another source of oxygen. She asked her abacus, "Where's Professor Sun?"

The suit answered, "Professor Sun is in critical condition. Life signs fading."

Her stomach dropped; a lump formed in her throat. *Oh, no.*

Her abacus gave her Sun's position. The ocean currents were inexorably sweeping away his inert form, about two-hundred meters away. She struggled to catch up with his listless body, swimming as fast as her arms and flippered legs could propel her. Sun was pursued by a deep red plume, which trailed behind him and was gruesomely illuminated by the light beacons of his suit. Triton effortlessly kept pace with Taitano, letting her take the lead. She caught up with Sun, arrested his movement by taking hold of his dorsal fin, and looked into his eyes. "Sun, are you OK? Can you talk to me?" she asked him urgently, trying to prevent herself from crying inside her helmet.

Taitano's suit stated placidly, "Warning: one minute of oxygen left. Locate an alternative oxygen supply immediately." Sun heard the warning.

Sun's eyes were closed, but he forced them open. Only one of them worked. He managed a few feeble squeaks from the top of his head, which were translated into Taitano's helmet as, "Hello, Agana. Did we do it?"

"Yes!" she said with bitter pleasure. "We did it, Sun! What the heck happened to you?" She saw the seared scorch marks on his head and neck, the polymers of his suit having fused to his flesh, all the way down to the bone. Blood was everywhere and obscured her vision. She winced and started to cry, knowing the wounds were critical.

Sun screwed his courage to the sticking place, bore down on the pain, and replied, "Oh, this? I was a little busy while you were disarming the device. It's nothing. I'm gratified you were able to shut it down. I hope the Enneans will be safe now." He paused his song to draw another ragged breath and then exhorted her, "Try to make this right when you return to the station and Earth-Ocean." His breathing became erratic, and his eyes closed. His body was wracked with spasms. He opened his eyes again and looked deeply into hers, "It's my time. Take my electrolyzer and make it back to the station. You have to make this right. You have to tell everyone back home what happened."

"I'm *not* taking your oxygen, Sun!" declared Taitano, truly horrified by the suggestion. She desperately continued, "We're going to get you back to the station, and you'll be fine." She did her level best to look confident and to reassure him, but failed miserably.

She perceived a gentle pressure on her shoulder. It was Triton. She projected thoughts in his direction. *Can you save him?* She received back from the alien, not words, but waves of sorrow and empathy, which she could feel in her mind: *Not enough time.* Sun also understood Triton's meaning, even if it was not expressed in the words of a human or the songs of a dolphin. Sun's injuries were too severe for him to make it back in time to one of the stations for such extensive medical attention. In addition, there was only one working electrolyzer between the two of them, and Taitano's suit was about to run out of air in the next few seconds.

Triton took gentle hold of Sun's electrolyzer, carefully twisted the mechanism in his ophidian-like arm, and apologetically liberated it from the casing that secured it to the ventral side of Sun's environmental suit. Triton held the electrolyzer before Taitano, offering it to her.

She refused to look at it.

Sun sang to her.

He instructed his abacus to transmit to her his unaltered and untranslated song. He was singing Agana's name to her, as he would have sung it to a fellow dolphin. It was an elegant, complex string of overlapping notes in B minor; the melodies intermixed with each other, rising and falling in irregular patterns that matched the failing rhythms of his damaged heart. He wanted her, just once, to experience the beauty of her own name in delphine terms. Sun gasped for air, as pain wracked his body, preventing him from continuing.

Coming up from behind them, Triton reached out an appendage and touched Sun's head through a rent in his damaged suit. In an instant, the alien communicated to him the final moments of their efforts to deactivate the devices. Taitano could see Sun relax, as he fully learned what had happened while he was dealing with the drone.

Switching his abacus back to translation mode, Sun courageously drew upon the last of his strength to utter, "Agana, we did it. *You* did it. You fixed the final sequence before activating it. If not for your obsessive-compulsive urge to double-check it—what I would call the *inspiration* to do so—it would have been wrong, and all this would've been for nothing." Sun struggled to draw breath from his ruptured suit, but the immense water pressure prevented him from filling his lungs. "It was you and your uniqueness that allowed us to save the Enneans—together. Now take the electrolyzer ... make it back. Knowing you ... has been ... one of the best experiences of my life. We all live ... we all die ... my time has come ... you have much left to do .... As your beloved Blake said, live in eternity's sunrise. Think of me ... now and then ... and remember the good times we had together." He faltered again and with his last breath managed to say, "I wouldn't trade them for anything."

Taitano tried to reply, but could only choke on the staccato sobs wrenched from her throat—her soul.

Sun locked his lone good eye with hers one last time. This was for her benefit more than his, for he was taking his "last look," as only a dolphin could, using his echolocation. He savored the beating of her heart and the slow rise and fall of her lungs and knew that she would make it back. With that, Sun turned and gracefully faded into the gloomy darkness of the sea.

Taitano was overwhelmed with grief, as she guiltily connected Sun's electrolyzer to her suit. She activated it, and oxygen came flooding back into her lungs.

Triton took her hand in one of his appendages and nimbly lifted her towards the orb that was patiently awaiting them near the selenium stream.

She felt compassionate waves of sympathy, love, and understanding emanating from Triton during the several hours it took to surf the selenium stream back to Station-1. Utterly spent from the events that had transpired, she drifted in and out of consciousness. In her more lucid moments, she tried to recall all that had happened, but when she did so, the death of her mentor was a sputtering electrical wire filling the otherwise tranquil sphere with stinging sorrow. She recoiled from it and then retreated again into slumber. Once or twice more during the journey back to the station, she awoke and tried to focus her thoughts, but was immediately reminded of what had happened and was enveloped once more by the anguish of her emotions, as the grief of Sun's passing enshrouded her in a deathly tomb of despair.

# CHAPTER 16

# RETURN

Taitano lay in her bunk, languidly gazing at the stellar vista outside the viewport of her chamber. She relished the simple sensation of not being in an environmental suit, quietly reclining in a loose-fitting dress. *Finally, I feel like I can breathe again. No suit. No kilometers of water pushing down on me, threatening to flatten me like a grilled cheese sandwich.* The air of her chamber was a perfect twenty degrees Celsius; the humidity at forty percent. She had asked the computer to play an ambient version of one of her favorite movie soundtracks from the twentieth century. It was a tale of high adventure—of the days when humans killed each other for land and power. *Well, I guess recent events prove that those days are still with us—or at least not as far in the past as we'd like to believe.*

*Ardanwen* was on her return voyage from Ennea to Earth-Ocean. The exchange program, intended to foster closer relations and understanding, had suffered a set-back, to be sure; but it would continue. Once Moon had recovered from the initial shock of Sun's death, the first thing she did was to co-author with Captain Saddiq a report to the United Nations Commission for Ennean Cross-Cultural Exchange, detailing in excruciating detail what had transpired. Saddiq and Moon, fully aware that they were violating their non-disclosure agreements with the Commission, copied the worldwide media channel on their report to ensure a cover-up was impossible. With all that had taken place—including the murders of Tiberius and Sun and the displacement and imprisonment of dozens of Enneans—they were both more than content, and even eager, to risk their careers in order to ensure that the truth was known to all on Earth-Ocean.

Judging from the return message, which came a few months later, the public of Earth-Ocean was outraged. Everyone on the Commission not only resigned, but also went into early retirement. Some were even facing criminal charges, but that would take many years to sort out in human courtrooms and dolphin community circles. Church, who had been confined to quarters on *Ardanwen*, had been officially stripped of his position in the *communiqué* from Earth-Ocean, with a recommendation that he spend the entire return journey in isolation.

The first act of the reconstituted Commission was to formally rescind its instructions about the relocation of the Enneans and the aquaterraforming of Ross 128b. Instead, the Commission ordered research on the possibility of constructing self-contained biospheres for humans and dolphins that did not adversely impact the native environment. The imprisoned Enneans were returned to their Ocean, and Taitano had even been asked, during the trip home, to work with Moon, Nereus, and Proteus to record a message of apology that the Enneans might understand, which would be transmitted to the Enneans from all four Earth-Ocean stations. Those remaining on the stations were also in the process of assessing the damage that the aquaterraforming devices had caused to the delicate balance of the Ocean, especially the selenium stream, and of devising methods to restore the native equilibrium of the subterranean marine ecosystem.

There was also the matter of the one-hundred-thousand-year-old remains of the hominids, which Taitano had stumbled upon in the rock station floating in the Ocean of Ennea. She had given to Moon a detailed account, along with the data recorded by her abacus; and Moon had included it in her report back to Earth-Ocean. This discovery smote the scientific community like the hammer of the gods; and raging debates—as well as much speculation—were underway to try to explain what could be the answer to this ancient riddle from across the stars. A full archaeological team was to be dispatched on *Ardanwen's* return journey to get to the bottom of this enigma.

There was an audible chime, and Taitano replied, "Yes?"

Patel's voice spilled into the room, interrupting Taitano's thoughts, "Agan-n-a, w-w-where the heck are you? *Jiu-jitsu* class started ten minutes ago, and w-we're all waiting down here for you. Even Fastcatch is getting in on the action today."

Patel's voice was filled with irritation and affection—and was badly slurred. His neurons had been damaged by the photonic pulses of Church's submersibles outside Station-1. In their damaged condition, the strain on his brain from the selenium tether's interface with his cybernetic implant had just been too much. When he returned to the station, his implant had to be surgically removed—permanently. In addition, he had suffered minor neurological damage, including to his speech centers. He would lead a healthy and happy life until the end of his days, but in a reduced capacity. His main pleasures on the return journey were eating, reading, and *jiu-jitsu*—although Taitano was now easily able to outmaneuver him on the tatami and get him to tap out, whereas before she had been no match for him and his cybernetically enhanced reflexes and superior repertoire of moves and strategies.

They were apparently now minor celebrities back on Earth-Ocean. She had mixed feelings about that, as she had never been one to seek that type of nonsense. Maybe she could use the attention to advocate for further social and environmental changes that were still needed back home. *We'll see. No rush. With the time dilation, by the time we get back, we'll probably be long forgotten. At the moment, I just want to rest.* Her ankle was slowly healing, but not quite there yet. She had been on old-fashioned crutches for a couple of weeks, when she was not floating in aquatic parts of the ship. She noticed that her foot and ankle ached terribly when they encountered gravitational anomalies, the way her grandfather's knees used to throb during a storm and the accompanying increase in barometric pressure. When the pain got particularly intense, she went to see Triton to alert him so he could recalibrate the vectors of their careening course through space-time to account for the differing gravitational planes. She was never one-hundred percent sure if Triton understood her, but she noticed that the ride always got smoother after her "chats" with him about her ankle.

She responded to Patel via the internal transmission system, "Saiyam, I'm chilling right now, and my ankle isn't feeling so well. I'm passing today. I just need some down-time, OK?"

There was silence on the other side of the transmission that lasted a little too long. Patel then replied, stuttering a bit, "Wa-wa-wa-well, if yer gonna make excuses, fine. But next time yer gettin' your butt whooped."

"That'll be the day, Saiyam. Send everyone my regrets, and I'll see you all at dinner, OK?

"Yeah, OK. See ya later."

The transmission ended. Thinking of her grandfather's aches and pains brought him to her mind. He had passed away during her time on Ennea. It was difficult news, but she weathered it with grace. He had reached a ripe old age undreamed of in most of humanity's past and had enjoyed a good quality of life; and yet it was always a challenge to emotionally accept that a person—along with everything they were, all their unique experiences and knowledge—was simply gone from the Universe. Lost forever.

In his last transmission, he had given her an update on his never-ending work, how things were going in the house, scandals at the university, a bit of local politics. He complained—always in a humorous way, to buffer his true feelings—of how much he missed her, but also told her how proud he was of her for going on the journey to Ennea. Before signing off, he had attached his latest story, explaining to her, "Remember what I told you about your cultural heritage and the special responsibility that comes with it. You must always use your powers for good, to protect others—never to destroy. And I know that is exactly what you will do. I had you in mind when I wrote this story. Maybe it will be my last. You never know. Hope you like it. My publisher's already found a fantastic illustrator and wants to put it on-line as soon as the images can be copy-edited and meshed with the text. I love you, Taibo … and I'm proud of you."

She tapped an icon in her grandfather's message to bring the story up before her as holographic words. She began to read …

### The Fable of the Wasp and the Bee

by Matapang Hofstadter


*Maior rerum mihi nascitur ordo, maius opus moueo.*

A higher order of things is born to me;
I set a greater work into motion.

*The Aeneid* – Publius Vergilius Maro


Once upon a summertide, an industrious honeybee

was flitting from flower to flower through a vast expanse of yellow and black faces. The pollen on her back glinted in the luminescence of Sol amidst a field of a million tiny sunflowers, children of the sun. A large black and yellow wasp whisked by the bee, circled back, and landed on the edge of a sunflower near the honeybee.

The wasp said to the honeybee, "Why, madame, whatever are you doing to that poor, defenseless sunflower?"

The bee replied a bit incredulously, "I am collecting nectar."

"Whatever for?" gasped the wasp.

"Well, to make honey, of course."

"Well, well, well! That is much too much work. Why not just sting some unfortunate and unsuspecting grasshopper and then gobble him up. It's a mite tastier, as well."

The bee looked stunned, "I would rather think the grasshopper might have a thing or two to say about that proposition!"

"Oh, that's the way of things," said the wasp.

"Well," said the bee, "it's not *my* way of things; and even if I desired to engage in such barbaric behavior towards a fellow soul—which I most certainly do not, mind you—I would refrain from doing so for my own sake." And she went on sucking up her delectable nectar and getting pollen all over herself.

"But why do you say 'for your own sake'?" asked the wasp.

The bee, starting to look a bit perturbed, once again ceased her labors and turned around to face the wasp,

"I, sir, am a honeybee. If I sting someone, I die."

The wasp was nonplussed. He tried to mentally process this statement. When the bee discerned his bewilderment, she patiently explained that her stinger was connected to her internal organs and had barbs on it. Once she stung someone, the stinger remained in the body of her target, and any attempt to remove the stinger took her entrails with it.

Now the wasp had a truly horrified expression on his face. As a wasp, his stinger had no barbs and was independent of his internal organs; so he could effectively sting someone as many times as he fancied, or was able, without undue risk to life and limb. He managed to stumble out the words, "How positively terrible for you. I am most sorry. Please, I beg your pardon."

The bee replied, "It's quite alright. Would you care for some nectar to quench your thirst on this glorious, but parched, summer afternoon?"

The wasp politely declined, but stayed perched on the sunflower, continuing to fix his gaze upon the bee and her labors.

"Is there indeed anything else with which I can help you?" asked the bee, becoming irritated again.

"Well, I was just wondering where you got all that hair and why you don't find a decent coiffurist to give you a bit of ... shaping ... shall we say," the wasp commented, trying to be helpful.

There was apparently no way for the bee to rid herself of the meddlesome wasp; she thus ceased her work and gave the wasp her full attention, "Yes, I had noticed how hairless and smooth you are. It might help you capture the unhappy souls you sting and then devour—or aid your efforts to outrun the ones who fight back. And that slender body of yours may help you fly with great alacrity. But my more rotund and hirsute body helps me to collect pollen and to bring it back to my hive for our queen and the next generation of bees—our children. True joy is in giving, after all."

The wasp reflected on that, "Well, I will grant you all that. But what happens if you have to defend yourself or others. With that silly integrated, barbed stinger of yours, any fight would be a suicide mission!"

"This is true," murmured the bee thoughtfully. She continued in quite a serious and resolute tone, "But, when I sting someone, I fully commit. And my determination, along with my stinger, remains with my adversary. There are no hit-and-run missions for a honeybee. And there is no greater joy than to give your life for someone you love. It's all part of the Great Balance."

"The 'Great Balance'?" queried the wasp.

"Yes, the 'Great Balance.' Please don't tell me," queried the bee, softly moaning in dismay, "that you've never heard of the 'Great Balance.'"

"No, I haven't," answered the clueless wasp, "Should I have? In any event, don't be coy, madame. Do tell me what it is."

The bee paused for a moment, reflecting on how to explain it to the wasp. Finally, she continued, "All living things are part of the Great Balance—even rocks and rivers. It's a crazily complicated cycle of death and renewal, pain and loss, bliss and birth. If you were to look at the Earth from very far away, you would see it as a seething cauldron of life that never stops changing. It's never static. An eclectic collection of different individuals who are completely dependent upon the Earth and each other. No individual could survive alone; and, although there are peaks and valleys, and individuals and species come and go, the Balance—as a whole—is always preserved. All serve the Balance."

The wasp listened attentively; he rubbed his antennae together and asked thoughtfully, "What about bears? I heard that, last year, a bear destroyed an entire honeybee hive down by that farm past the river. Was that part of the Balance?"

The bee pensively shifted back and forth upon the delicate, unstable petal of the flower, bouncing gently up and down, "Yes, I heard about that, too. And it *is* distressing when things like that happen—especially for the bees of the hive," she said quietly, looking off into the distance and in the direction of the river. "But we bees have gotten used to bears eating our honey and destroying our hives every now and then; and so there are a lot of hives and a lot of bees. Enough for the bears to have some honey and enough for our species to endure—and even thrive. We are all in balance."

"Are humans part of the Great Balance?" asked the wasp, undaunted.

The bee got a sour expression on her face. "Humans are indeed part of the Balance, but they have lost their way. They've strayed from the byways that traverse the Balance. Their minds grew faster than their hearts. They've become mixed up with the technological toys they created, and they decided they were better than the rest of the creatures in the Balance. Humans need to grow in courage and wisdom, and then they will someday remember that, in the end, they all return to the Balance—each one of them. It's just a matter of time. But it's difficult for them to learn all this during their short lives, and they don't always pass on what they have learned to their children. They are capable of doing terrifying damage to the Balance, which will eventually come back to haunt them. Haunt us all. But who knows? It may come to pass someday that humanity's *penchant* for destruction, like a forest fire, is also part of the Balance. It's impossible to say. One day, we may know. But that day will be long after you and I are gone."

Over the next days and weeks, the wasp and the bee spent time together debating the advantages and disadvantages of being a bee and being a wasp. There were heated debates and sometimes reluctant, but good natured, concessions, such as when the bee agreed that the wasp could fly faster than she could due to his smoother and narrower body. Or when the wasp admitted that wasps did not always eat other insects and feed them to their young, but rather also enjoyed sweet nectar in the late summer and fall when their young had hatched and no longer needed so much care. There were also epic polemics about whether it is better to build a nest from wax or chewed wood. But the bee and the wasp grew to enjoy their amiable altercations and even to look forward to them with anticipation. They soon became fast friends and spent time together each day for the remainder of the summer.

On a chilly day in late October, the honeybee was returning to her hive to deliver the last of the day's harvest of nectar, when she saw a baby bear shimmying up the tree where her hive was located. Hundreds of her fellow bees had already mobilized and were harrying the bear in a futile attempt to dissuade him from his course of destruction. But the bear had smelled the honey and would not be deterred. His hide and hair were thick, and the bees could not penetrate them. When one of the honeybees managed to sink her stinger into the bear's soft nose, the bear swatted it away, disemboweling and killing the defender.

The hive was doomed.

Without hesitation, the honeybee began to fly with all her speed at the bear to defend her home, but was unexpectedly bumped off her course. She spun out of control and landed in a pile of crusty brown and red leaves. When she regained her composure, she looked up in time to see a sleek yellow and black form buzzing around the bear's head. The bear vigorously tried to swat the insect away, but it was too fast. It repeatedly stung the bear's nose and the soft tissue around his eyes, plunging its stinger over and over again into the sensitive, exposed parts of the bear's face. Finally, the bear had had enough and began to retreat down the tree, just centimeters from the juicy, sweet hive filled with honey. But before the bear's winged tormentor could move to a safe distance out of reach, the bear managed one more swing of his massive paw, which connected with the flying insect, sending it swirling far away from the tree and into the dirt.

The honeybees rejoiced in their salvation. The hive would slumber intact for another winter and be resurrected in the spring.

The honeybee flew over to the one who was to thank for the survival of her colony's fragile abode. As she approached, she could see the crushed body of a wasp. Her heart already told her who it was. She slowly turned over the shattered body and looked into the face of her friend.

"How can we ever thank you?" said the bee.

The wasp could barely speak. His body was broken and oozing ichor. He was missing an antenna, and the other one was bent at an unnatural angle. As the bee cradled the wasp's head, the wasp managed to say in labored tones, "There's no need to thank me, madame."

The bee persevered, "You saved our home, our children. You saved us all. With that refined and un-barbed wasp stinger of yours."

The wasp croaked, "I did it not only to save the hive, but also to save you. To save my friend. And you were right. I have never experienced joy and happiness like this. You were right, my friend. Thank you for that."

And with these words, the wasp passed into another realm of both light and darkness—and peace.

The bee carried the body of her friend back to the hive and told her friends and family about their friendship and the sacrifice of the wasp. They buried the wasp at the base of the tree where the hive was still safely suspended; and, as the wasp's body decomposed over the months and years, his life force and essence once again became one with the forest.

And when the bee met the end of her own days, she experienced a profound tranquility in the knowledge that she, too, would soon return to the place whence she had come and would soon join her friend in the

Great Balance.

Taitano was weeping by the end of the story.

Salty tears traced tracks down her face and then shattered onto the floor beneath her. She consciously decided not to wipe away the tears, but rather to fully experience the wet sensation on her skin. *This is part of life. Don't block it. Accept it.* Feel *it.*

The tears eventually drained into the ducts in the corners of her eyes and then into her nose. She inhaled and exhaled, slowly and steadily, taking her time and allowing herself to bask in the piercing emotions.

Grief gradually and gracefully gave way to gratitude. *Good-bye, Sun. Good-bye, Grandpa. And thank you for everything.*

# EPILOGUE

"We saved the last one for you."

Agana Taitano Hofstadter felt the wall of air—the atmosphere of Earth-Ocean—washing over her face, whipping her onyx hair in all directions and inundating her ears with a deafening crush of air molecules that crashed over her in waves.

"What's that?" she absent-mindedly replied to the boyish engineer beside her on the vessel. She searched her memory for his name: Sergei.

Sergei smiled at her, came a bit closer, and raised his voice to be heard over the stentorian din. "I *said*—we saved the last one for you. We finished clearing this area over a year ago, but we decided to keep the last munition until you returned. Kind of sentimental, I know. We thought it would be a nice touch, not to mention a good photo op with Earth-Ocean's newest celebrity scientist."

She was on the sailing yacht (S/Y) *Oceania*, a scientific research vessel of the Polish Academy of Sciences' Institute of Oceanology. The International Commission for the Remediation of Sea-Dumped Munitions—ICRSM—had commissioned the *Oceania* for this last recovery and remediation operation. There had been talk of rechristening the ship *Taitano*, but she had flatly refused to give her blessing to *that*. Following the designs of shipwright Zygmunt Choreń, the vessel was built in the late twentieth century in the Gdańsk Shipyard. She sported three thirty-two-meter-high masts, with vertical rectangular sails, and was equipped with a wide range of laboratories to support experiments and environmental data collection missions. Her old diesel engines had been decommissioned, recycled, and replaced with photovoltaic sails that could collect and store more than enough electricity to run the systems of the vessel, including the propeller, when needed. Gone were the days when being on a ship at sea meant the omnipresent roar of a fossil-fueled engine and the gagging stink of partially burned diesel fuel. At full sail, the *Oceania* was a marvel to behold, and the journey through the Baltic, North, Norwegian, and Barents Seas to arrive at the northern coast of Novaya Zemlya had suffused Taitano with aching awe and wonder at the beauty of her home planet. They were currently anchored off the coast of Novaya Zemlya, in an area that was considered, somewhat arbitrarily, the "border" between the Barents and Kara Seas.

Shortly after Taitano's return from Ennea, Cornell University appointed her as the Ann Druyan Professor of Applied Sciences, and the ICRSM offered her a seat on its governing board—which she graciously accepted. She was content to split her time between teaching at Cornell and helping to manage the affairs of the Commission, which was focusing its efforts on clearing all of the nuclear waste out of the Ocean, now that the remediation of submerged chemical munitions was almost finished. The Commission had slightly delayed the recovery operation of the very last sea-dumped chemical weapon so that Taitano could be involved—a gesture of gratitude for all she had done for the environmental health of not only one world, but two. It was also a good public relations move for the Commission, which was always on the hunt for new financial backing. Taitano was honored and did not mind her rather exaggerated reputation being used to raise the Commission's public profile and help it generate voluntary contributions for its vital work to restore the health of the Ocean—a task that was well underway, but that would take generations to fully complete. The Ocean had, in fact, proved to be more resilient than once anticipated, and once humans had stopped using it as their own personal dumping place, the microorganisms, plants, and animals that dwelled there had finally begun to regain their former state of mutual balance.

Taitano fixed her attention again on the engineer, "Well, yes, it was most kind of you all to leave the last one for me. I hope you isolated it in a static polymer casing, while you were waiting. I would hate to think any toxic chemicals leaked into the sea on my account."

The engineer's visage simulated a mock expression of shock and wounded pride, "Yes, of course we did, Dr. Taitano! Perish the thought. It is safe and sound down there. I am *personally* monitoring it to ensure there is no leakage. All you have to do is go down there, make sure the fuse is deactivated, check the seal on the overpacking, and attach it to the recovery line. We'll then bring it up, toss it into the static detonation chamber, hit the switch on the good ol' plasma arc— and watch it burn. We'll even capture the resulting gases so that not a single $CO_2$ molecule is released into the atmosphere." He checked a gage on his panel, and then returned his attention to Taitano. "So, you're all cleared to go. If you hurry up, we can even make it back to the research station at Stolbovoy for dinner," he said, letting a charming smile spread across his schoolboy face before adding "— with me, perhaps."

Taitano rolled her eyes, smiled in a good-natured way, and responded, "In your dreams, Sergei."

"Well, I at least had to try, right?"

"You do realize, don't you, that I'm *decades* older than you," she playfully chided him.

"Yes, but only in relativistic time," he parried with a wink.

She did not verbally respond, but crinkled her eyes and returned his smile.

She fastened the seals of her helmet, gave a thumbs-up sign, and fell backwards off the side of the *Oceania* into the frigid Kara Sea. The weights on her belt immediately dragged her down. She managed, with a fair bit of effort, to swim to the cable a few meters away that had been affixed to the *Oceania*, at one end, and anchored, at the other end, to the seabed at the munitions dump site below. Reaching the cable required a great deal of physical coordination on her part, as she was still acclimatizing to the relatively lower gravity field of Earth-Ocean, as compared to Ennea. Nevertheless, she was relieved to be back in the water and to have the pressure off her ankle, which still ached from the fracture she had received during her descent from *Xanthus* to the surface of Ennea.

When she reached the cable, she hooked her carabiner to it and then gave herself over to gravity. She descended rapidly, the gravitational forces of her home planet pulling the mass of her body (and the belt weights) towards its center. She checked her oxygen and pressure gages. All good. She then double-checked them. It was good to be in a normal wetsuit again—albeit a heavy one—rather than the environmental suit that she had pretty much lived in while on Ennea. She felt more connected to her surroundings and rejoiced in the cold of the Arctic Ocean.

She basked in the explosion of life that surrounded her. A young ringed seal swam past her, quickly checking her out before moving on to conduct its business elsewhere. There were fish of all sizes and hues, jellyfish, krill, and plankton, which seemed to fill every square centimeter of the water around her. By comparison, Ennea was a sterile, barren place, with only its Ennean inhabitants to break the bleak absence of life.

And the light.

Unlike Ennea, which had been a paralytic darkness, the sea of Earth-Ocean was suffused with scintillating bands of light, piercing the sea in curved shafts of white, blue, and green. But even as she sank lower into the depths and it became increasingly difficult for the light of Sol to penetrate the thick layers of water that towered above and buried her, there was still *some* illumination, whereas on Ennea she had been perpetually encased in a lonely and fragile orb of light generated by her environmental suit—and also the radiance of the selenium stream. As the water pressure increased, her body was compressed into a shape of less volume, and her buoyancy decreased accordingly— which, in turn, caused her to sink faster towards the bottom. Her breathing was slow and smooth. After another minute, she observed the perimeter lights of the dump site, in the middle of which was a lone munition awaiting her.

She came to rest beside the munition. She keyed her abacus to scan the fuse of the chemical weapon that had been dumped there over two-hundred years ago. She thought about the government officials who had signed off on such offences against the environment. *Evil comes in many forms. It's not always monomaniacal villains like Church. Sometimes it simply takes the shape of an unquestioning or indifferent bureaucrat. Did anyone involved in this dumping operation ever stop to ask whether it was the right thing to do? Or was he just doing his job at the time? It's taken us a long time, but we are, slowly, breaking the cycle, Grandpa. Setting out on a new path to fix the mistakes of our ancestors. Rather than standing by and watching yet another destructive chapter in humanity's story unfold, we saved the Enneans—and maybe ourselves, too. At the very least, we're trying. There's still so much to do, but all we can do is to try to make a little progress in the right direction. Like the migrations of our ancestors across the globe, small steps, over time, can take us long distances.*

She analyzed the fuse of the munition and prepared to key into her wrist-mounted abacus the appropriate radiogenic frequencies that would dissolve the fuse without triggering the arming sequence. She had done it hundreds of times before and worked with ease and confidence. She still, of course, manually double-checked the amplitudes of the frequencies that would be emitted to ensure they were correct. She smiled to herself as she then *triple-checked* the frequencies, accepting that this was who she was and that it was not a bad thing. She scanned the explosive device again to confirm that the fuse had been disabled and that the seal on the overpacking was intact. They both were.

She hooked the retrieval line to the metal loop on the top of the overpacked polymer casing that contained the munition and signaled Sergei that he was clear to bring it up. She grabbed onto the line to hitch a ride back to the surface. As she ascended and the pressure on her body began to wane, she witnessed the waxing light penetrating the water from above.

The events on Ennea had brought her life into focus for the first time. The poem of her life, which before had no rhyme, now at least had a semblance of rhythm. She thought of Sol, seemingly suspended in the sky: the star, one-hundred and fifty million kilometers away, that had fostered all those who had come before her and that would sustain all those who would come after, on this modest—and yet extraordinary—world bursting with life. She thought of Sun. She missed him. She would always miss him. But her sorrow had already begun to transmogrify into a melancholy satisfaction that their lives had touched—that they had connected in their brief time together. For all life is a cycle of endings and beginnings to be repeated over and over, until Sol swelled into a fiery red giant and finally engulfed Earth-Ocean. When her head broke the surface of the Ocean, she turned herself to the blazing orb in the ceiling of the world and felt upon her face its nourishing warmth and light.

*The End*

# DRAMATIS PERSONAE

**Humans**

    Abdul-Noor Saddiq

    Agana Taitano Hofstadter

    Cassian Tiberius

    Frank Church

    Matapang Hofstadter

    Pution Mangabao

    Saiyam Patel

**Dolphins**

    Fastcatch

    Moon

    Quickbite

    Sun

**Enneans**

    Benthesikyme

    Triton

**Artificial Intelligences**

    Nereus

    Proteus

# Timeline

The timeline below uses the Gregorian Calendar and lists dates from the spatial-temporal perspective of Earth-Ocean. All years mentioned are in the Common Era (CE).

## 20th Century

1910s–1980s Over one million tons of chemical weapons are dumped into the Ocean

## 21st Century

2030s Global recession; collapse of insurance/reinsurance system due to environmental impacts of climate change

2040s End of international banking system

2050 Almost all states miss their net-zero carbon emission targets under Paris Agreement

2052 Casings of sea-dumped chemical weapons in the Baltic Sea erode and release their toxic chemicals into the marine ecosystem, killing almost all remaining life there

2061 Earth-Ocean's star (Sol) enters a phase of increased solar flare activity, causing ecological and social chaos across the planet; Enneans arrive and make fist contact

2062 Political upheaval across Earth-Ocean; governments replaced with next generation of leaders dedicated to sustainability and environmental remediation of ecosytem; Great Restoration commences; Enneans reconfigure the electromagnetic field of Earth-Ocean and prevent its destruction from massive solar flare; formation of United Nations Commission for Ennean Cross-Cultural Exchange; refit of *Ardanwen* commences

2072    Humans and dolphins make first contact; refit of *Ardanwen* completed

2073    Commencement of *Ardanwen's* first journey from Earth-Ocean to Ennea

2075    Earth-Ocean (finally) achieves carbon neutrality (sixty years after adoption of Paris Agreement)

2085    Last nuclear weapon decommissioned

2092    Dolphin appointed as full professor for first time at a human university (at Groningen University in Netherlands)

2097    *Ardanwen* arrives back at Earth-Ocean after its first journey to Ennea

## 22nd Century

2102    Dolphin appointed as Secretary-General of United Nations for first time

2168    Taitano orally defends dissertation and is awarded PhD at Carl Sagan University on Island of Tinian

2169    Taitano departs Earth-Ocean for Ennea

2193    Taitano returns to Earth-Ocean

2194    Taitano appointed to International Commission for Remediation of Sea-Dumped Munitions and as Ann Druyan Professor of Applied Sciences (at Cornell University); she disarms the last sea-dumped chemical weapon on Earth-Ocean off the coast of Novaya Zemlya

# Acknowledgements

I am so grateful to Tatjana, Grace, Shelly, Evan, and Steve for reading the manuscript and giving me their honest and valuable feedback. They saved me from making many errors and provided insightful comments that enhanced the story. Jason shared with me his expertise on characterization. I also owe thanks to Grace and Henry, my steadfast reading companions, for all the adventures we have shared together. Any deficiencies in the final product are my own.

Brent at Desert Wind Press assisted me in negotiating the publishing process, and Max brought the climax of the story to life on the cover of the book.

This book was inspired by my work on forcible and environmental displacement, international environmental law, and the remediation of sea-dumped chemical weapons. Having researched and written on these topics in an academic context, I wanted to also raise awareness through a work of fiction. The book is meant to address humanity's weaknesses and destructive power, while still acknowledging the potential we have to learn from our mistakes and do better. Evil must always be opposed, and a group of committed and well-intentioned individuals can make a difference. In this way, I have attempted to infuse the book with hope in order to motivate us to keep trying.

# About
# the Author

Grant Dawson earned a Bachelor of Arts in Classics from Columbia College in New York City, a Juris Doctor from Georgetown University Law Centre in Washington, DC, and a Doctor of Philosophy (PhD) in international environmental law from Groningen University Faculty of Law in the Netherlands. Dr. Dawson has served in a variety of legal positions in academia, non-governmental organizations, private practice, government, and international organizations. He has researched, written, published, and lectured on a wide range of international legal topics. This is his first work of fiction.

Printed in Poland
by Amazon Fulfillment
Poland Sp. z o.o., Wrocław
04 September 2024

86f687a8-3593-46cc-9f9b-4163cd94bf01R01